SMALL LIGHT OF DISCRETION

A NOVEL OF FACTUAL HISTORY
REGARDING TREACHERY AND THE
EXPULSION OF THE UTES

BY

J. HOOLIHAN CLAYTON

AUTHOR OF *COMMENDABLE DISCRETION*
AND *WITH GREAT DISCRETION*

WITH ILLUSTRATIONS AND ENGRAVINGS
FROM HARPERS WEEKLY

DOG SOLDIER PRESS

TAOS

Published in January 2023 by
Dog Soldier Press, PO Box 1782,
Ranchos de Taos, NM 87557
dogsoldierpress.com

Graphic Design: book interior and cover
Ananda M. Sundari, Alchemy Arts
AlchemyArtsllc.com

Library of Congress Control Number: 2022951993
Printing: Ingram Sparks
Print ISBN: 978-1-7371362-9-3
ePub ISBN: 979-8-9874524-0-0

*"It appears, by his small light of discretion,
that he is on the wane; but yet, in courtesy,
in all reason, we must stay the time."*

Midsummer-night's Dream, Act V, scene I
- William Shakespeare -

Condemnant quo non intellegunt.

*"The Agent sat for hours in a hot room filled
with tobacco smoke, and listened to speeches of
which he understood nothing, and during all the
time he said nothing - silently representing the
government of the United States."*

- Nathan C. Meeker, Indian Agent,
White River Ute Agency (signifying himself) -

Los Pinos Indian Agency, October 2, 1879

*To the chiefs, captains, headmen, and Utes
at the White River Agency:*

You are hereby requested and commanded to cease hostilities against the whites, injuring no innocent persons or any other further than to protect your own lives and property from unlawful and unauthorized combinations of horse-thieves and desperadoes, as anything farther will ultimately end in disaster to all parties.

OURAY, *Head Chief Ute Nation*

"We do not want to sell a foot of our land that is the opinion of our people. The whites can go and take the land and come out again. We do not want them to build houses here."

"The agreement an Indian makes to a United States treaty is like the agreement a buffalo makes with his hunters when pierced with arrows. All he can do is lie down and give in."

- *Ouray,* Chief of Tabeguache band of Utes -

"There is one spirit governing the heaven and earth; he looks down on me, and sees upon the earth as well as in heaven. Therefore, I cannot speak anything but the truth."

- *Quinkent* (Douglas) in testimony to the Special Ute Commission convened in Colorado, November 13, 1879 -

DRAMATIS PERSONÆ

CARL SCHURZ Secretary of the Interior, U.S. Department of the Interior.

GUSTAVUS JOCKNICK Bureau of Indian Affairs employee, trusted by Secretary Schurz.

SIDNEY JOCKNICK Son of Gustavus, former employee of Los Pinos Indian Agency.

ALONZO HARTMAN Former cow boss of Los Pinos Agency, rancher.

GEORGE BAGGS Rancher on Little Snake River.

JOHN LAWRENCE Rancher, businessman in Saguache.

FREDERICK PITKIN Governor of Colorado, mining investor.

W.B. VICKERS Newspaper editor and private secretary to Governor Pitkin.

FELIX BRUNOT President of the U.S. Board of Indian Commissioners.

JEROME CHAFFEE Mining investor, U.S. senator, banker.

HENRY TELLER Investor, U.S. senator, lawyer, future Secretary of the Interior.

HORACE TABOR Known as "The Silver King," Lt. Governor of Colorado, U.S. Senator.

ALEXANDER HUNT Ex-governor Colorado Terr., Denver & Rio Grande Railway Director.

EDWARD MCCOOK Ex-governor of Colorado Terr., removed from office.

OTTO MEARS Russian immigrant, government contractor, toll road and railroad builder.

GENERAL CHARLES ADAMS Ex-Indian agent & post office inspector, trusted by the Utes.

JAMES B. THOMPSON Ex-Indian agent of Denver Agency, brother-in-law of Gov. McCook.

HANNIBAL PECK Store owner on Yampa River, friend to the Utes.

MAJOR THORNBURGH Commander of Fort Steele in Wyoming Territory

NATHAN MEEKER ("Nick") Founder of Greeley, failed entrepreneur, Ute Indian agent.

ARVILLA and JOSEPHINE MEEKER Nathan Meeker's wife and daughter.

OURAY Principal chief of the Uncompahgre (Tabeguache) Utes.

CHIPETA Wife of Ouray, Ute delegate to Washington D.C.

RED JACKET JANE Ute woman, slave of Judge Carter at Fort Bridger, learned English.

SHAVANO War chief for Uncompahgre (Tabeguache) Utes.

JOHNSON (Canalla) Principal Chief of the Utes.

DOUGLAS (Quinkent) Principal Chief of the Utes.

CAPTAIN JACK (Nicaagat) Principal Chief of the Utes.

COLONEL EDWARD HATCH (Brevet Major General) Commander of 9th U.S. Cavalry.

EZRA A. HAYT Commissioner of Indian Affairs, U.S. Department of the Interior.

ALFERD PACKER Cannibal.

Foreword

The Ute people (*Nuuchiu*) are ancestral inhabitants of the Great Basin, Great Plains and the mountainous region extending from northern New Mexico Territory to southern Wyoming Territory. After acquiring the horse through trade with Spanish colonists, the Utes were the first Indian tribe to introduce the animal into their culture. As their mobility greatly increased, the *Nuuchiu* became accomplished buffalo hunters and imposing warriors who commanded respect from surrounding tribes and Spanish settlers.

In 1846, during the Mexican-American War, the U.S. Army came marching into *Nuevo Mexico*. During this initial period of armed residency, several skirmishes took place between Ute bands and the U.S. military. Both sides eventually became convinced that peaceful relations would be preferable, although each had disparate goals and differing perceptions in regard to the negotiation process. The Treaty of Abiquiú was signed in 1849 and ratified in 1850, providing for safe passage of settlers crossing Ute territory and placing Ute peoples "lawfully and exclusively under the jurisdiction of the Government of said States: and to its power and authority they now unconditionally submit."

In the early 1850's, Ute chiefs met several times with David Meriwether, Governor of New Mexico Territory (encompassing much of what became part of Colorado). They reasonably asked for firearms (to enable them to hunt and defend themselves from the Arapahoe, Comanche and Cheyenne, now migrating into Ute ancestral lands), food, recognition of traditional territory and, of course, the rations and medicine to be provided according to the 1849 treaty. In the summer of 1854, several of the most prominent Ute leaders met in council with Governor Meriwether, Christopher "Kit" Carson (an Indian agent appointed in 1853), and several other Anglo-American authorities. When the council had concluded, the Utes were provided with presents, among which were blanket coats.

The *Moughwach* and *Kapuuta* leaders departed the 1854 meeting much disappointed in the proceedings. Before many days had passed, all of the chiefs who had met with the governor and Agent Carson, and received coats from them, became sick with smallpox and died. They unknowingly infected many of their people, leading to an epidemic that claimed numerous lives. By the autumn of 1854, the dispersed remains of Ute smallpox fatalities could be found in abundance around the San Luis Valley. Conflicts and depredations increased as the Ute people sought vengeance and found themselves starving as game decreased and rations failed to be dispersed.

In 1858, gold was discovered on the confluence of Little Dry Creek and the South Platte River. By 1863, the *Tabeguache* band had ceded the San Luis Valley to the U.S. government and in 1868, three Ute reservations had been established in Colorado Territory. By 1873, the Ute people were forced to surrender their beloved Shining Mountains, known by whites as the San Juan region. Over the next few years, hunger for mineral wealth drove Indian policy in the region and the U.S. Indian Bureau was influenced by powerful Colorado politicians and capitalists whose leverage reached all the way to Washington D.C. In 1878, a new agent was strategically assigned to the White River Agency, ultimately leading to fortuitous consequences for political and commercial interests in Colorado and catastrophic ramifications for the Ute people.

Prologue

He had always considered himself to be a reasonable man, a man of vision and fortitude. Against all these qualities, he found he hated these people. He despised their earthiness and swarthy faces, their false pride, their childlike worship of Nature. Most of all, he loathed their inability to see that he knew what was best for them. He was the bearer of civilization and erudition. He was their benefactor and they remained impervious to his ministrations. But now he would show them. When the soldiers came and they saw that might and right were one and the same…then he would take them in hand and they would be sorry for their calumny and their betrayals.

AN EXPERIMENT WORTH TRYING.

EXPERIMENT

1

The wind blew incessantly. It seemed to yank all warmth and gladness from his flesh. Finding the woman's grave had produced a general angst. A profound aversion to his current surroundings reinforced it. Charles Wolfe Collins sat at a table finishing an inadequate breakfast, sipping coffee that had grown cold and pondering a slip of paper in his hand. He smiled at a small and ragged boy peering through the window. The child made a rude gesture, one with which he should not have been conversant, and skipped away into the crowded street beyond. Collins folded the paper and put it in a breast pocket. He did not really care for children anyway.

The telegram had arrived fortuitously. Having performed a simple task for Allan Pinkerton regarding a wealthy mine owner's absconded wife, Collins was delighted at the opportunity to shake the proverbial mud and copious manure of the streets of Cheyenne from his heels. Reveling in the boom of unfettered grazing and cattle, the town was not given to much beyond ostentatious luxury, gambling and the general reinforcement of proud ignorance. C.W. was surfeited with posturing men, their tooled gun belts, silken neckerchiefs and ridiculously high-heeled boots. He suspected that the legitimate cow hands were out on the range, risking life and limb in the service of making money for big investors from back east and overseas.

Leaving behind the relative serenity of the café, he braved the busy storefronts to purchase an entirely new outfit, including a pristine black Stetson and stylishly tailored ready-made suit. He sent a telegram accepting the commission and asking for further details. A mere five months previous, he had been in the Secretary of the Interior's employ and he remembered with chagrin that the outcome had not been auspicious. Interesting then, he thought, that Carl Schurz would be requesting his services once again and so promptly. He would have to postpone his journey to Montana Territory for a while longer.

C.W. had already wired Pinkerton with his final report of the missing wife. She had been unfortunately seduced then discarded by a charismatic drummer, set adrift in Wyoming Territory and had swiftly succumbed to debauchery and despair. Collins had found her in the outskirts of Cheyenne, occupying a forlorn mound of earth marked by a narrow stave of cedar. It had not been a providential end to an exceedingly unpleasant investigation. Impatient to move on, he had required that the outstanding remuneration for the case be wired to him posthaste. When the funds from Pinkerton and a supplementary communiqué from Schurz finally arrived, he was quite prepared to embark upon a fresh enterprise.

Collins was to proceed to Denver, there to meet an agent of Schurz' by the improbable name of Gustavus Jocknick. Pinkerton had telegraphed a request for him to investigate a robbery in the Cheyenne vicinity, since he was already in residence, but he had responded that this recently concluded and tragic case would be his last for the Pinkerton National Detective Agency until further notice. He could well imagine the spree of invective this message would inspire in the humorless Scotsman.

C.W. purchased a ticket for the train to Denver and packed his bags. The trip was uneventful, although rowdy passengers made it difficult to nap or engage in deep thought. He perused the latest edition of the *Cheyenne Daily Leader* and intermittently watched the uninteresting blur of prairie landscape out his east-facing window. In the end, he was grateful that the journey was not overly long.

On arrival to the flourishing cosmopolitan city of Denver, he checked into the Alvord House, a respectable establishment run by a Mrs. M.A. Alvord, a fussy and energetic little woman. He delighted in the tasteful appointments of his room and the impeccable service. He occupied the rest of his first day walking the crowded and colorful avenues, amidst fashionably dressed ladies and dapper gentlemen. C.W.'s mood was somewhat darkened by the occasional encounter with Indians, who seemed to be ubiquitously inebriated. He had read that the notorious "Denver Agency," presided over by the equally renowned Major James B. Thompson, had been disbanded. He was surprised that a handful of Utes remained upon the city streets as characters for amusement and derision. It saddened him to witness another example of the patent disintegration of a viable indigenous group, the unavoidable byproduct of mining camps and western expansion.

His rendezvous with Mr. Jocknick had been scheduled for noon on the following Wednesday in a nearby restaurant. On the day, Collins sat in a corner of sunlight at a small table, enjoying black tea in a delicate china cup. The fine china and linen napkins naturally turned his thoughts to Chicago Joe. He failed to notice the rather tall and Nordic looking fellow standing before him. A polite clearing of the throat brought him around to the man's presence.

"My apologies," Collins said, standing. "You are Mr. Jocknick?"

"I am as you say." Mr. Jocknick possessed a faint

Swedish accent and a rather impressive blonde moustache, shot with gray. Collins thought he recognized him.

"Please sit down," C.W. said, gesturing to the other chair at the table.

They sat and Collins lifted the teapot as an inquiry. The other man nodded.

"Were you in the war?" he asked, carefully filling the man's cup.

"I was a captain." Jocknick seemed a trifle taciturn.

"Now a representative for Mr. Schurz?"

"I am."

Collins decided to curb his attempts at conversation and wait on the man to illuminate him as to Schurz's reasons for requesting his services. He gazed out the window at the bright summer day. He suddenly remembered the reason for his recognition of this man, Jocknick. In 1873, the man's image had featured prominently in the newspapers accompanying articles regarding his exoneration for the "Blount Frauds" with the eastern Cherokee in North Carolina. He had been with the Indian Bureau for quite some time then, C.W. mused.

"Secretary Schurz has spoken of you many times," Jocknick said, breaking the silence.

Collins turned to look at him.

"He has remarked upon your...delicacy." Jocknick dabbed his painstakingly decorous moustache with a napkin.

Collins waited. He poured more tea.

"There is a situation developing in Colorado. It is, indeed, delicate."

The waiter came over to see if they required luncheon. They ordered steaks. Mr. Jocknick glanced around after the waiter left, as if gauging the privacy of their intercourse.

"There are factions in the state determined to dispossess the Utes of all their remaining lands. We are speaking of millions of acres of land rich with timber, grazing and mineral ores. Powerful men in the Colorado political echelons are creating a situation that could escalate into further armed conflicts with the Indians and the massacre of homesteaders and prospectors encroaching upon the borders of Ute lands."

"I must claim small sympathy with those who trespass upon treaty lands, Mr. Jocknick. Perhaps I am poorly suited for this commission."

The man scrutinized him for a moment. "On the contrary," he said. "It is for your known sympathies with the Indian that Mr. Schurz has contacted you specifically. As you no doubt are aware, he was not inordinately fond of President Grant, but, as I believe he told you last winter, he has come to respect Grant's peace policy. Although Secretary Schurz remains unconvinced that the president was an astute judge of character, he has come to respect you and your abilities."

Collins examined the traces of tea leaves on the bottom of his cup. He had heard there were Chinamen in San Francisco who told fortunes by "reading" the patterns created by the residue.

"I have found that President Grant could be an excellent judge of character when not played upon by spurious actors. Be that as it may," C.W. said, looking up, "I must be thoroughly briefed as to the nature of Mr. Schurz's plans for me before I accept any employment, delicate or otherwise."

The waiter arrived bearing plates laden with what was most probably Cheyenne beef. He carefully arranged the meal upon the little table, squeezing in condiments, dishes of potatoes and vegetables.

"I will adequately apprise you of his plans for you, Mr. Collins, never fear," Jocknick said when the waiter had gone. "I do not, however, feel comfortable engaging in such communication in so public a place. May we indulge in small talk until such time as we might remove to the privacy of your rooms in the hotel?"

In spite of their brief acquaintanceship, Collins sincerely doubted Jocknick's talents in the arena of small talk, but he nodded all the same. They gave their attentions to the excellent meal while the dining room filled to overflowing with the wealthier inhabitants of Denver. Collins and Jocknick did not, in point of fact, utter another word until their repast was completed.

2

In the tiny alcove, enclosing a table and two chairs near a window overlooking Larimer Street, the two men again seated themselves. Collins had found Jocknick to be reticent to the point of absurdity, but endured the man's tight-lipped affectation until they had gained the privacy of his rooms. He then braced the man with a piercing gaze.

"Enough, Mr. Jocknick. My patience is wearing thin and my mission cannot be as secret as all that."

Jocknick fastidiously produced a spotlessly white handkerchief and wiped his nose. "On the contrary, Mr. Collins," he said, sniffing. "In the Queen City, you never know who might eavesdrop on a conversation, especially on a topic as politically incendiary as the one upon which we are about to embark."

Collins stifled a chuckle at this latest pedantic assertion. "Oh come now, Mr. Jocknick, what exactly are we discussing? For, frankly, other than the fact that political factions are intent upon dispossessing Indians of treaty lands, I am entirely uninformed regarding this supposed topic. Also, I might presume to point out that this certainly is not a novel occurrence in the recent history of the western territories."

"Colorado is a state," Jocknick said, again wiping his nose and returning the linen to its pocket.

"Oh for...yes, it is a state and not a territory. God's teeth, man, will you not advance our discussion?" C.W.

willfully distracted himself by taking out his pipe.

"The governor of this *state*," Jocknick said and looked meaningfully at Collins, "is Mr. Frederick Pitkin. Mr. Pitkin has made his fortune on silver plundered from Ute lands in the San Juan Mountains. He has not been alone in this enterprise and most of the good and true men of Colorado politics come from similarly dubious backgrounds. There remain vast reserves of mineral wealth in Ute lands, as well as timber and other resources previously mentioned by me. Interested parties, most notably allies of Mr. Pitkin, are determined to author ruinous conflicts created to force the Indian Bureau to remove the Utes from any remaining and profitable regions... In order to open it up for further development, of course"

Jocknick fumbled in another pocket and produced a newspaper clipping. He cleared his throat. "I procured this from the *Denver Tribune* some time ago. It was written by the current secretary to Governor Pitkin, one William B. Vickers."

He handed the clipping to Collins, who puffed thoughtfully on his pipe as he read the article.

The Utes are actual, practical Communists and the government should be ashamed to foster and encourage them in their idleness and wanton waste of property. Living off the bounty of a paternal but idiotic Indian Bureau, they actually become too lazy to draw their rations in the regular way but insist on taking what they want wherever they find it. Removed to Indian Territory, the Utes could be fed and clothed for about one half of what it now costs the government. Honorable N.C. Meeker, the well-known Superintendent of the White River Agency, was formerly a fast friend and ardent admirer of the Indians. He went to the Agency in the firm belief that he could manage the Indians successfully by kind treatment, patient precept and good example. But utter failure marked his efforts and at last he reluctantly accepted the truth of the border truism that the only truly good Indians are dead ones.

"This is potent vitriol," C.W. said. "I will not dispute the point."

"Vitriol indeed. Political ballyhoo. The article has been reprinted in newspapers around the state under the title, 'The Utes Must Go!' Public orators and anyone with their sights set on political office have made this their rallying cry."

"'*Delenda est Carthago*,'" Collins mused.

Jocknick started in surprise. "'Carthage must be destroyed.' You, sir, have read your Plutarch."

He nodded. "The comparison is not much of a reach. Pray continue."

"Secretary Schurz and I are convinced there exists a cadre of powerful men in Colorado creating mayhem with the express purpose of gaining such popular support so as to entirely rid the state of all Indians. We believe that Vickers is one of the leaders. As it is, he has recently become part owner of the Denver Tribune, as well as its editor."

"Truly? That certainly is telling. What is it that Secretary Schurz wishes of me specifically?" Collins asked.

"To investigate. To learn the identities of the ringleaders of this potentially disastrous campaign, beyond the obvious politicians with outspoken agendas such as Chaffee, Teller and Pitkin. Men behind the scenes willing to resort to extreme violence with impunity. Mr. Schurz needs you to discover the extent of their malfeasance and stop them, if possible."

Collins laid aside his pipe and stretched in his chair.

"I will be frank, Mr. Jocknick. I am at a loss as to how to proceed. It will take me a good deal of time merely to learn the lay of the land, the politics, the players involved. It would seem as if the denouement of these events is imminently pending and I am unsure as to whether I will be able to deal my hand in early enough to be relevant."

Jocknick sniffed peremptorily. He twisted the waxed end of one of his moustaches. "I appreciate your forthrightness, Mr. Collins. I am, however, certain that you are completely capable of dealing your hand in, as you say. I know much about your history, having personally visited with President Grant vis-à-vis yourself."

This quite took Collins aback. "You met with President Grant?"

"I did, indeed. I have known him for many years. Although being ideally discreet, he did, in fact, apprise me of your abilities and his confidence in your...shall I say, circumspection."

"I am gratified, Mr. Jocknick." Collins said, gaining a measure of droll interest in his companion. This fellow was thorough if nothing else. "I, nevertheless, remain ignorant as to where to begin."

"I have a small list of persons with whom you should first consult." He removed a piece of paper from a vest pocket and unfolded it. "Some you may trust, some you may not. All will possess useful information," he said, handing it over.

"Nathan Meeker, of the White River Agency," C.W. read aloud.

"The agent. A ridiculous gentleman. A protégé of Horace Greeley... mentioned in the Tribune article as having given the Utes every opportunity to abide by his new direction and, in a remarkably short period of time, as having despaired of their redemption."

Collins recollected that he had, in point of fact, read essays written by Meeker, published in eastern newspapers. "He is a pietistic disciple of Fourier who has embarked upon a great Utopian experiment just north of here."

"Yes. The Union Colony, now known as Greeley."

"What, pray tell, can he possibly have to do with darkling political machinery? He would seem to be one of our last American idealists."

"I must admit to a grave dislike of Meeker. He is self-aggrandizing and blinded by his own sanctimonious nature. He is surely behaving as a willing marionette to these men bent on the destruction of the Utes."

"How?" Collins asked.

"Since having been appointed agent to the White River Utes, he has been applying his intractable sense of superiority in all matters. Apparently, he intends to have the Utes dancing to his own puritanical tune... despite his aversion to dancing."

"Please elaborate," C.W. requested, now thoroughly amused by his companion.

"He is, according to my sources, in terrible debt and seeks to ameliorate this through employment by the Indian Bureau. He is under the influence of those who seek to use his compulsive journalism as the voice of experts. He is an inveterate complainer."

"I understand." He consulted the paper in his hand. "Ooorey? Owray? What is this?"

"Pronounced Yu-ray. He is a most illustrious light of the Ute tribe, almost universally beloved by the whites."

"This would render me most suspicious of him."

"Exactly. I do not think him above lending his influence in the aid of those who would make a profit from agency business." Jocknick sniffed and narrowed his eyes. "Assess him for yourself, but know that Mr. Schurz is more than passing fond of him."

C.W. read the next name. "Charles Adams."

"Yes. He may be trusted, although his brother-in-law

is James B. Thompson of Denver Agency fame. Adams was Indian agent on the White River and Los Pinos agencies and is a good friend to the Utes. He may be a trifle naïve when it comes to the depths of political machinations being currently employed."

"And where may he be found?"

"He now resides near Manitou Springs, just south of here. Unfortunately, as post office inspector for Colorado and New Mexico Territory and, given his penchant for patrolling his routes most diligently, he is at present, unavailable. I will inform you of his return by telegram. You may have to accomplish an inordinate amount of traveling within a very short time in order to complete your mission."

"That, sir, is understood...Otto Mears," Collins said, referring again to the list.

"I believe he is currently scouting the route for another of his toll roads into mining country. Definitely not to be trusted. He is known to Adams and I believe admired by him, but this man is a nimble operator motivated solely by personal ambition. I suspect that he is tightly enmeshed in the aforementioned cadre of political interests. He worked diligently toward the election of Governor Pitkin."

Collins fiddled pensively with his pipe, spinning it upon the surface of the table. "How come you to know so much of Colorado intrigue? Do you not reside in Washington D.C.?"

"I do, indeed." He smiled slightly for the first time during their brief acquaintance.

"Well then?" C.W. asked, refusing to be put off the scent.

"I, myself, have been engaged to investigate certain matters in the past. This is not my first foray into Colorado. In truth, I maintain a small abode in this fair city." The ephemeral display of sardonic humor evaporated.

Collins suddenly realized there were vast reserves of

intricacies within this finical gentleman across the table from him. "I see," he said and turned back to the list. "John Lawrence."

"A prominent rancher near the town of Saguache. I do not know him well, but my impression is that he is respectable. He offered his services as interpreter for the Utes for the 1868 and 1873 treaty talks, speaks several Indian dialects, as well as Spanish, and is notorious for employing Indians and Mexicans on his ranch."

"Sidney Jocknick?" he read the last name.

"He is my son and has resided in Colorado since 1870. He worked under Charles Adams at the Cochetopa location of the Los Pinos Agency and under Agents Bond and Wheeler at the Uncompahgre location." He held up his hand at Collins' inquisitive glance. "There were two locations...the complications of which Sidney can thoroughly educate you. He has knocked about the mining country and is currently in need of gainful employment. I have been authorized to employ him as your guide and confidante. Be warned, he thinks highly of Mears, but President Grant assured me that you are one for assessing each situation upon your own counsel. Sidney is still quite young in many ways and slow to think for himself. Perhaps his association with you will prove profitable for him both monetarily as well as experientially."

"I assume he is to be my primary associate?"

"He will most assuredly expedite your travel and education. He has been in the vicinity of the recent boomtown of Rico. Having failed entirely in the arena of prospecting, he now endeavors to discover a source of cinnabar for sale to paint manufacturers." He glanced at C.W., realizing his tone had descended into the realm of paternal disappointment. He swiftly altered his tack. "I have secured your fare aboard the train to Alamosa for tomorrow and thence aboard the Barlow and Sanderson stage line into the San Juan Mountains and the town of

Ouray."

"There is a town called Ouray?"

"There is indeed," affirmed Jocknick. "A testament to the chief's popularity with the good people of Colorado."

"Does your son look for my arrival?"

"He does. He has received a letter and adequate funds. He should have all gear and provisions assembled in readiness for your arrival." Jocknick stood.

In the dimming light of the afternoon, he appeared to Collins to have wearied appreciably. He walked the man to the door. "I thank you for all the useful information. How shall I remain in contact with you?"

"Send telegrams to my residence here in Denver." Jocknick handed him yet another slip of paper. "Be discreet. I will see you off tomorrow."

3

His teeth set against physical discomfort and the robust brew of odors wafting from his fellow passengers, Collins peered out of the stagecoach window, mercifully unobstructed by the leather covering. The scenery was so stunning as to blessedly distract him from the suffocating restlessness imbued in him by the nature of his conveyance. Tall, shining peaks rose in an azure sky, their feet spread with cloaks of dense evergreens. The dramatic ranges of mountains seemed to create an impenetrable wall. Yet the hearty coach twisted, climbed and bounced its circuitous route farther and farther into the heart of the granite stronghold, sometimes passing men, carts, primitive sleds, freight wagons, buggies and beasts of burden trudging doggedly into this empire of accidental fortune. C.W. longed for the luxury of traveling alone. If only there had been time to send for his own transportation and outfit in order to pursue this latest investigation. Mr. Jocknick had remained adamant about the need for alacrity.

Shrugging off the insistent head of a sleeping passenger beside him, Collins observed that snow now covered the road, such as it was, as they steadily climbed to what was certain to be another pass. He had spent an uncomfortable night in Rose's Cabin, a stopover of questionable wholesomeness and cramped quarters. Charles Schaffer, the proprietor, was garrulous in the extreme and there had been talk of an event of cannibalism near

Lake City. C.W. had resolved to inquire as to the tale's particulars when united with Jocknick's son as, according to his father, he was a font of information regarding the San Juan region. Morning had found him crammed cheek by jowl in this battered coach penetrating deeper and deeper into the jaws of solid rock upon trails that did not deserve the name of "byway," let alone of "road."

He turned his perusal to the men with whom he was rubbing knees. The fellow straight across was undoubtedly a salesman of some type, wearing a store-bought suit of checked material, gold wire spectacles, and cloth gaiters over his scuffed shoes. The drummer was dozing with a worn satchel upon his lap, his unhygienic breath contributing to the unsavory atmosphere. The man in the middle appeared to be a plain laborer, perhaps a miner, not prosperous, but reasonably clean and built for strenuous exertion. His steely gray eyes met Collins' momentarily with an expression of friendly commiseration.

Caddy corner across from C.W. was another of the laborer class, but one of tattered vestments, filthy hands and boots near to rendering him barefoot, one wrapped in burlap and tied with twine. He, too, dozed fitfully, waking occasionally when the stagecoach lurched violently, glaring at the man across from him as if he had engineered the event, then resuming his slumbers. During one of his exuberant yawns, C.W. had observed that the gent was in sore need of dental care. The gentleman using him as a head rest was evidently a gambler type who seemed to be asleep most of the time. It seemed impossible to him that six grown men had wedged themselves into the tiny contraption. He had been previously reassured by the drummer that it was not unusual to have up to eight men crammed into the coach. He found this to be barely credible.

Glancing outward again, he could observe that the

carriage had labored almost to the apex of a majestic pass. Shortly thereafter, the horses were pulled to a halt and they heard the booming voice of the driver.

"Well boys, you are on a 'foot-and-walker line' so you have some work to do."

He demanded that all disembark the vehicle. Obligingly, the six of them climbed out into the brisk air of impressive elevation, stretching and cracking joints stiff from disuse. The driver and his companion extracted a two-man cross cut saw from beneath the pile of luggage upon the roof of the coach and handed it down. They directed the passengers to take turns at felling trees. Perplexed, Collins joined the stolid laborer of clean hands and took the first shift, climbing a short snowy bank above the road and unquestioningly commencing to cut through the trunk of a pine tree pointed out to them by Stokes, the driver. The saw had been recently sharpened and they were deep into one foot of diameter when Stokes replaced them with the gambler and the drummer. Puffing in the thin air, C.W. and the miner, who had introduced himself as Luke Walsh, slipped and slid down to the roadbed to spectate with the others.

"What are the logs for?" Collins asked Walsh as they watched the two decidedly unathletic fellows struggle with the saw.

"Why, to slow our passage down the grade." The man answered in a manner that suggested C.W. bore no greater mental competence than a small child.

"I am unacquainted with these mountains," Collins told him.

As they stood waiting, he caught an occasional whiff of some repugnant odor. Believing, at first, its provenance was most probably one of his fellow passengers, he said nothing. However, as the sun came out from behind the clouds and warmed the terrain, the stench became alarming.

"What, in god's name, is that smell?" C.W. asked his companion, uncaring that he might again be berated for his ignorance.

"You spoke the truth when you said you were not acquainted with these mountains, friend," Walsh said wryly. "That is the aroma of many and sundry beasts what have perished on this hazardous road."

"You mean to say that this emanates from dead animals?"

"Certainly. Follow me."

Luke Walsh walked over to the abrupt edge of the trail upon which they stood. Down the side, scattered across precipitous moraine left behind by prehistoric glaciers and partially obscured by melting drifts of snow, were the myriad carcasses of mules, donkeys and horses in varying stages of decomposition. Collins shook his head in disbelief at this evidence of wanton greed and the dearth of compassion. No wonder, he thought, the Utes were in danger.

Stokes and the relief driver, Perkins, had finally ceased being amused at the weak and pathetic efforts of the cardsharp and salesman to bring down the tree. They cursed with imagination and climbed up to push them out of the way. The tree was felled forthwith. The ragged miner and the remaining passenger, a fellow of youth and enthusiasm fresh from some eastern college, were directed to fell another evergreen nearby. The rest of them dragged the first tree down behind the coach, while Perkins stood at the head of the team to prevent a runaway. They took turns limbing the tree and when the other had been felled, limbed and similarly positioned, chains were removed from the boot of the coach and the logs were anchored to the undercarriage. Thus situated, the passengers were allowed to remount to their seats and the stage swayed wildly as Stokes and Perkins climbed to their perch above the horses.

Collins, not ordinarily daunted by physical danger, found the subsequent journey into the town of Ouray to be one of the most distressing events of his life. Not being the captain of his fate, wedged into a flimsy wooden box and confronted with precipices of indescribable depth, he experienced a realm of helplessness unknown since the war. Despite the logs dragging behind and liberal use of the brake, they seemed to descend at such breakneck speed as to defy the inadequate suspension of the stagecoach. The passengers jolted and bounced against each other and into each other's laps in a most disreputable jumble.

The coach emerged from a narrow and steep defile to turn into a jagged river gorge, and shortly thereafter stopped before a rickety bridge across a raging cataract. The driver spoke briefly with a man who emerged from a cabin tucked between a wall of rock and the roadbed. A barricade that blocked entry to the bridge was lifted. The lines snapped and the coach proceeded around a corner and down another pitch. Out of the window, facing upslope, Collins observed dramatic hanging curtains of gigantic icicles, pale blue and oddly threatening. He became acutely aware that the strait upon which they traveled was hewn out of solid rock and was just adequate to accommodate the width of the stagecoach. Occasionally, there passed an ominous shadow of overhanging granite.

Finally, the stage slowed as the driver pulled in the horses and they eased to the base of an enormous stone cirque. They subsequently plunged down yet another steep switchback until at last the carriage entered upon gentler terrain. Pausing momentarily to release the dragging logs and add them to a pile of others by the side of the way, the driver maneuvered the coach skillfully into muddy streets and pulled up in front of the stage office. The six wayfarers woke from their nightmare and disembarked with shaky legs and a variety of bruises, fetching luggage as it was thrown from the boot and the roof and parting from each other with brief farewells.

"Luck to you, sir," Walsh said to Collins, shaking his hand.

"And to you. Will you now try your hand at the color?"

"Perhaps. Most likely end up working for someone else, though," he said resignedly and directed his steps toward a nearby saloon.

Collins found his bags and gazed about the bustling center street of the town. Looking above, he observed that walls of rock surrounded the hamlet with only an outlet to the north. Everywhere the citadel was pocked with prospecting holes and adorned by yellow fans of mine tailings. A snow-covered mountain peak of mythic proportions stood as sentinel to the southwest. The tantalizing scent of food had just distracted him from inspection of his surroundings, when a tall, broad man with a bushy moustache and clear blue eyes approached him from across the road. The gent wore a flat-brimmed sombrero of dirty gray beaver felt and wide suspenders of a singular floral pattern. He was in his shirtsleeves, despite the cool temperature of late afternoon.

"Mr. Collins?" he asked with a voice appropriate to his stature. C.W. was only slightly taller.

"Yes. Are you Sidney Jocknick?"

"I am. We have a room in this hotel for the night." He gestured at the building nearby, which also housed the stage line headquarters. They walked into the three-story clapboard hotel and climbed the stairs to the second floor and their room. C.W. was pleased to see there were two small beds and that they would not be forced to "double-up," as he truly disliked sharing narrow mattresses with strangers. Jocknick was apparently tidy with his gear neatly organized by his bed.

Collins set his bags on the floor. "Is there a decent meal to be had in this village?" he asked.

"There is Mrs. Bronnon's place next door. She is more skilled with pies than meat and potatoes, but I do not think we will go amiss."

STAGECOACH

4

"Has your father thoroughly informed you as to what is required?" Collins asked as they sat awaiting their meal.

Their table was adorned with blue gingham cloth, as were the other tables, all the windows and Mrs. Bronnon.

"Not thoroughly. I would not say thoroughly, no."

Sidney bore little physical resemblance to his father and he had a slow, deliberate quality, seemingly born of habitual introspection and a modicum of caution. He certainly did not seem to be the youthful and impetuous character described by the senior Jocknick. Their stew, biscuits, coffee and apple pie arrived at the same time. All this was accompanied by fresh cream and butter.

"Well, gentlemen," Mrs. Bronnon said, after placing everything upon the table. "Will there be anything else? I have a large order for cakes and pies to bake and must be about my business." She was a beefy woman with a red face and no humor.

Collins shook his head and Jocknick and he began eating. They did not further engage in conversation for several minutes. Mrs. Bronnon disappeared into the kitchen. No other patrons entered and they had the place to themselves.

"I do not even know to what destination you intend," Jocknick said after a while.

C.W. was employed in lathering a thick layer of butter onto a biscuit. "Ouray," he said.

Jocknick stared at him a moment, a forkful of stew poised in front of his mouth. "We are in Ouray," he finally said softly.

Collins smiled. "Of course," he said. "I meant the man."

Sidney chewed and swallowed. "He is at Uncompahgre Agency, just north of here. We can depart in the morning."

"After which, we will have much traveling ahead of us."

"This does not pose a problem. I have good mounts and a worthy pack mule from Mr. Riley at the Watson Stables. They are being shod as we speak."

"I do not have a saddle," C.W. told him.

"I purchased one for you, assuming you would require it."

"Excellent."

They finished their meal, not toothsome but adequate, summoned Mrs. Bronnon in order to settle the bill and stepped out into the late afternoon.

"What of supplies?" Collins asked, putting on his Stetson and donning his coat against the growing chill of the high mountain air.

"They are purchased and being held at Rawles' dry goods store for our convenience."

"It would seem as if your father has chosen a most reliable guide and provisioner," Collins said, stepping into the road and walking casually toward the hotel. "I am grateful for your exhaustive preparations."

"Thank you," said Jocknick. They strolled down the street in the gathering twilight. "Are you a drinking man?" he asked after a bit. "Did you care to step into a saloon or add liquor to our stock?"

"I abstain as a rule. If you care to imbibe, I will repair to our room and you may occupy yourself as you see fit. I ask only that you be in fine fettle for the morning and do not make too much noise on your return this evening. As for liquor on the trail, I never require it and ask you follow suit."

"You mistake me sir," Jocknick said, stopping in his tracks and holding himself in a formal and rigid manner. "I decidedly do not drink except on rare occasions and do not require it at any venture."

Observing that his companion had been offended, Collins clapped him good-naturedly on the back. "Oh come now, Sidney, I was not implying such. Let us proceed together then and spend a restful night in anticipation of some rigorous travel."

Jocknick loosened his stance and once again accompanied Collins on his amble toward the hotel. They mounted the steps to their room in the midst of an animated argument between a grimy man in work clothing and a clerk behind the counter in the lobby. The discussion seemed to revolve around the exorbitant price of rooms. They shut their door against the din and prepared for repose. The sun had slipped behind the towering rock walls outside the only window.

MINERS

5

Collin's horse turned out to be a stout black mare. She had two rear stockings and a wide blaze down her nose between two savvy eyes, alert to all activity in her vicinity. He saddled her with the heavy and scuffed item provided by Jocknick. It appeared to be serviceable, but much abused. The mare, nameless according to Jack Riley the proprietor, remained calm as he placed the saddle on her back and adjusted the cinch and lengthened the stirrups. The stable was overflowing with animals, which Collins guessed were necessary to replace all those creatures profligately worked to exhaustion and cast aside upon the precipices of the San Juans. He surmised that, between animals living and dead, the summer fly population would have to be formidable.

Jocknick busied himself with a bay gelding that belonged to him, purchased while employed at the Uncompahgre Agency. Interestingly, Sidney had regaled Collins with a tragic story about his horse as they prepared for sleep the previous night. It seems he had been acquainted with Jim Beckwourth's nephew, George, who worked a mail route between the agency cow camp and the Cimarron River. While thus employed, he fell victim to a truly unfortunate accident involving a Ute pony herd, resulting in his consequent death. Jocknick had purchased one of the horses George had regularly used, avowedly out of pure sentimentality. This same animal, "Shoe String," was his current mount. Collins found the

Beckwourth connection between Wakalyapi, his cherished companion of erstwhile days, and Jocknick to be one of those small synchronies with which life was riddled.

The pack animal, chosen by Sidney for its size and docile temperament, was a draft mule of Belgian strain, similar to his own mule, Joey. It was a minimum of seventeen hands tall and more corpulent than any equine Collins had ever seen. Riley called him "Colorow" after an imposing Ute chief of past acquaintance. Jocknick thought it wise to rename him in the near future, as they would be traveling amongst the Ute people. Colorow could easily pack all gear and provisions required by them and more. Riley also assured them the mule would protect the camp from lions and bears, a statement that Collins knew to be accurate from past experience.

Having retrieved their victuals and being fully outfitted and adequately mounted, Jocknick and Collins rode north out of Ouray in early morning light, through a passageway bounded by steep cliffs and the Uncompahgre River. Occasionally, the sound of iron hitting stone could be heard and once they rode uneasily by the ungodly cacophony of a stamp mill, their animals restless with nervous displeasure. Above their heads, Collins again noted that the rock bore multiple scars of relentless prospecting, testaments either to desperation or extravagant optimism. He could not decide which.

After a reticent mile or two, Collins wearied of the prolonged silence and decided upon an attempt to divine information from his companion. His husky black mare, whom he had christened Mona, proved to be a calm and reliable mount and, given the general safety of their route, C.W. found himself to be really rather bored. Colorow's wide backside was monotonous scenery.

"What do you say to Felix?" Collins asked, being deliberately obtuse.

Sidney turned in his saddle. "What?"

"Let us rename Colorow the mule after the famed Indian commissioner, Felix Brunot."

"Suits me," the man said, smiling.

As the trail widened, Collins kicked up his horse to ride abreast with Jocknick. "What do you know of Nathan Meeker?"

Jocknick shrugged. "A citified gent who should never have been given the job of Indian agent…but then, I have seen more than one wrong man with the job."

"Such as?"

"Jabeze Neversink Trask."

Collins laughed aloud. "Surely you jest. There never was such a person."

"There was indeed," Jocknick said, smiling broadly. "He was the agent at the first Los Pinos Agency when I arrived."

"Explain that, if you please. Your father mentioned two Los Pinos agencies."

"Well, let us see," Sidney said pensively. "Let us begin with Trask. I recollect it was in the summer of '71. As you no doubt know, according to Grant's policy, various church boards were to recommend agents for Indian reservations. The determination was that the Utes were to have the guidance of the Unitarians exclusive. Mr. Jabeze Neversink was a Harvard man and fine example of Unitarian prowess."

He paused as they watched an osprey perform an arrow swift dive into the waters of the nearby river and rise with a silvery trout in its talons.

"Please continue," Collins encouraged. He found Mr. Jocknick to be a most competent orator when the spirit took him, quite unlike his father. He no longer despaired of weary miles of travel.

"By June of 1872, it became apparent that Mr. Jabeze was not an entirely successful designee. The first location on Cochetopa Pass was remote and not suited to growing crops and Trask was out of his depth. He was never accepted and did more harm than good, hiding in his house and hoarding supplies. That is when they moved General Adams into the position of agent to replace him. The discovery was made in Washington, however, that Charles Adams, no matter how adept he had proved as shepherd to his Ute flock, was a Catholic. The Unitarian hub of Boston made itself active and Henry Bond, a well-known Unitarian, replaced Adams. But the removal of Adams, a gentleman of experience and known and respected by several Indian tribes, was decidedly ill-advised. Bond was frail and sickly and perhaps not altogether honest. He was soon replaced by Major Willard Wheeler.

"It was in the summer of 1875 that orders came to pull up stakes and relocate the agency and Utes to the Uncompahgre country. So, as you see, there was the first agency in the mountains and the second on the Uncompahgre River. The second has a far more beneficial altitude for gardens and livestock. But I fear that serious trouble is indeed approaching between the Utes, settlers and miners."

"What more of Meeker? Any further knowledge of him?"

Jocknick snorted derisively. "I know enough of the Utes and of Meeker to tell you he is headed for a fall. 'Into the valley of death' as old Tennyson would say."

"As serious as that?" Collins asked, wrapping his reins around the saddle horn and uncorking the top of his canteen for a drink. The sun was quite warm and they had been steadily losing altitude. When finished, he wiped the rim and handed the flask over to Jocknick, who accepted it and took a long pull.

"Thanks," he said, handing it back. "Yes...I would say it is as serious as all that. I have imparted as much to my father. I have heard the talk and know that every dead cow, every forest fire, every missing prospector and every broken wagon axle is being blamed upon the Utes. And Meeker keeps penning those absurd essays for the *Greeley Tribune*."

"What is the import of these essays?" asked C.W.

"How the poor Indian must be brought into the bosom of civilization for his own good and some such. That fellow Meeker, to my understanding, has begun a campaign against the Ute ponies and I can tell you, they will not stand for it."

As if by prompt, Jocknick's horse, Shoe String, began to hop about in an odd manner. Sidney dropped the pack mule's lead rope in order to use both hands to bring the animal back under his control. It began to buck with a purpose. Collins grabbed the lead for Colorow, now Felix, and pulled him away from the commotion. It was then that he noticed a large diamondback rattlesnake coiled and buzzing beneath a nearby cluster of willows. Jocknick urged his horse ahead on the road. The animal minced along in a bunched-up stance, but was no longer bucking. Collins moved Mona after Jocknick, who was already heading farther down the trail. The mule followed with equanimity.

"Snake?" Sidney asked as Collins caught up to him.

"Big one."

"Confounded horse. No matter how many he encounters, he still comes apart."

It was plain to Collins that Sidney was inordinately fond of the unprepossessing gelding, due probably in part to his past attachment to George Beckwourth. He, himself, was pleased at the calm reserve exhibited by his new mare and the giant mule. It seemed his fortune to be graced by exceptional animals.

"Have you actually met this Meeker?" C.W. asked, returning to their original topic of conversation.

"Nope. I have had my fill of sanctimonious old gentlemen." Jocknick pointed to the west of them. "There is a hot springs pool over yonder. It was a lovely spot once, but now it is piled with garbage and has become a location for carousing."

"Do you believe Meeker to be politically motivated or merely blinded by his own good intentions?"

Digging a piece of plug tobacco from a breast pocket, Sidney took a bite and waved it at Collins, who shook his head.

"He may be a pawn, but I would say not knowingly," he told Collins around the wad of tobacco in his mouth. "But it has always been my opinion that well-meaning purveyors of disaster are no less disastrous." He spit a brown stream toward a clump of tall grass.

Collins smiled wryly. "Well said. What of Ouray?"

"The man or the town?" Sidney asked, turning to look at him with a twinkle in his eye. "He is frequently inscrutable," he said without waiting for an answer. "He has lost prestige since the Brunot Commission awarded him his thousand dollars per annum in '73. It has been paid more reliably than the other annuities."

"That is when the Utes gave up the San Juan Mountains?"

Jocknick senior had given Collins some notes to study on his train trip, mostly regarding the history of the Ute treaties and the duplicity of the Indian Commission. It was all so painfully recognizable to Collins, having been privy to the machinations of the U.S. government in regard to several situations involving Indians.

"For twenty five thousand dollars a year and Ouray's allowance. Brunot argued that if the Utes sold the mountains and there was no gold, then the whites would leave their mountains. Otherwise, there would be war and the Utes would get nothing."

"Tidy argument. Not the first time it has been employed."

Jocknick shrugged. "It is true. These Indians will lose everything, I fear, just as other tribes before them. There is no easy answer when white interests conflict with those of Indians."

"I suppose. But there must be some other solution," Collins said, tipping his hat back and scratching his forehead. "The traditional approach seems fairly simple to most; annihilate the Indians and all is expedient. I do not adhere to such thinking."

"Now you sound very similar in opinion to my father. He was the eyes and ears of President Grant in regards to Indian matters for several years. It is how he came to be suspected of stealing lands from the Cherokee."

Collins was astounded. "He spied for Grant?"

"I do not know if I would call it spying," Jocknick said, sounding a bit guarded. "He reported back to him on sensitive matters."

"Of course, I did not mean...and how much did your father actually inform you as to my present mission?"

"Not much. Just to tell you all I know and take you where you require. He implied that prudence was desirable. I presume, from our present destination of Ouray's farm, the import of your questions and the fact that Mr. Schurz employs my father, this has some what to do with the Ute difficulties."

"You deduce correctly, Mr. Jocknick," Collins said, and took out his pipe.

GRANT

6

The fire lit a warm halo about them as Collins smoked and relaxed after supper and Jocknick occasionally spat tobacco juice into the flames. A vixen cried plaintively in the darkness. According to Sidney, they were nearly halfway to Ouray's farm, having traveled until almost dark. The summer night became quite cold once the sun had descended and C.W. sat wrapped in a blanket.

"May I prevail upon you to tell me of the cannibal of Lake City?" he asked Jocknick.

The man appeared to be pleased by the request. "Certainly. I was well acquainted with him."

"In truth?"

"Indeed. I was wintering in the Los Pinos cow camp on the Gunnison when the first of his company arrived. They were near to dead from starvation and exposure. Ouray had given them shelter at the Uncompahgre, where he was staying for the winter. He would have extended it for the duration of the season, but they were eager to push through to new strikes in Summit County before spring and so had come to us. They had originally set out from Provo in early winter despite warnings of the pending severity of the season. As they were unfamiliar with the country, the landlord of the Provo boarding house where they were domiciled directed them to a guide supposedly schooled in the Colorado byways. This fellow, Alferd Packer, happened to be in some difficulty with the local law, but if they paid his fine, he would work it off by guiding them into gold country."

"Alferd?"

"Alferd or Alfred. I have heard it both ways. When the man spoke his name, it was difficult to tell which, what with his broken front teeth." Jocknick reached to refill his coffee cup.

"Well, in truth," he continued, "Packer had never actually ventured through Colorado. Many men were acquainted with the route in '73, so they would have been far better off with another guide. Eventually, after surviving episodes of freezing cold, starvation and bad judgment, fifteen of the original twenty-one members of the party became accounted for at the Los Pinos Agency...the one at Cochetopa, that is. Ouray sent a runner, Lovo, to find out what had occurred. When he came by the cow camp, we figured out that Packer and five others were still unaccounted for. I left Jim Kelley with the livestock and went with Lovo and the cow boss, Alonzo Hartman, to see Charles Adams at the agency headquarters. When there was no further news, he and his wife left for Denver. Supplies were running low, what with all the extra mouths to feed that winter. Ouray and Chipeta, his wife, arrived from the Uncompahgre and not many days after, a big white man came walking into the agency carrying a coffeepot of coals. He appeared to be in damn good health, considering."

Collins banged out his pipe on a rock. "Was there a Lake City at the time?" he asked.

"No. Desolate country then, especially in winter. According to his story, the party of men had forked off the Gunnison River too early and had followed the Lake Fork rather than the Cochetopa Creek up to the agency. He told us that the others had abandoned him when he had become snow blind. He acted surprised that they had not yet arrived to the agency. We asked what he had been living on all that time and he told us he had found some roots, berries and the like. Ouray was looking him up and down as you would a prize pig at a county fair and he did not seem to believe him. I remember Alonzo asking some impolitic questions and the man was decidedly taciturn."

Collins got to his feet and fetched more wood for the fire. When he was settled again, Jocknick resumed his story.

"I traveled back to the cow camp to take up my duties and I heard this fellow went on down to Saguache. Me and Jim kept an eye out for the rest of Alferd's party, but no one showed and spring arrived. Otto Mears told me later that Packer took a job bartending, but he seemed flush and was gambling quite a bit. Mears suspected him of foul play when he noticed a Wells Fargo draft in his wallet. This was after some other prospectors from Provo told him that Packer was broke when he left and he had been in trouble with the law for passing counterfeit money. Charles Adams had come back from Denver and was in Saguache on his way to the agency, so Mears induced him to devise some story to get Packer back up to the agency, where Adams had full legal jurisdiction. The plan was to get him up there and hold him prisoner until they could investigate. I was back at the agency when they reached there with Packer. He had been led to believe he was to guide a search party for the missing men."

"Describe this Packer," Collins asked as Jocknick bit off another chew of tobacco.

"As I said, he was big." He paused to arrange the wad in his mouth. "He wore unruly long hair and a beard. He was missing his front teeth and his eyes were deep set and shifty with a gray color that held no warmth and never looked right at a body."

"What happened when they got back to the agency?"

"Let me think. I recollect it was early May and the

country had opened enough to where it was known that Packer's group had never reached any of the settlements in the San Juans. We were all convinced by then that they had frozen to death or Packer had murdered them. Charles Adams braced Packer with forceful manner and demanded he tell the truth of what had occurred. That is when he confessed to killing the men with a hatchet as they slept."

"How is it possible that none of them awoke during the procedure?" Collins asked.

"I pondered this as well until one of the Provo men told me he knew Packer to have carried a packet of morphine. He used it to sleep and must have employed the soporific to drug the others in contemplation of murdering them."

"Quite the lad."

"I would not have chosen him as a traveling companion on looks and manner alone."

"Did he then confess to eating his victims?"

"Aw hell no. He never confessed to that. Adams sent out an expedition, with Packer as scout, to find the bodies. In short order, Packer made an attempt to murder Herman Lauter, the man Adams had put in charge."

"How was that?" Collins asked.

"He pulled a knife from his boot, according to Lauter. They brought him back to the agency since he refused to take them any farther, convinced they were about to hang him. He was taken to Saguache and placed in the local jail. Adams put the word out for all prospectors traveling through to keep a sharp eye for the bodies of Packer's victims."

"There was yet no thought of cannibalism?"

Jocknick shook his head. "Nope. Although I believe that Ouray had developed the theory when he was examining the man's stature and apparent health."

"Had he said aught?"

"No. Ouray is savvy enough to skirt making such accusations of white men."

Collins nodded in understanding. "What occurred next?"

"One of the first parties into the Lake City vicinity that year included a fellow named Randolph. He stumbled onto five bodies covered in blankets and purportedly all lying together but one. The heads had been bashed in. The fifth cadaver was a distance away, shot and decapitated. There were signs of struggle and it appeared this fellow, Bell, had made a fair fight of it. A crude shelter stood hard by and it was evident that old Packer had holed up and devoured most of poor Bell. As he had not eaten much of the rest of them, it was surmised the murders had been committed for profit. Randolph is a competent artist and made some grisly sketches of the scene for *Harper's Weekly*. Sadly, Packer had already escaped from jail in Saguache and nothing has been seen of him since."

"You mean to say he is out there somewhere?"

"He is indeed," Sidney told him, grinning wickedly. "Makes a person a bit perturbed to think on it. No telling where he might be."

CANNIBALISM

7

The following day dawned cloudy. There was a stiff breeze blowing from the west as they followed the Uncompahgre River's meanderings through narrow canyons and open bottomland, thick with cottonwood trees. After encountering the bustling tent community of Gold City, at the confluence of Dallas Creek and the river, they skirted the raucous noise and gangs of unwashed men and rode back into untrammeled countryside. They were forced to ford the stream more than once when their route became crowded between water and rock. High above them loomed a distinctive sawtooth skyline covered in snow, hewn jagged with pinnacles of raw granite, fierce and menacing. After a while, they broke out into open terrain of wide river bottom bounded by juniper-covered mesas on the west and sandy hills on the east. Ahead, Collins espied an impressive plateau rising in the north.

When the wind permitted, Jocknick told C.W. tales of hunting on the Gunnison River and stories of eccentric bovines and horses of distinctive personality and quirks. By late morning, they arrived to the second Los Pinos Agency, also known as the Uncompahgre Agency. An American flag snapped above the various adobe buildings situated in the open grassy valley west of the river. A log barn and rather large log bunkhouse sat farther back nearer to the Uncompahgre River. There were several bands of horses scattered about and some came trotting up to sniff at their mounts. Mona squealed and kicked at a fellow who became too inquisitive. They dismounted in front of the building nearest the flagstaff, secured their stock to a hitching rail and loosened their cinches. Collins shooed the other horses away. Some men stood staring at them from the corrals.

Jocknick pointed his chin at a hill to the northwest. "There lies George."

"Your friend Beckwourth?"

"That is he," Sidney said mournfully and stepped onto the small porch to knock on the door.

They entered at the invitation of a voice coming from within. Behind a typical government issue desk sat a fleshy gentleman of authoritative bearing and ruddy complexion.

"How do you do, Sidney," the man said without enthusiasm. "I had no idea you were back in the vicinity."

"Good afternoon, Major. May I present Mr. Charles Collins?"

The agent stood and shook Collins' hand across his desk. "What brings you to the Uncompahgre?"

"Hunting and prospecting," Collins answered before Jocknick could respond. He refrained from glancing at his companion, but felt his eyes upon him.

Major Wheeler sat down and waved his hand in an invitation to follow suit. Collins and Jocknick sat in chairs arranged along the nearby wall.

"When last I heard, Sidney, you were prospecting over in the Dolores River country."

C.W. noted the disapproving fatherly tone the agent used. He was certain it rankled his companion.

"His father and I are old friends and Sidney has been kind enough to offer his services as guide," Collins interjected, adopting slightly punctilious and effeminate mannerisms and gesticulating expressively with his hands. "As this is my first sojourn west, I am most grateful for his invaluable expertise."

"Did you wish to spend the night here at the agency?" Wheeler asked in a manner that was less than welcoming.

C.W. wondered about the history between the two men. "No. But I thank you for the invitation," he said, knowing there had been nothing of the kind. It seemed to him that Jocknick had lost his power of speech. "I am determined to spend all of my nights out of doors in an effort to pursue an authentic western excursion." Collins stood. "Are you prepared to venture forth, Sidney? We must find a commodious campsite before night over takes us." He turned to the agent. "Might I send a telegram?"

"Of course." Wheeler stood and handed him a pad of paper and pencil. "You may leave it with me and I will see that it is sent."

"Thank you," Collins said, scribbling an innocuous message to Jocknick the senior, letting him know they had arrived to the agency. He wrote the address at the bottom and laid the pad on Wheeler's desk.

"What a convenience. And squarely in the middle of the wilderness," he said, fastidiously adjusting his clothing. "Well Sidney?"

Jocknick stood. They bid Agent Wheeler a good day and left the building.

The men rode north through dry grasses cropped short by cattle and horses. Occasionally, they encountered boggy ground. Mona balked a few times at the squelching noise her hooves made in the mud. The wind began to abate as the sun came out from behind the clouds. Collins was smiling to himself in regard to his recent mummery. Of a sudden, Sidney began to laugh heartily. Shoe String crow-hopped a few jumps to exhibit his disapproval.

"That was quite a demonstration of the theatrical," he said at last. "Had I not known better, I would have been convinced you were a sissified dandy from the East."

"I did not care for the man and desired us gone," Collins explained.

"In truth, we could never abide each other and that is why I left the employ of the agency."

"I would not imagine he is courteous with the Indians."

"No. Mr. Adams was the best to be had for the Utes. Bond might have adjusted but he was forced to resign due to some missing cattle and various accusations made by Ouray."

"Missing cattle?" Collins asked, giving his companion a dubious glance.

"None of my doing, I can assure you," Jocknick said. He appeared to be a trifle indignant. "It had been a hard winter and many a slow-elk had fallen to a hungry miner's gun."

"'Slow-elk?'"

"Government cattle."

Collins smiled. "Thereby, I take it, entered Major Wheeler."

"In pomp and circumstance and godlike manner."

They rode in silence for a while as the afternoon progressed. The sun had become quite warm and the pungent scent of willow brush emanated from the river bottom nearby. They came to an open stretch of water and rode over to allow the animals to drink. A blue heron rose majestically from its perch in a dead cottonwood tree.

"Tell me about Ouray," Collins said, as they continued on their way.

"What do you care to know?"

"As much as you do."

"Well, let me see," Jocknick said, looking pensive. "He should be somewhere around forty-five years old. He is becoming rather stout and I have heard that his health may be failing."

"What of his history?" Collins interrupted. "How has he become so prominent?"

"Well, he is only half Ute. The other half is Apache. He grew up around Taos, down south, and he speaks excellent Spanish and really rather proficient English. I have heard he had been a friend of Kit Carson for several years."

"Carson?" C.W. asked in a deprecating tone.

Jocknick looked over at him. "You have had dealings with Kit Carson?"

" 'All his virtues…do in our eyes begin to lose their gloss, yea, like fair fruit in an unwholesome dish, are like to rot untasted.' "

"And did not bear him good will, I take it. Is that Shakespeare?"

Collins nodded. "I bore Carson no good will. But the man is now dead and can no longer author injury to anyone. Please continue. I wish to know all I may before meeting this fellow, Ouray."

"He left the Taos area around '50 to live with his mother's people, the Tabeguache Utes. He has told me that he witnessed the United States Army invade Taos and realized then that the Mexicans and the Indians would be driven to capitulation."

"How has he gained so much trust and status with the whites?"

"I guess it began when Ouray defended a group of whites from attack by the Moughwach Utes back in '55."

"And yet the Utes follow him as their chief?"

"Only some of them. Some would kill him if they could."

Now that the wind had died down, C.W. took out his pipe. "Pray, continue," he said.

"From what I have heard, Ouray was an aggressive and successful warrior and hunter. His first wife died and his only son was taken by the Sioux and traded to the Arapahoe. He has never been able to get him back, although Felix Brunot made many promises in that regard."

"So he has no wife?" Collins asked.

"No, he has taken another wife named Chipeta. They seem to be inseparable. He has no other children. It is peculiar, but he does not seem concerned by this."

"Perhaps he knows there would be no viable future for his progeny."

Jocknick nodded. "Perhaps. That had not occurred to me. In any event, he became friends with Lafayette Head, the Ute agent appointed at Conejos, a little village in the San Luis Valley. From what I have heard, Head was less than honest, brokered in Indian slaves and made a fortune off the appointment. He was a pal of Carson's and hired Ouray as his interpreter. They went together to Denver in '62 to meet with Evans."

"Evans?"

"John Evans, Territorial Governor."

"Why was this?" Collins asked and struck a match to relight his pipe.

"The Utes strove to trade their friendship with the whites in return for the preservation of their territory, some breeding livestock and annuities. The agreement was meaningless, however, as it was not sanctioned by the U.S. government. In 1863, Head took Ouray and some other chiefs to tour the East, ostensibly to make a deal with President Lincoln. In truth, it was to impress them with the might and sophistication of white civilization, thereby rendering them more agreeable to negotiations that would not be in their favor. Later, back in Conejos, a treaty was drawn up to move the Utes out of San Luis Valley and away from the eastern slopes of the Rocky Mountains. Ouray was officially recognized as chief of all the Utes by the U.S. government."

"Also by the Utes?"

"Aw hell no. They did not choose him. I understand from my father that it was much the same up north with Red Cloud. The whites thought he was the leader of all the Sioux, but that was not what the Sioux believed."

"So I have heard," Collins said, smiling and remembering.

"The upshot was that they gave up the San Luis Valley, most of Middle Park, recognized the supremacy of the U.S. government, and would allow roads to be built within the reservation. In return, the Utes would receive all sorts of provisions...I do not recall all that was told me by Mears."

"And then?"

"Well, the War of Rebellion was raging and often the government forgot its promises. I believe this is when Ouray might have decided to become a negotiator rather than a warrior. Or maybe it was after Sand Creek. Who knows? After the war, in 1866, another attempt was made to force the Utes onto a confined reservation. It failed. The following winter was brutal and when promised provisions did not arrive from the government, the Utes began to starve. Many were forced to beg to survive."

Collins sighed. "And this served to prove they were primitive children and dependent on the whites in all ways."

Jocknick nodded. "Just as you say." He pulled up his horse. "We are nearing Ouray's homestead. Do you wish to hear more prior to meeting him?"

"Perhaps not at the moment."

"I will certainly have the opportunity to provide further details at a later time."

"No doubt."

"I must tell you that he may or may not choose to speak English with you. If he speaks only Spanish, I will not be able to interpret."

"I speak some modest Spanish, so perhaps all will be

well," Collins said, easing Mona back into a walk. Her ears went stiffly forward at the sound of whinnying from the river bottom. Felix brayed loudly, startling Shoe String into a modest display of bucking.

8

Ouray's house was a single story but spacious adobe dwelling. Jocknick informed Collins that the house had been constructed by Otto Mears, having contracted with the government to build it. Inside the house there were all the appointments of a refined home. Collins thought it a sad affair, as if the couple were striving with all their might to appear to be assimilated, according to the ideal American proposal for the reformation of savage Indians. Civilization or extermination was the cause embraced by most U.S. politicians.

C.W. found Chipeta to be a comely woman, slightly shorter than her husband, graceful of bearing and with an air of quiet intelligence. She made all effort to make Collins and Jocknick welcome. They sat at a table adorned with an embroidered tablecloth and set with a Haviland china service. Ouray sat laconically at the head of the table while his guests were served coffee. Chipeta retreated to the kitchen and could be heard busying herself with pots and pans.

"We sometimes have a girl who cooks for us, but Chipeta always cooks for guests," Ouray told them. "Good to see you again, Sidney."

"Nice to see you."

"How is your father?"

"He is well. He was nearly appointed as agent for the Wind River Agency for the Shoshone and Arapahoe tribes, but I believe that Secretary Schurz decided he could not do without him."

Ouray nodded. "Your father's wisdom and sympathy for the Indian must be of great value to Mr. Schurz."

Collins deduced that communication would not be problematic and noted that Ouray spoke with a Spanish accent. He was surprised at his apparently comprehensive knowledge of the English language, especially as Jocknick senior had led him to believe the chief's English was only passable, while assuring him that the man possessed the highest order of intelligence.

"Have you seen Charles Adams?" Ouray asked Sidney.

"Not for quite a while. He is busy with his postal routes."

"Have you been prospecting?"

Color came to Jocknick's face. "I have some. No good has come of it."

"And you, Mr. Collins," Ouray said, turning to address C.W. "Have you come to prospect?"

Collins decided to be completely honest. "I have not. I have come to visit this country and to see if the Ute people are creating all the mischief of which they are currently accused."

Both Ouray and Jocknick sat staring at him a moment.

Ouray finally spoke. "What are your aims, Mr. Collins?"

"I am sympathetic to the plight of the Indian and intend to discover the truth."

"And what will the truth serve?" Ouray asked resignedly.

"With any luck, a just Indian policy here in the state of Colorado. A circumvention of disaster for the Ute people."

The Indian man sighed deeply. "*Ay chingaso.* Disaster has already come upon us. It glitters with *plata y oro.*"

Chipeta came in and refilled their cups. She placed a platter of small cakes on the table and returned to the kitchen. In passing, she smiled at Collins. Although Sidney had assured him that she could not speak a word of English, he suspected that she probably understood much. As he knew from past experience, such dissembling was an adroit tactic with which to learn a great deal. He surmised that Ouray must occasionally descend into similar subterfuge.

"I am aware that the situation is difficult," Collins said. "But perhaps there are those of us who may work to prevent further calamity."

Ouray turned to Jocknick. "Who is this man?"

Jocknick shrugged. "My father sent him. I am to guide him wherever he desires to go and introduce him to folks he desires to meet."

"Who are you?" Ouray asked Collins directly.

"I am an agent working for Mr. Schurz. He seeks to discover the identity of political factions working behind the scenes to deprive the Utes of all their treaty lands."

"I do not think you are required to search behind the scenes for those working against us."

Jocknick nodded. "Most of the whites in Colorado are keen to be rid of the Utes," he said.

"Yes, I am aware of this," Collins said. "But your father and Mr. Schurz believe that there are those who may be seeking to prepare a momentous disaster. One in which many would be hurt or killed."

"Many Utes?" Ouray asked.

"Yes. And perhaps whites as well. It would be the shortest route to acquiring the rest of your lands."

"And if you find the identity of these men, what can be done?"

"That will be within the purview of Mr. Schurz." Collins told him. "I will provide the intelligence and he will provide the response. If I am able to thwart potential violence then, of course, I am charged to do so."

"Why have you come to me?" Ouray asked. "I have no information to share with you."

Collins realized the man was overly cautious. He was sagacious and perfectly aware of what was transpiring around him. He exhibited the manner of an individual once powerful and commanding, but age, experience and ill health had rendered him diminished. Also, C.W. suspected, he had handed away bits and pieces of himself in the interest of compromise. This, he knew, tended to chisel away the fabric and integrity of a man until he was substantially reduced. In Ouray, the Ute people had a diplomat, but no longer a mighty warrior.

"I have come to you for information regarding those Utes who may be the most easily handled. Those who might be played upon to create an armed conflict."

Ouray appeared to be digesting his meaning. He was silent for several minutes. Jocknick fidgeted with a teaspoon and ate a cake.

"I will think on this," the Indian said. "I am not eager to provide you with the identities of men who may be seen as troublemakers." He regarded Collins pensively. "Will you stay as our guests?"

"We will camp nearby, if this meets with your approval," Collins said and glanced at Sidney, who nodded in agreement.

"Very well. I desire that you join us for supper," Ouray told them as they stood up from the table. Chipeta came to stand beside him, looking at Collins and appearing to study him closely.

"It will be a pleasure," he replied. "You have a lovely home."

9

They made camp in a small grove of trees not more than a quarter mile away. Some Ute children from a nearby group of lodges came to shyly observe them, but could not be enticed to come closer or make conversation. Collin's mare was picketed, as she had shown a propensity to wander, while Felix and Shoe String were hobbled and turned loose to graze. There appeared to be horses scattered all over the countryside. Both Gustavus and Sidney had impressed upon Collins the importance of horses to the Ute culture.

As Jocknick broke limbs and stacked them near the fire ring, he asked, "Do you truly believe that Mr. Schurz or any other government faction is capable of putting a halt to the encroachment onto Ute lands?"

C.W. paused in his task of taking stock of the ample supply of canned goods, most of which appeared to be beans. "I cannot honestly tell you that, no," he said, straightening his back and stretching. "All we can achieve is to find the most determined factions bent on violence and report their identity to Mr. Schurz. Unless the Congress decides to act on behalf of the Utes, I feel certain that their lands will be forfeit."

Jocknick spat a stream of tobacco juice. "Well, if Ouray will not apprise you of various Ute firebrands, I can."

"I would rather gather the intelligence from him. His will be an inside perspective, if he is inclined to share it with me." Collins arranged all the canned goods back in the panniers. "You must have a genuine fondness for beans."

Jocknick grinned. "Not really. I am just not imaginal when it comes to supplies. I am well used to the abuse of others because of it. When at Los Pinos, I was never allowed to provision the cow camp. Oddly, my first employment there was as cook."

"We will not starve on the trail, I suppose."

"No, but it may well be a windy voyage."

Collins laughed. " 'Blow, till thou burst thy wind, if room enough!' "

While they donned clean, albeit much wrinkled, clothing in an effort to show respect to their host, Collins sought further information from Sidney.

"How has Ouray held his position among the Utes despite the antipathy among some of them?" he asked, buttoning his vest. The sun was setting and a chill was in the air.

"Well you may ask," Jocknick said, smiling. "Back in '72, as I recall, six different individuals made an attempt upon his life."

"In ambush?"

"For all intents and purposes. His own brother-in-law, Sapinero, tried to do him in with an axe. When Ouray got the better of him, the rest of the crew took heel. Chipeta saved her brother from Ouray's wrath.

"Any others?"

"Oh surely. Ouray has never hesitated to murder his enemies, a fact much disregarded by those whites who wish to keep him in power. He killed a fellow named Suckett for chiding him over his friendliness with the settlers. He has also removed many others...such as 'Old Nick,' 'Hot Stuff,' 'Dynamitz,' 'Jack of Clubs' and supposedly another fellow called 'Campbell,' who was a breed from down south."

"What colorful sobriquets all these Indians seem to

have," Collins said, half in disbelief.

"I assure you, I am not being inventive."

Their boots wiped, clothes brushed and the camp arranged, they walked back up to Ouray's farm. He was seated on a chair outside the house. The aroma of roasting meat came teasingly from within.

"Come. Sit. Let us speak together again," Ouray said and indicated two more chairs nearby.

They joined the chief. Collins took out his pipe. "May I smoke?" he asked.

"*Si. Por favor,*" Ouray said. "How is your tobacco?"

"Rather good. Would you care to smoke?" Collins asked.

Ouray went into the house and returned with a flamboyant meerschaum pipe. He accepted Collin's tobacco pouch and filled the bowl. Collins took out his match safe and offered a light. As the night moved upon them, they sat smoking companionably while Sidney spat the occasional stream of tobacco juice. The man appeared to be mildly choleric.

"If I speak candidly with you, will I be offering tales to pass on to government authorities?" Ouray asked abruptly.

Collins waited a moment, then said, "I assure you, I will not commit any act that increases the danger to the Ute people. If you share information about certain individuals that might be construed as malcontents, I will not use this in an effort to court disaster, but rather prevent it."

"It is at White River that trouble will most likely come," Ouray said.

"That is what I understand from Sidney and his father."

"*Bueno.* I will share some information that may be useful."

"I would be most grateful."

Chipeta came to the door of the house and called to them.

"We will eat now," Ouray said and stood. "Later, we will speak of these things."

Inside, they were met with a delicious meal of roast beef, mashed potatoes, gravy, baked apples with cinnamon and custard pie. Chipeta served the men and then sat down to join them. There was little conversation as they ate. Collins became convinced that Chipeta could teach the finer points of culinary excellence to Mrs. Bronnon of the blue gingham. When the dishes had been cleared and coffee served, Collins and Ouray again smoked while Jocknick judiciously refrained from his preferred use of tobacco. Chipeta lit a hurricane lamp suspended from a rafter and sat at the table with a cup of aromatic tea.

"There is one man you can trust," Ouray said, at last. "A man known to Sidney. His name is Shavano."

Collins looked over at Jocknick, who nodded.

"He is a war chief and possesses much medicine," the chief continued. "He does not always agree with me and is not as friendly with whites, but he is honorable."

"Is he at White River?" C.W. asked.

"No. He is hunting in the Shining Mountains, but he will return soon. I will send him to you and he will guide and protect you."

"That would be beneficial," Jocknick said. "Someone who can speak Ute."

"Where are you planning to go next?" Ouray asked.

"I thought we would ride north to White River," Collins said.

"You must not...it would not be safe. It is best to wait for Shavano. There are many angry young men roaming north of here. Even though they are not causing the trouble for which they are accused, they would not hesitate to pick off easy prey...such as two men with good horses and many supplies they would undoubtedly see as prospectors"

Chipeta coughed and looked pointedly at her man. They spoke to each other in what Collins assumed to be the Ute language.

"She says I must tell you now of those who may be perceived as causing trouble," Ouray said.

"Yes. That would be useful information," C.W. said, looking at Chipeta. He thought he detected a slight nod.

"Captain Jack is the most likely. *Nicaagat.* He is a big man now that he has returned from scouting for the army. He wears his uniform and has taken many followers from *Quinkent.* Most of the young men follow Jack"

"He is at White River?" Collins asked.

"Yes."

"Who is *Quinkent*?"

"He is known as Douglas by the whites," Sidney told him. "A Yampa. Nice fellow."

"Nice, yes," Ouray said, "*pero* becoming very angry with Nick."

" 'Nick?' "

"Their name for Agent Meeker."

"Why is Quinkent angry?"

"Meeker has moved the agency fifteen miles down river onto good pastureland and the Utes' traditional track for horse racing. Also, he intends to plow up the earth for farming. But even though he is angry, I do not believe Quinkent would make trouble."

"Who did Jack scout for?" Collins asked, curious.

"General Crook. Against the Lakota people."

"Oh," C.W. said, noncommittally.

"Jack was also very angry when the agency was moved. Meeker threatened him with soldiers if he did not move his band of people from the old site."

"What did Jack do?"

"He is mostly gone from the agency hunting. He trades skins for guns and ammunition at Peck's store on the Yampa River. Sometimes he trades for whiskey."

Chipeta said something to Ouray. He nodded.

"Yes. There is *Canalla*. Johnson, my sister's husband. Canalla is running out of patience and may commit a reckless act. He is trying to guide this agent, but the man is stubborn and never doubts himself."

"This is not uncommon among whites," Collins said, musingly.

"Perhaps all these men suffer such arrogance," Ouray said.

" 'A hell-hound that doth hunt us all to death.' " Collins quoted.

"He is fond of Shakespeare," Jocknick said, answering the chief's quizzical glance.

"Ah…yes, Shakespeare. I have heard of this Englishman."

"Anyone else who may be accused of creating dissent?" C.W. asked.

Ouray spoke briefly with Chipeta. "*Colorow*," he said.

Jocknick and C.W. smiled at each other, thinking of their mule.

"He is a Moughwach Ute," Ouray continued. "Older and uninterested in the agency. He had his fill of whites while living near Denver. His band only comes in for sugar, coffee and the like. There are also *Pi-ah* and *Ka-neache*."

"But in your estimation, none of these men are creating the havoc or depredations of which they are accused?"

"No. Not yet. Perhaps later if events unfold that drive them to it. Or if too much whiskey clouds their judgment."

"*Nuair a bhíos an braon istigh bíonn an chiall amuigh.* When the drop is inside, the sense is outside."

"That was not Shakespeare," Ouray said.

"No. That was my own native tongue."

Ouray nodded. "Our young men often feed their sense

to a bottle."

Chipeta spoke to him again, gesturing toward Collins. "She wants me to tell you of Jane," the chief told him.

"Jane?" Sidney interjected.

"*Si*, Jane. She speaks English very well and understands much. She is married to a loafer named *Pauvitz* and now lives at White River. For many years she was servant to a wealthy white man at Fort Bridger up in Wyoming Territory. She is *muy linda* and it is said that Nick is fond of her. More fond of her than she of him, *comprende?*"

"So there is a bit of Lothario in the old man," Collins said pensively.

"You mean lecherous?" Sidney asked.

Collins nodded.

"I have heard this as well. There were tales out of the Union Colony… now called Greeley."

"There is also talk of his daughter," Ouray said.

"His daughter?" Collins asked.

"Josephine." Jocknick explained. "She supposedly flirts and smokes and plays cards with the men on the agency."

C.W. raised his eyebrows. An unruly daughter flouting convention amid Meeker's fold might be ruinous to his cause. "Interesting…But this Jane will be helpful?" he asked.

Chipeta nodded, a gesture not lost on C.W.

"Jane would be very helpful," Ouray said. "There is also Henry Jim, a young man I recommended and who is working at White River," he added.

The lamp above began guttering. Collins realized how fatigued he was and stood.

"We must not overstay our welcome," he told Sidney, who also stood up from the table.

"Come for breakfast. We always wake early," Ouray said.

"We will come," C.W. said. "Thank you very much for

a delightful evening," he added, looking directly at Chip-eta. "The meal was delicious. *Muchas gracias.*"

10

Collins woke the next morning to a light rain. The day was dawning clear, however, and he shook out his bedroll and draped it across the limbs of a nearby tree to air and dry out. Sidney was snoring musically, so he stirred up the fire and set the coffeepot to heat. He then began packing most of the gear, waiting for the coffee. A rooster crowed from the direction of Ouray's homestead. His companion finally stirred when Shoe String wandered over to blow in his face.

"Thanks," Sidney said, sitting up and accepting the steaming cup of coffee that Collins brought to him. He waved a hand at the horse to chase him away. The animal moved a few feet and regarded him with a saturnine expression.

C.W. smiled and hunkered down near the fire to warm himself. "If we cannot proceed cross-country to White River, what do you propose we do?" he asked.

"Well, I have been contemplating on that. We could bear off down the Gunnison and head for the old Los Pinos Agency. From there we are able to travel to Alamosa where you can get the train back to Denver. We should visit Alonzo at the old cow camp along the way."

"Why would I need to return to Denver?"

Jocknick was up and packing his personal gear. He appeared surprised by Collins' question. "Why, because Ouray has told you that to continue north is dangerous."

"Yes. Perhaps we shall need to find an alternative

route, but White River remains my destination."

Jocknick shrugged. "You will still have to take the train north through Denver to catch the Union Pacific to Rawlins. It is the only other route to White River without travelling north. Unless you plan to cross Middle Park and travel over Gore Pass to Bear River and that will be just as perilous. Either way, I will need to get these animals back to Mr. Riley at Ouray."

"You did not purchase them?" C.W. asked incredulously.

"No. They are merely let, except for Shoe String, of course."

Collins glanced fondly toward where Felix and Mona were grazing. "You mean to say that you would return these splendid creatures to certain death on the ramparts of the San Juan Mountains?"

"No choice." Sidney said pettishly. Collins had become aware that his companion was susceptible to swiftly altering moods.

"There is, in fact, a choice. I will provide you with the funds for their purchase and take them with me. When I have arrived at Alamosa, you are free to return to Ouray and settle with Mr. Riley."

Collins poured the remaining contents of the coffeepot on the fire and walked in the direction of the chief's house. After a moment, Sidney followed. Ouray was standing in the open door. The sun was just sending rays of early light across the landscape. Wisps of fog rose ghostlike above the river.

"Come," the Ute chief said when he saw them. "There is coffee and food."

Inside they were met with the pleasant aroma of fresh tortillas. Collins had developed a taste for Mexican food during a prolonged episode in New Mexico Territory. Chipeta served plates of eggs, tortillas and beans smothered in spicy red *chile*.

"I must tell you again to be careful of Captain Jack,"

Chapter 10

Ouray said as they ate. "He is always angry, especially since Nick has arrived to White River. If he thinks you have come to help the agent there will be trouble for you. He cannot be trusted, but he is smart and has reasons to hate Nick."

"For example?" Collins asked, dipping a piece of tortilla in egg.

"*Las vacas*. Cows."

Jocknick grinned. "Cows?"

"*Si*, milk cows. Agent Meeker wanted his band to raise milk cows. He told them they would be *muy rico*. Jack believes his people are scared of cows and that the smell of milk would make them sick. The truth is that we are horse people. We are not *vaqueros*. It was an insult."

Chipeta said something.

"My woman says to tell you to talk to Peck. He knows all the Utes in White River."

"He does that," Sidney agreed.

"You are convinced I cannot ride north to White River?" Collins asked the chief. "It would save much time."

"I think it would be *muy malo*. Very bad. Take the train to Rawlins. I will send Shavano to meet you there. He will come in from hunting soon." Ouray looked at Jocknick. "Will you stay with him?"

Jocknick shrugged. "I have to return south to the Dolores River country. I will ride with him back across Cochetopa Pass to Alamosa."

"You are always very changeable, Sidney. You are like spring weather."

Jocknick became surly. "I am not changeable. And I have better occupation for my time than working for my father and Secretary Schurz."

Ouray raised a hand in pacification. "My apologies, Sidney. I should not have spoken so." He turned back to Collins. "Shavano will be excellent company and will guard you well."

"I am most grateful," C.W. said, wondering how he would fare if the promised guide failed to arrive in Rawlins. He finished his coffee. "Sidney's father thought it imperative that I make all possible haste. We must depart."

Everyone stood. Jocknick and Collins found their hats and the couple escorted them a small distance toward their camp.

"Thank you again for your hospitality," C.W. said, offering his hand to both of them. "If only my entire journey could be so agreeable."

Chipeta smiled. She spoke to Ouray.

"Chipeta says you must be very safe and come back to see us."

"Tell her I will certainly do so," Collins said, smiling.

"*Adios*, Sidney. You are always welcome."

"So long, Chief." Jocknick said, visibly holding a grudge regarding Ouray's earlier comment.

As they walked back to prepare for their journey, Collins wondered why Ouray had intentionally provoked his companion. Perhaps, he thought, it was of no importance.

11

Collins leaned on the top corral railing and observed the cows and calves within. Although he knew little enough about animal husbandry, he could tell these must be the hard luck cases, since all the others were out on the nearby range. One small fellow wore a hide that had been skinned from another calf, matching the brindle color of the mother cow. The sun was just coming up and Collins was restless. Now they were back-tracking their route and it would be some days before he was in a position to continue his investigations, he did not care to tarry in visiting even such a desirable host as Alonzo Hartman.

The old cow camp for the original Los Pinos Agency was situated on the north fork of the Gunnison River at the tail end of the Elk Mountains. It was set in a pleasant stretch of river bottom and was now known as the Dos Rios Ranch. Hartman, a long-time acquaintance of Jocknick's and former cow boss, had taken over the location after helping relocate the agency. He had managed to acquire title from the U.S. government. He was reserved, but possessed a dry wit. His cowhands were obviously devoted to him and his abilities in raising livestock were apparent in the health of his animals, his burgeoning prosperity and the tidiness of the buildings and surrounding grounds of the ranch headquarters. Sidney had seemed a trifle "off his feed" since their arrival the day before and Collins suspected Mr. Hartman's success was not a source of great satisfaction for him. Jealousy was never advisable, he mused. As Shakespeare had written in *Othello*, "It is the green-eyed monster which doth mock the meat it feeds on."

He wandered over to the large pen where Mona, Felix and Shoe String poked their noses around a pile of hay. A bird sang uproariously in a neighboring tree, changing its cadence and tune with each new phrase of warbling. Collins smiled at the beauty of the morning and the sweet smells of grass, river bottom and cow manure, mingling in the gentle breeze. He noticed that Hartman was approaching from the ranch house, a modest two story affair of pine logs surrounded by large cottonwood trees. He carried two cups of coffee and handed one to C.W.

"Morning," he said softly through his thick moustaches.

"Thank you," Collins said, accepting the coffee. "You have quite a splendid ranch here."

"Thanks," Hartman said, gazing around their surroundings as if seeing everything for the first time. "I just could not bear to leave this place."

"I certainly can understand your inclination to stay."

They drank their coffee in silence, leaning on the corral rails and listening to the bird song, the bawling of calves in the distance and the low talk of the hands as they prepared for work.

"How long have you known Sidney?" Alonzo asked unexpectedly.

"Not long. He was hired as my guide by his father."

"And he has been taking you on a tour of the San Juans? That is all?"

C.W. glanced at his companion. "In a way."

Hartman's silence was eloquent.

"What are your sentiments regarding the Utes?" Collins asked after a moment.

"I hold them in high regard. Their ways are changing and soon they will be forced to live as white men. It will be a tragedy. I have always desired to live as they do."

"What of Ouray?"

Hartman shrugged. "Pleasant enough fellow. Seems more white than Indian these days. Sidney told me you were visiting his homestead?"

Collins nodded. "I had hoped Sidney would be more circumspect."

"You have some business here in Colorado that requires circumspection?"

"Yes, quite a lot of circumspection," C.W. answered smiling.

"I am sympathetic to the Utes, if that is what you are after."

"But, I take it, not many white ranchers see the situation in the same light?"

"Greed is not usually insightful."

Collins smiled again. "No, not usually."

Alonzo sighed. "These people have been earmarked for penury and destruction ever since the first discovery of mineral wealth. But there seems to be a faction now working its will behind the scenes, fomenting conflict and manipulating sentiments."

"Organized?"

"It would seem so. I have become increasingly concerned."

"Is it your opinion that Ouray is protecting his people or merely himself?"

He shrugged. "He endeavors to convince the Utes that diplomacy and compromise are their only hope and I believe he is sincere. He has assiduously taken care of his own security, however."

Collins finished his coffee and wiped his moustache with a shirtsleeve. "Any suppositions as to why Ouray would attempt to anger or estrange Sidney during our visit?"

Hartman chuckled. "Ouray is always pestering Sid. In the past, he has exhibited ...how shall I say it? A hesitation at engaging in risky situations. The fellow will not gamble in any sense of the word. Some of the Utes think him a coward. I believe he is merely cautious.”

Collins considered that here was a man who attempted to think the best of all those around him. An admirable trait and one he did not, himself, possess. Experience had disabused him of such niceties. They turned to see Jocknick headed toward them.

“I thought we should try our hand at fishing,” he said to Collins as he neared.

“I, perforce, need to keep traveling. My commission is paramount.”

Jocknick scratched his ear in a peevish gesture. “Very well.” He turned on his heel and headed back to the bunkhouse wherein they were billeted.

“Poor Sidney,” Alonzo said. “He seems incapable of attaining any sort of maturity in purpose or mien.”

“*Is maith an scáthán súil carad.* A friend’s eye is a good mirror.”

Alonzo looked over at him. “Indeed. A valuable mirror.”

“He can be quite sociable when the mood is upon him.”

“And when it departs…” Hartman nodded toward Sidney’s back. “A surly companion, indeed.”

Collins and Hartman caught up the horses. C.W. saddled and bridled Mona and Shoestring while Hartman arranged the packsaddle on Felix.

“A well-mannered mule,” he observed.

“I wish to prevent the return of the mare and the mule to mining country. May I send them to you when the time comes?”

“Certainly. Provide me with their price and an address to which I may wire funds.”

Collins shook his head. “Provide them a safe haven and humane treatment and I, no doubt, will owe you for care and feeding.”

Alonzo smiled. “Then let us say I am keeping them for you. You are a singular fellow, Mr. Collins. I hope you will return as my guest when more leisure is available to you.”

"Nothing would afford me greater pleasure."

MINING COUNTRY

12

As they rode down the east slopes of Cochetopa Pass along a poorly maintained stage road, Collins sought to gain more information from Jocknick regarding Ouray and the history of the Utes. It seemed apparent that the man had regained his equipoise. The wind was calm and the weather warm. They could see the Sangre De Cristo Mountains spread along the far horizon across the wide basin of the San Luis Valley.

They had spent the previous night in the vicinity of the old Los Pinos Agency. Most of the buildings had already been cannibalized for useable logs and other materials, but the location was agreeable. C.W. could see how its mountainous elevation would have made successful agricultural efforts difficult, however.

"Who were Ouray's predecessors as chief?" he asked Sidney.

"Well let us see," Sidney spit out a wad of tobacco. "Chief *Nevava* had been head of the northern Ute bands. When he died, there was a shift in the power structure within the tribe. *Chico Velasquez* was probably the most notorious, but he died of smallpox back in the fifties. Each band has their own leaders and they can change. When Ouray was in on preventing an attack on a wagon train back in '55, the whites began to notice him."

Collins recalled some of the history notes provided by Gustavus Jocknick. "So there was another treaty in 1868?" he asked, encouraging the continuity of conversation.

"Yes," Sidney answered. "It was at that time the U.S. government officially recognized Ouray as the negotiator."

"And, as you said, all the Utes did not accept this?"

Jocknick laughed. "No. The Northern Utes were angry that one of theirs was not chosen, mostly due to the fact that Ouray and the Tabeguache had given up territory in the past without their blessing. A goodly number of the Southern Utes were patently uncooperative as well. Even so, in early 1868, Ouray and nine other chiefs were sent to Washington D.C. in the company of your pal, Kit Carson."

Collins waved a bee away from Mona's ears. "Hunt was the governor at the time?"

"He was. In fact, the treaty of 1868 became known as the 'Hunt Treaty.' " Sidney grinned. "It also became known as the 'Kit Carson Treaty.' I guess since he died on the way home. It was meant to ensure that more than fifteen million acres of land would belong to the Utes in perpetuity."

It was C.W.'s turn to laugh. "Perpetuity? The government does not comprehend the word."

Jocknick smiled. "Eleven years later, it does not mean much. But at the time, it only meant that the Utes would be giving up land that the whites had already stolen, such as North and Middle parks and the Yampa Valley. They had already given up the San Luis Valley here," he waved a hand at the expanse before them. "Things have not worked out quite as the Utes expected, I guess."

"An astute observance."

Sidney's horse picked its way daintily through a stretch of rugged lava rock. Collins assumed he was on the watch for snakes.

"Was the treaty ratified?" C.W. asked as their route opened into grassy hills.

"By the summer of 1868. That was when the White River and Los Pinos agencies were built."

They rode in silence for a while. Collins hummed an Irish ditty and admired the terrain. There seemed to be outcroppings of chalk in nearby ridges. He could see a flock of sheep on a slope far in the distance.

"As I said, Kit Carson died on the trip home from Washington. And it was in 1868 that Ouray began receiving his first rather modest annual pension," Jocknick said, breaking the lull in conversation. "This did not sit well with the other chiefs."

"Do you believe he is mainly concerned with his own prosperity?"

He shook his head. "No. He has told me that he thinks it best for Utes to become farmers. That he must set an example."

"I see."

"But you are dubious?"

Collins shrugged. "Perhaps."

They finally dropped down to bottomland and easy riding. In a while, they angled over to a nearby stream and let the animals drink.

"It was somewhere around here that Lieutenant Marshall developed such a bad toothache he was inspired to seek a shortcut to Denver," Jocknick explained. "Thereby discovering Marshall Pass."

"Is this significant?"

"Otto Mears is at present constructing a toll road over the pass, which will lead to greater returns and respect."

" 'And so may I, blind fortune leading me, miss that which one unworthier may attain,' " Collins quoted.

"I would not deem Mears unworthy," Sidney said defensively. "*Lieutenant* William Marshall could not have benefited from his discovery, at any odds, being a military man."

"My apologies to Mr. Mears," C.W. said contritely and turned Mona from the creek to resume their journey. "Will we see Mears at Saguache?" he asked when Jocknick caught up.

"If he is not supervising the construction of his road. He possesses great instincts and is truly inspired in choosing the most fortuitous routes."

"Does he also build roads on the Ute lands?"

"Sometimes. The 1868 Treaty made provisions for roads and railroads to pass through the reservation."

Collins smiled to himself. He was quite curious to meet Mears. He was ever suspicious of someone who consistently prospered by way of government contracts, which definitely seemed to be the man's *métier.* "Please continue with your history," he said.

"The 1868 treaty was intended to encourage all of the Utes to give up their nomadic propensities and to ensure their protection from white encroachment," Sidney began, noticeably pleased by the request. "But when government surveyors began to delineate some of the finest hunting regions as areas for white settlement, and prospectors did not cease their explorations in any manner, the Indians became outraged. Ouray refused to ratify the survey, but pressure was placed upon him and a false promise of military protection induced him to sign."

Felix, doggedly following the horses with his lead rope slung across his packs, passed a prolonged bout of melodious wind. Both men laughed heartily.

"I hope you did not feed him some of our beans," C.W. said.

"He is musical all on his own. There is no need to lend assistance," Sidney told him, grinning.

"What came after the treaty?" Collins asked.

"By 1869," Jocknick continued, "the first agents were appointed to Los Pinos and White River agencies. Charles Adams was placed at White River and a fellow named Lieutenant Speer was the first to be assigned to Los Pinos. He did not begin well, but managed to bring in a sawmill and build several houses, the remains of which you saw yesterday. Otto Mears constructed this road we are traveling from Saguache to the new agency and supplied much of the cattle and goods."

Mears again, thought C.W. What a fellow. "Did he have a monopoly on all supplies to the agency?" he asked with curiosity.

"No. John Lawrence, a notable rancher of these parts, also supplied grain and goods."

"A rivalry?"

"Of sorts. Lawrence is a Democrat and Mears is a Republican."

"And after Speer came Mr. Neversink Trask?" he asked.

"Indeed," Jocknick answered, smiling. "He actually walked from Denver to the agency, being unwilling to spend the money for transportation."

"Alas, he was replaced nonetheless."

"Yes. My father was sent to investigate complaints. Trask was inept in many ways and frequently refused to issue rations. Oddly, the Indians also objected to his eccentric attire."

"Such as?"

"Green goggle glasses, old fashioned swallow-tailed coat and ridiculous beaver hat. The peculiar style of his garments became renowned throughout the region."

"No doubt. And what did your father discover?"

"That the Utes were exceedingly vexed by Trask. Upon hearing of my father's imminent arrival, they intercepted him six miles away from the agency. Even Ouray strongly objected to Trask...mostly as a result of his meanness with supplies and rations. His ledgers were in complete disarray and he had an absolute disdain for the Indians. Ouray volunteered to travel to Washington so as to demand a replacement. Shavano threatened to take Trask on a hunting trip into the mountains and abandon him there."

"Not auspicious, to be certain," Collins said, slightly concerned about this newest revelation regarding Shavano.

Jocknick tipped his hat to scratch his forehead. "No.

Not a bit. My father camped with the Indians on his journey back to Denver. They had many complaints of whites trespassing upon their lands and confusion over reservation boundaries. His report put an end to Trask's sojourn at Los Pinos, although I arrived in time to enjoy a brief acquaintanceship with him."

"Your father arranged your appointment?"

Sidney's countenance darkened. "Not actually. He did provide me with a letter of introduction to the governor. It was entirely through my own efforts that I obtained an appointment with Agent Thompson in Denver and thereby continued on to Los Pinos."

"And then Trask was replaced by Charles Adams?" C.W. asked, ignoring Sidney's peevish response.

"There was a fellow named Merrill for a month or so. He came and went rather swiftly as a result of an altercation with Shavano."

"What occurred?"

"Merrill demanded that Shavano remove the pistol from his belt whenever he came into the agency. The man was quite apparently terrified of the chief. Shavano refused to relinquish his weapon and took to sneaking up on Merrill, meaning no harm except to further illustrate the man's weaknesses. In the end, the agent confronted Shavano in a sort of hysterical paroxysm. The Indian just stood there and stared at him. The Utes have an abiding disdain for any exhibition of fear."

Collins recalled with irony what Hartman had told him about Sidney. "So this Merrill resigned?"

Jocknick chuckled. "Not really. He disappeared one night, never to return to the agency."

"Was everyone certain that Shavano had not 'done him in,' as they say?"

"He turned up in Colorado Springs, clerking in a dry goods store."

The day had progressed so that the sun began to sink

beyond the mountains behind them. "Shall we make camp?" Collins asked.

"There are many places we could put up in Saguache. There is Mears' hotel."

"I prefer to camp, if this meets with your approval. The weather is far too pleasant to withdraw indoors."

Sidney seemed about to protest when a grouse exploded out of some rabbit brush nearby. Predictably, Shoe String shied and engaged in a fit of bucking, which soon disintegrated into a pitched battle between Jocknick and his mount. Unable to lend a hand, C.W. retrieved the mule's lead rope and kept his own horse out of the fray. At length, Sidney seemed to be gaining a modicum of control over his animal until some invisible force perpetuated a renewed outbreak, resulting in Jocknick sailing over the gelding's head into the dirt.

Collins dismounted and went to help him onto his feet. "In one piece?" he asked, as Jocknick brushed himself off.

"Damn horse." He walked stiffly over to where the animal stood trembling and contrite. The horse did not attempt escape as Sidney reached for one of the bridle reins. To his credit, the man did not retaliate with physical abuse and the beast visibly calmed.

"We could camp over there," C.W. suggested, pointing toward the creek to their south.

Jocknick made no response except to begin leading Shoe String in the indicated direction. Collins followed, thinking it might be more pleasant traveling in the company of a recalcitrant Ute war chief with a pistol than this young man, his errant horse and his rapidly shifting temperament.

I AM YOUR FATHER

13

A small campfire of dried brush and juniper crackled cheerfully as Collins sat in silence, smoking his pipe and allowing his mind to wander. Jocknick had remained reticent throughout the evening meal and he had not attempted to draw him out. Not being one for widely varying humors, C.W. was limited in patience for those who were. An owl hooted in the rocks above the stream and he recalled how many of the Mexican peoples of the Southwest tended to be exceedingly superstitious concerning such birds. He was rather fond of them, coming from a cultural tradition associating owls with wisdom and the divine, as opposed to malevolence and a foreboding of imminent death.

"You really should meet with Otto Mears," Sidney said abruptly.

Startled out of his reverie, Collins took a moment to answer. "If he is in Saguache, I thought I would visit with him, yes. As you say, he may be absent working on his road."

"Could be."

"How are you feeling? Will you need to rest up?"

Jocknick appeared to take umbrage at his question. "No. I have taken worse spills."

"Very well. We will ride into Saguache and seek out Mears. What of Lawrence? Is he a man of information?"

"Could be," Jocknick said again, bluntly.

Collins knocked the contents of his pipe out on a rock

and put it away. He stood, stretched and went to check on the horses. There were only a few scrubby juniper trees about, now they had dropped out of the high country, so he had tethered Mona to a large rock. She had dragged it a small distance, but was clearly not going to be traveling far. The mare stood gazing at the place where Felix and Shoe String stood together, about fifty feet away in the gloom. C.W. had the distinct sense that her feelings were wounded by their exclusivity. He patted her neck and scratched her jaw.

Back at the fire, Sidney was rolling out his bedding. Collins followed suit and soon they were both supine as the fire began to die.

"Do you wish to hear more of the treaties?" Jocknick asked out of the growing darkness.

"If you care to relate further information, it would certainly be useful," Collins answered.

"After 1868," he began, "the general attitude among the whites was that the Utes had no right to stand in the way of progress. They wished to be rid of the Indian, the same as they would be rid of bears and wolves. Governor McCook, Hunt's successor, gave a speech in 1872 denouncing the size of reservation lands and demanding another treaty. He threatened to put pressure on the Utes to allow miners access to mineral wealth. What he proposed to do was anyone's supposition."

"It was around that time when President Grant established the U.S. Board of Indian Commissioners with Felix Brunot as president."

"Yes." Sidney shifted in the dark. "By late summer of 1872, miners were crawling all over the San Juans and a stamp mill had even been freighted into Baker's Park. Whenever confronted by authorities, the miners insisted that the Utes liked having them there and that they were always made welcome by them."

"Do you believe this to be true?"

"Hell no. Finally, in August, a meeting was held at Los Pinos Agency. Almost half of the entire population of Utes arrived. Governor McCook was there along with James Thompson, Agent Arny from New Mexico, Brunot and a fellow named Curtis who was chosen as interpreter."

"Were you there?"

"Yes, I was there with Adams and Ouray. John Lawrence came to observe. Mears was gone at the time. As expected, the Utes expressed their reluctance to give up any more land and the whites used various arguments to convince them they should. Nothing came of it except bad feelings."

Collins sat up, retrieved his pipe and began packing the bowl. "What happened then? Did everyone go home?"

"They did. Shortly thereafter, the commission sent out General Hatch to renegotiate, but Ouray was uncooperative and kept inquiring how the government could want more land a mere four years after the 1868 treaty. He also complained about the fact that few of the original agreements concerning rations and livestock had been adequately honored. Hatch returned to Washington without reaching any agreement. In November of 1872, Adams was told to send a Ute delegation to Washington. Mears went along with Ouray, Chipeta and several others. After touring the East for two months, they returned home."

"Did Ouray tell you about it?" C.W. asked, the glow of his pipe lighting his features.

"He told me he appreciated the visit and he was pleased by the strange animals he saw, but he did not care for the food or the noise and bad odors."

"Understandable. What did Mears say?"

"He was fairly frustrated by Ouray and the others. He sees their removal from Colorado as inevitable."

"Their departure would certainly be lucrative for him,"

Collins observed.

"Maybe. I do not believe he is working against them."

"Perhaps not. 'Poor man! I know he would not be a wolf but that he sees the Romans are but sheep.' "

"Romans?"

"No matter. What occurred next?"

"The commander at Fort Garland was given orders to remove all miners and prospectors from Ute lands. There was immediate protest from newspapers. Their foremost question was why should Americans be excluded from their own country?"

"Why indeed?" Collins said sardonically.

"Of course the military took no such action. As a result, many new claims were staked. Brunot met again with Ouray and several of the chiefs, telling them he had heard they wanted to sell their land and he was there to help."

Collins finished his pipe and lay down to stare up at the luminescent stars. "Did they intend to sell?"

"I do not think so. Not at the time, in any event. Shavano was there and raised a fuss about how reservation boundaries were made to jog around newly claimed mines. Ouray began to become cooperative on the second day. He hinted that they might be willing to sell the mountains, but this was after Brunot pointed out they might as well get paid for what they would surely lose to white settlers by pure attrition. In the end, Brunot brought Mears from Saguache to add his voice to the argument. It seemed that Ouray acquiesced to giving up the mountains after he was offered his substantial salary. I cannot say this for sure."

"How did Shavano take this?"

"Very hard. He departed and we did not see him for many a long day. The new treaty turned quite a few of the Utes more strongly against whites. Even Ouray, in spite of his salary, seemed to be more disdainful. Adams thought all had been served by the agreement, but he truly knew that the whites would have taken the mining district one way or another."

"Is this why the Los Pinos Agency was moved?"

"Ouray wanted to move to the Uncompahgre to help protect the agricultural lands there. As soon as the miners got the San Juans, there was a push into ranching and farming country. Some of the young Ute men began attacking surveyors and trespassers, especially after several women and children were killed by whites up near Rawlins."

Collins yawned and stretched, finding he was nearly asleep. "We had best continue this in the morning. I thank you for your excellent account. Sleep well."

"And you," said Sidney, settling deeper into his bedroll.

Watching the stars pulse in the night sky, C.W. wondered briefly if friends, far to the north, could be looking at them as well. It was a comforting thought.

Despite his fatigue, he awoke in the middle of the night and could not find sleep again. Unsettling memories came to him from his youth. His thoughts went back to Ireland and a time when he was walking along the beach, gathering kelp. His father was dead and he and his mother were living on her skill at weaving and whatever could be wrested from the sea. It was the time of the famine and they were blessed to be on the coast, where a body could find foodstuffs not controlled by the English overseers. He had come around a rocky outcropping at low tide and stumbled onto the emaciated and salt encrusted bodies of several children and the wasted corpse of their mother. They appeared to have huddled in a shallow depression of rock above the waves and, for loss of hope or strength, had stayed to perish. Their eyes were closed and sunken. The smallest child lay across the woman's lap.

Collins, quite young himself, had run back to his own mother as swiftly as possible, relieved to find her at her loom in their cottage. Taking his hand, she had led him to the village priest to relate his discovery, so the poor souls could be retrieved and given last rites and proper burial. Collins had always credited this event with his mother's renewed determination to take them to America, away from death and despair. The pale faces of the tragic family haunted him still, in spite of some of the far more disturbing scenes witnessed by him during the war.

Faint light began to appear over the peaks to the east and he finally slipped into a fitful nap.

14

The morning was already warm as they mounted up and began riding east. Jocknick had been sore and slow to move and so their start had been delayed. Collins wished to be covering more ground, since time was of the essence, but for the present he was forced to remain in Sidney's company. He looked across the San Luis Valley at the Sangre De Cristo range in the distance.

"There seems to be a large amount of disturbed earth at the base of the mountains over there," he said, pointing. "Are they mines?"

"Those are sand dunes," Jocknick told him

"Sand dunes?" he asked skeptically.

"It is really quite remarkable. No one is certain how the sand got there. Some say this was once a sea."

"But we seem to be surrounded by lava rock."

Jocknick shrugged. "I know little of geology."

"It is in the black protuberances all around," C.W. explained

"Yet there are large dunes of sand not far away," Sidney pondered. "I also heard that all of San Luis Valley was once a lake. Maybe that is the answer."

"Maybe. But sea or lake, such an amount of sand piled at the base of the mountains seems odd, indeed."

They followed Saguache Creek through an extensive herd of crossbreed cattle. Shortly thereafter, they passed a log building and corrals filled with horses. Jocknick told C.W. it was a stage station set up by a fellow named

Hougland. Someone waved from near the corrals and they waved back. Farther along there were more sheep and cattle and a house and barns.

"Who lives there?" Collins asked.

"That is Lawrence's ranch but I doubt he is there. He has a house in town."

As they rode down the valley, C.W. noticed more dwellings and farm fields, some pastures displaying luxuriant growth in the temperate lowlands. Occasionally, he could hear geese or the bleating of goats and sheep. They followed the stage road down to the town. Settled at the head of San Luis Valley, Saguache was a modest collection of adobe and board and batten buildings, including one that appeared to be a courthouse, and at least three churches. The structures were mostly aligned along one main roadway. In spite of being near the creek, there were no trees to be seen anywhere, except for some regularly planted rows of seedlings. A few people were about and Collins nodded at them as they rode by. Sidney led him, past the newspaper office and a large edifice that housed the Masonic temple, to a low building farther down the thoroughfare near where the creek bore south.

"This is Otto's store and that is his house behind."

"Humble," C.W. observed.

"He has several houses, a hotel and many other places of business," Jocknick said, as if defending Mears from opprobrium. "This is but one."

They dismounted and tied the animals to a rail, next to four sad looking burros. The log building was packed with goods and several men who were apparently purchasing supplies for an expedition into the mountains. A thin, sallow-faced man stood behind an oak counter, observing them. Jocknick walked over with Collins following.

"Is Mr. Mears in town?" he asked the man.

"In back," he answered.

Without invitation, Sidney walked around the end of the counter and disappeared into the rear of the building. Collins stood out of the way and perused the store's contents. There seemed to be a preponderance of gold pans, picks and shovels, as well as cheap blankets and shoddy ready-made boots. Jocknick returned, followed by a diminutive fellow in shirtsleeves and vest. He was bearded and so remarkably small in proportions as to cause Collins to think humorously of gnomes.

"This is Otto Mears," said Jocknick, with a pretentious air.

"My pleasure," said C.W., reaching down a hand to shake. "I am Charles Collins."

"Mr. Collins," Mears said, in a heavy accent and husky voice slightly incongruous with his size. "Sidney tells me you wish to see me." He seemed to be completely unaffected by having to look up at both his visitors. "Would you care to come back to my office?"

"Thank you." C.W. followed Mears and Sidney to the inner sanctum behind the counter. The clerk was busy coming to monetary terms with the customers.

"No deals, Howard," Mears instructed on his way by.

"No sir," the clerk answered respectfully.

Mears took them to a rather large and much cluttered office and took a seat behind a wooden desk piled high with paperwork and ledger books. He indicated a couple of chairs nearby. Collins and Jocknick laid aside more ledgers and sat.

"Why did you wish to see me, Mr. Collins?" Mears asked unceremoniously.

Collins did not care to be too forthcoming with this man, but he required more information. He chose his words judiciously. "I have been sent by Secretary Schurz to investigate current circumstances with the Utahs in Colorado. I was informed that you were quite knowledgeable regarding this situation."

Mears made a tent of his child-size fingers. "Schurz told you this?"

"I am not at liberty to discuss the totality of my connections in this matter."

"I certainly let him know you had much to do with the Utes," Sidney interjected.

Mears glanced dismissively at Jocknick. To Collins he said, "What exactly do you wish to know?"

"Do you believe that events will transpire to force the Utes from this state?"

An artful expression came over Mears' face. "I believe it is possible."

"And is it your opinion that a belligerent episode would precipitate a swift banishment of the Indians?"

The man examined him silently for a long moment. "Would that eventuality not demand their removal?" he asked slyly.

Collins had the distinct impression that he had just received an admission of culpability. Mears was studying him for a reaction.

"It would, indeed," he said, noncommittally.

"Was there anything else you desire to know?" There seemed to be a wealth of menace and challenge in the simple question. Mears was plainly suspicious of him and not a bit inclined toward providing any further intelligence.

"Not at present," Collins said, standing. It was astonishing to discover the calculating iniquity and puissance in this tiny man. He experienced a strong desire to remove himself from Mears' company, no longer reminded of gnomes but rather of hobgoblins. "I thank you for your time."

"Not at all," Mears said, not bothering to get to his feet. "Nice to see you, Sidney," he said disingenuously.

They exited the building and retrieved the animals.

"Where can I find John Lawrence?" Collins asked Jocknick as they mounted their horses.

"I am unsure as to where he might be. We should have asked Mr. Mears."

"I would prefer that particular gentleman to have short knowledge of my whereabouts and business," C.W. said, unable to shake a vague sense of foreboding.

Sidney looked at him askance. "I would have thought you could have gotten much more information from him. We spent very little time."

Convinced that Jocknick did not deal well in subtleties, he said, "He seemed busy. I thought it best to leave him be."

They rode down the dirt street until they happened upon a young Mexican fellow walking by.

"Can you direct us to John Lawrence's house?" Collins asked.

"*Si*, I can that," the man said. "*Pero* he is at his *rancho*. He spends most of his time out there. Ride west along the *rio* for three miles and look for a long white house with two chimneys. That is *Señor* Lawrence's *casa*."

"Thank you," Collins said, turning his mare back toward Cochetopa Pass.

"*De nada*."

Containing his angst as best he could, Collins said, "We should have stopped at Lawrence's ranch on the way here." He suspected Sydney had wanted to direct him to Mears first.

"I told you I was not sure where he was," his companion responded defensively.

"It is not in the best interest of my mission to retrace three miles."

"I did not know," Sidney insisted in raised tones.

Despite his aggravation, Collins decided to relinquish the argument as pointless. Sidney was in a sulk again and nothing would be served. He settled back into the saddle and reviewed the meeting with Mears. Although brief, many valuable insights had been gained.

15

A rather plain woman of Spanish heritage answered the door of the impressive adobe house. It was a rambling one-story building with white-washed walls and numerous paned windows. She took his hat and invited Collins into the dining room, as it was dinnertime. It was the only reason, he supposed, that a prominent rancher could be found inside the house during the day. According to some purpose of his own, Sidney chose to remain outside with the livestock.

"John," the woman said, "this is Mr. Collins. He wanted to see you."

The big man at the head of the table beckoned him into the low-ceilinged room. "Sit down, Mr. Collins. There is plenty of food. You must eat with us."

C.W. joined the array of what he took to be ranch hands and a variety of other workers at the expansive table. Several of the men and women appeared to be Indian. Various plates of food made their way in his direction. He helped himself to beef and some unknown dishes of Mexican origin. It was all excellent. In short order, the hands began leaving the table, with Lawrence occasionally providing instructions to some of them. A couple of times, he spoke what seemed to be Spanish mingled with an indigenous tongue of some sort. John Lawrence had a copious moustache and thinning hair, both salty with middle age. His eyes were clear and bespoke a keen intellect. When the room had emptied, the woman began to clear the table.

Lawrence stood up. "Come, Mr. Collins. Let us retire to my office."

Collins followed the rancher into a spacious room decorated with Navajo rugs, elk and bighorn sheep antlers and various Indian artifacts.

Sitting in a large upholstered chair by a window, Lawrence directed Collins to another nearby. "What is it I can do for you?" the big man asked.

"I have been told that you are kindly disposed toward the Utes."

Lawrence considered him a moment. "This is true. I am unashamed of my friendship with Utes, Apaches, Navajos or any of them."

"May I ask an impolitic question?"

"You are most direct, Mr. Collins," Lawrence said, bemusedly. "Yes, you may ask."

"What is your opinion of Mr. Otto Mears' intentions toward the Utes?"

The man raised his eyebrows in astonishment. "Mears? What is your interest in *that* purveyor of connivance?"

Collins chewed his lower lip a moment, weighing his words cautiously in spite of the confidence this man engendered. "I am interested in whether Mears could be part of a scheme to...precipitate the expulsion of the Utes from the state of Colorado."

Lawrence stared at him in disbelief. He finally spoke. "You, sir, are indeed impolitic. Why would I discuss my opinions on such a subject with a perfect stranger?"

"I have no time for niceties. I believe that an instigation of violence may be imminent. That key figures in this state, and some in subterfuge, mean to resolve the issue of the Utes forthwith. I have been sent to investigate and report back to Washington in this regard."

The man turned to gaze out the window. A ranch

hand passed by, driving a team of horses pulling a sickle mower. "Mears is my business partner in many enterprises," he said, after a moment.

"Again, Mr. Lawrence, I must impress upon you that urgency must needs preclude delicacy. I sense you may do business with him, but you neither trust him nor hold him in high regard."

"This may be true," Lawrence said. "But why should I trust *you*? Who is your master in Washington?"

Collins smiled. "I have no master. I am an agent for hire and am currently in the employ of Secretary Schurz."

"I see. And have you met with Mears?"

"I have."

"And did you share this information with him?"

"I did."

Lawrence shook his head. "That was imprudent. You are correct...I do not trust Mears and have reason not to. He is a dangerous man and will not hesitate to take any action in order to protect his interests. I would not be at all surprised that he is at work plotting an event with which to destroy the Utes. He will not be working alone, however. He has built a network of allies within the government and mining concerns. Be wary, Mr. Collins. You may have tipped your hand and compromised your safety." He got up and walked over to a whiskey decanter on a sideboard. He poured himself a glass and waved the decanter at Collins in inquiry. C.W. shook his head and the man brought his glass back to sit down again.

" 'There is a mystery...in the soul of the state,' " C.W. said. "Time is short and I must flush out the villains."

"How do you know I am not such a one?"

"I have been at this for a while. My instincts go rarely astray."

Lawrence smiled and visibly relaxed. "Then your instincts have not betrayed you. Will you accept advice?"

"I will and gladly."

"Are you headed for Denver?"

Collins nodded.

"Alter your mode of travel. I will send you by wagon to Cañon City, where you can catch the train to Pueblo. Also, be forewarned that now Mears is alert to your purpose, so will many others be in short order. What are your plans?"

"To meet with other key figures involved with the eventual disposition of the Utes. To gather intelligence and thwart calamity if possible. I will accept your offer of transport to the railway in Cañon City. May I request another favor?"

"I will grant it if possible," the rancher said, nodding.

"May I prevail upon you to send a man with my mare and mule back to Mr. Hartman's ranch on the Gunnison River?"

"I know Alonzo well. I will gladly send him the animals and I might even take them myself. I owe him a visit."

"Excellent," Collins said, standing. "Shall I be able to depart today?"

Lawrence got to his feet. "Stay the night as my guest and I will see you off early in the morning." He stretched and stood looking out of the window. "Is that Sidney Jocknick out there?" he asked, peering sideways through the glass.

"It is. He has been my guide. He desires to return to prospecting and will, no doubt, be pleased to leave my employ."

"He is easily influenced and has always been a disciple of Mears'"

"He is at least an admirer. May I go out and take my leave of him?"

"Please do. I do not wonder that he did not come in. We have been at odds on many occasions."

Conjecturing that Mears was probably the basis of

their disagreements, C.W. left the house and walked around to find Sidney sitting on the ground with his back against the side of a chicken coop, tossing rocks at an overturned bucket. Their horses were ground-tied nearby. He stood up when he saw Collins approaching.

"Are we leaving?" he asked eagerly.

"I am staying. You are free, at last, to pursue your own objectives. I assume your father will remunerate you for your invaluable services."

"You are dismissing me?" he asked dubiously.

"You expressed your desire to return to the Dolores River country. I have made arrangements for the mule and mare. I will give you the cost of their purchase and you will therefore be shed of us all."

Jocknick scuffed a boot in the dirt. "Where are you going?"

"North. I wish to thank you for all your information and admirable company. May we cross paths again in future." Collins put his hand out to shake. Sidney accepted it indifferently.

"Mr. Riley will want a good price for these animals," Jocknick replied, shaking a thumb at the mare and mule.

C.W. produced three gold double eagles from his vest pocket. "This should be sufficient, should it not?"

"It should," the man said, pocketing the coins and turning to tighten the cinch on his saddle. He swung onto Shoe String. "I wish you luck," he said as he turned his horse and loped back toward Saguache.

"*Ag duine féin is fearr a fhios cáluionn an bhróg air,*" Collins said to himself as he watched his erstwhile companion ride away. The wearer best knows where the shoe pinches.

VAQUEROS

16

Lawrence spent the afternoon showing Collins around his farm, recounting the hardships he had endured for the twelve years he had been building a lucrative trade in agricultural products and livestock. He told of his involvement in politics, his penchant for racing horses and his partnership with J.B. Woodson, whose wife was the woman Collins had met on his arrival. He seemed to be a modest man, despite his accomplishments and his established leadership in the small community.

"Woodson is in Leadville," he told C.W. as they walked through a flock of ewes, many with half-grown lambs at their sides. "He has an interest in one of the new mines there."

"From what I have heard, Leadville has already produced impressive tonnage of high grade silver."

"The population there has been growing by the thousands this year. It can boast over eighty saloons, some twenty hotels, ten lumber yards and several gambling houses." Lawrence snatched up a puppy that was playing nearby and held it to his face. "Delightful bugger," he said, handing it to C.W.

Collins cradled the animal in his arms. It chewed on his hand and squirmed. He missed his own dog, left behind in the care of a friend's daughter. "What about Tabor?" he asked. "Could he be part of an initiative to manufacture a contentious event? An excuse to expel the Utes from Colorado?" He gave the puppy back to its anxious mother.

"Could be. Although my take on the man is that he is more lucky than intelligent. He most definitely wishes to engage in politics and has become Leadville's first mayor, but I doubt the man's cleverness. He has nothing of the cunning of those such as Pitkin, Chaffee, McCook, Teller and the like."

"In your visits to Denver have you happened upon individuals who may be at work behind the scenes? Those who may be operatives for these more principal men?"

They passed through a gate and crossed a ditch into a fragrant hay field. A slight breeze had grown and brought a chill off the never melt snowfields in the mountains to the east. Lawrence stroked his beard.

"There is one such. Vickers. He has been the editor of both leading newspapers in Denver and is currently serving as secretary for Governor Pitkin. He used to own an interest in the *Greeley Sun,* organized by the fellow who is now the Indian agent for White River. Several of these prominent men took an interest in the man's appointment there."

"Meeker?"

"That is it, Nathan Meeker."

C.W. removed his hat to scratch his head. He carried it a while to enjoy the warmth of the sun on his brow. "What causes you to suspect this Vickers?" he asked, recalling that the elder Jocknick had mentioned the name.

"He is a shifty sort who seems to be ubiquitously involved in every issue that concerns the state government. His new master, Pitkin, was instrumental in obtaining the San Juan mining district from the Utes, his current wealth being the product of having trespassed on Ute lands. Vickers was never a miner, but he has become wealthy as an agent and mouth piece for Republican politicians such as Pitkin. It is just such a man who would be ideally suited to arranging events in their interest."

"And then there is Mears," Collins said, placing his hat back on his head.

Lawrence paused to gaze at a small bunch of mule deer bounding across the field. "I must caution you again, Mr. Collins. Colorado has been built mainly by grasping and ruthless men. This is not a bastion of honor and integrity."

"And yet you are here."

"I have been ruthless in my time." He resumed his measured stride over the hay pasture. "It is nearly the twentieth anniversary of my departure from my home in Iowa. I have never desired to return."

"Does this make you ruthless?" Collins asked, smiling.

"I have been committed to making a life here and have made mistakes. I am in business with questionable partners."

C.W. thought perhaps that Lawrence harbored regrets. "I will be cautious," he told him. "I am ever vigilant."

They walked in momentary silence. "Yes...then there is Otto Mears," Lawrence finally said. "He was one of the electors who supported Chaffee in becoming U.S. senator. He also had much to do with Pitkin becoming governor, but I am not able to relate particulars, as I am not in his confidence. I am a Democrat, you see. Mears does not trust me."

"He is ambitious, I take it."

Lawrence made a noise in his throat. "That is a small word for so great an attribute. Mears has never passed up an opportunity to further enrich himself or expand his empire of roads and commerce. He possesses no scruples that I have ever observed."

" 'Let a beast be lord of beasts, and his crib shall stand at the king's mess,' " quoted Collins from *Hamlet*. "Is it merely wealth that gives him so much influence?"

"No, the 'beast' has a network of agents," Lawrence told him, smiling. "Men who have had no success in any other enterprise and are willing to perform most any chore for sufficient reward. This is the provenance of my suggestion that you alter your route."

"I must admit to you, I was uneasy in his presence."

"Not without cause, I assure you."

The men angled toward a set of corrals on their return to the house. A mongrel black dog found them and followed at their heels. Inside the pens were several horses, some which appeared to be blooded stock. A big sorrel stud wandered over and blew in Collins' face. The dog departed on some business of its own.

"That is Red Buck," Lawrence said. "I have won several races with him."

They patted the animal and a few others that came up to them. It was peaceful and C.W. never tired of the company of horses.

"Tell me more of Mears," Collins requested.

"He has the mail contracts for this entire region. A premium, no doubt, from his cronies in politics. I believe now he is jockeying for the position of Indian Commissioner." Lawrence rubbed the chin of a young chestnut horse. "Here is a telling anecdote... Several years ago, there was a fellow killed during a fandango held hereabouts. After the burial, all the men were making too lively a time of it, so the women went up to Mears' store and broke up the whiskey kegs. Mears never said a word, but later on he charged the men hundreds of dollars for the whiskey that was wasted. They had no choice but to foot the bill, as they were bound to continue doing business with the man."

"Rather unscrupulous."

"There was also the affair involving cattle bound for the old Los Pinos Agency. According to Lieutenant Speer, the agent at the time, Mears held back fifty cows contracted to the Utes and supplied, instead, fifty old hides he had on hand, stating the cows had died on the drive."

"And you believed Speer?"

"Mears has always boasted that the U.S.I.D. brand for the Indian Department stands for 'You steal, I divide.' Chief Ouray has had many dealings with him, but does not trust him."

"Sidney told me you know Ouray quite well."

"I have known him many years. He is tired and sick now and not one to stand up to the rigors of protecting the Ute interests. I still respect and care for the man."

"What of Shavano?"

Lawrence smiled and shook his head. "He is a powerful man; intelligent and calculating."

"He is to be my guide into the White River country."

"Well, if he is loyal to you, you could ask for no better ally. If he does not take to you, I would not give you two bits for your chances. Ouray is sending him, I take it?"

"Yes."

"He is generally loyal to Ouray. You should survive his acquaintanceship."

They walked along and Collins made a point of visiting Mona and Felix one more time. He went into their pen and scratched behind their ears and spoke to them at length. Lawrence waited patiently, leaning on the top rail. Later, as they wandered through the pasture nearest the house, Lawrence related another episode involving Mears.

"There has been a drought here in southern Colorado for the past several seasons. I have been able to hold out, but many of my neighbors have been forced to sell their cattle and will most probably be forced to sell more if this warm dry weather continues. Mears and some of his partners...I am not among them...have been taking advantage of their hard luck and are buying the livestock on contract for the government. They will be driven to the Uncompahgre Agency and Mears will realize a handsome profit on the backs of his neighbors."

Collins felt confident that Mears and the man Vickers were plotting against the Indians. Secretary Schurz must be aware of Mears, he thought, as Gustavus Jocknick had mentioned him as a possibility. Now, leaving the next day for Cañon City, he was undeniably proceeding in his inquiry. With luck, he would not be waylaid or murdered. Whether he would be able to aid in the prevention of what now seemed a credible disaster was decidedly uncertain.

17

Supper was eaten at the same large table with all the hands. Mrs. Woodson and a young Navajo woman served. It became apparent to Collins that Lawrence spoke at least two dialects of Indian language as well as fluent Spanish. A fellow named Bob Morrison joined them, welcomed as a regular visitor and close associate. The food, again, was a blend of American and Mexican. Collins was introduced to *sopaipillas*, deep-fried triangles of tortilla dough eaten with honey and used for sopping up the chile sauces on many of the dishes. It reminded him of fry bread, eaten by reservation Indians in the Southwest, deluged with a surplus of government flour and very little else. As he had learned many years before, fry bread had been originally prepared out of dire necessity at Fort Sumner, during the brutal incarceration of Navajo and Apache peoples at the behest of General James Carleton.

Conversation around the table was limited to ranch work, the care of livestock and plans for supplying meat and produce to the Leadville market. C.W. was only able to follow the essence of discussions in English and a little in Spanish. As the dishes were being cleared away, Lawrence informed Bob Morrison that he desired him to drive Collins to Cañon City the next day. Morrison appeared surprised.

"I thought we were headed for Fort Garland to see if we could get up a race with Toben. Mr. Collins can take the stage."

"It can wait until you get back. Besides, you need to deliver those sacks of oats I owe Rudd. I want you to look after Mr. Collins here. There might be a problem or two." Lawrence looked at him pointedly.

"Oh," was all the man said. He rubbed at a spot on his shirt front.

The hands all left the table, taking their leave with varied expressions of deference in their respective languages. Each was notably acknowledged by Lawrence. Collins recognized in him a natural leader of men and one capable of inspiring loyalty.

"Why are you headed to Cañon City, Mr. Collins?" Morrison asked in order to make conversation.

"To catch the train for Pueblo," Lawrence answered. "Please do not be overly inquisitive, Bob. Mr. Collins' business is his own."

Mrs. Woodson brought coffee and dessert, breaking the awkward moment. Dessert was unrecognizable to Collins, except as some type of upside down pudding. Lawrence noticed him picking at it tentatively.

"It is called *flan*. It is quite good."

C.W. took a spoonful and found it so. "Custard?"

"Of a sort. Mrs. Woodson has the touch."

Collins found their arrangement rather unusual, with Mr. Woodson absent and his wife doing for Mr. Lawrence. Odder still was that Mrs. Woodson and Lawrence seemed to not care for each other one whit.

After dessert, Morrison, Collins and Lawrence retired to his office. Lawrence poured whiskey for himself, offered some to C.W., who declined, but pointedly did not proffer a drop to Morrison.

"Bob and I have a wager. If he drinks or plays cards for money at any time before Christmas, he gives me that chestnut horse colt you saw this afternoon. If he does not, I am to give him a colt worth comparable value."

Chapter 17

"I have my eye on the black," Morrison said.

"Then he shall be yours, should you hold fast."

Morrison grinned, pulled leather cord from his pocket and began to work on some braiding. Collins took out his pipe to smoke. Lawrence stood to replenish his whiskey.

"Do you care to go down to town and look around?" he asked Collins.

"No thank you. But please feel at ease to do so yourself. I plan to employ my bedroll rather early."

"Nonsense. You shall sleep in the house. You and Bob can share the room in the back."

Mrs. Woodson came into the room. "*Señor* Mears is here."

"What about?" Lawrence asked, apparently not pleased.

She shrugged. "*No se.*"

Lawrence sighed and paced the room. "Be judicious, Mr. Collins...and Bob, no mention of the journey to Cañon City."

Morrison appeared to grasp his import.

"*Bueno,*" Lawrence told Mrs. Woodson. "Bring him in."

She departed and after a moment Mr. Otto Mears entered the room. He walked to the decanter and poured himself a glass of whiskey. Collins noted with amusement that the man's child-size hand could barely encompass the stout glass.

"Good evening, John," he said in his heavy accent, lifting the glass to Lawrence. He turned to look at Morrison and only then noticed Collins, sitting quietly observing him.

"Ah, Mr. Collins," he said perching on the edge of a small divan. "So you have come to see my friend, John Lawrence." He made a show of searching the room. "And where is poor Sidney?"

"I would hazard that he is now *your* guest," Lawrence said under his breath, resuming his chair.

Mears smiled craftily. "Perhaps." He sipped his

whiskey. "Have you apprised John of your mission?" he asked C.W. "He is quite fond of the noble savage."

Collins considered him coldly. "What is your purpose?" he asked bluntly, placing his spent pipe in a jacket pocket.

Mears was all affronted innocence. "My purpose? Why Mr. Collins...I have come for a sociable visit with my friend John." His eyes narrowed, glinting dangerously. "What, one may ask, is *your* purpose?"

Collins got to his feet. "Thank you for a very enjoyable evening, Mr. Lawrence. I will leave you to your other guests and find comfort under the stars."

Lawrence nodded. "Bob, would you be good enough to show Mr. Collins out."

Morrison stood and ushered C.W. out of the room. When they were out of earshot, he stopped.

"Damn, but that little fellow always gives me the jitters. What is his interest in you?"

"I am unsure."

They resumed their progress to the outside door. "You are welcome to share my room," Morrison told him.

"Many thanks, but I will be more comfortable out of doors, especially given the balmy temperatures."

"See you on the morrow, then."

Collins shook the man's hand and walked away from the house, conscious that he was being watched from a window and who was watching him.

18

Collins was up with the sun, having found a genial location to roll out his bed away from the house, pens of livestock and piles of manure. The main irrigation ditch, or *acequia madre* as Lawrence called it, was nearby and offered the shelter of leafy brush and fragrant plant growth. He fancied he could detect mint among the herbage. After packing his gear, he carried it to a shed where his recently acquired saddle was cached, then made his way toward the house. He fairly stumbled on Morrison urinating on a clump of snakeweed.

"Oh, beg your pardon," the man said, buttoning up. "I was just on my way to find you. John asks that you come for a quick breakfast before the others arrive."

"Very well."

They walked together into the house and Collins' appetite was quickly kindled by the tempting odors of food. Lawrence was sitting at the table and they joined him.

"So you decided to sleep out of doors after all," Lawrence observed.

"As I was bent on withdrawing from Mears' company, I thought it most expedient."

"Of course."

Mrs. Woodson brought in platters of eggs, beans, tortillas and roasted chilies. They helped themselves and began to eat. She returned with cups and a pot of coffee. She made to sit, but Lawrence said something in Spanish and she withdrew.

"Bob, Mears was altogether too interested in Mr. Collins here. You need to give Saguache a miss on your way to the pass. Mrs. Woodson has gathered together provisions and camping gear and placed everything in the buckboard. José already loaded the oats for Rudd. Hitch up Frank and Sam. While you are in Cañon City, see Mr. Collins safely onto the train, then deliver the oats and see about that contract with Mack and Kennedy for poles. Afterward, beat it back here so we can go get up a race with Toben and the soldiers."

Morrison nodded agreement, as his mouth was full.

"And Bob...no whiskey or cards."

Morrison swallowed. "No, John. We have a bargain."

"See you remember it."

After breakfast and as the hired hands were wandering in to eat, Lawrence, Collins and Morrison went out to pack Collins' gear on the buckboard. While Morrison was catching and harnessing the team, Lawrence and C.W. stood together by the wagon.

"What do want done with your packsaddle and other tack?" the rancher asked.

"Keep it. I intend to have my own outfit when I proceed south from Rawlins."

"I certainly sound like an old woman, Mr. Collins, but watch your back until you are on that train. And keep Bob off the hooch if you can."

"You really think that Mears believes I pose a threat?"

"Schurz is a threat to his plans and you are employed by him. He insinuated to me that you might present a problem. In truth, he fancies himself as an 'empire builder' and says so often enough. Tell me, if you find proof of a cadre of men engineering a violent conflict with the Utes, what then?"

"I will report the intelligence to Secretary Schurz. He will, hopefully, attempt to employ the military and his myriad political connections in an effort to forestall disaster. If there is a way for me to avert a conflict, I will do so."

Lawrence sighed and shook his head. He poked a finger in his ear and dug around. "Pardon my skepticism, but powerful forces shoe-horned this territory into statehood, despite some mighty opposition in Washington. Whoever might be orchestrating a calamity is backed by the same forces. My opinion is that you and Schurz do not stand a chance...nor, for that matter, do the Utes."

"I have my mission. I must do my utmost."

"Of course, of course." They stood silently a moment, watching several cranes fly overhead, emitting a cacophony of calls.

"There can be such beauty in the world," Lawrence observed.

"For some," Collins replied. "It seems our friend Sidney does not see much of it. What is the matter that sits between you? Is it Mears?"

"It is. I do not quite understand the nature of his worship for the little Russian, but I have tried on several occasions to dissuade Sidney from this friendship. I have often been convinced that Mears was pumping him for information about various plans of mine. Information such as I wished to keep close to my chest. Sidney is not the best judge of men, I fear. We finally parted cordial company and he has been steadfast in his loyalty to Mears since."

Morrison arrived, leading two rangy geldings in harness, both chestnuts, but with varying blazes and snips. One was a hand or so taller than the other. Lawrence helped hitch them to the buckboard.

When all was made ready, Lawrence held out his hand. "Well, Mr. Collins, good luck to you. I will see your animals to Hartman and keep an ear to the ground for your success. Remember, you are always welcome here."

Collins shook his hand. "Thank you for your hospitality and advice. And please give my regards to Mrs. Woodson. It was a genuine pleasure."

Morrison climbed aboard the wagon and Collins followed suit.

"No whiskey, Bob."

Morrison grinned. "Yes mama."

Lawrence gave a humorous salute and headed back toward the house as Morrison turned the team to move out of the ranch yard. C.W. craned his neck to catch a final and affectionate glimpse of Felix and Mona, then the wagon rounded the corner and headed east toward town.

Taking a southerly route, they avoided Saguache, then turned northeastward to skirt a small range of mountains. They forded a couple of shallow streams, the horses appearing to be calm and heedless of any obstacles along the way. Some birds flew out of a thicket of brush and they remained steady. The men were quiet at first, enjoying the late summer day and perusing the scenery, but after a while Collins asked Morrison about his friendship with John Lawrence.

"I came to Saguache in '66. We became friends early on and have stayed so since."

"So you have known Otto Mears for about as long," Collins observed.

"Nobody knows Otto Mears...only the man himself. I give him a wide berth. As I have told you before, he gives me the willies. Cannot say why for sure."

"And J.B. Woodson...what sort of man is he?"

"Good business man, reliable and fairly honest. I know John thinks quite a lot of him. I do not think he cares a tinker's damn for me. Thinks I am a sour influence on John. Mrs. Woodson can be damn cold at times, when we have been at the cards or racing horses."

"She seems to be the matron of the household."

"She is and can throw a tantrum such as you rarely see. That is when Woodson, John and I seek other lodging for a time."

"She seemed very mild and obliging."

"She is a damn unalluring creature, yet she possesses all the common female traits."

Collins smiled to himself. Obviously, here was a bachelor who no doubt claimed more intimacy with the idiosyncrasies of women than true personal knowledge would warrant. And the man's own lack of stature and unattractive physiognomy allowed for narrow censure of others.

The buckboard offered little in the way of suspension. C.W. shifted his weight on the hard wooden seat. He removed his heavy serge coat and placed it under him by way of a cushion. He noticed a small herd of elk off to the south and pointed them out to Morrison.

"There were large herds of them hereabouts, back in the sixties. The sheep and cattle have forced them into the high country. Hardly see any bears, cats or wolves either. They were all hunted out."

"Now it is the Indians' turn, I suppose," Collins said, half to himself.

Morrison turned to look at him. "What would you suggest? There is no room for both ranchers and Indians. Not unless they learn to work the land and live as white people. John is stout-hearted in his defense of Ouray and his Utes, but God meant for whites to have this land."

Not wanting to begin a quarrel, Collins let it go. It seemed Mr. Morrison possessed the more prevalent attitude toward the Ute dilemma, in spite of his close friendship with Lawrence.

Changing the topic, he asked, "How will we traverse the mountains ahead? They appear to be impregnable."

Morrison snapped the lines and spoke to the horses. They were headed up a slight grade and bearing toward a more northerly direction. The wide valley was narrowing and the Sangre De Cristo Mountains rose as a granite rampart, shining with patches of ice and snow from the preceding winter.

"There is a pass over yonder," Morrison said, tipping his head and indicating a landmark indiscernible to Collins.

"You know it well?"

"Well enough."

This did not reassure Collins, but as he was at the man's mercy, he would have to make do. The team certainly gave him no pause.

"There are hot springs over there," Morrison informed him.

"There seem to be a preponderance of hot springs around southern Colorado."

"What?" Morrison asked, giving him a look.

"Quite a lot."

"Oh right. Yeah, I suppose so. These are real hot. Good to cook out the symptoms of a binge."

"No doubt. Why is Mr. Lawrence so adamant about keeping you sober?"

"Adamant?"

"Determined."

"Oh...that." Morrison was silent for a long moment. "There was an occurrence with an Indian boy a few years ago. I was drunk and fired off a couple of rounds. In the morning John found the boy dead. Been trying to get me sober ever since."

"How is it you did not go to jail?"

Morrison fired him a surly glance then shrugged. "John got me pardoned. Think he feels he done wrong now." After another lengthy pause, he added, "Kid was a slave, all the same. Always in trouble and not worth John's abiding protection."

They fell silent again. The wagon progressed toward the mountains, steadily gaining altitude. Collins decided he was not inclined to be overly congenial toward Morrison. He began contemplating solutions regarding the future of all Indians in the United States. Given the differences between the average white person's bias and the pragmatic reasoning of the Indian, there seemed no possible outcome except annihilation or complete subjugation. Little Phil's adage that the only good Indian was a dead Indian might be amended to account for those who sought to live as whites, such as Ouray. With such examples of effective assimilation, the moralistic luminaries of bureaucracy could pat themselves on their collective backs for the beneficent processes of civilization. Rip the heart out of a culture and people and justify it as a benevolent undertaking. He experienced the usual melancholy associated with such rumination. He reckoned that many indigenous groups, including his own, could never stand against the aggressive self-interest of colonization. Suddenly, the apparent pointlessness of his mission seemed overwhelming.

GOING TO LEADVILLE

19

Having slept hard and reluctant to wake, Collins forced himself out of his bedroll into the deep chill of the high mountain dawn, tending to the fire with celerity. Morrison was already awake and absent. Unconcerned, Collins began organizing the gear and packing it in the wagon. By the time Morrison had returned, there was coffee made and bacon frying and C.W. was in the midst of harnessing the team.

"Hey, thanks," Morrison said, pitching in to help. "I was just having a look around."

Collins thought he detected an odor of whiskey on the man, but neglected to comment. They finished harnessing and hitching the team, then packed the rest of the outfit. They ate as they worked. By the time the frost had disappeared, they were wending their way, cautiously, down the steep eastern slopes of the Sangre De Cristo Mountains. The climb up to the pass had been alarming, but the descent was reminiscent of his extraordinary stagecoach journey into the village of Ouray.

Morrison was uncommunicative. C.W. perused the magnificent vista stretching toward the rising sun and occasionally contemplated his own demise, given the precipitous route they traveled. The team labored slowly, placing each foot with care and ever mindful of the weight of the wagon, clearly having taken this route before. Morrison made consistent use of the brake. The road, at last, found even terrain and eventually merged with the southern bank of the Arkansas River. They stopped to water the horses. The animals drank deeply, lathered in sweat from the strenuous journey down the mountains. A trio of raccoons watched from a nearby tree, arrayed as furry ornaments among the branches.

When they resumed their journey, Morrison began to tell C.W. about the newspaper Mears was preparing to launch in Saguache. "It will be called the *Saguache Chronicle* and will assuredly be filled with news gilded for his own egoism."

" 'His very genius hath taken the infection of the device,' " quoted Collins.

"Pardon?"

"It is nothing. It is always prudent to manage the flow of information when one is meaning to handle local opinion."

"Well, I do not know about that, but it is certain that Mears seems to manage many enterprises."

Collins thought about this a moment. "That would mean he has quite an interest in moving the Utes off their remaining lands and expanding said enterprises."

"Is that what John told you?" Morrison asked, glancing at him.

"No. But it seems manifest."

Morrison abstained from conversation for a while, appearing to be mulling this over. "Come to think of it, he advanced himself as the main interpreter for the San Juan Cession treaty, even though John was far more capable in such a role," he finally said.

"The San Juan Cession?"

"In '73, when the San Juan Mountains were given over by the Utes."

The day progressed and the road took them through arid canyons before climbing onto open mountain parks offering breathtaking views of the mountains behind them. Shortly thereafter, the byway descended into a winding narrow creek bottom bounded by steep slopes covered in piñon and juniper trees. There was evidence of sporadic prospecting in the rocks above. Occasionally, they passed fellow travelers on foot, in carriages and some riding horseback. There were also several freight wagons, loaded with goods. Morrison speculated that most of the traffic was headed for Leadville. Farther on, they crossed the river over a ramshackle bridge and stopped to rest the horses and eat some cold meat and tortillas packed for them by Mrs. Woodson. Morrison described the impressive rocky gorge south of them and Collins regretted not having the leisure to visit this wonder of nature.

After a hard pull over a long and steep hill, they descended into Cañon City, passing an extensive prison and flourmill and coming straight into the town itself. The sun was setting as they boarded the horses in the Sartor Livery Stable. Morrison sent word to the fellow Rudd that his order of grain had arrived. Lawrence had suggested to Collins he stay at the McClure Hotel. As they maneuvered through the busy main street, bustling with pleasure seekers of dubious social strata, Morrison angled toward a well-lit saloon. It exhibited a large sign advertising billiards.

"I have acquaintances here at the Murray," he told Collins. "Will you not come in a moment?"

"I think not. I will seek the hotel and a robust meal. What of your wager with Mr. Lawrence?"

"He will be none the wiser," he said, smiling. "I will search you out after a brief interlude."

C.W. felt this would be improbable, but as he required nothing further from the man, he was not inclined to interest himself in Morrison's proposed recreation nor to engage in lectures on the benefits of abstention. They shook hands and Collins thanked him for his aid in getting him to Cañon City, after which they parted ways.

As he walked along the thoroughfare, Collins studied the burgeoning humanity around him. Not for the first time, he observed that the siren call of gold and silver attracted the dregs of the country's populace. His empirical proof was the loutish bearing of most of his predominantly male companions, jostling each other in the avenue. Abruptly, a tousled young man approached him, breathless and alarmed.

"Sir...can you please help me? I have just been robbed. I have nothing left."

The youth seemed near sobbing as he pulled on Collins' arm, propelling him toward a side alley between a two-story brownstone and a clapboard storefront building. C.W. forcefully halted their progress and removed the man's hand from his sleeve.

"Calm yourself, youngster," he said. "I am not the law."

The fellow endeavored to drag him farther along and managed to move him closer to the side of building. "Please, they are getting away."

Collins had become entirely wary and strove to extricate himself from the boy's implacable grip. Just as he noted a wily alteration in the young man's countenance, he was set upon by figures that moved out of the shadows. He was forcibly dragged into the alley behind a pile of refuse and broken kegs, at once filled with regret at having left his revolver with his belongings in the stables. Unsure as to the number of his assailants, Collins vigorously resisted their attempts to overpower him until a stunning blow to the back of his head rendered him incapable of self-preservation. He dropped to his knees, feeling a flow of warm blood down his neck. A hand took a fistful of his hair and kept him from slumping into prostration.

"Your presence is no longer desired in Colorado," whispered one of his attackers in an unmistakable Confederate accent. "Has this message been made clear to you?"

Collins felt his consciousness slipping. The pain was almost beyond bearing. "Who sends it?" he asked with great effort.

The answer was another tremendous blow to his head. He vomited and lost all sensibility. In the darkness of his oblivion, he wandered hallucinations of past tragedies and unbearable events, concomitant with a vague awareness of being roughly transported to some other location. He struggled for a return to cognizance, but it remained persistently elusive.

KU KLUX KLAN

20

After an interminable passage of drifting through amorphous nightmares, Collins became sluggishly aware of a redolence of whiskey accompanied by the scent of soap and something medicinal. His perceptions sharpened and he became sensible of being face down on a clean pillow, whilst unknown persons discussed him from above. Sunlight filled his periphery.

"Will he live?" asked a slurred voice.

"I believe so," said a woman's voice. "Where did you find him?"

"On the shit...sorry ...on the manure pile behind the livery. I thought he was dead, but he moaned and scared the shit...sorry...the bejeezus out of me."

Collins attempted to roll over. Strong hands moved him onto his back, adjusting the pillow in a manner intended to ease the pressure on the back of his head. He squinted through an upsurge of pounding between his ears and perceived a handsome middle-aged woman and a large and unkempt man standing over him. The woman knelt down beside the bed.

"What happened to you?" she asked, and C.W. thought he detected a European accent.

His mouth seemed incapable of action. She turned and retrieved a wet cloth, pressing it to his crusted lips. She wiped the rest of his face and tested the bandage on his head.

"Now then, can you tell me what happened?" she

asked again, still kneeling beside him.

"Say, have you got anything to drink here?" her companion asked.

"Go on, Timmy…You know better than that," the woman chided affably. "Everything I have here is remedial."

"I shall be departing then," the fellow said formally, albeit unsteadily.

"Thank you for bringing him," she said, getting to her feet and giving him a coin from her purse.

The man bowed and went out. From the sound of his retreating steps, Collins surmised they were on a second floor. The woman pulled over a chair and sat down.

"Can you speak?" she asked, after again pressing the moistened rag to his lips.

"I…I believe so…" His voice was as creaky as an old door.

"What happened?"

Collins decided the woman must be French, according to her accent. "I was set upon."

"By whom and for what reason?"

"I know not by whom, but I may be able to conjecture the reasons. Oddly, and I am certain this will sound absurd, my assailants were costumed as members of a lawless brotherhood of the southern states."

"The Ku Klux Klan?" she asked. Her face betrayed disdain.

"I am aware that my assertion is not plausible," he said apologetically.

She placed a hand on his arm. "No, no, *mon cher*… I do not disbelieve you. This community is rife with such men. Unfortunately, there are also those who choose the disguise in order to camouflage their identities while bent upon mischief. There is no use summoning the authorities."

Collins waved his hand dismissively. "I do not wish to summon the law. It would be counter to my purposes."

Her warm and sympathetic face filled with curiosity.

Chapter 20

"Your purposes?"

He shook his head on the pillow. The motion caused him to wince with pain. "It is nothing," he said. "May I enquire as to the identity of my inebriated benefactor?"

"*Comme il faut*," she said. "His name is Timmy Foster. He shovels out the stables down by the prison and endeavors to drink himself to death between times. He was a thespian in Denver many years ago and fell upon difficulties. I know nothing more."

"And you?" C.W. asked, squinting at her through swollen eyes.

"I am a doctor, having studied in Heidelberg and believing that the untamed frontiers of America would welcome my services. *Plutôt*, I have endured hunger in many scenic locations. Being a medical woman is an infamy *trés formidable*."

"Yet Timmy trusted you."

She smiled. "Only because he knew I would not charge him for my services."

"How long have I been here?"

"Just since early dawn. You must rest now. Are there people I should notify?"

Collins shook his head less vigorously than before. "Unless there is a fellow named Bob Morrison still at the Murray Saloon, but I could not ask you to enter such an establishment."

She laughed musically. "*Oh lá*," she said. "I go there *tout les temps*...all the time."

Collins was confused. "You play billiards?" he asked.

She laughed again, throwing her head back in an appealing gesture. "I take care of the ladies in the back rooms...their diseases and pregnancies. I discovered that this was acceptable to the townspeople and made it possible for me to eat. I work in most of the houses here." She became serious. "*Alors*, these poor women desperately need the care of someone who loves them and does not judge."

C.W. regarded her thoughtfully.

"You repudiate me, *n'est-ce pas*?" she asked.

"On the contrary. I respect your empathy and courage. Also, I am most grateful for your ministrations."

"*Ce n'est rien*... and you should rest. I will search for your friend, Morrison, at the Murray. If he is not there, where else shall I seek him?"

"I do not know. He may be more intoxicated than Timmy, in any event."

The woman shrugged. "I will try, nonetheless." She lifted his head gently and gave him a drink of medicine. "Now rest. I will be back and you are safe here."

"Wait," he said, as she was about to depart. "What is your name?"

"Madeleine De Jussieu."

"*Docteure* De Jussieu."

"*Merci beaucoup*," she said, curtseying. She smiled and exited the room.

21

The laudanum caused sleep to take Collins for several hours. When he awoke, he could hear someone moving around in the next room. He attempted to sit up and managed to slump halfway up the headboard. The creaking of the bedstead brought the woman.

"How are you?" she asked.

He considered the question a moment. His head did not ache as fiercely. "Better."

"*Trés bien*. Hungry?"

"No. Thirsty."

She stooped to prop him up with pillows and went to bring him a cup of water. She steadied his hand as he drank.

"Thank you."

"*Mais oui*." She placed the cup on a nearby table and sat on the edge of the bed. "I am sorry to say I could not find your friend."

"Not to worry. How soon do you think I may be able to travel?"

The woman's face showed disapproval. "No, no...you must not think of that yet."

"I must," he said forcefully. "I have important business in Denver."

"Your head has been broken," she told him, with equal vehemence.

He smiled. "Is that medical terminology?" he asked.

She laughed with a rich and bell-like tone. Her abundance of thick auburn hair released a tantalizing scent of lavender and she had a glossy olive complexion with tiny creases around her mouth and eyes. Collins realized with a twinge that he needed to move on as soon as absolutely feasible. "I will make you some soup," she said and left the room.

When he awoke again, Morrison was leaning over him. The doctor hovered in the background.

"You okay?" Morrison asked. He smelled of whiskey and appeared to be painfully unsteady.

"As you see," C.W. answered, sitting up with success.

"Come, come, *monsieur*, he needs rest," the woman insisted. She attempted to pull the man away from the bedside.

"John will skin me alive for letting this happen," Morrison said. "I got word that the tosspot who mucks out the livery stables found a corpse on the shit pile. Glad you are not deceased."

"Thank you."

"You cannot help him now," Madeleine told him, her voice rising in frustration. "You reek of spirits and need a bath. Come back when you are sober. He needs to eat."

Morrison straightened up with the artificial dignity of the drunkard. "I, madam, am as sober as a priest."

She made a disparaging noise. "*Exactement*," she said and began pushing him out of the room.

"Do not fear, Collins, I will return and get you on that train," Morrison said as she closed the door on him.

"*Merde*. What a fool," she said, wiping her hands one on the other in a gesture of a task completed. "Now..." she told him sternly, "you will eat."

Returning with a bowl of steaming soup, she pulled up a chair and began to feed him. He very swiftly wrested the bowl and spoon away from her so he could feed himself. The flavor of the potage reminded him of sumptuous stews consumed in the finer restaurants of New York and San Francisco. He finished his meal.

Chapter 21

"Better?" she asked, taking the bowl from him.

"Much. Thank you."

The doctor left the room and returned with the laudanum. "You must have more sleep."

He waved the bottle way. "No...not now. Are you familiar with the train schedule to Pueblo?"

She sat down, holding the bottle, and measured her answer a moment. "Perhaps."

"Where are my clothes?"

"Torn...ruined."

"My spare clothing is with my kit over at the Sartor stables. Any chance you would send for them?"

"*Oui.* Now?"

"Please."

Madeleine went out reluctantly and he heard her leaving the building. Collins tested his head, neck and shoulders and felt around the bruises on his face. He eased himself out of bed and onto his feet and moved around the room. Naked beneath a woolen nightshirt, he lifted the garment to examine the contusions on his ribs. The damage was extensive, but not unbearable. Mears must have meant for him to receive an unambiguous message without excessive impairment...nothing that might incite inquiries from interested parties in Washington D.C. Getting back into bed and admiring the tasteful décor of the room, C.W. helplessly contemplated the many delightful virtues of his benefactress. He conjectured that a swift exit was not only advisable, but cardinal.

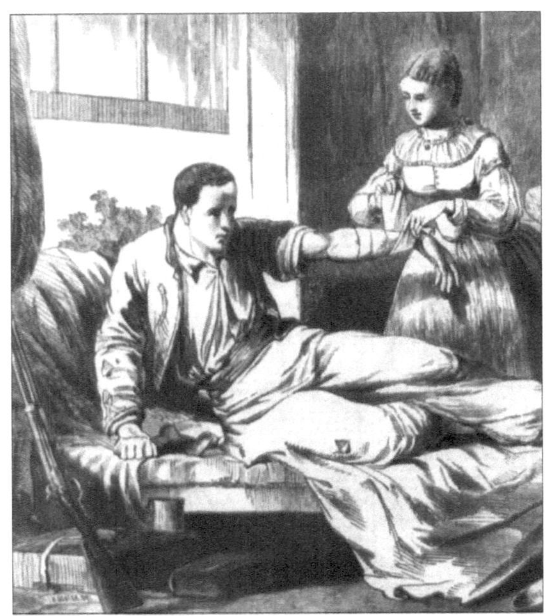

DOCTOR

22

Collins stepped out of the D.& R.G. Express office, having sent two telegrams. One had been sent to Gustavus Jocknick, apprising him of this most recent delay of his investigations and requesting that he meet him in Manitou Springs. Having inquired after the rather renowned gentleman, "General" Charles Adams, C.W. discovered that the fellow had returned home. Wanting to expedite his travels, Collins hoped to meet with both men during his stop in Manitou and proceed with all speed back to Cheyenne and on to Rawlins. He then intended to embark on a southward expedition to the White River Agency posthaste so as to ascertain, at the earliest opportunity, whether Mr. Meeker was a willing participant in political intrigues or merely an implement in the chicanery. This seemed to be the best course of action, with or without the aid of Ouray's war chief.

The second telegram had been sent to Fort Laramie, requesting that his friend and post commander, Major Evans, arrange to have his outfit, saddle horse and his pack mule, Molly, waiting for him at a livery stable in Rawlins. With all the rest of the dangers and uncertainties awaiting him, at least he would have no doubts about his livestock and equipment. His other mule, Joey, and his little dog, Gal, would have to remain in the care of Captain Collier, an old acquaintance from the war, and his delightful daughter Lucy. He squinted into the hot sun and walked toward the McClure Hotel, to which he had removed himself after exiting Madame De Jussieu's care.

Thinking of her now, he regretted the necessity of an imminent departure. Rarely did he meet women of her character and fine attributes. He was unable to discern whether she returned his admiration, but she certainly had exhibited indignation when he quitted her apartments. Entering the sybaritic lobby of the hotel, C.W. felt a twinge of longing for past attachments and those he must presently eschew. Romantic entanglements, however, were the least of his worries as he chafed at this unanticipated delay. Critical events, no doubt, were progressing.

He retrieved his key and ascended the wide stairway to his third floor room. In the midst of packing his belongings in preparation for the morning, there came a gentle tapping at his door. Reaching for his revolver, he walked over and stealthily stepped onto a chair intentionally positioned nearby. Peering through the transom window, he recognized the woman below. He descended, slipped the .45 beneath a pile of clothing on a small couch and opened the door.

"*Bonjour*," said M. De Jussieu. "I came to see if you are feeling well."

"Come in," he told her and stepped back to allow her entrance.

The woman glanced about and noticed the evidence of departure. "You are leaving yet today?" she asked.

"No. Tomorrow. An early train." He motioned to an empty chair, lavishly upholstered in satin brocade.

"How do you feel?" she asked, perching on the edge of the chair. "Are you in pain?"

Collins perceived a shyness about her. "Some, but not inordinately so. My head persists in aching, as one would imagine after being broken." He smiled. "Shall I send for tea?"

"*Mais non*," Madeleine said and got to her feet. "I will not further intrude."

Collins went to her and softly swept a tendril of hair from her cheek. "You are not intruding." Her presence had moved him beyond prudence and into appetency.

Folding into his arms, she pressed against his chest and sighed. He rested his cheek on her perfumed tresses. "Will you stay?" he asked quietly and felt her nod hesitantly. He stepped back from her and braced her with his eyes. She looked down at the carpeting then up again, meeting his gaze with the steady gray of her clear scrutiny. He bent to kiss her mouth and knew that his farewell on the morrow would be onerous at best.

Later, tangled in bedding and clothing and the warmth of her body, Collins told her a little about himself and his mission.

"You truly think there are political powers in this state that want to get rid of all the Indians?"

"I do indeed. I believe there are greedy men who will stop at nothing."

"*Mon dieu.* So that is why they attacked you," she said, lightly kissing a bruise on his ribs.

"And that is why I must depart tomorrow without delay."

She propped herself on an elbow and looked down upon him in disdain. "Do you think me some clinging vine? I am a woman of independence and duty. There will be no tearful pleading."

He smiled with his eyes. "Forgive me. I did not mean to imply such."

"*D'accord*," she said, resuming her position in the crook of his arm. "You are forgiven."

"Perhaps I will succumb to tearful pleading," he said, kissing her ear. "I did not care much for Cañon City until now."

"You may shed tears if you please. I will greet them with cold indifference," she said, coquettishly.

"No mercy?"

"No, *merci.*"

Collins rolled over and resumed his attentions. The woman did not resist, but met his embraces with vigor and enthusiasm.

TRAIN TO PUEBLO

23

The rocking of the train carriage did not lull him to sleep. Collins' thoughts were uncomfortably upon the woman he had left behind and the possibilities that had expired with his departure. As promised, she saw him off in a stoical and reserved manner. Although remotely affectionate, there had been no residual trace of the passionate and responsive partner of the previous evening. There were no pledges made between them to meet again or to write. For this he was grateful.

The land over which the train was passing leveled out onto rolling plains. Late summer was inspiring a soft blanket of golden grasses spreading into the horizon. His ruminations turned to Morrison and he wondered what had happened to the man and whether Lawrence would discover his duplicity. Odd, he thought, that Lawrence had taken it upon himself to look after Morrison. He did not seem to be his equal in intelligence or integrity nor did he seem to be a person of conversation or erudition. Perhaps Lawrence was limited by the available reservoir of acquaintances. Certainly, Mears was more his equal, but hardly a desirable associate. C.W.'s head ached. He was reminded of a blow from a coup stick in a camp up on the Yellowstone River and hoped his skull could withstand all the misuse.

C.W. finally yielded to slumber and awoke as the train jolted to a halt. He looked out at the depot and saw he had arrived in Manitou Springs. Placing the Stetson upon his head and wincing at pressure placed upon his head wound, he retrieved his jacket and carpetbag and climbed out of the car. Someone spoke his name and he turned to see Gustavus Jocknick standing nearby.

"Mr. Jocknick," he said, walking over to shake the man's hand. "I see you received my telegram."

"I did. I had hoped you would be farther along by now," he said in a disapproving tone. Collins was reminded of a querulous schoolmarm.

"Well, I have certainly had my share of unforeseen impediments," C.W. told him as they walked into the depot. Collins made arrangements to have his baggage held for him. They exited and Jocknick steered him up a rutted dirt road toward the rocky backdrop of a little village.

"How are your injuries?" Jocknick asked.

"Improving. My assailants did not intend that I should expire."

"And who do you think was the author of this attack?"

"I am disposed to believe it was Otto Mears. I may have told him a trifle too much and tweaked his nose a bit."

A small whirlwind twirled past them on the dusty lane. The air smelled of yellow pine trees.

"What of my son?"

Collins hesitated. "He has chosen to return to the Dolores River country."

"You did not discharge him?"

"I did not."

Gustavus sighed. "I see."

"He was a valuable companion and provided me with much information. Ouray has made arrangements for another guide."

Jocknick paused in the road. "What guide?" he asked in mild alarm.

"A warrior named Shavano. John Lawrence warned me he is not entirely reliable."

The man seemed to relax. They resumed their leisurely amble. "He is entirely reliable. Especially as Ouray is sending him to you."

"I have heard much to the contrary."

Gustavus smiled. "I believe he delights in this. He is fond of pranks...you should be on your guard. That is all."

C.W. was unconvinced. "Would you willingly journey through unknown territory in his company?"

"Unquestionably. The man has a highly developed sense of probity."

Taking this statement as further evidence of Jocknick's respect for Indians, C.W. relinquished any reservations about his impending association with Shavano. He had enough preying on his mind as it was.

Ahead, he noted a charming clapboard house in a grove of cottonwoods. It was painted cerulean blue with a lighter blue trim and offered a shady, generous porch. Sitting in a rocking chair in front of an ornately carved mahogany door, as if on guard, was a diminutive woman eyeing them suspiciously. As they drew nearer, she stood and C.W. was reminded of a small but fierce mammal.

"Good day, Mrs. General," Jocknick said.

Collins glanced over at his companion. This singular nomenclature was undoubtedly derived from the objectionable woman in one of Dickens' serial novels.

"Good day, Mr. Jocknick," the woman responded in a piping and infantile female voice of a type that always put Collins on his guard. "The General is expecting you."

They mounted the steps and Collins was introduced. It was made clear that, as Collins was not immediately perceived to be a person of importance, Mrs. General would maintain mere civility in her dealings with him. They followed the woman into the coolness and oddly acidic odor of the house. A large man rose from a desk in a back room and strode toward them.

"Gustavus," he exclaimed enthusiastically in a Teutonic accent and bent to embrace the shorter fellow.

Jocknick accepted the gesture indifferently and straightened his jacket.

"Hello Charles. This is Mr. Collins. I sent a telegram."

"*Ja in der Tat.*" The big man held out a hand. "Welcome." He ushered them into a well-appointed parlor cluttered with décor of European affectation. "Some tea, Mama?" Adams asked his wife while his guests found seats among the collection of impractical furniture. The woman left the room reluctantly, as if fearful of missing essential conversation. "So, Gustavus, why have you brought Mr. Collins to me?"

"In truth, he is sent by Mr. Schurz."

Adams leaned forward on his chair. "*Ja*? Is this true?"

Collins nodded.

"For what purpose?"

Smiling at the directness of the question, C.W. said, "To discover details about the political machinery of this state as it especially relates to the Ute peoples."

The stolid Prussian considered this. "Why you?"

The dearth of racket in the kitchen suggested to C.W. that Mrs. General was not quite attending to the tea. "Due, I suppose, to certain experience I bring to the commission."

Gustavus coughed pointedly. "He is skilled in enquiry. He has powerful allies in Washington."

The large man relaxed in his seat. "What can I tell you?"

It was Collins' turn to be direct. "Of all the individuals in the state, which ones would you hazard as willing to inspire mayhem, so as to rid themselves of the Ute dilemma? With no regard to losses on either side?"

Adams raised his eyebrows in astonishment. "This is a bold assumption. Is it that of Schurz or yours alone?"

"Schurz and others in the Indian Bureau," Jocknick answered. "It is mine as well."

The General stood and stalked the confines of the room with his hands clasped behind his back. "I have been reluctant to give my fears credence." He stopped and studied Collins. "I have seen you somewhere. You were in the Southwest during and after the war."

"Perhaps," Collins said cryptically.

"I was scouting for the army. I remember you."

Tact, thought Collins, was not one of the man's strengths. "I was there," he said.

"You were known to be sympathetic to the Indians. You reported the plight of certain tribes in stringent terms."

"I did."

He bent to clap Collins on the shoulder. "I can trust you." Adams resumed his seat. "Where is the tea?" he demanded in elevated tones.

His question was answered by a subsequent commotion in the kitchen.

"You must understand, Collins. I have many dealings with many men. Some of them I may not choose as an intimate of the bosom, but I live here. I am a practical man as well as a friend to the Indian."

"I must admit to the possibility that I am less practical than you," C.W. said. "What do you see as the probable destination of the Utes, given all the animosity and pressures being heaped upon them?"

Adams glanced at Jocknick, who responded. "Secretary Schurz has a plan to assign individual title to lands, thereby civilizing the Colorado Utes. It is his assertion that this will leave several million acres open to white settlement, thereby relieving some of the political pressure."

" 'Forty acres and a mule.' Sounds too reminiscent of erstwhile political failures and equally altruistic policies," Collins said. "And does the current governor's administration support this notion?"

Mrs. Adams entered the room, following a hefty servant girl bearing a loaded tea tray. She directed that the girl place it upon a sideboard and ordered her from the room in gestures.

"You must teach her English, Mama," Adams told her.

"She is an Austrian bovine and will not learn," she answered impatiently. The woman filled cups and handed them around, offering milk and sugar. When everyone had tea, she offered her guests cakes and sandwiches. After she had settled on an ottoman near to her husband, the conversation resumed.

Adams wiped crumbs from his moustache with a napkin. "Governor Pitkin does not approve of allotting any lands to the Utes...nor does any politician in the state."

Collins rose to place his cup and saucer upon the sideboard. He again framed his question. "In your opinion, General, who would most benefit from a calamity between the whites and Indians?"

Adams appeared to be discomfited. He also came to his feet and rid himself of his cup and cake plate. Standing beside Collins, he looked across to Jocknick.

Irritated by the procrastination in response to his inquiry, C.W. said, "Come, come, Mr. Adams. You are fully aware by whom I have been employed and what is being sought. Why so circumspect? Mr. Jocknick, you assured me I would receive vital intelligence here."

Mrs. General spoke up in stridently childish tones. "We are people of means and respect in this state, Mr. Collins. Who are you to question us in our own house?"

Disinclined to engage this capricious female in conversation, he turned to the man beside him and said, "I do not believe, Mr. Adams, that I need to explain or defend my commission to your wife."

Adams turned to address Mrs. General. "Will you please leave us, Mama? We have important matters to discuss."

The woman departed the room in outraged fury.

A door on the second story was heard to close forcefully. Adams was noticeably flustered and an ensuing lull reigned temporarily in their discourse. He finally sat down and Collins followed suit.

Unwilling to countenance further delays, C.W. swiftly resumed the topic he had been pursuing. "I reiterate my question. Who has most to gain from an orchestrated catastrophe between the Utes and whites?" he asked.

Jocknick responded without an appealing glance from Adams. "All Colorado politicians, the railroads, mining interests, most white settlers and specific parties in Washington. Remember, Secretary Schurz is not seeking the identity of those who are outwardly hostile, but those who have the will and the wherewithal to precipitate a fatal incident with the Utahs without warning."

"'...The great ones eat up the little ones.' Am I correct in assuming that absolutely no white man in Colorado, including Mr. Adams here, is completely and utterly on the side of Indian interests?" C.W. asked.

"You presume upon my civility, sir," Adams exclaimed.

"Not at all," said Collins, rising to his feet and giving full vent to his frustrated displeasure. "I see that you must be quite protective of your livelihood and home. Your wife would insist upon it...that is plain enough. I do not have the time nor the inclination for diplomacy. An entire race of people is o'ershadowed by the Sword of Damocles and you are playing puss and mouse with me. I have been charged with the ponderous duty of discovering a method with which to allay disaster and, in order to achieve this, I must first ascertain who are the masters and who are the players and who are merely by-standers. You, sir, are a friend of Mears. This either makes you a player or a bystander. Which is it?"

The large man had visibly deflated beneath C.W.'s indignation. "It is true, Mr. Collins. I am at all cross-purposes. I am cordial with many factions in the state that are of a supremely determined conviction. The Utes, as has been reiterated orally and in print *ad infinitum*, must go. As Gustavus here knows, I helped Pitkin to be elected governor through the German vote. I did not know at the time that he would be so...virulently adamant about the removal of the Indians. Chief Ouray warned me, but I did not heed him. *Ja, es ist wahr*, I am also a friend of Otto Mears. He has never been against me, but now you tell me he has been working against the Utes and I can see that this must be. What may I do?"

"I suggest that you embrace your inherently honorable nature," Jocknick interjected. "You are a man of integrity and have always maintained amity with the Indians. Can you not now play a double game and use your connections with men such as Pitkin to another purpose?"

Collins studied Jocknick, again astonished at the complex permutations of the man's character. He took his seat and said, "This is excellent advice, General. You could be of great help to Secretary Schurz and myself."

The big man slapped his knee. "Then, by *Gott*, I will do this. I will attempt to descry the clandestine maneuvering of those with whom I am convivial, including Mears. And, meantime, you will be pursuing the ultimate duty to obviate a disaster for the Utes and their subsequent removal?"

"I will," C.W. answered. "I plan to visit the White River Agency to assess the situation with Agent Meeker."

"*Ja*, Meeker. I was an agent on White River for a short time. We wintered there and were unable to bring any order to the Ute bands. I remain very fond of the people, especially Douglas and Ouray and, of course, Chipeta, but it is a difficult task to bring consolidation to such autonomous and nomadic peoples." He looked at Jocknick. "I seem to recall that Meeker has moved the agency?"

"Yes. It is a more commodious location, but imprudently placed on Ute grazing lands and a tract favored for horse racing."

"Do you know this Meeker personally?" Collins asked Adams.

"I have not met him, but have heard much of his inability to negotiate well with the Indians."

"What of the possibility that he is in league with Mears, Pitkin, Vickers, Chaffee and the others?"

"It was Senator Teller who selected Meeker for the position. He has ever been one of the loudest proponents for Ute removal," Jocknick told him. "I do not, however, believe he is disingenuous enough to be working behind the scenes."

"Of all the men you have mentioned," Adams said, "I fear that Pitkin and his man, Vickers, are the most devious. And...Mears *vielleicht?*"

"But," said C.W. to Adams, "it would be useful to know whether Meeker is an agent in a larger sense or a pawn chosen for his righteous and undiplomatic propensities. Can you find this out?"

"I will try. I must be cautious."

"Yes." Jocknick said. "Do what you can. I am certain you will become further involved as events progress. Also, be...wary...of relating too much of our discussion to Mrs. General." He took a handsome silver watch from a vest pocket and noted the time. He turned to address Collins. "We must go. Our train north shall be departing shortly."

UNION PACIFIC

24

Vexed by a minor delay in Cheyenne, Collins was forced to revisit this town of recent acquaintance and endure its distasteful climate. He dined in the hotel wherein he was domiciled and kept to himself until the scheduled departure of the Union Pacific Number 3 for all points west. He settled into a railway carriage by a window and sorted through the notes on Meeker provided to him by the efficacious Gustavus Jocknick. The locomotive abruptly jerked away from the depot, pulling a long line of passenger cars. Collins glanced briefly at his fellow travelers, mostly men and many of them military, no doubt headed to Fort Fred Steele on the North Platte River or other postings farther west. Out of the window he could see vast lots full of lowing cattle awaiting the next train east to the Chicago stockyards.

It was a brilliant morning and the immense expanses of prairie grasses stretching beyond the narrow conveyance seemed limitless. It called to mind the cherished days of his youth, many of which were spent afloat in a tiny coracle on the gray Irish waters of Sligo Bay. He thought back upon his early years roaming the countryside, climbing Benbulben and Knocknarea and exploring the rambling shoreline. C.W. barely noted the passing terrain, until painful memories forced his attention to the packet of notes upon his lap and a renewed study of its contents.

Meeker had taken the position as agent of White River in the spring of the previous year. He had promptly begun working on the relocation of the agency to pastureland called Powell Park, near the confluence of the White River and Strawberry Creek. By early spring of '79, the move had been completed, much to the chagrin of most of the Utes, including a woman named Jane, as mentioned to him by Ouray. Meeker had ill-advisedly reported a putative conversation he had had with the woman and submitted it for publication in the *Greeley Tribune*. In this discourse, he had informed her that the land of the agency belonged to the government and not the Ute people. He had also, imprudently, informed her that if the Utes did not do as he directed, the land would be taken away and given to white settlers. Collins read the publication, included in the folder, and inwardly cringed at the arrogance and lack of sagacity exemplified in the man's diatribe.

According to Jocknick's notes, Meeker's report in the *Greeley Tribune* had inspired William Vickers, secretary to Governor Pitkin and editor of the *Denver Tribune*, to pen and publish the caustic article entitled "The Utes Must Go!" as shown to him by Jocknick during their initial meeting in Denver. The man, apparently, was an inveterate propagandist for the expulsion of the Utes and, either with or without Meeker's collusion, found the agent to be useful in his arguments. Several of the Utes had held Meeker accountable for the opinion expressed in the article, especially regarding good Indians being dead Indians. Despite his denials, all trust was destroyed. Meeker persisted in plowing and fencing the Utes' pastureland and race track, engendering greater animosity. This, apparently, was where the matter remained. Collins was quite interested in assessing the situation himself and was determined to make his way south as swiftly as possible. He had the nagging sense that matters were escalating and they would soon come to a dramatic culmination.

C.W.'s journey took the better part of the day. The railroad skirted a small and unimpressive range of rocky hills then turned north of the Medicine Bow Mountains, which were of greater altitude and craggier peaks. Fort Fred Steele, a prominent military post approximately twenty miles east of Rawlins, saw the disembarkation of most of the passengers. It was late evening as the train pulled into Rawlins, a nugatory collection of buildings facing a dusty lane. He stood in front of the modest depot and perused his surroundings, noting that the only bright lights emanated from a nearby procession of saloons and gambling houses. The train hissed and chugged away toward the Pacific coast, leaving Collins with the vague sensation of having been left stranded.

As cool night air softened the heat of the day, Collins sighed and picked up his bag. He had just stepped from the platform when a quiet voice came from the shadows of the side of the building.

"*Señor* Charles Collins?"

He started and spun around, his hand on the butt of his Colt. "Who is there?"

A figure stepped out to become substantial, moving into focus in the borrowed light of the nearest saloon. "Shavano. I have come for you."

In the dim incandescence, C.W. discerned a moderately tall and powerfully built man with finely chiseled and handsome features. He wore a mixed array of white and aboriginal clothing, shoulder length hair, that was unbound, and a large silver hoop in each ear. His most conspicuous feature was the revolver worn prominently at the front of his waist. The man was redolent with wood smoke and sage.

"I thank you," said Collins. "I must go to the livery stable to see if my animals and outfit have arrived."

"They are here. They are at Rankin's stable."

"How do you know this?"

"I have been watching for you many days."

Collins was taken aback. "Again, I thank you. Where are you staying?"

Shavano let out a gruff and caustic laugh. "Do you suppose it is in one of the fine hotels hereabouts? Or do you suppose that Indians are not allowed?" He spoke in deep and melodious tones.

"My apologies. I have no such prejudices. I will camp with you after we fetch my outfit."

The man shrugged and walked up the road toward town. He possessed an athletic, swinging gait, silent in ornately beaded moccasins. C.W. strode beside him and they soon turned off toward a large barn surrounded by jack-and-rail pens of various sizes. Almost at once he espied his horse and mule, standing head to tail by a hay bunk. Climbing into the pen, he was immediately advanced upon by both animals. Molly, the mule, rubbed her forehead on his back while Ulysses, his stocky buckskin, blew hot breath in his face. He spoke to them lowly, momentarily overwhelmed by sentiment at the reunion.

A stout fellow emerged from the barn and approached the pen. "Hello Shavano. I see your Mr. Collins has finally arrived."

Collins turned to see the Indian standing just behind him. He found the gate and walked over, followed by Shavano. "I am Charles Collins," he said, holding out a hand. "I am glad to find you at this late hour."

"Joe Rankin." They shook hands. "I generally sleep here. The rest of your equipment is inside."

Rankin led the way into the faintly lit interior. He jerked a canvas tarp off of a pile of goods and Collins recognized his saddle. They went into the office to settle the bill while Shavano remained behind.

"You intend to travel in his company?" Rankin asked, nodding in the Indian's direction as he wrote a receipt for payment.

"I do. He was sent to me by Ouray."

"Shavano is a war chief and no easy customer. I do not dislike him…nor do I trust him. Watch your scalp."

"I would trust him before many white men," C.W. said, honestly.

Rankin looked him over. "I do not know who you are, friend, but that is a judgement I would keep to myself, if I were you."

Without comment, Collins took his receipt and exited the office to find that his gear was sorted and all his tack was missing. Outside, he found his horse saddled and Shavano in the process of arranging the packsaddle on Molly. Rankin helped him transfer the rest of his belongings to the panniers. C.W. slung his carpetbag on top of the load and roped it in place with a diamond hitch.

"Thank you, Mr. Rankin. Where would you suggest we purchase supplies on the morrow?"

"France's store just up the way. He is the best equipped with dry goods and has been at it since '68. He and Shavano here are friendly."

The chief grunted. Collins had noted that the man did not speak in Rankin's presence. Rankin and C.W. shook hands and he turned to find Shavano headed down the street, leading Molly behind him. Taking Ulysses by the reins, he followed. They angled away from the town into the night. After a short distance, they came to what appeared to be a deserted homestead. Collins saw the shapes of two horses in a dilapidated corral.

"We will stay *aqui*," Shavano said, leading Molly to the corral. They unloaded and unsaddled the animals and put them in with the other horses. After the usual squealing and kicking, they settled down. Collins laid out his bedroll nearby and the Indian disappeared into a primitive tipi-style shelter of branches. Sitting on his bedding, C.W. smoked his pipe and watched the stars. He was now prepared for the next leg of his journey. Fate would author the outcome.

25

Collins could not help but smile at the man's preposterous whiskers. James France, proprietor of the first and foremost dry goods store in Rawlins, was a tiny gentleman with a tremendous beard. It hung to his waist, where it was tucked into his waistline. Lacking a moustache, the facial hair reminded Collins of Mormon patriarchs common to Deseret. While C.W. chose various supplies and stacked them on the counter, France regaled him with stories of recent White River history. Shavano stood by the door and said nothing, apparently not as friendly with France as Joseph Rankin had presumed. It was quite early and no other patrons were present.

"Most years, the government do not send adequate rations. And these are not some handout. It is what is owed to them in exchange for lands what were sold to the U.S. When them Utes roam around looking for means of survival, settlers from all over the region put in concocted claims against annuities for damage of tumbledown buildings, dead livestock and broken machinery."

Collins took out his pipe and packed it with tobacco offered by France. "How has it been since the arrival of the new agent last year?" he asked, striking a match.

"No more settled than before. A few goods have come in. Not much. I delivered them myself, having the contract for hauling supplies, but Meeker has the Indians in an uproar." He glanced over at Shavano.

"Can you explain?"

"Well...a lot of it has to do with Jack. After scouting for General Crook up north, he returned as a conquering hero. He speaks English, being he was raised by Mormons, but does not think highly of whites. He now seems to consider himself to be the true leader of the White River Utes since Douglas is getting older. After Meeker presented him with a scheme involving dairy farming, Jack told me that fighting the whites, in the way of Sitting Bull and Crazy Horse, is the only way to get what the Utes need. He has drawn in a large following and has stolen several lodges away from Douglas' band."

While Collins smoked, France fetched the rest of the requested items and added them to the pile. He tallied the balance due and C.W. tendered the required amount in coins from a leather pouch he kept in an inside pocket of his jacket. France gave him the change and wrote out a crude receipt.

Looking over at Shavano, impassive in his place by the door, Collins asked, "Do you require any supplies?"

France chuckled, organizing the stacks of goods on the counter. "He cannot speak much English...only mimics what he hears."

Shavano met Collins' eyes and gave an almost imperceptible shake of his head. Collins added more tobacco, ammunition and an extra pipe to the rest of his purchases. Making several trips, France, Collins and Shavano packed the supplies into panniers and bundles on both pack animals. The Indian's ponies were short and stocky, especially the little brown paint pack horse that seemed to be almost as wide as it was tall.

"Give my greetings to Agent Meeker and his family," France said as they mounted their horses. "And tell George Baggs, if you happen to see him, that his new rifle has come in."

Collins thanked the man and he and his Ute guide headed south out of town. The air was clear and cool and the distant mountains rose distinctly to the east and south. Ulysses was skittish after limited activity for such a prolonged period of time. He balked and snorted while Molly brought up the rear with equanimity. Collins wondered how they had enjoyed their sojourn at Fort Laramie. They appeared to be quite sound and in excellent condition.

Their surroundings were empty and expansive. Antelope herds dotted the landscape and the occasional coyote trotted across their periphery, ears back and tail down. He could well imagine that buffalo had once been a common sight throughout the region; hunted out, no doubt, by the residents of the town and nearby fort. The morning grew warm as they traveled steadily across sweeping arid terrain and he was forced to remove his coat and stuff it behind him on the saddle. Shavano rode ahead without any alteration of posture or casual word to break the sustained monotony of silence. The Indian gave the impression, however, that he was acutely aware of his environment and all movement therein. Collins was curious about the chief and had seen little of the intelligence or humor reported about the man. He relaxed into the saddle and felt the miles pass beneath his beloved gelding, at last settled and tranquil, as they drew perceptibly nearer to the southern mountain ranges.

The sun was reaching its apex when the horses began to climb toward the first scattering of trees along the foothills of a looming plateau. Collins saw a hawk awkwardly take flight with a rabbit in its talons. He had recently read one of the books written by Dr. David Livingston. According to Livingston, when brutally attacked and shaken by an African lion, he had ceased to feel fear, pain or apprehension. From the experience, the explorer had surmised that this was most probably the state produced in all animals of prey when slain. Watching the raptor come to rest on a sandstone boulder and begin to tear at its victim, Collins hoped this supposition was valid.

Realizing this to be a philosophical point upon which he might draw out his guide, Collins nudged Ulysses forward. "I have a question," he said to Shavano.

The Indian turned to look at him in mild surprise.

"Do you think that a rabbit is in a condition of abject terror or acceptance at the moment of its death?"

Shavano contemplated him a moment. "When a creature performs its purpose, it is content."

"If a puma sprang upon you at this instant, would you be fulfilling your purpose?"

An impish glint flashed in the man's eyes. "If *I* sprang upon you this instant, would you be fulfilling yours?"

Collins grinned. "Perhaps not, but I certainly hope I would not die in a state of abject terror."

The Indian made a low, throaty noise and they rode side by side for a short distance until the narrowing of the path forced Collins to pull up and resume his position behind the paint packhorse. The way rose more steeply and after a protracted climb, they came to a small open park where Shavano halted to let the animals blow. There was a pleasant view of their back trail and the plains to the north. In the distant southeast, smoke from what must have been a momentous forest fire created a towering plume.

Collins dismounted and loosened the cinches on his animals. He stretched and removed his Stetson hat to wipe perspiration from his forehead. Taking the canteen from his saddle, he drank deeply, then offered the bottle to Shavano. The man slid nimbly to the ground and accepted. After a long pull, he handed it back.

"We all have a purpose," he said, quietly, "but much has changed."

"For you?" C.W. asked, looping the canteen strap back on his saddle horn.

"For me," he answered, looking off into the distance. "For the *Nuuchiu*, the Ute people."

Sighing, Collins sat on a nearby rock. "What did Ouray say when he sent you to me?"

"He asked that I take you to Nick. *Todo.*"

Ulysses stamped and bit at a fly on his leg. A light breeze whispered past them in the trees. "Secretary Schurz wants me to find out about impending violence between whites and Utes."

"To be made so we can be removed from our treaty lands?" the Indian asked, sagaciously.

"Yes. What do you know of this?"

He squatted on his heels beside Collins. "There are bands of white men roaming around making fires and stealing livestock in a way that the Utes will be blamed. Someone is paying them."

Collins turned to look at Shavano. He noticed for the first time that the man's left eye appeared to have been damaged. "You know this to be true?" he asked.

"*La verdad.* I have seen it."

"I must learn more about this."

"It will do no good," Shavano said and stood up.

"I must try. I must attempt to stop any conflict that would cause the Utes to be sent away. I have given my word to Mr. Schurz," Collins said, getting to his feet and walking over to his horses.

"*Si*...if you have given your word, you must try." The war chief mounted his horse. "I will take you to White River Agency."

AGENCY

26

"Why do you call him Nick?" Collins asked as he poked at the fire. The sun was down and they were preparing for sleep.

"You mean the agent at White River?" Shavano was sitting on a log smoking the rosewood pipe that Collins had presented to him earlier.

"Yes."

"He writes his name as 'N. C. Meeker.' I think this is the reason."

"You can read then?" C.W. asked, feigning nonchalance, but wanting to know more about this man.

"Not very much," Shavano said without a shade of apology. "I read well enough and there is Peck."

"Peck?"

"An *amigo* who owns a store on Yampa River. He tells the Utes of things we should know. Things he reads in newspapers. Things he hears."

"Will we see him on our way to White River?"

"We can." He emptied his pipe and stowed it in a pocket. "Perhaps we should."

The next morning, they were on the move at first light. Collins could not shake a sense of imminent doom. They skirted the highest slopes of the rugged Sierra Madre range and dropped down to Muddy Creek. By early afternoon, Collins could see a sizeable collection of ranch buildings among the cottonwoods and willows along the Little Snake River.

"This is Baggs' ranch," Shavano told him. "We will spend the night here."

"Will you be speaking?" Collins asked facetiously.

"No. I do not speak English. I only mimic what I hear," the chief said.

They rode in amongst the unpretentious log buildings and were greeted by a woman with an impressive bosom, inadequately restrained by a faded green dress. She was carrying a basket of clothing to a line strung between two trees

"Welcome stranger," she said, addressing only Collins. "Come to stay the night?"

"We wish to camp nearby and visit with Mr. George Baggs, if he is available," Collins told her, dismounting.

"There is a place just along the river there. You will find hearthstones and a tether line for your animals. George is out and about. I am Maggie Baggs, his wife. Come to the house when you are settled."

C.W. walked in the direction indicated by Mrs. Baggs, leading his horse and mule. Shavano followed. About a quarter of a mile down the river bottom, there was a tidy clearing in the trees with a large rock fire ring. Collins and Shavano unsaddled their animals and turned them loose to forage. Collins hobbled Ulysses as a precaution, knowing Molly would never leave him behind.

They arranged their camp and found an ample supply of wood left by a previous inhabitant. Sitting on a stump by the fire ring, Collins drank cold water from his canteen, replenished from the Little Snake River. The Indian came over and joined him.

"I will stay in camp," he said. "There will be much talk and I do not need to listen."

"Is this Baggs unfriendly to the Utes?"

"No. His wife does not like us, but Baggs has always claimed to be our friend. But he talks very much and I have heard most of his stories."

Collins smiled and stood to brush the dust from his blouse, vest and trousers. He carried his jacket in the warm afternoon. Leaving his Colt and belt on his bedroll, he gave a casual nod to Shavano and walked along the river back to the ranch. Sundry items of clothing now waved gently on the line and he angled toward what appeared to be the main house. He noticed an old man with braided red and silver hair sitting cross-legged beneath a neighboring cottonwood tree.

"Howdy, friend," the man said.

As C.W. approached, he observed that the old-timer was deftly working on a piece of leather, producing a pouch of some kind. He was attired in a predominantly Indian costume, breechclout and all.

"Good day," Collins said, hunkering down beside him.

"Jim Baker. No doubt you have heard tell of me." His voice was reedy with age.

A tall and muscular man walked over. "Jim, you old hide... what lies are you telling this fellow?"

Collins got to his feet.

"Why, I did not get the chance to tell him nothing," the old man replied plaintively from his seat on the ground. "You rudely interrupted our meeting."

"My name is Charles Collins. I was hoping to visit with you, if you are George Baggs. And if you are amenable." He held out his hand.

"By all means," the man said. "I am George Baggs and I am quite amenable," he said, shaking C.W.'s hand. "Maggie told me I had visitors. What have you done with Shavano?"

"He chose to stay in camp down the way."

"He never was very chummy. How come you to be in his company?"

"He is guiding me to the White River Agency. Ouray sent him to me."

George raised his eyebrows. "Very interesting. Come

into the house and we will talk. You coming Jim?"

"Later, George. Monkey will skin me if I do not finish this for her," he said, indicating the partially manufactured pouch.

"Monkey?" Collins inquired as they walked away.

"One of two Snake women who have been with Baker since God was a pup. They are staying on the ranch just now. We are old chums."

The rambling log house was cool and filled with the smell of fresh baked bread.

"Maggie?" Baggs called loudly.

There was no response.

"Hmmm....must be out in the cook shack. That woman does keep herself busy," Baggs said, sitting down at a battered but sturdy oak table. Collins joined him.

"Care for a snort?"

C.W. shook his head.

"Well then, coffee or some cold buttermilk? We have a very good cellar...keeps everything chill in the summer and frost free in the winter."

"I will have some coffee, if it is made."

"Aw hell," said Baggs, "we have coffee on at all hours, being a sort of way station on the White River Road. Not much traffic lately, though. Too much Indian trouble."

A door banged and Maggie entered.

"Found each other, did you?" she asked and fetched cups and the coffeepot.

Pouring three cups, she set the pot on a cast iron trivet and sat down.

"It is far too hot," she said, wiping the hair back from her forehead. "Looks like another drought."

"Well, let us hope that all will be well. It has been a tough couple of years," he told Collins. "Maggie, this is Mr. Charles Collins," he said.

"How do you do," Collins said. "Thank you for your hospitality."

"Surely. We are happy to have you," the woman told him.

"You mentioned Indian trouble." C.W. said, looking at Baggs. "What exactly do you mean?"

"Oh…lots of folks have reported fires being set, livestock killed…there have even been reports that they have burnt Major Thompson's house to the ground."

"The Denver agent?" Collins asked.

"Why, yes. He has a ranch on the Bear River now."

Maggie set her cup down hard. "They need to go. There are too many good people need land to farm. Damn Indians do nothing but raise heck and hunt out all the game."

"Now, Maggie, such talk for a sweet girl," said George, reaching out a hand to take hers. "Live and let live is what I always say. I have been neighborly with the Utahs for many a moon and have had no trouble."

Maggie took her hand back and left the table abruptly.

"Any other incidents?"

"Some surveyors were supposedly attacked, but from what I heard, they were surveying on reservation lands."

"No strangers that have passed through here?" Collins asked, fiddling with his empty cup.

"None that have come through here. There was somebody…now who was it?…Oh yes, Charlie Perkins. Has a store and hotel down the way. He told me a few days ago that he had a gang of fellows come through. Said he thought they was shady and not long on information. Plumb belligerent is how he put it."

"Not prospectors?"

"Well, I asked the same question, but he said they bought nothing but ammunition and some grub and he saw no tools to speak of on their pack animals. They also showed no interest in the breed girls he keeps on the side, which he found unusual."

Mrs. Baggs returned with a plate of fresh sliced bread, butter and jam. "I guess I was rude before," she said. "You traveling with Shavano and all. Sorry." She poured more coffee and sat down. "Have some bread. Just baked."

"Maggie's daddy was killed out in Minnesota by the Sioux," George said, by way of explanation.

Collins took a bite of bread. The mingling of cool butter, hot bread and thick chokecherry jam was delicious. He said as much.

The woman's ruddy cheeks flushed more acutely and she smiled, revealing a couple of missing teeth. "You will stay for supper?"

"I will. Thank you. Oh yes...Mr. France wanted me to tell you your rifle has arrived."

"Good news. Been a while coming." Baggs licked jam from his fingers then asked, "Why were you asking about strangers hereabouts?"

"Just curious. Could it be that some of the crimes attributed to the Indians might be the work of whites? It would be an efficient manner with which to foment discord. It seems to me there are more than a few factions interested in pushing the Utes out of Colorado."

"Too true, too true," said George, nodding his head. "Perhaps..." The man seemed to be mulling over the suggestion.

"What is your business, Mr. Collins?" Maggie asked. "Do you mind me asking?"

"Not at all. I am in the employ of Secretary Schurz and am on my way to visit Agent Meeker."

"You work for the Interior Department?" Baggs asked. "In a way."

"Why is Shavano with you?" Maggie asked. "You could have found your route to the agency without him."

"Now, Sugar, that would be his business," George told her.

"I am content to answer," Collins said. "Chief Ouray sent him to me for protection. I also suspect he wanted me to learn more of the Utes."

"Excellent," said George.   "Although conversation might be limited."

"Yes," said Collins. "I was hoping you might speak Ute."

"Only very little. You need to go see Peck. He speaks as much Ute as you could ask for."

Old Jim Baker came in. He precipitously began a story about grizzly bears and fermented oats and no more information was available from Baggs or his wife. The evening passed with good food and a battle of wills between Baker and Baggs. Each one of them sought to outdo the other with the most outlandish tales. C.W. found it passingly entertaining, but somewhat exhausting, and found an early excuse to remove himself from the company.

CATTLE DRIVE

27

The following morning, Shavano and Collins secured their animals to a tree and went to the house to bid George and Maggie farewell. The Indian remained outside the door as C.W. knocked and was beckoned inside. George, his wife, and another fellow sat at the table over empty plates and coffee.

"Breakfast?" asked Maggie. "We have finished ours."

"No, thank you very much. We are just departing." In truth, the previous night having been interminable with stories of regional settlement, hunting and neighbors, he now knew why Shavano had chosen to stay in camp. He was ready to take his leave.

"Mr. Collins. This is Bill. He brings our mail when he is down this way. Happens he has a telegram for you. I was about to take it to you."

C.W. nodded at the young man. "I appreciate that. Do you have it handy?"

Baggs took it out of his shirt front. "Here it is."

Collins accepted it with thanks and placed it in his jacket pocket, despite Baggs' obvious curiosity. "My gratitude for your kind hospitality and fine food," he said.

"Our pleasure. Do come back and see us. We enjoy visitors."

Amidst supplementary expressions of leave-taking, Collins exited the building and found Shavano visiting with an Indian woman nearby.

"Ready?" he asked.

The chief nodded. Collins looked at the woman, striking in middle age and neatly attired in a deerskin dress decorated with colorful cotton flannel across the shoulders. She glanced at him then turned her eyes to the ground shyly.

"This is *Frijoles*," Shavano told him. "She is Baker's woman. She has seen strange white men in the hills, south along the Yampa River. She was visiting relatives there not long ago."

"Does she possess any further information?"

"No. *Es todo.* That is all."

Collins and Shavano mounted their horses and crossed the river at the ford just east of the ranch. They turned south through parched terrain of cactus and sage. It looked as though rainfall in the early spring had inspired the grass to grow, but it had since become dry and brown. Powdery dust was raised in wisps by the tread of their animals. By noon, they had crossed a small pass and dropped into a valley threaded by a substantial creek. They dismounted and stretched. Collins retired into the brush to relieve himself. On returning, he saw that Shavano was watering his two horses. C.W. loosened the cinches and led his own animals to a wide pool in the creek.

"You had a telegram," Shavano said, as they ground-tied the horses under wide, shady cottonwoods and sat down.

Collins glanced at him sharply. "How do you know this?"

"I heard. Are you going to read it?"

Smiling, Collins got up and went to his saddle to fetch his jacket. Clearly, he thought, this man missed very little and, in truth, he had forgotten the message. Resuming his seat, he took out the telegram and, noting it was from Gustavus Jocknick, he read it aloud.

" 'Adams found close connection between Vickers and Mears. None to Meeker beyond employment promoted by Teller. Chaffee possibly involved. Indications of clandestine forces behind escalation of conflict. Two Utes accused of burning home in Middle Park. Meeker attempted delivery of suspects to authorities. Tensions growing. Ouray asked Pitkin to remove Meeker. Work quickly to forestall disaster. Send reports of progress.' "

"Bennett and Chinaman," Shavano said.

"What?"

"The two young men accused of burning the house. They are innocent."

"Could this be the work of the white men you spoke of?"

"Possibly."

"Why would Meeker attempt to turn them over? Does he not know they are innocent? Is he *that* ignorant of the people in his care?"

"'The people in his care,' as you call them, are not known to him. Nick is blind to the *Núuchi-u.* He is blind in many ways."

Collins folded the telegram and slipped it into a pocket of his vest. "Do you believe he is willfully working against them?"

"This I do not know. It is possible. *Pero* it does not matter. It will not go well for the Ute people."

Collins shrugged. "Perhaps. Perhaps not," he said, getting up. "We should keep traveling."

They rode in silence for a while, passing a distinctive rock outcropping reminiscent of a medieval castle.

"Does this have a name?" C.W. asked.

"The whites call the rocks and creek by the same name. I do not remember."

The White River Road followed the creek and occasionally their passing flushed out flocks of birds from surrounding trees and, once or twice, groups of mule deer bedded down in the unrelenting heat.

The day wore away and the route was somewhat monotonous. Collins resolved to learn more of his companion.

"What about Otto Mears? Is he a friend?" he asked.

They were riding abreast on the wagon road and Shavano turned to look at him. "Mears?"

"Yes. He is a friend of Ouray. Is he a friend of yours?"

Shavano was quiet for a time. Then he spoke almost inaudibly. "I do not know you, *Señor* Collins. I do not know you at all. You seem to want to help the Utes, but I have only your word for this. I do not trust you. I do not trust any white man. I will take you to Nick. This is what I was asked to do."

Collins did not expect this. He found he was infuriated as much by this taciturn Indian as he had been by the evasive Prussian, General Adams. "I see," he said, bitterly. "And since you have already succumbed to the inevitability of the destruction of your people, what are your plans?"

"You are angry?"

"I am angry because I know what forces are aligned against the Utes. I have seen it before with other Indian tribes. But I have not heard a war chief who speaks as you do. You are fatalistic."

"Fatalistic?"

"You have given up."

The Indian pulled in his horse. Collins halted as well. He suddenly felt vaguely unsafe and time seemed to have been suspended. Shavano studied him coldly. The angled sun intensified the sharply defined features of his face, making it appear to have been struck from iron. He fingered the butt of his revolver. The ubiquitous glint of sardonic humor in his eyes was gone, replaced by a frozen animosity.

"What are you saying?" he asked after an eternal moment.

Collins held his eyes, knowing it was considered to be rude behavior among most Indian people. "Secretary Schurz, Mr. Gustavus Jocknick, Ouray and General Charles Adams are hoping I can find a way to protect the

Utes from absolute calamity. You heard the telegram. I was given the job of discovering the identity of whites who are most deadly to the cause of a settled Ute reservation in the state of Colorado."

Ulysses began pawing the ground vigorously, forcing Collins to pause. "Perhaps you are right," he said after a bit. "Perhaps it will do no good." He swatted irritably at a fly buzzing around his face. "Hell, you do not have to trust me. I am only asking that you help me. There is still a chance."

Shavano remained as a statue, retaining his posture and his hand upon his pistol. But something had imperceptibly softened in his manner. C.W. took a breath and waited.

"*No entiendo*. You seem to care very much," Shavano said at last, shifting on his horse and removing his hand from the revolver. "Why would a white man care about the Utes in this manner? They must be paying you for this."

Collins laughed, partly from relief and partly in response to his companion's entrenched cynicism. "Truthfully, they are not paying me enough to risk your displeasure. I am not here to deceive you, although I know well why you do not trust me nor any white man. As I said, you do not have to trust me...merely help me discover what enemies are arranging catastrophe. Perhaps Secretary Schurz has the authority to thwart these men."

The Indian shrugged. "Perhaps. Nothing stopped the selling of the Shining Mountains and nothing stopped Byers from stealing our hot springs and driving us from our lands with soldiers. Nothing has stopped the surveying of reservation boundaries as suits white settlers." He nudged his pony back into a walk.

Collins rode beside him without response, thankful the strained moment had passed. He was frustrated with himself for crossing the forbidden boundary of practical insult. He knew from experience this was unwise and he suspected that he had come perilously close to bodily harm.

"Mears is *muy malo*." Shavano said abruptly. "He is dangerous and cunning as a coyote. I know this to be true."

"So do I," Collins said pensively. "So do I."

28

Peck's store was a one room structure situated near the main ford across the Yampa River. Collins had discovered that Bear River and Yampa River were one in the same, the whites generally using the former name to designate the prominent stream. He and his guide camped nearby, having arrived rather late. Come morning, they had made their way to Peck's and found him drinking coffee. He was sitting on a sack of oats in the disarray of goods and mounds of green hides piled around the floor of the building. At first glance, Collins observed that the store was amply supplied with guns and ammunition, above all else.

"Shavano," Peck said enthusiastically, jumping to his feet. "Good to see you! What are you doing in these parts? Last I heard you were out east hunting buffalo."

The Indian shook hands with Peck, white man style, and said, "I have not been hunting buffalo for several moons. I am taking this man to see Nick."

Peck was as unkempt and disheveled as his place of business. There were tobacco juice stains on his shirt, alongside patches of grease and soot. His slight frame, tall and gaunt, was inadequate to fill out the ready-made clothing he wore. C.W.'s first impression, however, was favorable, due to the man's unpretentious air and open manner.

"How do?" he asked, reaching to shake Collins hand. "I am Hannibal Peck, but one and all refer to me only as

Peck, including my wife."

"My name is Charles Collins. Pleased to meet you."

Peck fetched heavy ceramic cups and poured coffee. "Sugar? I know Shavano will have some. He has quite a sweet tooth. Has been known to sit and devour an entire jar of jam." He poured a goodly amount of sugar from a small cotton sack into the Indian's cup. Collins only occasionally carried sugar on the trail. He resolved to purchase a supply.

A young child began crying somewhere nearby. Collins saw there was a door in the back and made the assumption that the Pecks lived on the premises.

"Shavano told me you keep the Utes apprised of newspaper content when it applies to them," he said, sitting on a large bundle of unknown contents by the east wall. The pot-bellied stove in the middle of the room emitted a scant amount of heat, but the morning was already warm.

"Apprised? Well I read to them. Mostly the shit that Vickers and Meeker write."

"And you sell them guns?"

Peck put the coffeepot back on the stove and narrowed his eyes. "What is that to you?"

"Nothing. Just a testament to your good relations with the Indians." Collins placed his cup upon the floor and took out his pipe. "May I smoke?"

"Have at it. Just mind your ashes. Those are kegs of powder over there."

Shavano helped himself to more coffee and sugar and perched on a stool by the open door. "This man is looking for white men who are making trouble for the people. White men starting fires, killing animals and stealing so that Indians can be blamed."

Clearly, thought Collins, Shavano spoke freely in front of Peck.

Peck again eyed Collins suspiciously. "Why?"

"I am a special agent for the Interior Department.

Chapter 28

Secretary Schurz hired me."

The man raised his eyebrows and smiled wryly. "That will not make you very popular with certain local politicians."

"Decidedly not," he said, smiling back.

"Charlie Perkins was telling me of some men that came through. They just did not smell quite bonny fide to him."

"George Baggs told me of this."

"I, myself, have not seen them," Peck said, shaking his head. "I would not be surprised that hired men are raising hell, though."

"I have seen them," said Shavano. "I saw them starting a fire near the pass road up by the Smart place."

Collins looked at him, surprised by this revelation.

"No shit?" Peck asked.

"No shit," said Shavano.

"Any idea who they are?" Peck asked.

"A bunch of white men. I watched them for a couple of days. I saw them steal two young cows from the Crawford ranch and butcher them. When they left I went down to see. They wasted much meat and left behind an iron-tipped arrow, fletched in the way of the *Weeminuche.* Any stupid person would know that the people would not waste meat in this manner."

Collins was listening with interest. Shavano was much more forth-coming with his friend Peck, he noted, than he had been on the trail. "How long ago was this?" he asked.

"One moon, maybe less."

"What exactly is your job?" Peck asked Collins. "I mean, what can you do to stop all the bullshit about the Utes?"

"I can find out who hired these men and inform Washington."

Peck shook his head. "We have some powerful politicians running back and forth between Colorado and

Washington. Will Schurz take your word over theirs?"

Collins shrugged. "As I told Shavano, I am honor bound to perform the task for which I was hired. If we can prevent an irreparable conflict between whites and Indians, there remains a chance that Schurz' plan for an inviolate Ute reservation could be achieved."

The storekeeper went over to a table piled high with papers, bills of lading and stacks of newspapers. He picked up a copy of the *Denver Tribune.* "Well then, you need to hear this," he said to Collins, bringing the paper back to his seat on the oats. "And so do you, my friend," he told Shavano. The man snapped the pages straight and began to read.

> Though not particularly quarrelsome or dangerous, the Utes are exceedingly disagreeable neighbors. Even if they would be content to live on their princely reservation, it would not be so bad, but they have a disgusting habit of ranging all over the state, stealing horses, killing off game, and carelessly firing forests in the dry summer season.

Peck tossed the paper on the floor. "Never mind that their rations were held by the Union Pacific until spoiled due to an unpaid freighting bill left by the contractor and that for the next two years there were no supplies sent at all," he said, disgustedly. "Vickers goes on to write that '...every year they threaten some of the white settlers with certain death if they do not leave the country.' What the hell? If the settlers are squatting on Ute lands, what are they supposed to do? I would like to punch this Vickers square in the nose."

"How do you get along with your white neighbors?" Collins asked Peck.

"Passably," he answered smiling. "The wife is the

postmistress and she has a pretty good handle on all their dealings. Nobody gives me too much grief, even though I sell guns and ammunition to the Utes. Perkins does the same at any rate. The sale of weapons has been prohibited on the agencies."

"Well, I would say that those of us hoping to defend the Utes against ruination," Collins said, looking pointedly at Shavano, "have a rough road ahead. It is a worthwhile enterprise nevertheless."

"Worthwhile," said the Indian. "But useless."

It seemed to Collins that Shavano was baiting him. " 'By treason's tooth bare-gnawn and canker-bit, I come to cope,' " he quoted. "Of what use are proclamations of doom?"

"No use at all," said Shavano, grinning and taking out his pipe. "Have any tobacco?" he asked Peck.

INDIAN POLICY

29

Having purchased an abundant supply of sugar and composed a telegram to be sent to Gustavus Jocknick regarding this new information about hired agents, Collins was prepared to resume their journey. Shavano acquired some ammunition for his Maynard rifle. It was habitually suspended by a strap from the makeshift affair of naked and archaic saddle tree, cinches and colorful blankets he used as a saddle. It seemed an unusual weapon for a Ute chief, but Collins was swiftly learning there was nothing usual about his companion.

They left the confluence of Elkhead Creek and the Yampa River, crossed at Himley's Ford and angled southwest to rejoin the White River Road. The day was quite warm and there was a complete dearth of clouds upon the horizon. Drought brought desperation, thought Collins, and desperation always prompted acts of aggression and self-preservation. Nature was playing the Utes false. The summer progressed without a break from unrelenting heat and with complete absence of precipitation. Even if these mysterious agents were not exacerbating the already strained relations between Utes and whites by provoking distrust, the weather would have made matters worse.

"It is too dry," Shavano said, as if reading his mind. "There will be more fires, even if they are not deliberately set. *No está bien.*"

They were climbing the slopes of a small range of

mountains, not remarkably steep or high, but rugged.

"There is no doubt that the Utes will be blamed for everything that occurs," Collins said, attempting levity.

"For gold playing out on Pike's Peak or an outbreak of measles."

"Or the drought itself."

An enormous gopher snake slithered across the road in front of them. They pulled in their horses a moment to let it pass.

"The Zuni people would say this snake shows someone is thinking bad thoughts about us," Shavano told Collins with a slight grin. "But we already know this to be true."

"Where were you born? Was it somewhere in the Southwest?" Collins asked, reaching down to scratch the back of his knee. Ulysses stamped impatiently and he nudged him forward down the trail.

"I am Shoshone and Ute. I think I was born somewhere near what is now Fort Washakie in Wyoming Territory. I spent most of my youth up north. Later, I took up with the Tabeguache peoples near Taos. This is where I met Ouray."

They came to a modest pass in the mountains and began to descend through a narrow canyon. Below, Collins could see a creek delineated by scattered cottonwoods and bounded by sandstone rim rock.

"Where were *you* born?" Shavano asked. "I think you are from some other place."

"I was born in Ireland," C.W. answered, unsurprised by the man's insight, having come to the realization that Shavano was particularly observant. "My people were dying from starvation and we had no choice but to sail to America," he continued. *"Bíonn súil le muir ach ní bhíonn súil le tír. There is hope from the sea but none from the grave."*

"For the Utes, there is no sea. Only starvation and loss."

Chapter 29

They were forced to travel single file as the trail became more treacherous. Finally, they came down into the creek bottom and rode over to an open pool in order to allow the animals to drink.

"The sound of your language is pleasing," Shavano said. "It is Irish?"

"It is."

"Say something else. I wish to hear more."

Collins thought a moment. *"Nineart go cur le chéile. There is no strength without unity."*

They forded the stream and followed the road along the creek through low hills. Some ducks flew out of the creek, wings beating furiously.

"La verdad. Alone, we can be weak," Shavano said, pensively. "Sometimes with the Utes it is difficult,"

"I have seen it with other peoples. The Irish have always been weakened by fighting amongst ourselves."

The horses kept a steady pace. The men ate dried meat and apples purchased at Peck's store, not wanting to stop for a noonday meal. Before long, the road came out into a small valley and then into open grasslands. It had become quite warm and Collins felt the perspiration rolling down the back of his neck. He paused a moment to drink from his canteen.

Magpies chattered nearby and he looked to see a desiccated carcass about a hundred feet to his right. It looked to have been a deer, now a mangled shell and a prize to be fought over. Five angry magpies were pestering a lone coyote, sniffing the jerked carrion to see if there were any worthwhile bits remaining. A whiff of death came to C.W., bringing unpleasant associations.

As the day waned, they dropped down into another creek bottom at the base of some mountains to the south. After choosing a place to camp, Shavano took care of his animals, then stalked off saying he was going to hunt. Collins arranged camp as the sun went down.

He was quietly smoking his pipe when the Indian returned with a brace of rabbits.

"I will cook them," Shavano said and began skinning them out.

"I have some salt here," Collins said, reaching into a jacket pocket.

As the sun began to set, the camp was quiet and the rabbits were roasting on a spit. The men were smoking and staring at the fire, lost in their own private thoughts. All at once a dozen or so horses materialized out of the darkness and surrounded them. Collins and Shavano jumped to their feet and reached for their rifles near to hand. Their horses, tethered nearby, whinnied and stamped. Molly brayed loudly in alarm. A young Indian man slid off his mount and came over to Shavano. They began speaking to each other in furious tones, in a language unfamiliar to C.W. The young man became aggressive, gesturing assertively in Shavano's face, causing him to lean back. Shavano deftly reached a foot around and felled the young man abruptly. He pulled the revolver from his belt and used it to keep the youngster on the ground while pointing his rifle at the others, still on horseback, agitated and shouting. Collins also aimed his rifle at the mounted warriors, following Shavano's lead.

The chief spoke loudly. *"Uvusi maa!"* All became quiet and the intruders controlled their skittish ponies.

Collins noted that they all appeared to be well under twenty years of age. Shavano spoke extensively and forcefully in his language, while allowing the boy to get to his feet. The entire group looked chastened and contrite. Shavano pushed the young man back toward his horse with the butt of his rifle. The boy swung onto his pony and said something at length to the chief, seemingly with deference. Then he and his companions disappeared into the night at full gallop.

Shavano slid his Colt back into the holster at his waist, leaned his rifle against a nearby rock and bent down to check the roasting meat. Collins put down his Winchester, checked on their livestock and resumed his seat near the fire.

"What the hell was that?" he asked the chief.

"*Chingaso!*" Shavano exclaimed, burning himself as he pulled the rabbits from the fire. "That was the other problem for the Ute people." He sighed. "Those are angry young men who roam about attacking the occasional prospector or surveyor. Mostly they posture and make noise and do nothing, but it offers another excuse for the whites to say that the Utes must go away."

Collins accepted the juicy portion of meat handed to him. He cradled a tin plate on his lap and ate with his fingers. After a moment he said, "Ouray seemed to think it was not safe for me to ride north from the Uncompahgre to the White River Agency. That is why I came around by way of Rawlins and he sent you to guide me. Are you saying there really was no danger?"

Shavano chewed and swallowed. He wiped his mouth on a sleeve, apparently formulating his response. "Ouray had his reasons. Perhaps it was dangerous. Perhaps he preferred to have you travel in my company rather than with young Sidney."

Collins mulled this over. "I am glad," he said simply, stripping flesh from bone with his teeth.

YOUNG MEN

30

"What did you say to our guests last night?" Collins asked, as they climbed farther into the mountains the next morning.

"I told them they were fools and to mind their manners." Shavano said. "I told them they were playing into the hands of the white politicians and to go home."

"What did they say to you, if you do not mind me asking?"

"That they wanted to kill you." The Indian paused a moment and smiled faintly. "They told me the only future for the Ute people will come from fighting. They may be right. They also reported having seen a group of white men, heavily armed, roaming around and causing trouble. They said they tried to get them to fight, but they refused, which the young men thought was strange. There were many of them and they had all manner of weapons and they refused to fight."

"Interesting," Collins said.

"How can you find out who these men are and who hired them?" Shavano asked.

C.W. shrugged. "I have no idea."

The road climbed upward until it reached a rather unremarkable mountain pass. They paused to rest the stock in the shade of a grove of quaking aspen trees. Collins loosened the cinches and stood with Molly and Ulysses a moment, scratching their foreheads and speaking to them softly. A breeze soughed through the trees, making the leaves shiver and flutter. The animals nibbled at bunches of grass.

"We will be at the agency soon," Shavano said, walking over. "This mule has a U.S. brand," he said.

"Yes, it was once an army mule."

"Did you steal it?"

"In a way. I borrowed it and never gave it back."

Shavano reached out to run a hand along the mule's neck. "I once knew a white woman with *pelo*, hair, of this red color. *Muy rojo...muy lindo*."

"Did you have affection for her?" Collins asked, intrigued.

"Yes, but she did not know," he answered, looking at Molly and scratching her jaw. The mule seemed to be pleased with the Indian's attentions. "She was the wife of a schoolmaster I knew in Denver. He taught me English."

"And very well, I must say," Collins said, taking some jerky from his saddlebags and sharing it with Shavano.

"*Tog'oiak'*...thank you." Shavano added, "I went many times for lessons. It was the only way I could see this woman with the hair." He walked back to his ponies.

Collins smiled to himself, pondering the notion of a fierce and dignified warrior held in thrall by a redheaded woman. They continued on their way, crossing the pass and beginning their descent. They dropped down into a narrow canyon laced with seams of coal and eventually passed what appeared to be a coal mine. The road lost more elevation and opened into a wide valley with low timbered ridges to the south. Angling to the west, they were approaching the agency buildings by early dusk, just along the north side of the Rio Blanco on open grasslands. Collins could see where there was newly plowed ground downriver. It looked like an open wound on the otherwise unscathed floodplain.

Shavano pulled in his horse. "I will leave you here," he said.

"What?"

"This Nick bothers me very much. And his daughter is too…friendly with me."

Collins looked at the chief with his flat crowned hat set at a rakish angle, the silver hoops in his ears and his intelligent and striking face. He could imagine a girl finding him more attractive and romantic than the middling farm boys who, no doubt, filled the ranks of her father's cadre of disciples.

Ulysses whinnied and was answered by several ponies in a herd grazing along the river near a group of Ute lodges. Collins patted his neck. "I had hoped you would stay and help me catch these men causing all the trouble."

"I will find you. You interest me."

Collins smiled. "You interest me as well. I will see you later, then," he said and nudged his horse toward the buildings, feeling Shavano's watchful eyes upon him.

He rode into the small community, coming onto a significant thoroughfare leading due west. Oddly, he saw no one about. Crossing a simple wooden bridge across a large irrigation ditch, he arrived to what appeared to be the agent's house and office. A young woman was on the porch, shaking out a tablecloth. She was thin and boyish with a beaked nose pressing upon the upper line of her mouth, creating a prudish effect. Collins rode over and dismounted.

"Is Agent Meeker about?" he asked.

"And who are you?" the woman asked with an affected bravura.

"A gentleman who is inquiring as to the whereabouts of Agent Meeker. Is he within?" he asked quietly, in a perfectly civil tone.

Collins was aware that some women, especially homely women, tended to behave peculiarly in his presence. He stood patiently, awaiting her response. A mourning dove called from a nearby rooftop.

Holding the bundle of tablecloth before her, she stared down at him for a long moment, as if unsure of what manner to next adopt. He found it rather unusual that her hair was cropped to her shoulders and she wore it loosely.

"Agent Meeker is inside," she finally said, almost belligerently. "He is my father. We have just finished supper."

"Will you tell him I wish to see him?" Collins asked.

She shrugged offhandedly and turned to enter the house. C.W. tied his animals to a nearby hitching rail, eased their cinches and waited. After a few minutes, an older man, tall but slight of build, came out of the house. He seemed to Collins to be quite wary and hesitant.

"You wish to see me?" he asked. "Are you from the governor?"

"I do wish to see you, but I am not from the governor," Collins said, climbing the steps onto the porch. He held his hand out to shake. "My name is Charles Wolfe Collins. I am acting on behalf of Secretary Carl Schurz."

The agent adopted the mannerisms of an eager school boy. His careworn face seemed suddenly to attain the blush of youth. "Secretary Schurz sent you. That is fine. That is very fine. Now I will receive the assistance I require. Yes...yes indeed. Welcome to you. You are most welcome."

Collins half expected him to begin wringing his hands and dancing up and down with glee. "I beg your pardon," he said. "But I am not here to assist you in any way."

The man appeared confused and became even more agitated. "What? What? Not assist? But you said..."

"I said I am in the employ of Secretary Schurz. That is all."

Somewhat deflated, he did, in fact, begin wringing his hands. "I do not understand. I have been writing letters to Commissioner Hayt, Secretary Schurz and Governor

Pitkin. These Indians have ceased all agricultural endeavors and are constantly plotting against me. I cannot perform my duty of civilizing them if they simply will not cooperate." He began rocking nervously on his heels with his hands clasped behind his back, all the while studying the planks on the porch floor.

C.W. observed him for a moment. "Secretary Schurz is concerned with preventing any type of hostility between Indians and whites," he said.

"That has nothing to do with me," the agent said defensively, looking up to face Collins. "I am here to help… only to help. If only they would cooperate." His pale and watery blue eyes seemed to become even more damp. "No one will listen. That Peck up on Bear River riles the men with falsities. The military refuses to engage. And now…after telling me I must keep my Indians on the reservation, with no suggestions as to how to do that, the Indian Bureau and Carl Schurz send you to do what? What? To spy on me?"

It was now manifestly clear to Collins that this man was disintegrating. He made an attempt to calm him. "I am not here to spy. I am here to assess the situation so that I might advise Secretary Schurz as to the most expeditious approach to deescalating tensions between whites and the Ute people. I do not believe this is counter to your purpose."

"Perhaps not…perhaps not," the agent said, wringing his hands again.

Just then, a woman came out the door. "Dearest? Is everything all right?"

This woman bore facial characteristics akin to those of the younger woman, with similar nose and mouth, but to a greater degree. She did, in fact, appear to be in the presence of a very disagreeable odor. She also looked to be a few years older than Agent Meeker and so Collins surmised this must be his wife and not another daughter.

"I am fine, Mother. This is an agent of Secretary Schurz. He has come to see me...although I, as yet, do not understand where lies his purpose." The last assertion was spoken under his breath in the mode of a recalcitrant and sulky child.

"Shall we not invite him in? Have we given over all proprieties?" She took Meeker's arm in a conciliatory way. "Have you had supper?" she asked Collins.

"I do not require anything, ma'am. I only desire to speak with your husband. I will make camp and tend to my animals. In the morning I will return for a visit, if that would be acceptable."

Agent Meeker was rocking again and seemed to be adrift in his thoughts. His wife was forced to arouse him by shaking his arm gently. "Dear? Is that acceptable? May this gentleman return in the morning to meet with you?"

"What?" the man said, coming back to himself. "Why yes. I will expect you in the morning, Mr. Collins. Do you have everything you need?"

C.W. nodded.

"Well then, be careful as you go...these Utes can be treacherous. Do not disturb them. They cannot be trusted." With this, he turned to the house and was gone.

"My husband is not quite himself," Mrs. Meeker said. "He is under a great deal of strain. I trust you are here to advise him...that is just as well. And my daughter, Josie, she is in need of guidance, so perhaps you can help there. Sleep well," she said and went away. The door closed and Collins was left standing by himself on the porch.

31

Collins gathered up his horse and mule and began leading them toward the river, following a road that led due south in an unfaltering linear course. There was sufficient light, from a clear night and a half moon, for him to comfortably make his way. Passing what appeared to be a storehouse and blacksmith shop, he wandered in contemplation of the previous interaction. He was under the distinct impression that the entire Meeker family was *non compos mentis*. Perhaps "Nick" was not purposefully working mayhem for various political interests, but he certainly was no ally to the Utes. The man was evidently unhinged.

" 'Now see that noble and most sovereign reason, like sweet bells jangled, out of tune and harsh,' " he muttered to himself.

"What is that you say?" A female voice came out of the gloom.

Collins halted and sought the source. "Who is there?"

"I live here. The better question is who are you and what are you doing out there in the darkness?"

Collins detected a slight southern accent, but mingled with another, more subtle inflection. "In truth, I was quoting Shakespeare to myself and searching for a campsite. My name is Charles Collins. I am here to see Agent Meeker."

What for?" the mysterious woman inquired, stepping out of the shadows and onto the road.

"Will you not introduce yourself?" he asked, ignoring her question.

"I am Jane. That is my place," she said, gesturing toward a substantial lodge in the trees. There were some sheds and pens nearby.

"Nice. Is there a corner hereabouts where I might camp?"

"Down there along the river. No fires. It is too dry."

"Thank you."

"And now will you tell me why you are here?"

The gelding began moving about impatiently. Collins reached to rub his forehead. "You are Jane?" he asked. "The Jane who used to be at Fort Bridger?"

"I am."

"Ouray and Chipeta wanted us to meet. I traveled here in the company of Shavano."

"Where is he now?" she asked, placing her hands on her hips and glancing around as if not quite believing him.

Collins eyes had adjusted to the shadows well enough to observe that the woman before him was quite attractive, showing refined features imbued with evident force of character. She wore her hair fastened up in the style of white women and her clothing consisted of a cotton dress with apron and high-top moccasins.

"He did not care to meet Nick nor his daughter. He is out there somewhere."

Jane laughed faintly. "He is wise. You may place your livestock in my pasture. There is good grazing there."

She led the way through a grove of trees and out the other side to a wooden gate. "You may leave your outfit here," she said, helping him unload. "Everything will be safe."

Collins turned Ulysses and Molly loose in the pasture and watched them roll. He spread a tarpaulin over his saddles and goods. "May I bed down here as well?" he asked.

"You may. First, come to my lodge for some coffee and food. My useless man, *Pauvitz,* is away as usual. I do not have whiskey."

Collins wished to speak with this woman. He accepted the invitation and they made their way back to Jane's spacious tipi. Inside, he noted that the clutter of decorations consisted of a curious blend of European and Indian items. A porcelain figurine of a 17th century lady adorned a delicate sideboard draped with a Navajo blanket and two large floral rugs covered the dirt floor. The murky extremities were hung with bundles of herbs and intricately woven baskets. Off to the side there was a small brass bed draped with a buffalo robe and in the middle, with a pipe extending toward the smoke flaps, was a petite Acme cook stove.

"Sit," the woman told him, gesturing toward a tiny oak table upon which a cut-glass oil lamp provided illumination.

C.W. thanked her, taking a seat at the table. "I was told you spent many years in the employ of Judge Carter," he said.

"I was his slave. He did not pay me and I finally ran away. Do you want milk with your coffee?" she asked, setting a cup in front of him. "I have a very good cow."

"Yes, please," he said. He was curious about her history but sensed it would be impolite to inquire further..

After placing a small pitcher on the table, she brought a pie and sat down. "This is plum. They grow along the river," she said and cut a wedge.

Collins accepted the slice of pie and juggled it over his coffee cup. He took a bite and thought it might, perhaps, be the best pie he had ever tasted. "This is delicious. *Tog'oiak'*," he said, attempting to imitate Shavano's word.

Jane laughed. "You speak very bad Ute. But it is nice that you try. Why did Ouray want you to meet me?"

Collins poured milk in his coffee. He finished his pie and formulated a response. "I was sent by the Secretary of the Interior."

Jane sipped her coffee and studied him. "Why?"

"Secretary Schurz believes there will be a cataclysmic altercation between the Utes and whites. He thinks there are those who are trying to make this happen so that the Utes can be sent away." Collins began to feel as if he had explained his mission too many times.

"Do Ouray and Schurz think you can stop this?"

"I do not know. Only that they want me to find out about all contingencies."

The woman stared at her cup. "I have seen much. I have been privy to the ways of the whites. What they want they get. Are you being paid?"

"Yes."

"Then no matter what you find out, you get money."

"Yes, but I was chosen due to my known sympathies."

Jane held his gaze. "Your sympathies are with the Utes?"

"My sympathies are known to be mostly with the Indians."

She smiled sardonically. "And still you work with the government?"

"I am Irish. It is not easy to find employment."

Jane frowned quizzically. "You whites do not even get along with each other."

"No, sadly, we do not."

"Nick will fill you with lies about us," she said, getting up to pour more coffee.

32

The following morning, fortified by information provided by Jane and a restful night under the stars, Collins strolled up the dusty avenue back to Meeker's house. He climbed the steps and knocked on the front door. Mrs. Meeker let him in and showed him to her husband's office. The man was scribbling frenetically on a sheet of paper. Collins took a seat before his desk and waited. Mrs. Meeker retreated from the room without a word. After several minutes, within which he was never acknowledged, Collins finally spoke.

"I need to converse with you, Agent Meeker."

The man continued to write, splattering ink from the pressure of his quill. Only when he upset the inkwell did he look up, jumping from his chair and covering the spill with blotting paper.

"Who are you? Where did you come from?" he asked in bewilderment.

"I am Charles Collins. We met last night and I informed you I would return this morning. Mrs. Meeker showed me in and I have been awaiting a pause in your correspondence so that we may speak."

Meeker sat down and blinked. "I met you?"

"Last evening, out on your porch. I was sent by Secretary Schurz."

A glimmer of recognition appeared in Meeker's pale eyes. "But not to help me. Not to help," he muttered.

C.W. shrugged slightly. "Certainly not to hinder you. If you recall, I was sent to gather intelligence so that a collision between Utes and whites may be forestalled."

For a moment it seemed to Collins that the man came back to himself. His eyes focused, he took a deep breath and folded his arms across his narrow chest. "This is a bad lot of Indians. They have had free rations for so long and have been flattered and petted so much, that they think themselves lords of all. I have found it necessary to make a report of depredations by the Indians to Governor Pitkin, who then forwarded this report to the Commissioner of Indian Affairs."

"What depredations?" Collins asked, attempting to keep frustration from his voice.

"Destroying game, burning timber, driving off cattle." The man was altered. He seemed extraordinarily self-possessed.

"You have witnessed these acts committed by the Utes yourself?"

"I do not have to. They have been reported to me."

"By whom?"

The man's composure began to crumble. "Reliable sources."

Collins commenced a sustained attack. "Such as? Can you be specific? Remember, I am acting on the authority of Secretary Schurz."

"What was your question?"

"Who provided you with information that the Utes were committing depredations?"

The man's hands began to shake. "Reliable people."

"Do these people have names?"

"Baggs. George Baggs."

"That," Collins said, "is not possible. I stayed over at his place a mere two days ago. He reported no such thing."

"James B. Thompson...others."

Collins stood to pace the room. "Damn it, man, you are pouring fuel on a lit fire. It may blow back upon you."

"No profanity."

"What?" Collins glanced at the agent, not understanding. Meeker was fidgeting with a letter opener.

"I cannot abide profanity."

Chapter 32

C.W. drew breath and gathered himself so that he would not be further tempted to cuff the fellow alongside the head. "Mr. Meeker," he said quietly, walking over to the desk and sitting down. "Have you been hired to foment unrest and to create mayhem?"

Meeker seemed astounded by the suggestion. "Have I...? Mayhem? Mr. Collins, I will have you know that my mission is to bring these veritable children into the bower of civilization and our modern age. To introduce them to the wonders of the late nineteenth century and its advancements. Governor Pitkin and his compatriots are visionaries. They witnessed the success of the Union Colony and wished that Fourier's tenets be employed among the savages. Why, the successes here could lead to a consolidated approach to end all hostilities with the Indians here and in other regions of the West. This..." he said, standing behind his desk and waving toward the view out the window, "is only the inception...the nascence...of a grand apotheosis."

With this, Meeker sat and his visage held an almost ethereal sanctity. Collins was physically nauseated and no longer in doubt that the man before him was a tragic pawn, putrefying in the juices of narcissism and naiveté and caught irrevocably in the web of his mercenary masters, full of compliments and deceits.

Collins sighed. " 'I am giddy, expectation whirls me round,' " he quoted sardonically. He paused a moment, noting that the man appeared wholeheartedly confused. "And yet, you say, the Utes themselves do not share your philosophies?"

"They will be led to it. Spare the rod and spoil the child. I have been in contact with the War Department and Fort Steele."

Collins' rancor persisted despite all attempts at curtailment. "These, sir, are not children. They are people."

"I am their father!" the agent said, his voice rising to a pitch of pietistic rectitude.

"You are a fool!" Collins shouted, losing his temper entirely. He came to his feet again.

Mrs. Meeker swept into the room and straight to her husband's side. The man sat stunned and blinking, just as if C.W. had, indeed, struck him on the head.

"Mr. Collins! Why the raised voices? What has taken place here?"

Collins suddenly felt the guilt wrought of senselessly torturing a weaker creature. "I apologize. I lost my composure. You, madam, are in grave danger here. You should urge your husband to decamp immediately."

"No, no, no..." the man muttered, placing his hands over his face and shaking his head from side to side.

Mrs. Meeker patted her husband's shoulder in reassurance and turned to face Collins. "He would not abandon his post, even if we begged him to. We have placed our faith in god. We are his pilgrims and, despite Nathan's imprudent atheism, my devout prayers will protect us all."

Collins rubbed his mouth with his hand to quell any response that may have sprung to his lips. There were no more words to be spoken here and no rational ears to hear. He turned and left the room without farewell. A whisper of blood was in the gathering tempest.

33

"You should get clear of here," Collins told Jane, again sitting at her table. "There will be trouble... I can feel it."

Jane smiled down at her hands, folded in front of her, and nodded. "I can see you are right. I have felt it also. I will go to stay at the Uncompahgre Agency for a while. I have already sent my daughter down there. My useless man may do as he pleases. I have finished with him."

"What about Susan and Johnson? Are they nearby? Ouray desired I should speak with them...also a fellow named Henry Jim."

"Henry Jim has disappeared. It was said that Nick became angry and began waving a stick at him as if to beat him. He has not been seen for over a week. He has probably gone back to the Uncompahgre. *Canalla*, or Johnson as the whites call him, and Susan are just downriver from here, beyond my pasture."

"Meeker seems maniacal. Has he been thus since his arrival?"

"Not so much. At first, he was tolerable, but then he moved the agency and began treating us as servants. He has been writing lies about us in the newspapers and this makes us very angry. He says this, then that. He tells us the land is no longer ours, that we have given it up for beads and blankets. Canalla persists in advising him, but he heeds nothing."

"And what of Mrs. Meeker and the daughter?"

"Mrs. Meeker is old and tired. She seems baffled by

her husband most of the time now. I help in the house for extra money and also over at the boarding house run by Josephine, the daughter. She is another story entirely."

"Meaning?"

"She does not seem to value honesty and her parents are in ignorance of the time she spends with the men. She is paid to teach school, but the children have stopped coming."

"And what can be said of Douglas?" Collins pushed his chair back from the table to cross his legs. It had become rather warm outside, but the tree-shaded lodge was cool and comfortable.

"*Quinkent*...Douglas...He has lost many of his band to Jack, but he is strong with ponies and still has much influence. He has been very angry with Nick lately over the plowing and barbed wire."

Collins rose from his chair. "Once again, I thank you for your hospitality. I will go visit with others at the agency, if possible, and get the lay of the land. Then I will see Canalla."

"He should be there," Jane said looking up at him without expression. "Will you make a bad report of us to Secretary Schurz?"

He smiled at her. "No. I will make a bad report of Nick. You promise to begin packing?"

She smiled back at him. "I promise. Come to eat later. I will have food."

Collins strolled down to check on his stock and gear, then walked back into the agency. Outside the blacksmith's shop, he noted a beefy man sharpening the blade on a plow.

"Good day," C.W. said as he approached the man.

The fellow looked up and took his measure. "Good day. Where did you come from?"

"I have been to see Agent Meeker. My name is Charles Collins."

Chapter 33

"Shadrach Price." He did not cease his labors nor offer his hand. "I do most of the heavy work 'round these parts. Come from Kansas to Greeley…then here in early spring."

"I see."

"Come to stay?"

"No."

"Just as well. These Indians are none too friendly and, between you and me, I would relish if me and the boys had a chance at them."

"A chance?"

"Sure. It will come to it. Old Meeker thought he could learn them to act civilized, but the truth is, they only know one way. They start something, we will sure as hell finish it. You know," the man said, stopping a moment to train his empty eyes upon Collins, "I killed and scalped nine of them Pawnee bastards over Fort Omaha way. Still have one of the scalps."

Price returned to his work of honing the plowshare. Collins thought it already looked sharp enough to cut off a man's head.

"If you need a bed," Price said, "the wife works over at the boarding house. Can put up there if need be."

"Many thanks," Collins said and made a swift retreat up the lane.

As he explored the environs of the agency grounds, shaking his head over this prior exchange, he reflected on whether brutality was an inherent aspect of the human race. Presently, it appeared to be a defining characteristic of settlers and miners. C.W. wandered about, observing that there were some men busily engaged in chores and many more who seemed to be lazing about, unoccupied. On the face of it, Meeker was not a leader who engendered universal dedication.

Near the bunkhouse, there appeared to be a card game in progress. He went over to see. Four men and Meeker's daughter, Josephine, were smoking cigars and playing stud poker at a weathered table in front of the building. No one took note of him as he stood off a short distance to watch. Mildly astonished at the uncouth language being bandied about by the girl, along with the indecorous humor of the general assembly, Collins left the vicinity after a short while and determined there could be nothing else learned in the agency's surroundings. He departed along another of the arrow straight lanes that latticed the agency; the result, no doubt, of Meeker's notions of perfect order

Ambling leisurely back toward the river, pleased to be quit of the dusty lots and austere buildings of the agency, he angled past Jane's camp toward the west. Molly and Ulysses were grazing upon parched grasses along the river bottom. A bald eagle perched in a dead tree nearby, still and silent as a figurehead. Beyond, he saw two lodges buried in among the cottonwood trees. He approached the largest one, following a worn trail.

C.W. walked up to the tipi and cleared his throat loudly, according to courteous manners acquired from Indian friends far to the north. He could hear voices within. The discussion ceased. A stocky Indian woman, with bobbed hair and a pretty face, appeared in the doorway and stood looking at him quizzically.

"Good afternoon," he said, not really knowing the time of day. "Are you Susan?"

"I am Susan," the woman said in halting speech.

"I am Charles Collins. Ouray asked that I come to see you."

"Yes...my brother. Come in," she said, gesturing to the dark interior of the lodge.

He was unable to discern much of the furnishings, as his eyes had not adjusted from the bright sunlight of the outdoors. She motioned him toward a table and there he found Shavano sitting with another man.

"*Venga aquí*," Shavano said, grinning. "*Siéntate*. Sit down."

Collins sat and raised an eyebrow at his erstwhile companion. "You have been here all along?"

"Perhaps. Perhaps I have been keeping an eye on you." Shavano nodded toward the other man. "This is Canalla."

"Hello," C.W. said. "I am pleased to meet you."

Susan spoke to Canalla in her native language and left the tipi.

"She is going to help a woman with her baby," Canalla told C.W. "She is very good that way."

"You have met Nick," Shavano said.

"Yes."

"You believe there will be trouble?"

Collins assumed he had been conversing with Jane. "Yes, I do. And soon."

Canalla made a sound of disgust. "Nick is becoming more *KatÙsuYa*...crazy...every day."

"What do you plan to do now?" Shavano asked. "Go back to Washington and report this? Then what?"

"I plan to return to Peck's and send a telegram. If I sent it from here, Meeker would be privy to its contents. Then, if I can convince you to stay with me, I want to track the men who are starting fires and placing suspicion upon the Utes. I want to catch one."

"You will hunt them?" Canalla asked with seeming delight. The husky man had an artless mien.

"I want to find out who hired them," Collins answered. " 'Such smiling rogues as these, like rats, oft bite the holy cords a-twain.' We shall see if we cannot convince one of these rats to turn on his employers. Will you come?" he asked Shavano.

The man grinned impishly. "*Si*, I will come...if you promise to let me use my own methods. *El gato con guantes no caza ratones.*"

THE ONLY GOOD WHITE MAN...

34

Due to a sense of urgency, Collins convinced Shavano to depart before dusk. They took their leave of Jane and C.W. again made her promise to leave the agency. They rode all night in the light of the waxing moon and camped on the Yampa River as morning dawned. Finding he was exhausted, Collins ate little and reclined upon his bedroll, smoking. Shavano busied himself with cleaning his Colt revolver and then began braiding a new horsehair headstall for his bridle.

"How did you like our Jane?" Shavano asked.

Collins considered the question. "In what manner?"

Shavano grinned, but did not look up. "She speaks very good English."

C.W. pulled hard on his pipe. "She does that."

"Do you have a woman?"

"No. I have no woman..." He thought briefly of Madame De Jussieu and Chicago Joe, as well as other fleeting conquests made over the past few years. "Or rather I have several women, but none in my home."

Shavano gave a low laugh. "Perhaps you are wise. It might be better to keep them in different places." He laid his work aside and stretched his arms. "I find Jane interesting, but she has a man."

"Not one she likes very well."

"No, but she frightens me a little. She is smart... probably smarter than me. *A la verga...* She could outwit me."

It was Collins' turn to grin. "Yes, that may not be such a good quality," he said. "But sometimes smart women can be very intriguing." With that, he rolled over to let sleep take him.

They rode out in late afternoon, angling east to ford the river. As they tied their animals outside the store, Collins could see smoke coming from the stovepipe. Peck opened the door before they could knock, shaking their hands and appearing glad to see them.

"Come in, come in," he said. "Back so soon?"

Shavano and Collins settled on makeshift seats and accepted steaming cups of coffee.

"I need to send a telegram," C.W. told him.

"Oh sure. No problem. The mail carrier should be here tomorrow and he can take it back to Rawlins with him."

"Will it be secure?"

"We can seal it and it will not be opened until in the hands of the operator."

"Very well. Any news?"

"Jack is here," Peck said.

"*Nicaagat*," Shavano said, stirring sugar into his coffee with a finger. "He leads the largest band at White River."

"Oh right, I remember," Collins said. "He does not care for Nick very much."

"Not at all," Peck said. "He is really angry now about the reports claiming James Thompson's house has been burnt down."

Just then the door opened and in came a short, wiry Indian man in all animation. He saw Shavano and began speaking in his native tongue, gesticulating wildly and with obvious ill humor.

"Hey Jack," Peck interjected loudly. "Have some coffee."

He poured a cup and held it out toward the Indian and Jack accepted it. He seemed to visibly calm himself and went over to perch on a stack of crates. Collins noticed he favored large silver ear hoops similar to those of Shavano. His hair was in braids and he wore mostly ready-made clothing, with the exception of moccasins and a blanket wound around the waist of his trousers.

"I have been to see Thompson's house," Jack said in excellent English. Collins recalled he had been raised by Mormons.

"Is it burnt?" Peck asked.

"No, it is not. It is in fine shape. This is another lie." He gestured with his cup and sloshed coffee onto the floor planking.

"I thought that James B. Thompson was a friend to the Utes," Collins said.

Jack said something to Shavano, tipping his head in an unfriendly manner toward Collins.

"Speak English," Shavano told him. "This man is from Washington and he is here to sort out all the lies. His name is Collins."

"You came to help us?" Jack asked. "Come with me to see this Governor Pitkin of Colorado. Come with me to tell him that the Utes are not burning houses."

"I cannot," Collins told him, "I have another mission to perform, but it is a good idea... Peck, can you get away and go with him to Denver? Do they know you there?"

Peck chuckled. "They know me a'right. But I would be willing to go and see what I could do. At least to testify to the fact that the Utes ain't guilty of all these offenses."

"I need to tell Pitkin that Nick must go away," Jack said. "He is bad for the way people think of us. He threatens us with soldiers. Washington must send another agent right away."

"Last month he tried to get the commander at Fort Steele to force all the Utes hunting up north and around the Yampa to return to White River," Peck told Collins. "As far as I know, Major Thornburgh has received no such orders from his superiors."

"What about this Thornburgh? Is he reasonable?"

"Seems to be. What do you think, Shavano?"

Shavano drained his cup. "I think he is a soldier and will do what he is told. If Nick keeps complaining, the important men of Colorado will force the military into action. It is what they want. Meanwhile," he looked at Collins pointedly, "those others will commit more crimes and after a while no one will care if our people are innocent or not."

"Then, by god, I will go with Jack to see the governor," Peck said. "Maybe we can stall him off. Meanwhile, you could go to Fort Steele and see what Thornburgh has heard. If the soldiers have been ordered south, we need to know about it pronto."

Collins considered this. "We have a job to accomplish first. Afterward, it makes sense for us to go and meet Thornburgh. I want to be able to make an official report as to whether or not the Utes have been committing depredations on game and timber."

"We are not!" Jack shouted, coming to his feet. "We are not!"

"I know that," Collins said quietly. "I need proof and that is what I intend to get."

35

They picked up the trail just west of Hahn's Peak. Shavano said he figured there were around fifteen horses, no doubt including some pack animals, so possibly ten men. The trail was a day old or more. Night was falling and they made a cold camp. Collins spent some time with his animals, rubbing them down and feeding them carrots from Peck's garden. He shared the treat with Shavano's stocky little geldings.

"What was in the telegram you sent?" the Indian asked, coming up behind him.

"Damn it, man," C.W. said, startled. "Let a body know you are near."

The chief grinned. "You have sharp reflexes," he said, "but bad hearing."

"Why should I tell you what was in the telegram?" Collins said, smiling back at him. "You probably looked at it before Peck had the chance to seal it."

"No I did not. He was too quick."

"Very well," he said, scratching Ulysses' dun colored jaw. "I sent two telegrams. One to Schurz, telling him that I believe a conflict is definitely imminent and he might find a visit to Colorado to be advisable. The other was to Gustavus Jocknick, letting him know that Jack and Peck are on their way to see Pitkin. And that Meeker...Nick...has slipped the rails."

"Slipped the rails?"

"He is no longer in control of himself."

"*KatÙsuYa.*"

Collins attempted to repeat the word, but failed miserably. "We need sleep," he said and headed to his bedroll and a quick smoke.

As he lay back looking into the night sky, he thought about Wakalyapi. It had been several months since their parting, when she had left again for Fort Walsh. Of course, they could not correspond, given all the constraints, but he truly desired to have word of her. Rumor had it that Sitting Bull's band was requesting land and rations from the Canadian government, due to the scarcity of buffalo, and that the elders were having difficulty controlling the young men. General Terry had already forced a meeting with the great chief, bringing a message from the president that he should bring his people back to the United States. It did not bode well for his friend and he was apprehensive about her future.

C.W. and Shavano were in the saddle before sun up. The track turned southeast to follow a small creek. They found an abandoned camp and Shavano decided there were nine men with six pack horses. They were plainly catching up with their quarry and, as they rode, they discussed the possibilities of splitting one of the men from the bunch.

"It will be too difficult to sneak up on their camp," the Indian said. "There are too many of them."

"Could we bait one into going off alone?"

"Perhaps."

The crew of men were moving swiftly. Collins and Shavano had to ride hard to gain on them. As night fell, they left their animals tethered in a grove of trees and moved ahead on foot. In the hills at the base of Gore Pass, Shavano spotted a campfire among the timber. They stealthily approached as the darkness deepened. Finally, Shavano gestured for Collins to stay among the lower branches of a blue spruce and await his return. The interval seemed unduly protracted and C.W. was napping when a small noise woke him. Shavano crouched beside him in the secure bower of the tree.

"They are camped about a half mile away," the Indian said quietly. Collins could see him shake his head in the gloom. "*Chingaso!* They have dynamite, cases of ammunition and many, many weapons."

"Shall we get back to our outfit?" Collins asked. He had not brought his rifle and suddenly felt rather vulnerable without it.

They made their way quietly through the pine duff and underbrush until they were back with their livestock and gear.

"I have an idea," Shavano told Collins as they made another cold camp.

"That was what I counted on," he said to him, smiling.

"I make a very good turkey call. I will sneak up before dawn and choose a place. Then I will make my call and you can pounce on the first one who comes hunting me. Can you do this?"

Collins regarded him drolly. "There was a time when I was quite adept at pouncing."

"Good. But do not kill him. We need him alive."

"Without question."

In the dim hour before the first light of day appeared on the skyline, Shavano had ensconced himself in a shallow depression behind a granite boulder. Collins placed himself, with knife and makeshift club in the natural approach from the strangers' camp to Shavano's retreat. Collins' heart beat in anticipation as the horizon became laced with pale light and the war chief began emitting a most convincing wild turkey call. In unexpectedly short order, someone was heard battering his way through the brush.

Collins braced himself and, at the precise moment the dim figure came within range, he struck the fellow across the temple with the stout branch he had brought for the purpose. He trussed the man's hands and feet and gagged and blindfolded him before he could regain his wits. Shavano appeared and helped sling the man across Collins' shoulder, retrieving the man's hat and rifle and erasing all signs of a scuffle. Deeply grateful for the slight stature of the prisoner, Collins trotted as silently and surely as possible through the timber to their livestock. The captive struggled at first, but Shavano punched him in the head and he became perfectly compliant. They bent him face down over the packs on Molly and secured him with rope.

They descended the foothills in haste, deliberately crisscrossing creeks and rocky ground. When they hit the open parks, they galloped northwest toward the Yampa River. They angled into isolated canyon country where they would be safe from discovery. Choosing an ideally sheltered defile, they unloaded their prisoner, unsaddled and tethered their animals, built a fire, made coffee and ate a leisurely meal. The captive slumped against a dirt bank and writhed against his bonds, resembling a dusty caterpillar.

"Shall we work on him here or move farther into the hills?" Collins asked, as he set aside his plate and took out his pipe.

"I feel we are plenty hidden in this place. We can work on him here."

The captive began making muffled protests through his gag and struggled more vigorously. Shavano and C.W. enjoyed a smoke, while the Indian told stories of hunting wild turkeys. As the sun reached its apex, they finally dragged their prisoner close to the fire and removed the gag but not the blindfold.

"You feel the heat from our fire," Shavano told him. "We have hot irons and other instruments."

"Fuck you," said their captive, bucking defiantly

against his restraints. "Who the fuck are you?"

"You possess information we require," Collins told him. "It is very simple. Give it to us and we will set you free close to some settlement."

"Go against us," Shavano added, "and we will kill you slowly or give you to the young Ute warriors who are nearby. They will have interesting ways to use you."

"What the hell do you want? I am just a poor prospector," the man said.

"What is your name?" Collins asked.

"Fuck you. I will not tell you."

Shavano removed the man's boots.

"What are you doing? Stop!"

"What is your name?" Collins asked again.

"Fuck you...why are you doing this?"

"I spent time with the Apaches," the chief said to Collins in a conversational manner. "It is said they sometimes put honey on their enemies and then stake them out on ant hills. I never saw this, but it might be useful."

"Oh for chrissakes!" their captive shouted. "What the hell do you want?"

"Who do you work for?" Collins asked, hunkering down next to the man.

"I am a prospector. Just a poor prospector."

"You know," Collins said, "I have heard that pulling out the toenails is very painful. It might be simpler than finding an ant hill."

Shavano poked a stick at the bottoms of the man's bare feet. He let out a yelp. "I think this man is a coward," the Indian said. "Let us find out."

He took a smoldering branch from the fire and put it against the arch of the right foot. The man hollered in protest.

"Who do you work for? We know you are causing trouble for the Utes," Collins said. "If a small burn causes you so much grief then do not wait for more. Tell us now."

Shavano again placed the glowing end of the branch against the man's foot. He shrieked as if being eviscerated.

"You know," C.W. said, "I have always observed that the greatest bullies are the weakest men."

"It is true. Does your Shakespeare not have a word to say on it?"

"Of course. 'Thou mayst be valiant in a better cause, but now thou seem'st coward...Thou shalt not damn my hand.' "

"Well said," the Indian reflected. "I do not warrant it a crime to kill a coward."

Their prisoner lay quiet, as if believing he might be forgotten. Shavano blew on the smoking branch and placed it against the sole of the man's other foot. He howled and almost rolled into the fire.

"Look there, he almost burnt himself up," the Indian said. "Perhaps we should toss him into the fire. Here, let us build it up."

"No, damnit, no!" the man yelled. "I have had enough of you fuckers!"

"What is your name?" Collins asked, squatting down again beside him.

"Bill...Bill Burnett."

"Where are you from?"

"Blackhawk. I used to work in the mines there. Then I went to Denver."

"Who is with you?"

"No...I will not give up my pals."

Shavano took his knife and pressed the tip against the base of Burnett's chin. "Who are they?" he asked menacingly.

"We are mostly from around Denver. None of us had much employment until they hired us for this job." Burnett sounded as if he was almost in tears. "Please do not kill me. Please, for godssake."

"Who hired you?" Collins asked.

"There were three of them. They advertised in the Trib. ' Vigorous men wanted for outdoor labor.' Some such. We were to meet them at the American House. One was a politician I had seen around town at speeches and such. One was a slick gentleman who gave us our stake money and instructions."

"And the other?" Collins asked, believing he already knew the answer.

"Some little bitty fucker with a foreign accent. Honest, mister, that is all I know. We bought supplies and traveled out here. Can I have some water? I am mortal thirsty."

"What were your orders?"

"To go around starting fires, killing and running off livestock and stealing equipment and tools, all the while making it look like the Injuns were at it."

"What is the dynamite for?" Shavano asked.

"Dynamite? Who said anything about dynamite? Is he a redskin? He sort of sounds like a redskin."

Shavano stomped the man in the side. "What about the dynamite?"

"Ow, god damn it. God damn it..." Burnett said, bringing his knees up in pain. "We purchased dynamite in case we had the chance to do some prospecting. Or we could maybe find a chance to use it some other way. Are you gonna give me some water?"

"Can we kill him now?" Shavano asked, winking at Collins. "Have you heard enough?"

"Oh fuck...hey I am sorry what I said about you sounding like a redskin."

"Is that all you can tell us?" C.W. asked, standing up.

"Uh...I guess. I guess that is all I know. Jesus, are you going to kill me?"

"Did these men tell you why they wanted you to do this job?"

"Not really...just that they wanted the Utes to look bad

so they could get rid of them. I guess that is the answer."

"Well…" Collins said. "I suppose if you must kill him, you can. Or we could just leave him out here to die…all trussed up like a Christmas goose."

"Aw fuck…just kill me outright then, you fuckers. I shoulda stayed in the Crook's Palace and drank myself to death."

Shavano and Collins grinned at each other. Shavano picked up the gag and stuffed it back into Burnett's mouth. They packed up camp, tied the man on Molly's load and headed north.

36

They reached Fort Fred Steele two days later. Their captive had been deposited, barefooted and blindfolded, in the vicinity of Perkins' Hotel and Emporium, near the Little Snake River. Angling eastward, they had skirted Rawlins and made directly for the fort, riding hard and resting little. Collins was eager to discover the military's position on the overall situation at the earliest opportunity. Then he would send another telegram to Jocknick in order to convey all current information and their new intelligence about the hired agents, now verified by the unfortunate Burnett.

The fort was a warren of carelessly constructed barracks, dusty lanes, a railroad depot for the Union Pacific, a sutler's store with goods stacked in piles on the porch, a large hospital built of local stone, a powder magazine, warehouses, the blacksmith's barn and stables, various corrals, grain bins and shacks. One impressive edifice caught their attention, being a two-story building with several gables and lush vines climbing the porch latticework. Assuming this would be the commander's quarters, they rode over and dismounted. As they were beating the dust from their clothing prior to going in, a tall, able-bodied young man in uniform came out onto the porch. He stood at the top of the steps looking down at Collins and Shavano.

"What is your business?" he asked. "I am just on my way over to the garrison headquarters."

Collins noted his profuse sideburns. They reminded him of a fellow named Cooke, who had died at the Little Big Horn and whose mutton-chop whiskers had been scalped.

"May we accompany you?" Collins asked.

"Certainly," the officer said, coming down from the porch. "Bring your animals. They attract flies and my wife has a most developed aversion to the pests."

Collins and Shavano collected their livestock to lead them behind the military gentleman. C.W. noted the man's West Point ring, major's insignia and ram-rod gait. They proceeded to a one-story building built of logs. They again secured their animals and followed the man into the cool interior of the office. The post adjutant saluted his superior, but did not rise from his seat behind a table covered in documents.

"I am Major Thomas Thornburgh, post commander," the officer said, taking a seat behind a large desk on the opposite side of the spacious room. Shavano remained by the door, as was his habit when indoors, and C.W. procured a chair near at hand and placed it before Thornburgh's desk. Without invitation, he sat down and crossed his legs.

"My name is Charles Collins. I am an agent hired by Secretary Schurz."

Thornburgh appeared nonplussed. "Secretary of the Interior Schurz?"

"One and the same. I am on an intelligence gathering mission for him. I have some information for you, as well as several inquiries to put to you."

"I see." He looked over at Shavano. "And who is your companion?"

"Chief Shavano of the Ute people. He is my guide and advisor." Collins observed that the Indian held himself with dignity and looked Thornburgh in the eye.

"I see. I suppose this is concerning the Ute problem," Thornburgh said.

"It is. However, I do not particularly see this as a Ute 'problem' *per se*, but more of a political contrivance. May I smoke?"

"You may," the major said. "Why would you make such a statement?" he asked.

Collins took his time packing the bowl of his pipe. He lit it before answering. "It has become plain to me that the depredations attributed to the Utahs, such as forest fires, the killing of livestock and all the rest have not been committed by them, but by hired agents. White agents. Have you heard no rumors of this?"

Thornburgh raised his eyebrows. "Why yes…as it happens, I have heard from various local ranchers that they have observed a bunch of unknown white men riding about the territory. They supposedly killed some Ute women and children east of here a while back."

"That, doubtlessly, would be the men of whom I speak," Collins said, removing his pipe from his mouth. "They have been hired by those who wish to foment an armed conflict, authored to facilitate the expulsion of all Utes from the state of Colorado. I give you very sincere warning that I believe an incident is imminently pending."

The major turned his West Point ring round and round his finger pensively, gazing at the surface of his desk. He looked up and stroked his whiskers.

"Meeker," he said, almost to himself.

Collins nodded. "He is another factor of the stratagem."

Thornburgh appeared to rouse himself. "You have two telegrams waiting for you, Mr. Collins. I have them here. No one knew who you were."

"You read them?"

"Certainly not!"

"My apologies. May I have them?"

Thornburgh opened a desk drawer, took out the sealed telegrams and handed them to Collins. He slipped them inside his blouse front.

"I have heard a curious rumor," Thornburgh said.

"Yes?"

"Mr. Meeker has some sort of relationship with General Pope. From what I have surmised, he did Pope a favor while writing dispatches during the war."

"Favor?" C.W. asked.

"Lincoln appointed Pope as head of the Army of Virginia due to Meeker's glowing reports."

"That is ill-fated."

Thornburgh smiled. "Indeed. It might be genuinely ill-fated for the Utes. In any event, I am under the authority of General Crook, Commander of the Department of the Platte at Fort Omaha, but the White River Agency is encompassed by General Pope's Department of the Missouri. It seems that Meeker has recently departed for Denver. He heard Pope is there and intends to enlist his aid with the ... well, the problems he believes exist upon his agency with its inhabitants."

"Curious he made no mention of his departure to me," said Collins. "I was just down to meet with him a few days ago. I must tell you that he seemed to be clearly deranged." He placed his spent pipe in a vest pocket. "This is truly unfortunate news. It may well have been my visit that precipitated his decamping for Pope."

"How is that?"

"He appeared to be upset that Secretary Schurz had sent me on a fact-finding commission, rather than on a mission to lend him aid in his disintegrating relations with the Utes."

"There is more," Thornburgh said. "Captain Francis Dodge and his Ninth are presently in Middle Park investigating reports of forest fires set by Indians. I have been advised that Governor Pitkin has been writing stringent letters to the Commissioner of Indian Affairs in Washington. He is adamant about the fact that White River Utes, specifically, are causing all the fires and depredations on livestock. He is demanding they be removed to Indian Territory."

"And what is your personal opinion of all this?"

"Bunkum, not to put too fine a point on it. Back in late June and early July, I sent some of my men to visit ranchers and miners throughout the surrounding area and none of them reported any problems. Some of them reported hunting parties killing game, but many of the Indians have come to trade with local ranchers and have behaved with propriety. A few others have reported a peculiar band of mounted men frequenting the region, as I mentioned previously. About the same time, roughly one hundred White River Utes made their appearance at a mining camp near the head of Jack and Savoy Creeks, some sixty miles south of here. They engaged in hunting and trading without incident and departed after almost a week. According to the miners, there were no difficulties whatsoever. Some tie-men actually admitted to accidentally setting the fires on Brush and French Creeks."

"I wish Meeker had not gone to Denver," Collins said, shaking his head in dismay. "This will only lend credence to his tales of woe and reinforce Pitkin's arguments. Peck, proprietor of a store on the Yampa River, has agreed to accompany Jack, the Ute chieftain, to Denver in order to meet with the governor. I am unsure when they plan to depart."

"Perhaps it will do some good, but I doubt it. Pitkin seems to be singularly preoccupied with the removal of the Utes from Colorado at all costs."

"And may well be one of the employers of the mysterious company of provocateurs."

"Truly?"

"It is quite possible."

"And Meeker? He has been quite insistent that I send soldiers to reinforce his policies and force his wayward flock back onto the reservation. I have never received any orders from my superiors to compel these Indians to remain on their reservation. Do you believe he is in league with Pitkin?" Thornburgh asked.

"I have become convinced that he is an unsuspecting accomplice. He seems to be motivated solely by personal glory and gross misconceptions. He is, however, being led to create disorder by those who manage him. And, I must reiterate, I believe the man's reason is disintegrating."

The officer nodded. "Yes...this has been my impression. His nerves are entirely unstrung."

The interior of the building had begun to darken with encroaching dusk. Collins stood. "We must make camp," he said.

"Will you not be my guest?" Thornburgh asked. He clearly intended the invitation to C.W. alone.

"No thank you. We will camp along the Platte. I will return tomorrow in order to send necessary telegrams and, perhaps, request further information."

"Certainly," Thornburgh said, walking him to the door.

Shavano was already untying the horses and preparing to depart. They mounted and headed for the river as the first brilliant rays of sunset colored the sky.

37

" 'Here's neither bush nor shrub to bear off any weather at all, and another storm brewing; I hear it sing i' the wind: yond the same black cloud, yond huge one...' "

Shavano looked up from his careful arrangement of kindling as he was preparing a fire in their newly constructed hearth ring. "I believe you are speaking of trouble and not the weather," he said and returned to his task.

"You are correct," Collins said. He was occupied with plucking a grouse killed by a blow from a well-aimed rock only minutes before. The bird had been remarkably susceptible to the distractions provided by Shavano.

"Shakespeare again?"

"Again."

"You remember these things." It was a statement rather than a question.

"Yes."

C.W. skewered the bird and rested it upon the forked sticks that braced the crackling fire.

"What can we do?" the chief asked. He sighed and sat down on a nearby log.

Collins bent and stretched his aching back. "I do not know. I should read my telegrams."

He took a seat by the fire. Taking out his messages, he noted that the first was from Jocknick. He opened it and read aloud.

SIR: I am in receipt of your telegram dated 25th ultimo, relative to the emotional state of Agent Nathan C. Meeker and opinion of pending collision between whites and Indians. Have forwarded information to Sec. Schurz. Continue to stay apprised of local machinations and relate forthwith all tidings.

Shavano busied himself with filling his pipe. "Not much action and mostly talk."

"Ah well," Collins said. "I will send him news of our man Burnett and his pals tomorrow."

"What about the other telegram?"

Collins looked it over. "It is from John Lawrence of Saguache. I suppose he knew I would come to Fort Steele eventually."

The Indian leaned forward and turned the bird. "I know Lawrence from before."

Collins glanced up. "Oh right...from the days at Los Pinos. He says here that Otto Mears has been spending much of his time in Denver with Governor Pitkin. He believes that events will culminate soon."

"The storm that is brewing. Again, I ask...what can we do?"

Collins shook his head. "The only plan of action I can think of is to suggest that Meeker be removed at once."

"Is this possible?" Shavano asked, sending a puff of tobacco smoke into the night.

"I do not know," Collins said, shrugging. "If Schurz is clever, he will see that this is expedient."

"We will send more telegrams?"

"Yes. Then I will return to Peck and discover whether he and Jack went to Denver. Will you stay with me or go your own way?"

"Perhaps I will stay," Shavano said and fed the fire carefully beneath the roasting bird. "You may yet need my help."

Chapter 37

"Do you want pay? I should offer to pay you, as you have been requisite."

The Indian eyed him in an unfriendly manner.

"I am sorry," Collins said. "I was rude just now. I only meant that if I am being paid, you should be also. Please accept my apology."

Shavano regarded him quizzically. "You are the most polite white man I have ever met."

Collins laughed. "There are some who would not agree with that."

"I will stay with you. You make me think there is more to do before the storm comes."

They ate and settled down to sleep. Around midnight the horses woke them up, stamping and blowing nervously. Collins jumped up to grab his Winchester and Shavano reached for his Maynard rifle. Building up the fire, they saw an Indian man standing politely near their camp waiting to be invited.

"*Mique*," the young warrior said quietly. "*Táwache.*"

Shavano gestured for him to come closer. "*Üû.*"

The Ute man sat by the fire and spoke at length to Shavano in his native tongue. C.W. heard Peck's name mentioned a couple of times. When the conversation was over, the youth lay down on the bare earth by the fire and precipitously went to sleep.

"What is it," Collins asked quietly.

"Peck sent him. We must send the telegrams and then go to see him. He said not to stop by Baggs' ranch at all."

"This is interesting. We should pack and go. *Bíonn an fear deireanach díobhálach.*"

"Yes?" asked the chief.

"One should not leave things too late."

MEDICINE MAN SCHURZ

38

Collins composed his telegrams while Shavano stood by the horses, waiting. C.W. had to roust the telegrapher out of his room in the back of the office. The young Ute warrior sent by Peck had already left them to return to Yampa River. They mounted and rode south out of Rawlins, having decided to circumvent the fort and move quickly. It was still early morning.

"I informed Mr. Jocknick of our intelligence gained from Burnett. I also sent a message to Secretary Schurz that Meeker should be replaced as soon as possible."

"Will this do any good?" the Indian asked, skeptically.

"No telling," Collins said and sighed, feeling slightly melancholic. He could not shake a sense of looming disaster. It was, in fact, intensifying as the days passed.

"Peck wants us to get to him as soon as possible. He said it was important," Shavano told him.

"Why are we not supposed to stop by Baggs' ranch?"

"I am not sure. Something about a story he told regarding my people. Something about his cows."

"I thought he was friendly with the Utes," C.W. said, turning in the saddle to look at his companion.

"I have never trusted him."

They rode hard, skirting the Baggs ranch and crossing the Little Snake at a shallow stretch of the river then turned south along the White River road. Collins noticed a large herd of cows grazing along the river to the west of them. After a long day of riding, they camped by a small lake and arrived at the Yampa River by early afternoon.

There was a lodge pitched near Peck's store. Smoke rose in a thin trail from the top flaps. They watered their animals and unloaded and unsaddled them, turning them loose to graze along the river bottom, then walked over to the buildings. They noticed a woman near the lodge and Collins recognized Jane.

"Hello there," he said.

"Hello. *Mique* Shavano."

"Why are you here, my daughter?" the chief asked. "Charles told me you were going to the Uncompahgre."

Collins glanced at Shavano. He had never before referred to him by name.

"I have important news," she said. "It is why Peck sent Jimmy Tavapaunt for you."

"Is Peck within?" he asked.

"He is," she answered. "Come."

They went into the store and found its owner napping in a chair by the stove. The evening was becoming cool and breezy. He roused at their arrival and set about serving coffee and corn cakes.

"Glad you have come. Bad things are happening," he said, resuming his chair.

"Bad things?" Shavano asked.

Collins glanced at Jane and she nodded. "Very bad," she said.

"Something about Baggs?" C.W. asked.

"He has told lies, but there is worse," Jane said.

"What lies?" Shavano asked.

"He claims the Utes stampeded his cattle and slaughtered many for hides," the woman told him.

"What in hell?" exclaimed Collins, leaning forward on his seat of ammunition boxes. "He told me he was always on good terms with the Utes."

"Someone paid him," Shavano said. "Someone paid him well."

"There is worse," Jane repeated.

"Worse?" Collins asked.

"Meeker has accused Johnson of attacking him," Peck said.

"I thought he was in Denver," Collins said, balancing his empty cup on a nearby sack of oats.

"He has returned," Jane said. "He is determined now to bring the soldiers in."

"*Pinche* Nick," Shavano said. "What happened?"

"I was almost packed to leave for the Uncompahgre," said the woman. "Meeker came back from Denver, but he was in a bad mood because a wagon had wrecked and hurt his arm. He was also very sure of himself after visiting with the big general he knew from before. He gave that man Price orders to begin plowing the pony pasture. He gave him orders to plow right into my corrals and pasture. Antelope and I went to see Meeker. We told him to stop, but he was very angry and made insults and told this Price to keep plowing. The youngest son of Johnson and another boy walked beside the plow with rifles and told Price to stop, but Meeker ordered him to start again. This time, the boys shot over his head from the brush nearby. After that, Price refused to go back out there."

"This is terrible," Collins said, shaking his head.

"Meeker was crazy with anger," Jane continued. "Canalla thought he should speak to him. He thought he could reason with him. He went to the house and told Nick that the pony pasture and my corrals must be left alone. He said that he would not allow the plowing to begin again. That is when Nick told Canalla he should kill his horses."

A silence rested in the room. The fire crackled in the woodstove.

"He has learned nothing" Shavano said quietly.

"He told Canalla he had too many horses and that he had better kill some of them," Jane said.

Collins had the sense that this statement was tantamount to pure sacrilege to the Ute people. He had witnessed the affection and reverence they felt toward their horses and could well imagine his own wrath at the suggestion that he should kill his animals.

"What did Canalla do then?" he asked Jane.

"He told Nick it was not right to say such things. Then Nick threatened him with jail and told him he had always been a troublesome man. This made Johnson very angry as he had always tried to help Nick. He told Nick it would be better for another agent to come who was a good man and would not be sending lies to Washington and talking about prison and killing ponies. He took Nick by the shoulders and shook him. He pushed him out onto the porch, but that was all. Mrs. Nick began screaming and two men ran over. Johnson walked away without saying another word. He was so angry I thought he might come back and kill Nick, but he did not."

"Oh no," said Collins. "This is very bad."

"Nick has already sent telegrams," Peck told him.

"Telegrams?"

"One to Governor Pitkin and one to the Commissioner of Indian Affairs, Hayt."

"Did you get a look at the telegrams?" Collins asked Peck.

"I did. John Steele, who owns the mail contract for White River, had the messages and was taking them back to Rawlins. He had been to see Meeker and stopped over here on his way back. I stole a glimpse at them while he was sleeping."

"Dare I ask?"

"He told Hayt that he had been assaulted by Johnson and injured badly."

"This is a lie!" Jane said vehemently. "He was injured by the wagon. Canalla never hurt him."

"Go on," Collins told Peck.

"He wrote that his life and those of his family and employees were not safe. He requested that Pitkin convince General Pope to send the soldiers from Fort Steele."

"This is not good," Shavano said.

"What came of your meeting with Pitkin? Did you and Jack see him?" C.W. asked.

"That greasy damned secretary of his, Vickers, finally let us in to see him. I thought Jack was quite eloquent in telling Pitkin that many of the crimes blamed on the Utes were false. He also told him to not believe everything he heard from Meeker. He strongly requested a replacement for Meeker and Pitkin promised to write to Commissioner Hayt the next day...I did not believe him. Then we came home to this."

"Jack tried to talk to Nick about Canalla," Jane told them. "He warned him he better let it drop. That it was bad to make such a fuss. Meeker told Jack that he would call in soldiers to put them in chains and drive the Utes from their lands and that it really was not their land any way. Jack is very angry and has promised to fight the soldiers if they come."

Shavano looked at Collins. "Shall we go see Nick?" he asked.

C.W. shrugged. "What can we say? The machinery is already moving, and the man is hysterical...you know this to be true."

"Yes."

"Jack and his band are preparing to hunt up in Wyoming Territory," Peck said. "Perhaps this still might blow over if you can get to Schurz."

"Jane, can you get a message to the people at White River and tell them to get the hell out of there?" Collins asked.

"You mean the white people?" she asked him.

"No...the Ute people. They need to go to Ouray or into the mountains."

"This will only make Nick more angry. He has always complained about the people leaving the agency against his will," she told him.

"I do not think it matters now."

"We need to stop the soldiers from coming," Peck said. "How can we do that?"

"I need to get a message to Secretary Schurz and General Crook," Collins said. "Then I need to see Major Thornburgh. He has the closest military contingent, but he is not under Pope's command. No matter what Pitkin may try to do, Fort Steele is under Crook's authority. That is our only hope." He turned to Shavano. "Will you stay with me or go to your people?"

"I think you will need help."

Collins considered him sadly. "I really do not know what will stop this now. *Tar éis a chítear gach beart.* It is afterwards that events are best understood."

39

They left their pack animals with Peck, departing north at full gallop as soon as there was adequate light to see. Molly brayed loudly with indignation at the loss of her companion and Collins' heart went out to her. He could not believe they had to retrace their route again at such short notice and he worried about using Ulysses too hard, even though the horse was still young and strong.

The aspens were beginning to show sporadic golden and rose tints up on Yellow Jacket Pass. They rested their animals momentarily in a grove, drank some water and proceeded again at a ground-eating pace. Shavano led the way along trails only he could see, through valleys and over ridges, always bearing north and always sure of himself.

By nightfall, they had reached the first fringes of the high desert country south of Rawlins and their horses were played out. After making a cold camp near Muddy Creek, Collins lay on his back on saddle blankets and found he could not sleep in spite of extreme fatigue. He could hear the horses moving about, hungrily devouring grasses among the trees in the creek bottom. His mind raced in circles, retracing the inexorable snarl within which the Utes were ensnared. He could find no resolution to their dilemma, if the machinery of U.S. politics followed its usual course of injustice and perfidy.

"You are worried," Shavano said in the darkness.

"Yes."

"You will still try," he stated flatly.

"Yes."

They kept the horses to a brisk gait the next day, but held them back from the arduous pace of the day before, wanting to conserve their endurance for impending trials. Monotonous landscape and lack of sleep further depressed Collins' spirits. He was angry at Schurz and Jocknick for sending him on this patently futile assignment, especially when it had already been too late to impact the outcome. They arrived in Rawlins before sundown and the telegraph operator was still on duty.

"May I rely on your absolute circumspection?" Collins asked the gray-headed, fussy little man.

"Of course!" the man said, indignantly. "Why would you ask such a question? I am a Western Union telegrapher. We are held to a higher standard."

"Very well..." he said impatiently. "I have a delicate matter to relate. I require complete secrecy."

"Of course," the man said again.

"Firstly, do you have any messages for Charles Collins?"

The operator became agitated. "I have an urgent telegram waiting here for you." He reached into a cubby and pulled it out. "Here it is."

Collins opened it and read:

> Denver, Colorado Sept 14 1879
> To C. Collins Rawlins, Terr. Of Wyoming
> SIR: Secretary of Interior Schurz en route from Calif. to Denver to meet Gov. Pitkin re: Ute troubles. Agent Meeker's telegram of peril wired to Sec. Schurz due Comm. Hayt not present. Send latest intelligence at once. Sec. of War McCrary sending orders for military action.
> G. A. Jocknick, Interior Dept

He composed a comprehensive message to Jocknick, decided it was pointless to wire Crook or Schurz, and left the Western Union office.

"It has begun," he told Shavano, walking over to where he waited with the horses.

"Begun?"

"The military has been mobilized."

"There will be trouble."

"I fear as much. I must go to Fort Steele to see Thornburgh."

"What will you do then?"

"Stay with the troops and see what I can do to avert disaster. The rest will be in Secretary Schurz' hands. He should be in Denver by now."

They made camp a short distance from town and, again, Collins slept poorly. Early the next day, they stopped at France's store and C.W. purchased what few supplies they could carry on their saddle horses. The clerk was wrapping a small cut of beef in brown paper when France walked in.

"Alrighty, Tom, I can take over. Thanks for coming in on your day off." He turned to look at Collins.

"Hidy," he said. "Saw old Shavano outside. Figured you might be here. How is Meeker? I hope he can hold out."

"Hold out?" he asked with presentiment.

"Until Major Thornburgh can get to him."

"Get to him?"

France officiously tucked his beard deeper into the waist of his pants. "Major Thornburgh pulled out of here day before yesterday with some two hundred troops. The whole town turned out to see them off."

Collins groaned. In their haste, they had missed the column of soldiers.

"Lots of goings on," France continued. "Secretary of Interior Carl Schurz came in on a train naught but a day before the troops came through town. As I say, sure hope old Meeker can hold out. Them Utes been raising hell here bouts and no lie."

Collins did not care to disabuse him of his notions and gathered up his purchases. "Thank you," was all he said.

"Anything I can do, friend," the man said to C.W.'s back as he departed the store.

He packed the supplies in his saddlebags and tightened his cinch while Shavano studied him curiously, noting his haste.

"We need to go," C.W. said, mounting Ulysses and turning south out of town. Some distance later, he pulled up his horse to let him blow.

"What is wrong?" Shavano asked. "We are not going to the soldier fort?"

Collins shook his head in dismay. "They have already left. We need to catch up with them and talk sense to Thornburgh."

"*Chingaso*. When did they leave?"

"Two days ago. We missed them."

"They will be moving slow with men and wagons. We can catch them," the Indian said.

"Yes, but our horses are weary."

They rode at a swift walk back across the desert and Collins swore he never desired to see this region of Wyoming Territory again. Ulysses' head was heavy with fatigue when they stopped to make camp on Savery Creek, near where it joined the Little Snake River.

"We have traveled many times up and down," Shavano said conversationally to Collins as they smoked their pipes by the fire.

"When I took this commission, I was told I might have to do a fair bit of traveling."

"There may be more ahead," the chief said, staring into the fire pensively.

"I am obliged to tell you," C.W. said, knocking ashes from his pipe, "I have small hope of achieving any purpose now the soldiers have been mustered."

A cool breeze stirred the coals and a horse pawed the ground in the shadows. Collins could almost hear the noise of battle, distant in the plutonian night.

OFFICER'S TENT

40

By the time Collins and Shavano had caught up with Thornburgh and his troops, they were camped on Little Bear Creek near the castle-like rocks that Collins had noticed on his first journey south through White River country. They rode into the military encampment and, in its center, found a large Sibley bell tent, as favored by officers. Major Thornburgh was seated in a campaign chair in front of the tent, speaking with his adjutant. He looked up as Collins pulled in his horse and dismounted.

"Good evening, Major," he said, walking over.

Shavano slid off his horse, but did not approach.

"Good evening, Mr. Collins," the officer said, registering surprise. "What brings you out here?"

"I am heartily concerned that Mr. Meeker has caused such a fuss as to have the military mobilized. It is surely a fool's errand," Collins said, accepting a chair offered by Thornburgh's adjutant.

Thornburgh raised his eyebrows. "That may be, but we will have the truth of it soon enough. I have just now finished composing a letter to Mr. Meeker informing him of our imminent arrival." He looked over at his adjutant. "Lieutenant Cherry, would you be so good as to summon Mr. Lowry?"

"Yes sir." The man strode away.

"Now, Mr. Collins, please explain," the major said.

"It has come to my attention that the Utes believe your presence, so close to their reservation, constitutes a grave threat. They have vowed to fight you."

"Nonsense. They do not even, as yet, comprehend that we are near. Mr. Meeker does not know and so cannot have informed his Indians."

Collins glanced over at Shavano, standing well within earshot of the conversation. The chief made a slight movement with his mouth eliciting disdain for the officer's naiveté.

"I do not believe that there could be any movement of men through this country without the Indians knowing of their presence," C.W. said. "Surely your experiences a year ago with the Cheyenne taught you this. Meeker has threatened the Utes with their removal to Indian Territory, or worse, prison. He has lost his reason entirely and the Indians are more than ready to defend themselves against such contingencies."

Thornburgh laughed acerbically. "I believe you give them far too much credit."

Adjutant Cherry returned with a man in tow. The fellow seemed overwrought, especially when he observed Shavano standing by the horses.

"Major Thornburgh, sir, we are being spied upon," he said, without delay.

"What do you mean, Mr. Lowry?"

"I have spotted more than one Ute scout in the brush above."

The major looked at Collins. "You have sound information that the Indians intend to fight us?"

"I do."

"And your man, there. Where are his loyalties?"

Lowry coughed loudly. "Major…that is a Ute war chief named Shavano. I can tell you where his loyalties lie."

"Is this so?" Thornburgh asked Collins.

"Shavano here is a war chief and, no doubt, his loyalties lie with his people. He was, however, asked by Chief Ouray to guide me, so that I might avert a disaster such as the one I see lying imminently before us."

"Disaster?"

"This is exactly what the politicians have intended… that the military and Indians should clash, thereby opening up the last of the agency lands for mining and agriculture. You are a pawn, sir."

Thornburgh came to his feet. "I am no pawn. I have been ordered out to investigate the situation and render assistance to Agent Meeker if need be. That is all." Thornburgh turned away dismissively. "Mr. Lowry, would you be so kind as to ride to the agency with my letter to Mr. Meeker forthwith. Make haste, as I have been out of communication with him for ten days and require supplementary intelligence as to the state of affairs with him and his family."

"Yes sir," Lowry said, glancing at Collins and taking the letter. He departed swiftly.

Collins stood. "We shall take our leave as well. Perhaps I can meet with some of the Ute leaders and allay their fears as to your mission here."

"Very well, but do not be deceived. I will fight, if necessary. The Utes must obey their masters, no matter how misguided they may be. Colorado is a state, after all. It is no longer untamed frontier."

Shavano chose this moment to walk over to the major. He came close and looked him in the eye. "You should not be deceived. The Ute people have no masters." The chief turned, sprang onto his horse and loped south out of camp.

"Good god!" Thornburgh exclaimed, taken aback. "He speaks English like a white man."

Collins regarded him with scorn. "Many of the Utes speak Spanish, English and even some French, not to mention various Indian dialects." He walked to Ulysses and swung into the saddle. "I will see you down the trail," he said and rode in the direction taken by Shavano.

C.W. found his companion awaiting him on a small hill a scant mile south of the soldier camp. "That may not have been prudent," he told him.

"I should not have given way to anger," the Indian said contritely

"Understandable, considering," Collins said, smiling. "Nothing will make much difference at this point anyhow. '…The world, too saucy with the gods, incenses them to send destruction.' Let us ride to Peck's store."

When they reached the Yampa River and their old camp, they turned their horses loose to graze with the rest of the stock. Molly greeted Ulysses and he returned her civilities, whickering lowly. Collins and Shavano slept a couple of hours, worn out from the many hours in the saddle. They were awakened by a commotion and went to investigate. Captain Jack and a few other warriors were talking to Peck and loading what appeared to be cartridge boxes on pack horses.

"Hello there," Peck called to them. "Back so soon?"

"The army is coming," Shavano said simply.

"You could not stop them from coming?" Jack asked, eyeing Collins.

"No. But I think you should talk to the commanding officer before you fight them. He is not dead set on fighting you, as Nick has threatened. They are here to investigate."

Jack scowled. "Investigate what exactly?"

"Meeker's frenzied accusations. Let them come and see for themselves there is nothing amiss."

The Indian tossed his head scornfully and the large silver hoops swung in his ears. "Meeker has them all convinced he is in terrible danger. We tried to talk sense to Pitkin, but he only pretended to listen."

Most of the Ute warriors headed south toward White River with the ammunition, while Jack remained with Peck and watched them go. Shavano sat on a nearby stump, silent and alert. Collins looked around and saw that Jane's lodge was gone.

"Jane went to Ouray?" he asked Peck.

He nodded. "She will let him know what is happening here. What have you learned?"

"Secretary Schurz is in Denver with Pitkin. The Secretary of War, himself, ordered out the troops. This will be disastrous if the Utes do not resist fighting."

"And what will happen if we do not fight? Have you never heard of the Washita?" Jack asked feverishly. "We will not wait for the soldiers to slaughter our families."

"I have heard of Washita. You must get your women and children out of the White River Agency, above all else. Then wait and see. If the Utes fire the first shot, your fate will be sealed and no one will take pity on you."

"Our women and children have already been sent south out of the agency. Beyond that," Jack said, "we will see…we will see."

ARMY

41

Warm sunlight slanted through the cottonwood grove and heated his shoulders as Collins stood brushing his tired horse's back, crusted with salt where the saddle had rested for many miles of travel. Molly stood nearby, watching them. It was peaceful beside the Yampa River, but he felt it was a fragile peace and feared the days ahead. The sound of approaching horses diverted his attention. He turned to see two riders, one of whom he recognized as Joe Rankin from Rawlins. The other was Major Thornburgh's adjutant, Lieutenant Cherry. He watched them silently as they dismounted and watered their horses.

Shavano found him. "The soldiers have camped over on the Tom Ile Ranch about one mile from here," he said. "I have been to see."

"Why are those two here?" Collins asked.

"I do not know. We will find out."

They held back until they saw that the men had entered the building. Captain Jack came out from behind the store and joined them. He was accompanied by another Ute warrior, one who was called *Sowowíc*, according to Shavano. When the four of them stepped into the store, Peck was in the midst of explaining to the lieutenant that he had no more ammunition to sell.

"But we were assured that you always had ready supplies of cartridges," Cherry was saying.

"With all the current troubles, I am sold out," Peck

told him, obviously loath to report he had sold the last ten thousand rounds to Nicaagat and his men that very morning. He glanced uneasily at Collins who shook his head slightly to indicate he would not betray him.

Joe Rankin looked at Collins and Shavano. Suddenly his face filled with recognition. "Well hell, Mr. Collins, you still in this part of the country? I thought you would have moved on long ago."

"You are from the soldier camp?" Jack asked Lieutenant Cherry.

"We are. It is close by."

Collins thought it singular that there seemed to be no antagonism between any of the men present. It struck him that all were being played upon by powerful interests that would benefit none of them and could only serve to create havoc and destruction in their simple lives.

"I would go to see your officer," Jack said. "Is this possible?"

"I do not see why not," Cherry said agreeably.

Jack looked at Collins. "Will you come?"

He nodded.

Peck begged off accompanying the small group, insisting his wife was frightened and he must remain behind with her. Jack, Rankin and Cherry retrieved their horses and headed east along the river. Shavano and Collins saddled up and followed, overtaking them in short order. As they neared the camp, they began passing troopers fishing in the warm afternoon as if on a holiday excursion. Major Thornburgh was sitting at a small table writing dispatches in his tent when they rode up. He wiped his pen, blotted the writing and stood to greet them outside.

"We are met again so soon?" he asked Collins. He regarded Shavano thoughtfully then turned to peruse the other two Indians.

"Here is Nicaagat, or Captain Jack as he is known

among the whites, and Sowowíc, an important man of the Ute people. They desire to speak to you," Collins said formally.

Major Thornburgh sat on a campaign chair by the fire ring. There were several makeshift seats surrounding the smoldering pit. He gestured for the others to join him, but they remained standing except for Joe Rankin, who saw to the horses and then took a seat on a nearby camp stool. Thornburgh directed his orderly, Private O'Malley, to procure coffee and cigars. Cherry went off on some duty or other.

When everyone was settled, Jack said, "Nick is very bad. He should not have sent for soldiers."

"Nick?" Thornburgh asked.

"Agent Meeker," Collins told him.

"Oh...I see...Well, Mr. Meeker has the right, as Indian agent, to request military succor when expedient," the major explained,

Sowowíc became quite animated, speaking in the Ute language to Jack and gesturing with his hands.

"What does he say?" Thornburgh asked.

"He says Nick has been withholding supplies that belong to the people and has plowed up much pasture," Shavano translated. Rankin openly displayed astonishment at the chief's fluent English.

"He is also full of false promises and many bad intentions," Jack added.

The orderly offered cups of coffee and cigars around. Collins noted distractedly that the boy's ears stood almost perpendicular to his head.

"I would not credit these accusations as being worthy of threats to his life," the major observed, drawing deeply on his cigar.

Jack snorted derisively. "There have been no threats on his life."

The officer studied Jack a moment. "You say he is

not in danger?"

"No," Shavano answered vehemently. "But he has threatened the Ute people with terrible punishments."

Thornburgh sighed. "That may be so, but he is still an agent of the United States government."

"And we are people with treaty agreements that have been violated many, many times. Does that not count with you?" Shavano asked.

"I am only a soldier with clear orders to proceed to the agency and investigate rumors," the major said. "I must needs leave the rest to my superiors."

"Perhaps you could delay a little," Collins suggested. "At least until the situation with Meeker has been clarified?"

"By you?"

"By me, yes. I was, after all, engaged by Secretary Schurz."

"I regret to say that this would not be possible. My orders are quite clear."

"That is unfortunate, Major Thornburgh. I was in the war and often found that orders were sometimes best interpreted as per the situation on the ground."

"You, sir, could not have graduated from West Point. There we were taught that an order is not subject to interpretation."

Collins smiled slightly at the man's implacable manner. "And, thereby, have many brave men found untimely demise."

"You are no longer in the military," Thornburgh said scornfully. "May I assume you were dishonorably discharged?"

"No you may not," Collins said coldly. "And were I at leisure, I would give you reason to regret your words."

Major Thornburgh stood and bowed slightly. "I already regret them. Please forgive my insult to your honor as resulting from the anxiety of recent days."

The Indians silently awaited the outcome of this exchange. Shavano's hand rested upon the butt of his pistol. After a considerable pause, within which he strove to maintain his composure, Collins gave a nod and relaxed.

"You are forgiven, sir," he said. "But I would still caution you to avoid profligately falling into the web woven by Governor Pitkin and his cronies. Meeker is merely a pompous lunatic. This campaign was begun at the behest of those who would advance by it. Why do you imagine I was employed by Secretary Schurz?"

The major remained standing. He seemed about to speak then thought better of it.

"Yes, yes I know…" Collins said impatiently. "You have only my word that I was hired by the Secretary of the Interior Department."

"We must go," Captain Jack said brusquely. "Thank you for this fine cigar."

Sowowíc and Jack went to their ponies and trotted westward out of camp. Joe Rankin excused himself and wandered off toward the river.

"I must send a telegram to General Crook," Thornburgh told Lieutenant Cherry, who had returned and was standing nearby awaiting orders.

"Please excuse me gentlemen," the major said. "I invite you to dine with me tomorrow evening." He and his adjutant retired into the tent.

"We should go as well," C.W. said to Shavano.

They retrieved their horses and rode out of the soldier camp, heading back to the river.

"Would you have fought that man?" Shavano asked after a while.

"I do not know. Maybe. *Beó duine d'éis a anma, agus ni beó d'éis a einigh.* A man may live after losing his life, but not after losing his honor."

SOLDIER CAMP

42

The next day, the soldiers bivouacked in a meadow on Deer Creek and Collins and Shavano set up camp not far away. They had brought their pack animals and outfit from Peck's store so as to travel south with the troopers. The column had been delayed while Thornburgh's wagon master repaired a dray belonging to a supply train headed for the White River Agency. The troops were only about forty-five miles north of White River now and Collins knew if trouble were to come, it would be soon.

That evening, Major Thornburgh, Collins, Shavano, Lieutenant Cherry, Joe Rankin and an officer called Captain Payne sat by the fire and smoked more of the major's fine cigars. Just after dusk, several riders approached the group. Three of the men dismounted and walked over. A Brobdingnagian Indian man slid down from his horse and stood off to the side. Shavano got up and went over to him.

"Major Thornburgh?" one of the men asked.

"I am he," the major told the fellow, remaining in his chair.

"I am Wilmer Eskridge of the White River Agency. This here is John Augisley and that is Henry Jim. He guided me here."

Collins studied the young Indian man. According to Jane, he had disappeared after Meeker threatened to beat him, but must have returned. He wondered if Ouray had sent him back.

"Good evening. Will you not sit?" Thornburgh asked.

Eskridge and Augisley accepted the invitation, but the young Ute man remained standing.

"I am awaiting news from Mr. Charles Lowry. Have you seen him at the agency?" the major asked.

"Sorry sir, but I have not," Augisley said. "We brought you a letter from Agent Meeker. And that fellow over there is Colorow," he said gesturing toward the brawny Indian speaking to Shavano. "He says he is representing Captain Jack."

Eskridge handed a parcel of papers to the major who stood and went into the tent to read by the light of a lamp that burned within. Lieutenant Cherry offered cigars to the two agency men. Augisley accepted one and lit it with a stick from the fire. From the look of him, Collins surmised that Eskridge was new to the West. Henry Jim squatted on his heels in the shadows just outside the glow of firelight. Collins could hear Shavano and Colorow speaking in low tones.

When Thornburgh returned, he said, "I will give you the salient details, gentlemen. Mr. Meeker now states he wishes us to remain outside the reservation boundaries and to send a detail of five men to the agency. It seems the Indians are much perturbed by our presence and consider any advance of the troops as a declaration of war. Mr. Meeker claims he is attempting to allay their fears, but insists that our approach at this time would prove deleterious. What about this, Mr. Eskridge?"

"Things had been rather peaceful for several days after Price got himself shot at. We all thought that Meeker had panicked and we would pass a quiet autumn. But then Jack came to spread the news of soldiers coming and the place blew up like a busted bee hive. Now Meeker is fearful and wants you to wait."

Colorow and Shavano approached the fire. Shavano spoke. "This man is Chief Colorow."

Chapter 42

Joe Rankin made a deprecating noise in his throat. Major Thornburgh gave him a scornful glance. "You will be polite here in my camp, Mr. Rankin."

"He sure as hell ain't nothing more than a loafer, Major. There ain't no 'chief' to it."

"Must I repeat myself or will I be forced to ask you to excuse yourself?"

Rankin looked down at his feet and said nothing more. Shavano watched him for a long moment as if to see what he might do.

"Pray continue," Thornburgh asked Shavano.

Colorow spoke in his native language.

"He says that Captain Jack has given his word no harm will come to the five men who visit the agency," Shavano translated.

Colorow spoke again. He presented a stately figure, wrapped in a colorful Navajo blanket with his scalp lock twisted up and tied with ermine tails. Collins observed he was quite tall and massive enough to appear truly imposing. Something about the man reminded him of "Boss" Tweed of Tammany Hall.

"He offers to accompany you," Shavano continued. "That way you will have his protection as well."

Major Thornburgh appeared deep in thought. No one spoke.

At last he said, shrugging, "I suppose it could do no harm to send a scouting party to assess the situation."

Captain Payne, who had appeared to be struggling with the need to express himself for quite some time, sprang to his feet. "I emphatically disagree! We do not bargain with savages!"

"It would be foolish," Rankin said passionately.

"Sit down, Captain, and restrain yourself," the major said, placidly but with conviction. He ignored Rankin. "What do you think, Collins? Is this not what you counseled earlier?"

"It is, indeed, Major. Even a small delay may prove beneficial." Collins turned to Shavano. "What do you say?"

"I think it would be unwise to cross the reservation line at this time," the war chief answered. "Colorow says that the people are very afraid and speak of Sand Creek."

"Sand Creek? Oh yes...Chivington." Major Thornburgh said reflectively. "Good god man, I and my men would never..."

"But the Utes do not know that," C.W. interrupted. "Why would they?"

"Your point is well-taken. I have made up my mind," he said and looked pointedly at Payne, whose face was red with frustration. "Captain do come into the tent. I wish to have a word with you." He stood and addressed the group at the fire. "I will inform the agent that we will make camp on Milk Creek just north of the reservation. I will visit the agency with four of my men. Mr. Eskridge, if I send a message with you, will you take it safely back to Agent Meeker?"

"Yes sir, I will."

"Very well. Gentlemen, please excuse me," the major said and withdrew into his tent with Captain Payne following after.

43

On the following day, Shavano and Colorow went hunting. Collins stayed with the troops and accompanied them as they moved south ten miles along Deer Creek. While camp was again being organized and the tents erected, a man came riding up in an agitated state. He said his name was Eugene Taylor and he ran a sutler's tent on Milk Creek. According to him, a band of Utes had come in the day before and seized all his ammunition, after which they had intercepted the mail carrier from White River Agency at Peck's store.

Word spread through camp and the soldiers became unsettled. Thornburgh placed pickets in strategic locations to ease their fears about surprise attacks. Collins made camp about a quarter mile upstream from the troopers and leisurely gathered wood, awaiting Shavano's return. Around dusk, the major sent Lieutenant Cherry to invite him to dine. Collins wandered over to the soldier camp and found the major's tent. Captain Payne and Thornburgh were deep in conversation with a very excited fellow in unkempt civilian attire.

"I am telling you, it is not safe to cross the creek. The Utes are waiting," the man was saying.

"Hello, Mr. Collins," the major said as he sauntered up. "This is Columbus Henry, one of the bullwhackers from the ox train to which we lent aid a day ago. He is adamant that we will be attacked if we cross onto the reservation."

Columbus Henry pulled a crumpled paper from a breast pocket. "Here, Major, take a gander at this. It was under a rock in the middle of the road where somebody was sure to find it. Look at it," he said, handing it over.

Thornburgh perused the paper and handed it to Collins. It was a crude pencil sketch and appeared to portray dead soldiers.

"Fear not, Mr. Henry," the major said. "We have a plan. Now, join us for some supper."

Private O'Malley provided plates of venison stew, having shot two mule deer the day before. After they were finished, several of the men took out their pipes or accepted cigars from the orderly. Collins chose his pipe and smoked quietly while listening to the conversation of the others. Mostly, it revolved around military engagements with Indians and the Little Big Horn inevitably arose as a subject. He was grateful for the interruption caused by the arrival of Charles Lowry.

"Mr. Lowry, where have you been?" Thornburgh asked the man disapprovingly.

"Well," Lowry said, taking a seat, "I am sorry to say I drank a bit of whiskey and did some gambling on the road south. I finally got to the agency last night."

"And what is the state of affairs with Mr. Meeker?"

"I must report he is in quite a lather, there being only a few men folk there to protect the women and children. All the Indian squaws and babies have disappeared and the bucks are war dancing. They claimed they would burn the agency and murder old Meeker for calling in the troops. I calmed them down and they swore they would not do nothin' for now."

Shavano appeared out of the darkness and squatted next to Collins. Major Thornburgh finished his cigar, then adopted an official air.

"Orderly!" he called.

Chapter 43

O'Malley materialized out of the tent.

"Call the officers to a meeting immediately."

"Yes sir," the boy said and trotted into the darkness.

"Mr. Collins?"

C.W. looked up.

"I believe your Indian will make the officers nervous," the major told him.

"He is not 'my' Indian, Major. What exactly are you saying?"

"I will meet you in camp," Shavano said and walked away.

"I apologize, Mr. Collins, but a Ute war chief at an officer staff meeting would not be well received."

Collins tamped his pipe with a finger. "I take your point," was all he said.

When the officers had gathered, Captain Payne spoke first. "According to Joe, here," he said, gesturing toward Rankin, "the best place for an ambush is in Coal Creek Canyon. Ute warriors could shoot at us from either side or roll rocks down upon our position. If we ran for it, we would come right out into Jack's own camp there at the southern egress of the canyon."

"What do you suggest, Captain?" Thornburgh asked.

"The men could camp just north of the reservation while you and Lowry and maybe five soldiers ride on down to the agency. Then, after dark, the rest of us could make our way through the canyon and be in striking distance of White River by dawn."

There was a murmur of approval from around the fire. Collins withheld his opinion entirely, although privately he entertained doubts.

"Very well, Captain Payne," the major said, "we will follow your plan. I must now write a letter to Agent Meeker, letting him know we will visit on the morrow with a handful of men, according to his last communiqué. I will also send a request that he meet us on the road so that we will have the lay of the land before arriving to the agency. And tell him that he may bring such chiefs as he deems necessary to prevent an incident at the agency."

The group broke up and C.W. wandered back to his camp. Shavano was not there, so he checked on his animals. He saw that the chief's horses were nearby and wondered where he had gotten to. After building a fire and rolling out his bedroll, he lay looking at the stars. He could not shake his sense of anxiety about the coming day. At last he fell asleep.

44

Collins woke abruptly with a shape looming above him. He sat up and Shavano hunkered down beside him.

"We must go," he said quietly.

"Why?"

"First we must go. Then I will tell you."

They fumbled in the dim light from a cloud covered moon, packing their camp and saddling and loading their horses. Leading their animals past sleepy sentries and easing into the open country beyond to the east, they finally mounted and rode in the direction of Yellow Jacket Pass. As day broke, they stopped and built a small fire to make coffee and fry some bacon. While they were eating, Collins again inquired after the reason for the urgency of their departure.

"On my way back to our camp, I heard a horse moving quietly through the trees near the creek. I followed a rider, not a soldier, toward Major Thornburgh's tent. He slipped by those watching and went on foot to the tent. He was allowed in and I went closer to listen."

"Who was this fellow?"

"I did not learn this, but I heard clearly what he told the officer. He told him that he must take all the soldiers to the reservation at once and attack. He told him he must do this and forget all else. I heard him take out a paper and whatever was written on it impressed Thornburgh into believing him. I could tell that the major did not want to follow these orders and thought this was a bad plan. The other man threatened him with grave trouble, *muy malo*, if he did not do this thing."

"Aw hell," Collins said, removing his hat and rubbing his forehead in frustration. "Where did the man go? Is he still there?"

Shavano shook his head. "He left and went to his horse. I followed him north for some way and he took the White River road toward the *Rio Yampa*."

"We must watch and see what takes place."

They cleaned up, watered their animals at a small spring and found a thick and remote grove of aspens in which to hide their pack animals and gear. Riding north, they caught sight of the line of troops just as they were watering their horses at the last crossing of Milk Creek. Collins and the Ute chief pulled in their horses on a low rise and watched as the column proceeded toward the reservation boundary. It looked to Collins that Lieutenant Cherry, Joe Rankin and three soldiers were about a quarter mile in front of Thornburgh and the rest of the troopers. Far in the rear, they could see the military supply wagons and dust raised by the civilian ox train coming up behind.

Collins shifted in the saddle and watched as the soldiers moved through some cottonwoods.

"Now they are crossing onto the reservation," Shavano said softly. Then he said something to himself in his own language.

Collins glanced at the horizon for a moment and when he looked back at the soldiers, he noticed that Cherry was waving furiously at Thornburgh behind him. He pointed at the long ridge ahead and began waving again. Collins took out his old army-issue field glasses and scanned the ridge. His heart sank. There, lining the ridge top above Cherry's position were around fifty mounted Ute warriors.

"I think they will fight now," Shavano said.

Chapter 44

Joe Rankin rode back toward Major Thornburgh's position, where the officer was hurriedly deploying his troops in the bunches of sagebrush on either side of the road. Rankin and Thornburgh appeared to speak for a moment, then Thornburgh rode out ahead and stopped his horse. He waved his hat and Collins was surprised to see several Utes wave their hats in return. A few of the soldiers waved. Then a veil of surreal tranquility descended and all motion ceased. Collins chewed his lower lip in apprehension as the Indians and the soldiers faced each other in the late morning sunlight and a meadowlark warbled in the distance. He could hear a horse whinny from the rear of the column.

A movement on the ridge caught his eye and he observed that two warriors had dismounted and were coming slowly down the side of the slope toward Lieutenant Cherry's position. C.W. began to breathe again, believing a parlay was forthcoming. Cherry also dismounted and began walking in their direction, waving his hat again. Just at that instant, someone off to the west imprudently discharged his weapon and the moment exploded into indescribable chaos and irretrievable consequences.

Cursing ineffectively from his lookout, Collins watched as Major Thornburgh pulled his revolver, turned his horse and rode back toward the cottonwoods, presumably to bring up the rest of the troops. A shot rang out from a large caliber rifle and the major dropped to the ground. His body thrashed about haphazardly then became still. His horse bolted into the trees.

Collins sat on Ulysses, momentarily stunned by the events unfolding before him. One of the mules on Private O'Malley's ambulance crumpled in its harness. Captain Payne fell from the saddle as his horse was shot out from under him. A Ute warrior charging through the tall grasses suddenly toppled from his pony, clutching his chest. The soldiers held their own in the brush on either side of the road and Captain Payne was suddenly on his feet and taking command. He sent a rider toward the supply wagons and C.W. figured he was sending for more ammunition. The soldiers were fighting their way back north. Nightmarish cries and billows of dust and gun smoke accompanied the ascending conflict.

Shavano cuffed C.W. on the shoulder. "We must go," he said.

"Where?" Collins asked, coming back to himself.

"You can do no good here, but if we stop further mischief at White River, the Utes may not be blamed for what has happened here today."

He immediately saw the wisdom in this. They turned their horses and rode at full gallop back for their pack animals. It was midafternoon when they headed down out of the pass toward the White River Agency. Collins was fully aware that another catastrophe might lie before them.

45

"It was the man."

"What?" Collins asked, looking over at his companion.

They were riding through the bottom end of a narrow canyon. It was oddly quiet.

"The shot that was fired…I saw who fired it. It was the *Anglo* who was at Thornburgh's tent last night."

"I thought you said he headed north?"

"He did. I followed. He must have known I followed, then waited and doubled back."

Collins squinted in perplexity. "There was much confusion. How could you identify him?"

"The man wore black and white checked pants. They were curious. When a rider skirted the soldiers along the base of the ridge and dismounted by a big rock, I saw them again. It was from there that the shot was fired."

"Then the possibility of a peaceful resolution was willfully destroyed. Did you see where he went?"

"I looked, but could not see with the dust raised."

"Damn!" Collins said, shaking his head. "I have been outmaneuvered in every possible way."

"We will do what we can at the agency."

Collins sincerely desired that all was well with Meeker and his family, not because he bore them any particular good will, but for the sake of the Indians. They passed by Captain Jack's farm. A few horses grazed about, but otherwise there were no signs of activity or any people. They followed the road along the benchland above White

River and came upon a smoking wagon approximately five miles from the agency headquarters. Dismounting, Collins went over to investigate. Lying nearby were the bodies of an old man and an adolescent boy. They had not been brutalized other than having been shot and killed. Collins turned away from the tragic scene.

"This does not bode well," he told Shavano as he swung into his saddle. Someone else would have to bury these men.

"No. I think it is bad. I think we are too late."

Riding at a fast trot now, they came upon another body farther on. Collins recognized Wilmer Eskridge. They sat on their horses and contemplated the corpse. Ulysses danced around, not liking the smell of blood.

"This is the man who took a message to Meeker for Thornburgh," Shavano said.

"Yes." Collins nudged his horse forward, categorically uneager to survey what might lie ahead.

As they drew nearer to the White River Agency, they could see billows of smoke in the golden light of near sunset. Collins glimpsed a flag fluttering in the soft breeze. Riding into the agency, they came upon a field of devastation. Almost every building smoldered and some structures were still lit with flames. Every article of white manufacture lay strewn about; smashed or tossed as refuse in contempt. Ubiquitously there was evidence of rage and resentment, no doubt brought about by Meeker and his unwavering commitment to dismantling the Utes and their way of life.

In deep silence of foreboding, the two men dismounted and tied their animals away from the fires. Returning on foot, they made their way toward Meeker's house. It still burned furiously on one side and something made a small explosion within the wreckage of the building. Probably a can or jar, Collins thought absently, as he scanned the area for signs of life.

"Here," said Shavano, pointing at something a short

distance away.

Collins walked over and looked. The remains of two men lay close to each other and he was able to identify Price, the Kansas blacksmith, as one of them. The other man was rather young. Again, both were shot, but not scalped, mutilated or stripped of clothing. There had been swift dispatch in fury and nothing more.

"These things were done in haste," Shavano said.

"Yes."

They looked around and found that the storehouse was not burned. The ground surrounding the building was covered in flour and flour sacks, torn open in anger and scattered. Just inside the doorway lay another white man, flour sacks inexplicably clutched to his breast. Brain matter lay in clumps beside his exploded head. Not far away, lay the bodies of three more men, but none of them was Meeker. One seemed quite young and was crowned with blonde curly hair. Collins thought fleetingly of a mother, bereft of this golden boy.

Shavano called and C.W. went to see what further tribulation he had discovered. In the dirt at the Indian's feet lay Nathan Meeker, bastion of virtue, utopian philosopher and stalwart defender of benevolent civilization. Bizarre in nudity, the bruised and bloodied dead man lay upon his back with gray eyes staring blindly at the open sky. Looped about his throat was a heavy chain, used for skidding logs. He had apparently been dragged a few passes about the compound. What appeared to be a stave from a barrel had been ruthlessly jammed down the man's throat.

C.W. hoped that this final contemptuous act had been committed *post mortem.* Whatever fool that Meeker had been, he did not deserve to be wantonly tortured. Perhaps the poor man had been dispatched prior to any of the degradations to which his body had been subjected. What looked to be a bullet wound to the side of his head spoke to this.

" 'The baseless fabric of this vision, the cloud-capp'd towers, the gorgeous palaces, the solemn temples...yea, all which it inherit, shall dissolve,' " he quoted faintly, more to the corpse than to himself. Shavano took his arm and led him away.

The sun was sinking and they failed to find sign of any of the women. They made quick work of searching the rest of the agency grounds and found the milk house intact and nothing more except some household items scattered across a field to the south and the tracks of many horses following the river eastward.

"They are heading for the *Rio Blanco* ford and one of the old camps to the south of here. They must have the women. They are moving swiftly and we should not try to catch them. They will be afraid of what they have done and will be very dangerous."

"What is there I can do now?" C.W. asked, at a complete loss. "What can we do to save your people from the fate they have made for themselves?"

"We must try to help save the women. We must get Ouray to come and you must get a message to Schurz and Jocknick. If the women are harmed or killed, the whites of Colorado will take their revenge on every Ute man, woman and child. We must stop this thing before it happens."

Collins placed his hand upon Shavano's shoulder and looked him in the eyes. "We must try, my friend. We will try."

The Indian nodded. "*Bueno.*"

Night had fallen and the embers of the agency buildings flared eerily in a faint breeze, as if from the kindling of phantom lamps. Ghosts will walk here, C.W. thought morbidly, as they turned away from the scene of pathos and annihilation. Such is the end of most utopian ideals.

46

The glow of a campfire caught C.W.'s attention as they went to retrieve their animals. It was west along White River and hidden in the brush, but the moon had not yet risen and the light pierced dense shrubbery to reveal itself. He placed a hand on Shavano's arm and gestured silence, then pointed to the flickering blaze in the trees ahead.

Together, they stealthily approached to a place where they could observe the camp. Sitting alone on a wooden chair, no doubt pilfered from an agency building, was a white man in civilian clothing. Collins at once descried the white and black checked pants as described by Shavano. Making certain the man was indeed alone, they drew their revolvers and walked into the circle of firelight.

"Hello friends," the fellow said coolly, as if expecting them. "Your approach was duly proclaimed by the snapping of dry shrubbery."

"Was it now?" Collins asked. "And the presence of angry Ute warriors in the area gives you no pause?"

"They are long gone. I have been monitoring their shenanigans. They have the women and the spoils of their depredations. Now, they have gone off to their cherished mountain ranges and will be punished in due course. The denizens of Colorado will insist upon it." The man examined Collins and Shavano. "Yet here is a curious duo... What can your presence connote in this place of tragedy and comeuppance?"

Collins waved the barrel of his Colt .45 at the man. "I believe we will be asking the questions. Kindly remove your revolver from its holster."

"You may ask whatever you please," said the man with aplomb, complying with the request and gently tossing the pistol upon the ground some distance from his feet. "But first, I must insist you take a seat and partake of hot coffee," he added, waving his hand toward the pot near the fire. He possessed a slightly epicene and Southern style of expression that was vaguely disagreeable. Collins found him oddly reptilian in his mannerisms.

"No, I think not," he said with equal nonchalance. "I desire to know who has hired you to effect mayhem and incite conflict."

The man did not pretend to misunderstand. "You cannot guess? Why after Cañon City, I felt certain you would assign blame to correct parties."

"Mears," C.W. said, the truth dawning upon him.

"I beg your pardon?" the man asked, reaching into his inside jacket pocket. Shavano took a step closer. "Just a cigar, my friend. Might I offer you one?"

"Otto Mears, the Russian." Collins said to clarify his meaning.

"Oh quite," the stranger said and smiled widely. "No cigar?" he asked in feigned disappointment. "Ah well."

"What of Pitkin, Teller and Chaffee? Are they part of this?"

"Unquestionably. The actual and vigorous strategist is, however, William Vickers. The man is a patent marvel. He was astute enough to recognize my own peculiar gifts and recommend me."

"What might your talents encompass?" Collins asked in curiosity.

"I have no conscience, pure and simple," the man said, waving his hand dismissively. "This allows me to perform the most unspeakable acts, as witnessed by the precipitation of violent engagement on this very morning. Heavens, I actually thought for a moment that they were all going to commence glad handing one another. How disastrous that would have been."

"What was the letter you gave Major Thornburgh?" Shavano asked.

"So it was you who shadowed me?" the man asked artfully. "Well, I am afraid the letter's provenance and contents must remain inviolate...even under threat of physical torture. You see, its author insisted I not only deliver the message but take care of poor Thornburgh as well. Hell of a shot."

C.W. took a moment to absorb his meaning, truly offended by the outright murder of the principled young officer. "Then what of this tragedy hard by?" he asked quietly.

"Well..." The fellow smiled slyly. "I may have visited a few of the more easily influenced young men earlier in the week. I may have supplied some whiskey and incited them to thoughts of barbarity and turpitude. One young man seemed absolutely smitten with our Josie Meeker. My goodness, when I carry word of the furious rapine of those poor females, especially that of the aging wife of the noble and martyred Nathan Meeker, back to the saloons and drawing rooms of Denver, the population will be moved decisively toward the eviction of all savages from the state of Colorado. *Et la*, my work will be achieved. *Veni, vidi, vici.*"

"Enough of this," Shavano finally said and moved threateningly toward the man.

"I quite agree," Collins concurred. "We will take you with us and let you reveal the specifics of your employment to the proper authorities...outside the boundaries of Colorado, I might add."

The man sprang to his feet and produced an ugly little derringer from a pocket. "I think not, dear friends. I have much yet to accomplish."

Without hesitation and in one fluid motion, Collins raised his revolver and shot the scoundrel. Shavano glanced at him in surprise as the man dropped to the ground. He writhed in agony and expounded the vilest curses, out of character with the obsequious temperament of earlier discourse. Eventually he wore out and lay in subdued distress.

"He will not now be aggravating the situation with his lies," C.W. told his companion, not caring if the man was dead or not.

He occupied himself reloading the .45 and the Indian stepped aside to throw dirt on the fire. There was a rustle of vegetation and they turned to see that the man had disappeared into the surrounding thick undergrowth. His revolver had vanished with him.

"Let him go," Shavano said. "We have no time to search. We must get to the Uncompahgre agency in all speed."

"He will not survive," C.W. told him. "I shot him in the belly, thereby securing him a most excruciating and predictable end."

Moving quickly through the trees back to their horses, ever vigilant against an ambush from the wounded stranger, they departed the area with relief. They rode all night in the glow of a nearly full moon, heading west then south along Piceance Creek and out into the open country of Piceance Basin. Finally, by late morning, neither man nor beast could continue and they were forced to make camp and rest.

47

Having ridden hard, skirting the Grand Mesa and fording the Gunnison River, quite low due to the ongoing drought, Collins and Shavano rode into Ouray's farm late on the second day after the disaster at the White River Agency. Lamps burned within the Ute chief's house, in spite of the advanced hour. They unsaddled and turned their exhausted animals loose to graze. They then approached the adobe building, hearing agitated voices as they drew near. Collins knocked.

The door was opened by Henry Jim. He saw Shavano and motioned them both to come in. Chipeta, Ouray, another Ute man and Jane sat on various items of furniture in the parlor. They ceased speaking and looked up in surprise.

"Mr. Collins," Ouray said. "Why are you here?"

"There has been a calamity on the White River."

"We know. Henry Jim has told us. It is terrible news for my people."

"Yes, it is," Shavano agreed. "We must get the women back."

"How will we do this?" Ouray asked.

"You must send a message. Tell Nicaagat, Colorow and the others to stop fighting," Shavano answered. "Find out who were the ones that did the deed at the agency. We need to separate them out from the warriors who are fighting the soldiers."

"Yes," Ouray said, nodding. "I see the wisdom in this.

The fight on Milk Creek is a fight between warriors. Unlike the useless slaughter on the agency.”

“It was provoked by whites all the same,” Jane said bitterly.

The other Ute man in the room spoke to her in his own language.

“That is *Sapovanero*, Chipeta’s brother,” Shavano told C.W. in muted tones.

“How bad is this thing, Mr. Collins?” Jane asked.

“As bad as could be,” he answered. “We discovered that the battle was incited by a hired agent of white politicians. He willfully fired the shot that precipitated the battle. He also killed Major Thornburgh. Until then, it looked as if there might have been a peaceful resolution.” Ouray, Chipeta and Sapovanero had stopped conversing to listen to Collins. “We saw the agency,” he added.

“I was there,” Henry Jim told him. “It will not look good for us.”

“The *maricat’z* will be very angry when they find Nick’s body,” Ouray said.

“The *maricat’z*…the whites,” Shavano translated for Collins. “Yes, there will be lots of trouble, but even more if those women are killed or harmed. Are they still alive?” he asked Henry Jim.

“They were last I saw. They were in the summer camp near Piceance Creek. The old Meeker woman was slightly injured and was driving everyone crazy with her howling. She saw Nick’s dead body. She is with *Quinkent.* He will not harm her.”

“What of Josephine, the daughter?” Collins asked the young man.

“She was angry and bossy, as usual…like we were still under her father’s authority at the agency. *Pursune* has her and is giving her presents. Perhaps this will help.”

“Perhaps,” Shavano said. “I doubt it.”

“Do you have thoughts? Can you help?” Chipeta asked

Collins. It took a moment for him to register that she had spoken to him in English.

Ouray gave her a stern glance. "Please do not tell that my woman speaks your language," he requested.

"No, of course I will not."

"He will not," Shavano reassured the chief.

Collins gave him an appraising look and Shavano shrugged.

"Can you help?" Chipeta asked again.

"I will try. So far, my efforts have not achieved much," he said ruefully. "I have not had communication with anyone for many days. I do not know how the situation stands in Denver or with Secretary Schurz."

"We will go to Agent Stanley in the morning," Ouray said. "We will find out what he has heard."

"Agent Stanley? What happened to Agent Wheeler?" Collins asked.

"He was replaced. There must be many men who wish to be agents to the Indian."

"So they can steal from us," Jane said. "I will travel up to the camp where they hold the women," she added. "I will see if we are better off keeping them alive or killing them, so they cannot lie about their treatment."

Chipeta spoke to her in the Ute language.

"My woman says Jane must not say such things, but I think she may be correct," Ouray said.

Collins shook his head. "I cannot say what is best, but it would be good for Jane to go and find out what is happening there. If the women say they have been outraged, it could go very badly for the Ute people."

"It is what the whites will want to hear," Jane said in disdain. "Why would any Ute man touch those women? Even my useless Pauvitz could not drink enough whiskey to want to touch them in that way."

"Yes, the whites will be hungry for news of outrage and abuse," Shavano agreed.

"If it is possible, we must keep these inventions from being printed in the newspapers," Collins said. "I cannot say I am hopeful about this."

"The whites will write what they want," Jane said. "Nick always told lies and they were put in newspapers."

Chipeta left the room and returned with a graniteware coffeepot. She passed out cups and poured coffee. There was a lull in conversation.

"How did the agency look to you?" Ouray finally asked Collins in a worried manner. "I have Henry Jim's word, but you are white. How did it look?" he asked again.

"Meeker's body was the worst of it. Everyone else appeared to have been killed outright. No one was mutilated except for the agent."

"That was the young men," Henry Jim explained. "They had sport with Nick's corpse."

Ouray sighed. "It will make it bad, this thing happening to Meeker. I think he was much liked by the powerful white men of Colorado."

"Or they thought he was silly and something to be toyed with," Jane said.

"That is more correct, I fear," Collins told her. "But he will be even more useful to them now he is dead. They have a martyr for their cause."

"Martyr?" Chipeta asked.

"A person who has sacrificed themselves for something," Shavano told her. "The Spanish and whites love their *santos*."

"Yes," Ouray said. "Nick will be a martyr. And that will be *muy malo* for my people." He stood. "It is late. We can do no more talking around and around this thing. We will sleep and talk again at first light."

Shavano and Collins came to their feet as well. "We will camp," C.W. said.

"Come for food in the dawn," Ouray said. "We will talk more and see what we can decide."

Collins followed Shavano into the night. The moon illuminated their way. Without words, the two men checked on their animals, rolled out their bedding and fell asleep in exhaustion. Collins' last thought was that he was again adrift in the harried waters of Indian peoples. It was a questionable way to make one's livelihood and a distressing one, at that.

BATTLE AT MILK CREEK

48

"Jane left early for the north," Ouray said, wiping his plate with a piece of tortilla. "She was eager to find out about the women and discover if they can be a threat."

Chipeta set her cup down loudly. "She must not harm them."

"It may be best if they were out of the way," Shavano said. He had left the table and was standing near the door, leaning against the wall.

"I have sent Henry Jim to Agent Stanley to see what he has heard. We must find out what the whites are saying," Ouray told them.

"Do you think the news could have reached them by now?" Chipeta asked Collins.

"It depends. If someone got back to send a telegram, then the whole world knows," he answered.

They finished breakfast and Chipeta began clearing the table. The men took out pipes and Collins shared his dwindling supply of tobacco. They smoked in silence, deep in thought. After a while, someone knocked at the door and Shavano opened it.

"Agent Stanley," Ouray said, standing up from the table.

Henry Jim came in behind the agitated white man. The agent wore a crumpled suit. He removed his bowler hat and took the seat offered by Ouray. Henry Jim went to stand beside Shavano.

"This is terrible....terrible," Stanley said in potent dismay, nervously drumming his fingers on the table.

"What have you heard?" Collins asked.

"Who in the hell are you?" the agent asked, noticing him for the first time.

"This is Mr. Collins. He is a special agent for Secretary Schurz," Ouray answered.

"Truly? How did you get here so swiftly?"

"I was already here. It is a long story. We need to know what is being said about the conflict up north," Collins told him.

"A man named Rankin made a heroic ride to Rawlins. He reported that Major Thornburgh and several soldiers have been killed or wounded by Ute warriors on Milk Creek. The battle continues and many settlers fear an Indian uprising."

"There is no uprising," Ouray said. "The soldiers came onto the reservation when they had given assurances they would not. The Ute warriors are defending their people."

"What of the agency and Mr. Meeker?" Stanley asked.

"We know nothing," Collins said quickly. Rankin could not possibly know of the disaster at the agency, he thought, and therefore could not have carried the news. He noticed Shavano watching him carefully.

Chipeta brought Stanley a cup of coffee.

"What do you propose to do?" C.W. asked the agent.

"We need to send a message north to tell the White River Utes to stop fighting," Stanley told Ouray. "Can you send a message to your people?"

"Yes. Do you also wish to send a message?"

"I will send young Brady with an official request from the Indian Department that they cease hostilities. Can you send some warriors to give my man protection?"

"I will choose fifteen warriors. I will also send Henry Jim with a message to my people."

Chipeta spoke.

"My woman says she is very sorry this has happened."

"We may all be quite sorry before too long," the agent

said punctiliously. He finished his coffee and stood. "I will return to the agency and send Joseph Brady here to you with my message," he said to Ouray. "Send him north as quickly as possible."

"I will do so," the chief said.

Collins thought Ouray appeared quite fatigued and grey with illness. The agent placed his hat upon his head and took his leave.

"*Gracias*," Ouray said to Collins, after the agent had left.

"For what, pray?"

"For withholding your news of the agency," Shavano answered.

"What would that have served?" C.W. turned to Ouray. "What shall you tell the people up north? Can you convince them to stop fighting the soldiers?"

"I will send a very strong message. I will say that all hostilities cease against the whites." He looked over at Henry Jim. "You must go and find *Sapovanero*. You must both go and be very strong in relating my message to those holding the women."

The young man nodded and left the house.

"What will you do now?" Shavano asked Collins.

"Will you go to see Charles Adams?" Ouray asked. "He is our friend and might lend us aid in this terrible time."

"I will go to Denver. I must find Gustavus Jocknick," Collins answered.

"Young Sidney's father."

"Yes. And perhaps I can find Schurz in Denver. I heard he was there."

"That would be most beneficial. Mr. Schurz can help us greatly," Ouray said, nodding.

"I will wait here," Shavano told him. "You will come back to us."

"Of course. I leave my horse and mule here with you, that way you will know." He turned to Ouray. "May I borrow a pony to ride south to catch the stagecoach?"

"We will take you in our wagon," Chipeta told him. "We will be pleased to do so."

49

The return stagecoach journey from the town of Ouray to Alamosa was no less harrowing or unpleasant as the original expedition. Thirty-four long hours later, Collins waited impatiently for the eastward train of the D&RG railroad, tormented by an agitation born of dire urgency. He found he was less tolerant than ever of the inanities of his fellow white travelers, crowded together near the depot. They were full of news of the battle on Milk Creek and gleefully recounted fictional grotesqueries. C.W. was unwillingly privy to all the wrath and odium they could muster for the Utes. It was with great relief that he boarded a railway carriage and escaped into private reverie.

The engine labored toward the top of La Veta Pass, sending a hail of black cinders and clouds of smoke past the carriage, momentarily obliterating the scenery of thick timber, rock walls, steep precipices and the occasional bear. Collins turned back to the newspaper in his lap. Some fellow named Thomas Fulton Dawson was apparently reporting every piece of tripe expressed by anyone who cared to see his name in print. C.W. became enraged by the destructive propaganda filling the pages, sealing the destiny of the Ute people.

There was also, reproduced in the newspaper, a telegram sent to Governor Pitkin from Laramie, written by one Colonel Downey, a delegate from Wyoming Territory to Washington D.C. In the communiqué, Downey dramatically requested that Pitkin take "prompt action as will protect your people and result in giving the war department control of the savages." Of course, thought Collins, the War Department will make use of the event to revive their goal of gaining authority over the Indian Bureau.

Asleep when the train finally pulled into Pueblo, Collins awoke as several travelers disembarked and others boarded. He pulled his collar up against the chill of autumn that crept into the railway car. Ignoring attempts at idle conversation, authored by a neighboring passenger, he opened another copy of the *Denver Tribune*, purchased prior to boarding the train in Alamosa. The publication contained an auxiliary abundance of invective directed toward the Indians, masquerading as verisimilitude. Collins was deeply disheartened as he read one particular passage that declared, "...the governor's office is besieged by sturdy old pioneers and hot-blooded young men offering their services to the State in defense of their homes and to exterminate the savage horde."

Collins could well imagine local militias gathering in fervor, the drunkards banding together in saloons, as they had done prior to the slaughter at Sand Creek. Hatred and sanctimony would be more potent than cheap whisky, however, and would serve as heady fuel to authorize contemptible actions. Somehow, throughout human history, stupidity and cruelty went hand in hand. He recalled a quote from Shakespeare. "Wisdom and goodness to the vile seem vile."

During a stop in Colorado Springs, he purchased updated news in the *Colorado Springs Gazette.* Inside the newspaper, he found an editorial expressing the opinion that Pitkin was filled with "political vapors" and ambition regarding the Ute uprising. To illustrate this, the *Gazette* printed a statement from the governor in which Pitkin declared that the Utes should be obliterated, if the U.S. government did not remove them from Colorado. He claimed he could raise enough men in twenty-four hours to not only protect settlers but reimburse the expense of the endeavor by opening up millions of acres to white settlement and mining.

The editorial went on to state that one provoked attack on military forces, incited by unwarranted trespass upon reservation lands, did not constitute a general uprising. In addition, the journalist expressed the view that Ouray bore no blame in any manner. Collins was astonished that someone would hazard such a contrary viewpoint in the midst of a storm of patriotic vitriol. It was reassuring to find there were at least a few residents of Colorado who were not blinded by bigotry.

His train arrived in Denver after dark. C.W. gathered his carpetbag and ream of newspapers and stepped off into a bustle of pedestrians and news boys barking sensational headlines. He felt a light tap upon his shoulder and turned to see Gustavus Jocknick.

"You received my telegram," Collins said.

"I did. Let us have supper." Jocknick appeared weary and dejected.

"I need to find a room."

"I have booked one for you at the American House. We will take your bag there and then dine."

Later, seated in a private dining room in the back of a nondescript Chinese restaurant, Jocknick sipped jasmine tea and examined Collins pointedly.

"Yes, I know," C.W. said.

"What do you know?"

"I have failed miserably."

"On the contrary," Jocknick said. "You made a valiant attempt to thwart this calamity."

"To what end?" Collins said dispiritedly.

Jocknick did not answer, but deftly applied chopsticks to a bowl of sliced pork. After a while, he asked, "What of Meeker? Did you see him? Reports are only now filtering through of terrible atrocities committed at White River."

"No atrocities except for the brutal handling of Meeker's corpse." Collins swirled the tea in his cup. "Is Secretary Schurz still in Denver? Will I be able to speak with him?"

"Alas, he departed prior to the news of the disaster. He had a scheduled speech in Indian Territory. He could not tarry." Jocknick regarded him sadly. "Do not place too much store in Mr. Schurz' abilities to intervene in this. He must bend to compelling political maelstroms."

Collins stared at him in disbelief. "You do not...you cannot mean it. He *must* intervene. He sent me on this ill-fated mission. The future of the Ute people depends upon it."

"Do not be so naïve, Mr. Collins," Jocknick said, dabbing his elaborate moustache. "I was privy to many meetings that took place here in Denver earlier this month. Mr. Jay Gould was present for one of them."

"The railroad magnate?"

"Quite...he has promised to invest millions in railroad expansion here in Colorado."

"If the Utes are forced out," Collins said almost inaudibly.

Jocknick nodded and gave him a sympathetic look. "I am not unaffected by the injustice of all this, Mr. Collins."

"You led me to believe that we could avert disaster. You..." C.W. took a deep breath and regained his composure. "Tell me more of these meetings."

"Otto Mears was here for a couple of days. He had clandestine meetings with Secretary Schurz and, of course, Governor Pitkin. I did not attend any of these meetings and, therefore, cannot apprise you of their subject matter. I was, however, witness to Adams, Schurz and the Secretary of the German Legation, a man called Count Donhöff, happily reminiscing about the fatherland. The German vote is pivotal to American politics, you know."

"How delightful."

"Mr. Schurz was candid with all of us that a Ute conflict would probably result in the removal of Hayes from the

1880 presidential ticket. This, of course, would result in *his* removal as well. The Grant Republicans would see to it."

"I do not give a tinker's damn about the 1880 presidential ticket. I care what happens to my friends waiting for Schurz to come to their aid."

"I learned long ago," Jocknick said with a fatherly air, "that men need to remain in power in order to effect good. This is a complex situation for Mr. Schurz."

Collins rested his forehead in his hand, overwhelmed by a sense of futility. "It is vastly more difficult for the Utes."

"What of the women? Did you see them?"

"Not afterward. Ouray was intending to get them back, if possible."

The waiter brought more rice and tea. Collins thanked him in Mandarin, having learned some of the language in San Francisco.

"What of the fighting on Milk Creek?" he asked Jocknick.

"It has ceased. General Merritt from Fort D. A. Russell has taken control of the area and the Utes have scattered. Merritt is now focused on rescuing the captives."

"Then it is now a race to get the women back before the soldiers catch up with the White River Utes."

Jocknick nodded. "I must persuade Mr. Schurz to send Adams. He is the best choice for this commission. The Utes know and trust him."

"Yes. That is the impression I have gotten. I will go as well."

"I have been authorized to make final payment and release you from employment. Your term of service is ended."

"But I will not depart. There may be more I can do."

Jocknick shook his head. "Mr. Collins, there is nothing left but the housekeeping."

"I had not thought you to be so very cynical when first we met."

"Perhaps I am not...but time spent in our nation's capital, primarily concerned in Indian affairs, has produced decided acquiescence. There is no future for the Utes in Colorado now. Their insurrection and Mr. Gould's proposed investment have irrevocably decided their fate. Otto Mears, Vickers, Pitkin and company have done their worst."

"I am well aware of this. But I must return to lend assistance all the same."

"So be it, but I must needs remunerate you for your services. After which, you will no longer be under the auspices of the Department of the Interior." Jocknick raised an eyebrow and considered him. "Mr. Collins, you will be on your own and subject to whatever might befall you. Your friendship with the Indians may lead you into mishap."

"I understand," Collins said. It would not be the first time, he thought.

50

The next day, Jocknick found him at his hotel and delivered a telegram from Secretary Schurz. It informed Collins that he had a new commission to assist Adams in resolving the hostage dilemma. The communication relieved some of his anxiety in regard to his future plans. Collins suspected that Jocknick had aided his cause with the Secretary of the Interior, despite earlier pessimistic and jaundiced declarations.

On the eve of departure for the Uncompahgre Agency, they met Adams at the railroad terminal in Denver and then proceeded to join the celebrated Count August Donhöff for supper, according to Adams' wishes. In the midst of their repast, the count pleaded most obstinately to be allowed to accompany them, citing his friendship with Schurz as unassailable justification. How this qualified him to attach himself to an expedition bound for a potentially incendiary climax of events, C.W. could not fathom. Against common sense and Collins' firmly expressed views to the contrary, the count was accepted as a traveling companion by Adams. Even the reticent Jocknick articulated concern that if the count happened to be killed, it might incite an international incident. Adams remained intractable in the matter.

"I am certain that Mr. Schurz would want us to extend all courtesies to his friend," Adams told them.

"I will not be killed," the count stated. "It is an impossibility."

"How is that?" Collins asked, in spite of himself.

"I have been in two wars. I have been in danger and nichts ist passiert. I live a charmed life, you see."

Collins did not care for Count Donhöff. Although pleased to be imminently departing Denver, he did not delight in the count's flagrant anticipation of adventure and excitement. Adams appeared to be quite serious regarding his special appointment from Schurz and the responsibility of rescuing the three women who yet remained in captivity. Donhöff, on the other hand, virtually gamboled about like a small boy in the belief that he might encounter wild Indians and, perhaps, find the opportunity to shoot one of them. To make matters worse, the man was habitually and conspicuously attired in a green velvet jacket and hunting cap, both adorned with the family crest.

Upon departing Charpiot's Restaurant and Hotel, with its elegant ambiance and delectable fare, they took their leave of Count Donhöff. Adams, Collins and Jocknick proceeded as a group to an appointment at Governor Pitkin's home. Adams had been instructed to inform him of Schurz' plans, as well as garner an agreement to curb his campaign of political propaganda until the rescue had been effected. A servant answered their knock and ushered them into a parlor that bespoke of vast wealth and an intention to brazenly display its magnitude.

Pitkin entered the room in a smoking jacket and invited the company to take a seat. C.W. chose a chair off to the side, hoping to observe the man in relative anonymity. They were not offered any type of refreshment. The governor sat down in a leather covered Morris chair by the door. Collins wondered if he planned a speedy exit.

"So, Mr. Adams, what is the nature of this visit?" he asked, puffing on a large cigar.

"Secretary Schurz has asked me to inform you of my mission into Ute lands to rescue the Meeker captives."

"And who is sending you?"

"Why, Secretary Schurz of course. We hope to prevent harm to the women."

Pitkin smiled. "Surely it is too late for that," he said mordantly.

Jocknick spoke up. "We do not know that at all. Many of the Ute people have shown themselves to be trustworthy."

The governor eyed him with incivility. "Ah yes, Mr. Jocknick. It is well known that you are a great champion of the red man. Well, they have shown their savagery now and the good citizens of Colorado will not stand for their carnage and treachery. Ouray even sent a telegram insisting he was not party to the incident, but no one believes him. It will not make any difference, at any rate."

"Come, come, Mr. Pitkin," Adams said, "there surely remains the possibility of resolution. Secretary Schurz felt it was only courteous to apprise you, the governor of this great state, of our purpose. He also wanted me to ask if you would refrain from inflammatory rhetoric while we attempt a peaceful outcome to this predicament."

Pitkin laughed outright. "Why would I do that?" he asked. "And why would Schurz believe I cared a whit for your sad little escapade? If you are killed, I suppose it would strengthen my cause of having all the Utes exterminated. I clearly envision the future of this state and it does not encompass the continued residence of godless heathens. I will be making the most of the situation. Did you actually believe all this was some inopportune accident?"

"I know it was not," Collins said quietly.

The governor turned to look at him for the first time. "Pray, who are you and what in blazes could you possibly know?"

C.W. steadily returned his gaze. "I know a fair amount." There was a momentary unspoken challenge between the two men and Collins would have gladly answered it.

Pitkin finally averted his eyes and rose from his chair. "I think we have said all we need to say. Please leave. I care not what Schurz or any of his bootlickers here in Colorado have planned. The Utes are finished. And I take no interest in those idiotic Meeker women. Do as you will." He left the room. His servant returned in short order to show them out.

The meeting had been fortuitously brief, but long enough for Collins to have formed a decisive opinion of the governor. He had found the man to be infinitely more offensive than he could have anticipated prior to the encounter. Compassionless and completely motivated by political gain, Pitkin had seemed to exhaust the room of light and air.

"This was a pointless endeavor from the outset," C.W. said to the other two men as they walked away from the mansion. "You were correct, Mr. Jocknick, the Ute people were never going to survive men like Pitkin."

"*Ja*, but we had to try," Adams said. "They have been struggling to keep their homeland for many years. If we can but save the women, perhaps Carl may still intervene on their behalf."

"I am going to Washington," Jocknick announced. "I can do nothing here in Denver."

"Hopefully you can encourage Schurz to eschew politics and fulfill his duty to the Utes?" Collins asked.

He could see Jocknick shaking his head in the dim light of a street lamp. "I will do what I can and call in many favors. I do not know what can come of it."

They retreated into silence and went their separate ways.

The next day, Collins and Adams were met by Donhöff and they boarded the train to Alamosa. By this time, Collins had seen enough of Colorado to last him a lifetime. They arranged their luggage and settled into the railway carriage. C.W. had purchased a few newspapers and a

Harper's Weekly so he would not have to converse much with the Prussian count. Adams and Donhöff spoke mostly in German and Collins was content to withdraw into a refuge of the printed word.

The train had just pulled out of Pueblo when Adams asked, "I did not have the opportunity to inquire...did you discover hired agents creating mischief for the Indians? Gustavus hinted at something to that effect."

C.W. was engrossed in an article about Ulysses S. Grant in San Francisco.

"Mr. Collins?"

He looked up. "My apologies. You asked me a question?"

"*Ja.* I was wondering...did you encounter information about agents causing difficulties for the Utes?"

"I did indeed. One of these villains actually precipitated the battle on Milk Creek. He also assassinated the commanding officer."

"I had not heard this," the big German said incredulously. "How could you possess such information?"

Collins raised his eyebrows. "I spoke to him. I shot him."

Count Donhöff had been listening. "What do you mean you shot him?"

"I mean I gut shot him and left him for dead."

The count looked at him pensively, as if seeing him in a new light.

"Were there others?" Adams asked.

"That I shot?"

Adams chuckled. "*Nein.* Others who were committing acts against the Utahs."

"Shavano and I cut the trail of a gang of them. We captured one and questioned him."

"Questioned?" Donhöff asked.

"Frankly, we tortured him," Collins told him. "But we were pressed for time."

"What did he tell you?"

"Enough for us to learn they were paid off by a prominent politician, a 'slick' talking fellow and a small foreigner. I believe that our captive was referring to Pitkin, Vickers and Mears. It was all he had to tell."

"Did you shoot him too?" the count asked.

C.W. just shook his head.

"And you really are convinced that Otto Mears is one of the primary forces behind the recent catastrophe?" Adams asked.

"Absolutely. He is a devious fellow and has been making substantial profits from his involvement in all of the Utes' affairs. Now it behooves him to be shed of them. He is wholly ambition and avarice."

"*Scheisse.* I thought him a friend to me as well as the Ute people."

"Sidney Jocknick even implied that Mears helped Alferd Packer escape from the Saguache jail. He said it was because the little Russian thought the cannibal was bad for business."

Adams nodded. "I had always wondered about Packer."

"Who is this Packer person?" the count asked.

Collins let Adams tell the story to his companion. They fell back into their native German language and C.W went back to his reading.

About six hours later, they arrived in Alamosa. They gathered their gear swiftly at the depot and made their way to a nearby livery stable. There, the three men were met by Shavano and a young Ute man, called *Tatit'z,* both sent to them by Ouray in answer to a telegram from Jocknick to Agent Stanley. The vicinity was peopled with moody settlers, miners and off-duty soldiers from Fort Garland, scrutinizing the party with undisguised malice. The disheveled stable hand was phlegmatic and indifferent.

In the corral at the stable, Collins embraced both his equines openly and with great affection. Ulysses put his muzzle forward and blew in his face, while Molly stood by with her ears upright and alert.

"They are your family," Shavano said, coming up behind him.

"They are indeed. And how are you, my friend?"

"I am worried," the Indian answered quietly. "General Merritt is scouring the country, hunting for those who have the women."

"Jocknick went to Washington to see Schurz, but it looks bad. We must get to the women first."

Adams came over, with Donhöff trailing behind, and greeted Shavano warmly. "It has been a long time since I have seen you, Shavano," he said.

The chief accepted Adams' outstretched hand, but did not speak. The count was examining him as if he were an exhibit in a museum. Shavano turned back toward his horses and moved away.

"Is that Indian trustworthy?" Donhöff asked.

"I would trust him with my life," C.W. told him.

Saddles and cinches were adjusted with alacrity. The animals were loaded with supplies for several days and plenty of ammunition. The group departed along the Rio Grande as the sun was setting. It was agreed that they would not be stopping to rest. Ulysses and Molly had fattened on Ouray's farm and were in far better condition than when last he saw them. He knew Shavano was responsible for this and desired to express his gratitude, but had discovered that the Indian would not be speaking English in Donhöff's presence and did not want to give him away. Whether Adams knew of Shavano's aptitude with English, Collins could not tell. They seemed friendly enough with one another, but the chief remained diffident in Adam's presence.

Darkness and chill subsumed them. They followed the river and occasionally caught sight of oil lamps burning cheerily in windows. Adams explained that the route between Alamosa and Del Norte was mostly peopled by Hispanic families and sheep. They passed through the town of Del Norte and, at break of day, were approaching Wagon Wheel Gap. Pausing momentarily to stretch their aching limbs and relieve themselves, Collins managed a private word with Shavano.

"What else has been happening?" he asked.

"It is difficult. Ouray sent a telegram to Denver through the agency clerk. It stated that the White River Utes were the only ones involved. Ouray sent a separate message saying no one had need to fear the Tabeguache and that they are desirous to continue peaceful relations with the whites."

"Yes, I heard of this while at Governor Pitkin's house. He was full of scorn."

Shavano spat on the ground. "He is a bad man. I almost killed him once when he was trespassing in the Shining Mountains."

"I wish you had," Collins said, smiling. Then he nudged the chief and nodded at the approaching figure of the German count.

"You are a famous chief, *ja?*" the man inquired with enthusiasm.

Shavano contemplated him silently.

"Is he not Chawano, the chief of war?" the Teuton asked Collins.

"I believe his name is Shavano."

"And you speak with him?"

"No…only with gestures."

C.W. glanced at Shavano and pointed to his gelding, making signs of tightening his cinch. The Indian walked over and adjusted the saddle and pulled the latigo snug. He turned around and behaved as if awaiting further instructions. Ulysses bent his neck and pressed his nose against Shavano's shoulder. The Indian spoke to him in the Ute language and stroked his forehead. Donhöff rejoined Adams.

They mounted their horses and rode in the direction of Lake City. Adams told Count Donhöff all about the new settlement and Otto Mears' part in its development. C.W. was still not certain that Adams was convinced of Mears' duplicity. The small party rested again at noonday, while *Tatit'z* made a fire and brewed a pot of truly terrible coffee. They ate cold rations and grained the horses. C.W. had bits of sugar for Ulysses and Molly and he gave some to Shavano for his coffee. Farther on, they paused to survey the site of Packer's grisly crime near the lake. By late afternoon, the company was following one of Otto Mears' poorly maintained roads down Lake Fork toward the Gunnison River. Donhöff rode beside Adams, who continued to be distracted by entertaining his German companion with colorful stories of local history. Collins and Shavano were able to fall back with *Tatit'z* and speak freely.

"Ouray wants to propose to Adams and Schurz that the Utes who took the women be arrested according to white law," the war chief told Collins. "In this way the other bands will be left alone."

"What of the White River Utes who fought the soldiers?"

"Those warriors were defending their homes from attack. Ouray will tell Adams and Schurz that Thornburgh broke his word and came onto the reservation. You are a witness." Shavano gave him a questioning glance.

"Yes. I am a witness…I believe that Ouray will be wise to suggest this. I hope Schurz will pay heed."

Tatit'z spoke at length in his own language.

"He says he saw the women not long ago," Shavano told C.W. "He said they are well. He says the daughter is very angry. But she has always been angry."

The two Germans had stopped to examine a vein of quartz in a granite wall, while the other men rode on. They caught up with Shavano and Collins, precluding any further discourse.

"August hopes to find gold while he is here," Adams

told Collins.

"I see."

"Are you also here to find gold, *Herr* Collins?" the count asked him.

Collins did not respond, but urged Ulysses forward, tugging Molly gently behind him.

51

"It is very nice to see you again," Chipeta told Collins as she tossed corn to her little flock of white hens. He stood nearby in the warmish afternoon sun, content to be away from strong German accents and the ongoing discussion of plans for the next day's journey north to find the women.

"It is nice to see you again as well. Have you had any news from Jane?"

She picked up one of the chickens and held it to her breast. "Yes. She sent a message to say she thinks we should kill the women. She thinks it would be better. I think it would be very bad. *Tsashin,* or Susan as you know her, is keeping an eye on the agency women so that they will not be harmed."

"Well, in some ways Jane might be correct. If the women make up stories about how they were treated, it could be worse than having them just disappear. But in other ways, it might be better to save them so that only a few can be blamed for taking them captive."

"That is my husband's plan. Those stupid men who took them should be punished."

"I agree. Shavano told me of Ouray's idea. It is sound."

Chipeta put the hen back on the ground. It stayed by her a moment, then scurried over to pick at the scattered grain. Collins thought the woman appeared to be tired and worried. He had also noticed that Ouray was looking particularly ill indeed. Collins and Chipeta walked togeth-

er back to the house. Inside, they saw that Sapovanero had arrived from the north with news. Everyone was
crowded around the table. Chipeta went to make coffee.

"*Sapovanero* tells us that the women are still alive and
are being held on the *Mesa Grande*," Ouray told Collins.

"That is good," Collins said. "We will be able to get
them back and hold off the soldiers."

"*Mein Gott*," Count Dönhoff interjected. "You do not
want the soldiers to capture the heathens?"

"No, we do not want that," C.W. said coldly. "And
please remember you are a guest in Chief Ouray's house,"
he added, looking meaningfully at Charles Adams.

Adams spoke up. "August, please refrain from expressing too many judgements here. It is difficult to know the
situation at first glance."

Shavano came into the house and took up his position
against the wall by the door. Sapovanero nodded to him
and he nodded back.

"Shavano took a message to the agency for me," Ouray
said. "I wanted to send a telegram to Mr. Schurz asking to
punish only the guilty people, not all the Ute people."

Shavano spoke to Ouray in their language.

"The agent wants his clerk, George Sherman, to go on
this journey," Ouray translated. "Another of his people,
tambien…a Mr. Saunders. They will drive the supply wagon."

"We must have a wagon for the women," Adams said.

"*Si*, I will send my buckboard with Captain Cline. It
has good springs and will make a smooth ride. I will also
send my new tent for their comfort."

"Who is Captain Cline?" Collins asked.

"An old friend," Ouray told him. "He has been a scout
and trader for many years."

Shavano spoke again at length.

"He says the agent wants us to depart from the agency
in the early morning. He also tells me that the agent re-

ported that Merritt's soldiers have been told to halt their advance until Mr. Adams finds the women. Our friend Schurz has asked for this."

Chipeta came in and served coffee all around. Then she sat down.

"How many warriors do you intend to provide to me?" Adams asked.

"I will send young Colorow who is here. He is the eldest son of Chief Colorow and has many friends among the young men at White River. Shavano and Mr. Collins will go and Sapovanero. I will see who else wishes to go."

"I will go also. I am happy to go," the count said.

Shavano said something that Ouray chose not to translate.

"You are very kind," Adams said diplomatically.

Collins excused himself and left the house. Shavano followed him outside and they walked together to check on the livestock. Collins took out his pipe and smoked.

"This could get complicated with all the other agency men going along," he told Shavano. "Who knows if one of these fellows is in the employ of Pitkin or some other rascal."

"It is possible. I have found out that the Saunders man has been writing for newspapers and will be writing for the *Denver Tribune* in this."

"Damn! How did you find this out?"

"I heard him speaking to that man George Sherman. I think we should also watch Sherman. He could be hired by someone."

The day was waning and the air cooled substantially. A wedge of Canada geese rose out of the bottoms of the Uncompahgre River. There came the sound of dogs barking and children laughing in the distance.

"What will you do after the women have been fetched back?" Shavano asked Collins, while gazing off at the horizon where the sun was setting in a blaze of orange and magenta.

He took his pipe out of his mouth and contemplated his companion. "I cannot say, for I do not know. What will you do?"

"Try to help the people. Ouray is unwell. The people will lose heart if he dies."

"*Ní gnách cosaint ar díth tiarna.*"

Shavano turned to look at Collins. "*Sí?*"

"Rarely is a fight continued when the chief is fallen."

That may be true," the Indian said. "But the Utes have many chiefs."

52

Collins and Shavano joined the wagons and men from the agency as they passed by Ouray's farm. Ouray and Chipeta walked out to the road and Collins could see that the woman had been crying. He hoped the Meeker women would prove themselves worthy of her compassion. The chief had gathered ten of his warriors to join Sapovanero, Shavano and young Colorow. They came riding up and surrounded the wagons on all sides, glued to the backs of lively and unruly ponies as whole entities. Collins and Shavano chose to bring their pack animals so they could remain independent of the rest of the party, especially in the event they needed to make a swift departure. Neither one of them was assured of safety. The war chief was in danger of violence from the soldiers and Collins was in equal peril if a dispute erupted with the White River Utes.

The company departed Ouray's farm and proceeded north along the Uncompahgre River on an old wagon road built by Mormons many years before. Sapovanero had brought a couple of young men from his camp and sent them ahead to inform Quinkent of their approach. Sherman and Saunders, from the agency, rode in the supply wagon. Sherman took the first shift driving a team of green and rather intractable bay mules. After several miles and for no apparent reason, the animals suddenly balked and refused to proceed. Sherman began cursing in a most prolific manner and beat them with a whip that he brought out from under the wagon seat. The mules panicked, braying loudly in distress, pulling against each other creating outright chaos. In spite of this, Sherman persisted in striking them.

Collins had dropped Molly's lead rope and was headed back toward the wagon, when one of the warriors named *Yanco* loped to the head of the tormented animals and encouraged them to move forward by placing his little speckled mare in front of the team. The mules calmed visibly and followed the Ute pony to line themselves out and again travel down the road. Sherman was actually in tears from frustration and Collins was about to berate him for his cruelty when *Yanco* dropped back beside the wagon.

"White man bad goddamn!" he yelled at Sherman. "No more hurt!"

C.W. thought to himself he could not have phrased it better. Shavano rode his pony up beside Ulysses.

"*Pinche cabrón!*" he exclaimed.

"Precisely," responded Collins, not requiring any translation.

Their journey continued without further incident. Shavano and Collins dropped behind the group so they could converse.

"What is wrong with your people?" the chief asked.

"In what meaning?"

"They trample all things and use animals in such a way."

"That fellow is not *my* people," Collins told him. "All white people are not the same…Oh well, maybe they mostly are," he said as an afterthought. "The Spanish use the term *Anglos* for white people, do they not?"

"*Si,* that is their name for them."

"Well," Collins said, smiling sardonically, "the Anglos have been plaguing my people for many generations. Being white does not necessarily offer protection, especially from the likes of Mr. Sherman over there. The German count and General Adams, for example, are Anglo-Saxons…of the Teutonic race. That is where the term came from. "

Chapter 52

"What is the difference between your people and the Anglos?"

"My people are Irish. We were the people in our land before the Anglos came, much the same as your people were here before the whites arrived."

"You are an Irish Indian," Shavano said, chuckling.

C.W. grinned at him in answer.

The day was ending as they approached the Gunnison River. Having come about thirty miles, they forded the river and camped on the other side. Shavano and Collins chose a place downstream from the others. Yanco, Sapovanero and most of the other Ute men joined them. They built a fire and shared food amongst themselves. Collins made a pot of coffee. One of the younger men produced a pint bottle of whiskey, but the rest of them berated the youth and Saponavero took it and threw it away.

Shavano shook his head and said, "These young men do not see that whiskey is a tool of the whites."

"It is used against the Irish as well," C.W. told him. "An effective strategy to eviscerate a culture."

"Eviscerate?" the chief asked.

"Take out the guts."

"Ah, *si.* But more like cutting out the heart."

"Indeed. '…the grief that does not speak whispers the o'er-fraught heart and bids it break.' "Collins quoted.

"Your Englishman?" Shavano asked, having grown accustomed to Collins' practice of quoting Shakespeare.

C.W. nodded.

Yanco said something to Shavano.

"He wants to know if you can say more," he translated to Collins. "He admires your fashion of speech in that way."

"I can read," he said, pleased to be of service to this man who had so valiantly defended the agency mules. "I have my volume of Shakespeare."

"*Uvusi maa!*" Shavano said loudly and all became

silent around the fire. He explained what was about to happen, then turned to Collins. "Please, read now."

Collins opened the book and, getting to his feet, began to read from *Julius Caesar*, giving a dramatic recitation of Antony's soliloquy: "O, pardon me, thou bleeding piece of earth…" from Act 3, Scene 1, with much gesticulation. His companions expressed approval by nodding and smiling. He thought them to be a very polite audience. They requested that he continue and he read a long while and finally had to stop when he became hoarse. The Indians demonstrated disappointment but courteously expressed their gratitude for his performance. Some of them wanted to handle the book and he let them pass it around.

Later, while reclining on his bedroll and smoking, Collins said to Shavano, "I would very much like to ask you something. It is something I have wondered for a long while. But it may be an impolite question."

"We can talk. We are now *buenos amigos, que no*?"

"Yes."

"*Es verdad.* Ask."

"Why do some Indians scout for the whites against other Indians?" Collins asked. "Like Captain Jack scouting against the Sioux."

"I would never do such a thing. It may be that some of the people lose their way. Sometimes because of whiskey, sometimes because of weakness. Many of our paths are blocked now and it can be easy to become lost. I think Jack wanted to be a warrior again. Maybe that is also a reason."

"Do you think some of them regret what they have done?"

"Who knows?" Shavano said, shrugging. "Some acts mean that a person's spirit becomes corrupted and they no longer behave in an understandable way."

"Like most white people?" C.W. asked.

"Like most white people."

They finished their smoke in silence and settled in for the night.

Adams and Dönhoff came to rouse their camp just before dawn, but most of the group were already packing gear and saddling horses. The count approached Collins as he was securing his bedroll on Molly's packsaddle.

"This is a grand adventure, Mr. Collins. *Nicht wahr?*"

"Frankly, I find this entire episode to be tragic and disturbing."

"Bismarck has shown us the importance of unification. If the United States desires to be as strong as the German Empire, it must be willing to create struggle in order to win peace. These red men are like *kinder*. They must be taught."

Collins finished tying down his load and walked away without responding. The count stood awkwardly by the mule for a moment, then wandered over to where Adams was drinking a cup of coffee by the fire. Many of the warriors had mounted and ridden north. In the other camp, Cline and Yanco were employed with harnessing and hitching the team for the buckboard. Sherman and Saunders were already perched on the supply wagon in preparation for the day's journey. Collins saddled Ulysses and turned to find Shavano nearby, sitting on his stocky little paint.

"This is a nice adventure, Mr. Collins," he said in an amusing parody of Dönhoff's accent.

The two laughed heartily as Collins mounted and they proceeded to ride after the wagons that began to move up the trail.

GERMAN GENTRY

53

On the second day of travel, they reached Whitewater Creek by two o'clock in the afternoon. The day had been uneventful. Alongside the creek, the party stopped to rest the animals and cook a meal. While they gathered around the fire, Henry Jim and another man rode in from the village where the women were being held. Henry Jim dismounted and walked to where General Adams sat with Cline and the Prussian count. It was obvious to Collins that Adams and Henry Jim knew each other from before.

"Well, hello, Henry," Adams said jovially. "Do you bring us news?"

"Yes sir. Quinkent wants me to tell you that the women are safe and in fine shape. They are being held separately, but in the same camp up on the big mesa, east of here, south of the Grand River."

"How do we get there?"

"It is difficult. The easiest way is to follow the river to the next stream, then double back up onto the north edge of the mesa."

"That will take time," Adams said.

"Yes, and news has just come that the soldiers are once again moving south. Quinkent will not wait long for you to come."

Shavano spoke. He motioned to Henry Jim to translate for him.

"Shavano says there is a short cut, but we must leave the wagons. This route will save many miles."

"Did Douglas…or rather Quinkent… say he would let us come?" Adams asked.

"He is willing. Some of the others wish to hold the women until you have stopped the soldiers from advancing."

"*Scheisse*," Adams said. "Mr. Schurz has sent word to stop the soldiers. Why have they continued on?"

Shavano spoke again. The young man asked him something in their language and the war chief made another short statement.

"He says he can help," Henry Jim told them, "But we must keep traveling and not stop for the night here."

General Adams looked at the chief circumspectly. "*Gut*," he finally said, making up his mind. "I have never known Shavano to be dishonest. We will keep going."

The camp was swiftly broken. The wagon teams were turned loose to graze and the young Ute man, who had come with Henry Jim, volunteered to remain with William Saunders and George Sherman to watch over the livestock and wagons. Adams had wisely found adequate excuses to leave behind the agency men, one of whom, of course, was acting as reporter for the newspaper most antagonistic toward the Utes. Collins walked to where Sherman was pitching a tent and settling his own small campsite.

"You abuse those animals in any way, Sherman, and I will beat you."

The man, a natural and manifest coward, became immediately defensive. "What do you mean? Who are you to threaten me?" he asked in a wheedling tone.

"I mean exactly what I say. I will thrash you and I am just the man to do it. Take care of those animals and protect them with your life."

Collins strode away without giving time for response. He swung into the saddle and retrieved Molly's lead from Shavano, sitting patiently on his horse awaiting him.

Adams rode over to them. "Shavano," he said, "I am in difficult circumstances. I suspect that you understand

English and I believe you speak it also. Can you not abandon your subterfuge so that we may engage in discussion? The agency men are staying behind. I am begging you to let down your guard."

Shavano contemplated the big German for a long moment. Finally, he spoke. "General, I will do as you ask, but you must swear not to reveal this thing. It is best if most whites think me an illiterate heathen." The chief grinned at C.W.

"*Mein Gott*, you speak very well. I thought as much." Adams turned to look at C.W. "Did you know?"

He merely nodded.

The big man sighed and shook his head. "It is my fault that I did not know you better at Los Pinos."

Shavano shrugged.

"Now, do you truly know this route up to the mesa?"

"I do. We must leave now, but still we will have to travel some distance in the dark."

Shavano rode out toward the northeast, following the nearby creek. Henry Jim and Collins came up behind him in single file with Adams, Count Dönhoff, Sapovanero, Cline, young Colorow and six other Utes. The remainder of the warriors forded Whitewater Creek and headed north, wanting to spy on the soldiers moving closer to the Grand Mesa.

The sun was setting as Shavano led them across the stream and up a narrow trail that began to switchback along the steep slopes of the immense land mass towering above them. Shavano's small gelding and packhorse nimbly picked their way along the treacherous path, lending confidence to Henry Jim's pony. Molly's steady presence behind Ulysses reassured him and Collins gave him a pat on the neck occasionally and spoke to him encouragingly. Ouray's stout horses, ridden by the two Germans, seemed to be calm and trustworthy, but the horse borrowed by Captain Cline from the buckboard team was skittish without its constant companion. The Ute warriors finally forced him to let them pass by and made him bring up the rear. In the end, he lost his nerve and dismounted to lead the animal up the precipitous track.

It was fully dark when Shavano brought them all safely to the top of the great tableland of the Grand Mesa. They waited for Captain Cline, who at last came huffing up the trail, still leading his horse. He remounted and they rode on a few miles to a winding creek that fed a substantial beaver pond. The animals slapped their tails in consternation at the intrusion. They rested a while, watering their horses and smoking. In the early dawn, Cline prepared a brief repast of coffee, hard tack and beans. Shavano sent Yanco and Henry Jim ahead to ensure that their arrival was anticipated. He then led the rest of the group along the stream to a small rise from which they could look down upon a Ute camp in a shallow valley below. Henry Jim rode back to them at full gallop.

"Quinkent sent word that they held a council last night and will let you come in," he told Charles Adams. "He is in the next village. He will come to meet you."

Dönhoff and Cline had ridden off a short distance to admire the views and study some impressive rock formations on the far horizon. Adams turned to Shavano.

"What do you think?" he asked. "Can we proceed safely?"

The war chief shrugged. "Quinkent's word is good. I cannot say how many of the others are angry and fearful." He spoke to young Colorow, who then galloped down toward the Indian camp, his pony raising dust in the morning sun. "Colorow will speak to the young men. We should go down."

Shavano and Sapovanero rode first, with the rest of them following behind. The other Utes had already departed to find their family members and friends in the villages beyond. Henry Jim rode alongside Adams, bringing him to the lodges that made up a small camp where the women were supposedly held. Adams urged his horse toward the nearest tipi, from which a sallow face was peering through the door covering. Adams dismounted and a white woman came out. Captain Cline, Dönhoff and Collins rode over to the lodge. Collins recognized Josephine Meeker, but said nothing.

"Have you come for us?" she asked Adams when he drew near.

"*Ja*," he told her. "You are Miss Meeker?"

"Yes. You are Mr. Adams?"

"I am. We are here to take you home."

"I am so glad."

"Did you see who did all the killing? Did you see who killed your father?"

"No."

"How have you been treated?" Adams asked.

"Better than we expected."

"Are you healthy? Did they subject you to…indignities?" he asked.

"Oh no, Mr. Adams, nothing of that kind. But now you have come for us. I am so glad."

Collins thought the woman exhibited a great amount of sangfroid here in captivity. It appeared she wore a warm and fairly new outfit made of blanket material. She was not exactly in tatters.

"Where are the others?" Adams asked.

"Here. Perhaps some of them hid my mother and Flora Ellen. They knew you were coming."

"Get ready to leave this afternoon. I will find the others."

Adams rode to the next camp with Sapovanero, Collins and Shavano. They heard voices emanating from a big lodge at the edge of the village. Sapovanero hailed the inhabitants and two warriors emerged to argue with him. Shavano told Adams that the warriors were saying the other women had been hidden. Nothing could be done until Quinkent came to speak to them, so Shavano suggested they ride back to the first encampment to re-join Cline, Dönhoff, their pack animals and Henry Jim, who had stayed to protect them. Upon their return, they dismounted and loosened cinches, leaving the horses to graze. They lounged about a picturesque meadow, covered in golden brome grasses and withered wildflowers. Dönhoff took out a small notebook and began to sketch. After a while, Jane made an appearance, bareback on a stubby little grey mare.

"Hello, Agent Adams," she said, sliding down off her horse.

"Hello Jane," Adams said. "Have you come to help us find the women?"

"No," she said, frankly. "I have come to ask what you plan to do about the soldiers...Hello, Mr. Collins."

"Good morning, Jane," he responded.

"Which soldiers?" Adams asked.

"The soldiers headed down from White River."

A commotion arose as a group of mounted warriors rode through the neighboring cluster of lodges. Out in front rode a smallish man with ear length hair, the usual silver hoops as earrings, drooping whiskers and an intelligent and acute look about him. Collins recognized Sowowíc beside him.

Shavano came to his feet. "Quinkent," he said and strode toward him.

Quinkent, also known as Douglas, dismounted and spoke to Shavano. They walked together to where Adams and the others were sitting. Adams came to his feet and shook his hand. Douglas proceeded to have a lengthy conversation with Shavano. Adams sat down again and waited patiently. Collins was impressed by his calm assurance. Jane came and sat beside C.W. and gave him an engaging smile. Finally, Douglas sat down next to Adams. He flattened a hibernating ant hill and began to draw a map of the White River country in the dirt.

"Soldiers are still coming, General." he said to Adams,

showing him their route on the crude diagram. "Ouray sent word they would stop when you came, but they are still coming and building a new road."

"I know nothing of this," Adams said. "I was told the soldiers would halt their progress."

"They will be hostile," Quinkent said, nonchalantly picking grass seeds from his buckskin leggings. "We should keep the women until the soldiers stop coming. Then we will give them to you."

"I tell you again," the German said, "I was told by Washington that the soldiers would stop when I entered this country. Mr. Schurz told them to stop."

"And I tell you they are still coming. Will you go and see them and stop them?"

"I will go to their camp after you give up the women. I will go and send them away, but only after I have the women."

Quinkent came to his feet. "Come, we will go to my lodge to talk with the others, then I will decide." He turned to look at Dönhoff, Cline and Collins. "Not you. You will not come."

Shavano said something to him. Quinkent shrugged. "You," he said pointing his lower lip at Collins. "You come. Nobody else." He spoke to Henry Jim, who nodded and remained seated beside the other white men.

Jane stood up and walked to her horse. "We will meet again, Mr. Collins," she said, nimbly springing onto the mare. "I will go find Tsashin...Susan... and tell her what is happening. She has been very worried."

"Do not play mischief with the captives now, Jane," he said. "We need them."

"Of course not, Mr. Collins." She nudged her horse into a fast lope and rode away.

CAMP

54

The atmosphere within the lodge was unfriendly and dense with mistrust. Collins also found it to be thick with smoke and stifling. Adams spoke through Shavano, telling the Indians over and over that he would do nothing to help the Utes in their predicament until the women were released to him. The Utes insisted that they had done nothing wrong and that the troubles had been forced on them; that the soldiers had come only as a result of Nick's lies and betrayals. Adams paid no attention to their explanations and complaints. He wanted the women started for home and only then would he consider helping the Ute people.

The warriors said they no longer wanted any part of the government. They only wanted to live in their own country, live as they had before, without the interference of Washington. At this point, Sapovanero stood and gave an impassioned speech. Shavano did not bother to translate for Adams and Collins. The diatribe continued for quite some while. Collins heard Ouray's name mentioned several times. When Sapovanero had finished and resumed his seat, the Utes said they would give back the women and then Adams could do something for them if he would.

Adams had refused to smoke with the men until they agreed to release the women. Now he smoked and the mood became more relaxed. Sowowic, a favorite of Adams' according to Shavano, came to sit beside the German and slap him on the back. He did this several times, while smiling at him and nodding appreciatively. It seemed to Collins that the Utes now generally believed all would be well. Shavano shook his head at him and made a deprecating noise in his throat. He motioned C.W. out of the lodge. They stepped out into the clear daylight and breathed fresh air.

"Adams will not be able to help us," Shavano said. "Schurz will not be able to help us. It is good the women were not harmed, but this will not go well for us."

"Will you go to White River with Adams?" Collins asked him, as they strolled away from the boisterous group within.

"Yes, I should go with Sapovanero, Sowowic and the General. There will be bad trouble, even with the women released. Where will you go?"

"I will go back to Ouray. On the way, I will see the men Saunders and Sherman. I may be able to guess at how slanderous the newspapers will be. Then I will be able to pass this information on to Secretary Schurz."

"The newspapers will say we are like... red heathens. Bad children. That we need to be punished."

They saw Adams come out of the lodge and stretch. He strode to where Count Dönhoff and Cline awaited him. Collins and Shavano joined them.

"The *Frauen* are being brought to us," Adams told them. "They will be here soon."

Collins caught a movement out of the corner of his eye and turned to see an old woman, leaning heavily on a staff, heading in their direction. C.W. recognized Meeker's wife. She was accompanied by a younger woman, carrying a small boy in a blanket. Susan and Jane were with them. Most of the Ute warriors, now exiting the big lodge, came over as well. Arvilla Meeker shook hands with Adams.

"We are so thankful you are here," she said. "We were told yesterday that Washington was coming, but we could not believe it. Now you are here. When will you take us away?"

Collins thought the woman looked to be in remarkably good condition, despite an obvious limp. She wore a clean calico dress, shawl and sunbonnet. Her voice was clear and distinct.

"Very soon," Adams told the woman. "You will start for home tomorrow."

"We are very happy," said the other woman, dressed in an outfit made from blankets, similar to that worn by Josephine Meeker. Her head was sheltered by a large sombrero.

"You are Mrs. Price?" Adams asked.

"Yes. We are very happy," she said again. "When the Indians came to our tent and hid us in the willows, we did not know what was going to happen."

Adams drew her away from the crowd. Collins followed along while the others were distracted by Mrs. Meeker.

"Did you suffer any indignities? Were any offered to you?" the German asked, in a low voice.

"Oh no sir," she said. "They were very cruel in their ways and tormented us with various deceits. But they did not harm us in that manner. It was very hard, and we suffered greatly, but we were not harmed like that."

Collins had assessed her to be rather guileless and of limited intelligence and therefore believed her words. Apparently, Adams did as well, for as Flora Price walked back to rejoin Arvilla and her son, he asked, "Collins, may I trust you to send a dispatch to Secretary Schurz?"

"Of course."

"Please get it to him right away. Tell him these women were not outraged and that they are safe and on their way home."

"I will do so. They seem to be in excellent condition, do they not?"

Adams raised his eyebrows. "*Ja,* very much so. It is far better than I had supposed."

Collins saw that Josephine had been brought to the group, along with Flora's little girl. Adams went over to the assembly. Susan was fussing over the children and Jane had disappeared. Collins went to join Shavano and Sapovanero, who stood off by themselves.

"We will be riding for the main camp soon," Shavano told him.

Sapovanero walked away, leaving Collins and Shavano alone. Shavano took a small pouch from around his neck. He handed it to Collins.

"You must take this, *mi amigo*. You must take this and not forget the days we have ridden together."

Collins held the worn leather bag in his palm. It was pungent with cedar. "How could I forget, my friend?"

"It is possible. You will go far away now."

Placing the cord of the pouch over his head and tucking the bag into the front of his blouse, C.W. said, "I thank you." They shook hands loosely, Indian fashion. "Is there something I can give to you?" he asked. "Something you admire?"

"A saying," the chief told him. "Give me an Irish saying to take with me."

"Let me think...oh yes, this is appropriate...*Minic a mheath dóigh is a tháinig andóigh*."

"*Si?*" Shavano asked.

"Often have the likely failed and the unlikely prospered."

Shavano repeated the proverb. "The whites will certainly prosper," he added.

Collins placed a hand on Shavano's shoulder. "I apologize. I failed you and your people."

Shavano regarded him closely. "No...you did not fail. You tried very hard and I will not forget this."

They walked over to where Shavano's horses stood. Collins tightened the cinch on the pack horse and held the lead rope in readiness.

Adams and Dönhoff mounted up and rode over to them.

"Mr. Cline will take charge of the women," the General

told Collins. "You need not bother about them."

As the Indian swung onto his horse, he looked down at C.W. one last time. "Perhaps we will not see one another again," he said.

"Do not be so sure," Collins told him.

"Perhaps. *Adios.*"

Wheeling his gelding to follow the Germans, Sowowic and Sapovanero, the war chief took the lead rope of his pack horse from Collins' hand without looking at him. Collins watched Shavano disappear into the trees as dusk was falling. He lightly touched the pouch resting on his breastbone and turned away.

WHEN DIGNITY IS LOST

55

After a two day journey back to Ouray's farm, traveling ahead of the women and Captain Cline, Collins thought to remove himself from further events regarding the future of the Ute peoples. He did not tarry with the agency men, Saunders and Sherman, on Whitewater Creek. They were laconic and stubbornly unreceptive to his reports of the general welfare of the Meeker women. He certainly was unable to discover what information Saunders intended to provide to the *Tribune*.

Following a brief visit with Chipeta and Ouray, Collins went to the agency headquarters and sent a telegram to Schurz informing him that the women were in good health, had not been violated and were en route to the Uncompahgre. From there he rode to Hartman's ranch on the Gunnison River. He spent several days enjoying the rancher's prodigious hospitality and excellent conversation. One day, Alonzo brought him the news that there was to be an investigation regarding recent events. It was scheduled to take place at the Uncompahgre agency in mid-November. C.W. rode over to Lake City and dispatched telegrams to Secretary Schurz, requesting permission to be witness to the proceedings. After a couple of anxious days of waiting, Schurz sent word that he was authorized to attend. When the time came, Collins took his leave of Hartman and returned to the Uncompahgre.

Upon his arrival, Ouray extended an invitation to bivouac near his farm. The wind was raw fromy the northwest and he took up residence in the grove of cottonwoods where he and Sydney had camped not so long ago. Ouray was gracious enough to lend him a battered Sibley tent, the provenance of which he did not inquire. It made a snug domicile and his camp was located within easy traveling distance to where the White River Ute Commission would convene at the Los Pinos Agency on the Uncompahgre River. Ulysses and Molly had ample fodder among the trees.

Once settled, Collins made his way to Ouray's house, in response to a summons from Chipeta. Abundant smoke rose from the chimney and he could smell coffee. He knocked and the door was answered by Douglas, who beckoned him inside. Ouray sat in a rocking chair near the wood stove, looking ill. His skin had a yellowish gray pallor and his face appeared swollen.

"Collins, welcome. Sit," he said.

C.W. sat at the table with Quinkent. Chipeta came out of the kitchen with a coffeepot and cups. She smiled at him. "Good to see you, Mr. Collins," she said and poured him some coffee. She went back into the other room.

"I am surprised that you want to involve yourself with more of our difficulties," Ouray said. "Did Secretary Schurz send you to speak on our behalf?"

He shook his head. "I asked to come. I doubt I will be given the opportunity to speak on your behalf, but I will lend whatever support I may. Is Shavano coming?"

"He is far to the north," Douglas told him. "He does not involve himself with white doings. He loses his temper and scares people."

Ouray adjusted his position in the chair. "I am hoping he will come with me to Washington. He gives me good advice, even if I do not always listen. I am trying to convince Schurz to let us go there and be heard. We can find no justice in Colorado. All negotiations need to be in Washington with the general government."

"Do you think he will go?" C.W. asked.

"He may. If I convince him it is important enough. He has a strong voice."

Chipeta brought roasted pork, bowls of fragrant beans and warm tortillas. They all sat at the table to eat, but Collins noticed that Ouray barely ate. He could tell that the man was tormented by pain and anxiety.

"Who is this General Hatch that is to be head man of the commission?" Douglas asked.

"I knew him in the war back east," Collins answered. "He is a soldier, but has always seemed to be intelligent and reasonable." He dipped a tortilla in his beans and took a bite.

"I do not like Townsend. He will change our words," Ouray said.

"Townsend?" C.W. asked.

"He is to be the interpreter. Ute people dealt with him several years ago. He is not honest and is always for sale."

"Will you be allowed to interpret as well?"

"Some I think. I think General Adams trusts me."

Chipeta poured coffee and gave her man a cup of fragrant tea. She placed a hand briefly on his back then returned to her place at the table. "We have known him a long time," she said. "I hope he is a friend to us in this."

"Who are the men being summoned?" Collins asked.

"I am to be first," Douglas said. "I think the women have said I hurt them."

"When?" C.W. asked with concern. "They said at the camp they had not been harmed."

"Now they are saying terrible things. One of the women said I made her bed with me." Quinkent snorted derisively. "I am sick with it."

"But when?" Collins asked again. "When did they say this?"

"Adams and some people met with them in the town that Meeker built out on the plains,"

"Greeley?"

"That is it," Douglas said, nodding. "About ten days ago. The women told stories about us. Bad stories. It is the same as when Nick told stories about Johnson hurting him. The whites believe other whites. Never the Ute people."

"So they changed their story and said they had been outraged?"

"I believe Adams knows they are now lying," Ouray said. "Douglas told me the General questioned them carefully when he first found them."

"Someone must have paid them. It is the only explanation," Collins said. "You say this was ten days ago?"

"They were also in Denver. Before Greeley, they also told their stories in Denver," Chipeta said. "I was kind to them and felt sorry for them. I did not think they would harm us after that."

"I do not have a good opinion of the Meeker girl or the other one. I am sorry we tried to help them after they were taken by some of the young men," Quinkent said. "I think the old woman is silly and easily confused."

"Someone must have gotten to them in Denver. You must be careful in talking to the commission," Collins told them. "It is important that you keep your testimony simple and direct. Who is testifying after Douglas?"

"Johnson," Ouray answered. "After that they will summon Yanco, Sowowíc, a Tabeguache named Charley, Henry Jim, Captain Jack and the white man named Brady who works for Agent Stanley."

"And the women?"

"I was told they would not come. Someone will read their statements taken in Greeley."

"They do not wish to face us," Chipeta said.

"I believe you must prepare for a very unpleasant time," Collins told them. "I will watch and listen and advise you to the best of my ability. I cannot be seen to be helping you for I think they would expel me from the proceedings."

"We are glad you are here," Ouray said.

"I am so sorry I cannot do more. I am so sorry I could not have stopped this."

"You are not at fault," Chipeta said. "Mostly it was the gold and silver that caused this. White greed caused this. The hunger is endless and nothing can stop it."

PROSPECTORS

56

The men of the White River Ute Commission were seated behind three tables lined up on the southeast side of a large adobe building on Los Pinos Agency. There were General Adams, Brevet Major General Edward Hatch, John Townsend, interpreter, Mr. Caldwell, the stenographer, and George Sherman as clerk. First Lieutenant Gustavus Valois of the 9th Cavalry presided as legal advisor. Chief Ouray sat at the end. A witness chair was placed directly before and facing the tables. Agent Stanley, Collins and the Utes were seated on the west side against the opposite wall. It was clear to Collins this would be a very official and serious affair. Just before the proceedings began, Hannibal Peck, from Bear River, came in and took a seat by the door.

Douglas was called and he sat in the solitary witness chair. He was sworn in by Ouray. Douglas gave his testimony in the Ute language. Townsend interpreted nimbly, but after what Ouray had said, Collins was unsure of his accuracy. He surmised that if Townsend changed any of Quinkent's words too much, Ouray would object. The Indian gave background information about his dealings with Nathan Meeker. He told of how Meeker wanted the Utes to kill some of their horses and how he wanted to plow all the land for growing crops. Douglas also recounted how Meeker had stated that the land no longer belonged to the Ute people. That it had been bought by the government with blankets and such things. There was angry mur-

muring among the Utes present in the room. Ouray made a slight gesture with his hand and they became quiet.

The chief went on to tell of how Meeker threatened him with soldiers, that they would be coming soon to take them to some other place. He had told the agent that he should have some of the White River Ute men speak to the officers because the Ute people were afraid of soldiers. Supposedly, Meeker agreed to take four or five of the men to meet with the soldiers. Douglas said he had heard gunshots later the same day. He testified that he went to his lodge and he and his wife packed up and left around dusk. He claimed not to have witnessed any of the killings at the agency.

General Adams began aggressively questioning Douglas at this point, wanting to know who Douglas saw that day at the agency, whether he had seen the women, whether he knew of the fight on Milk River and so on. Douglas told how he found Arvilla Meeker and took her, so as to care for her, and how they later joined up with the others who had possession of Flora Price and Josie Meeker. Adams next inquired about two civil officers coming to the agency a couple of days before the attacks at the agency. The officers supposedly wanted to arrest two Ute men for the burning of Thompson's house on Bear River. Collins remembered that Captain Jack had said the house was never burned.

Douglas said, "I went to Meeker and told him I did not understand who was making those fires, and the agent said that was all right, and then the men left again."

Collins decided he needed some air. He departed the building into a chilly autumn day and walked behind the structure out of the wind, so he could smoke. He hunkered down on his haunches and packed and lit his pipe. He was baffled by Adams' adversarial tone in the proceedings. Perhaps he had orders from Secretary Schurz to not appear congenial toward the Utes. After he smoked for a while, Peck found him and sat down nearby.

"Good to see you again, Mr. Collins," he said. "Shavano here with you?"

"No. I have not seen him in a while."

"Probably best. He do have a temper."

"Why are you here?" Collins asked him, handing over his tobacco pouch.

"Thankee," Peck said and scooped out a small handful and stuffed it in his mouth.

Collins watched in amazement. "I take it you never smoke?"

"Naw, too much work," he said, working his tongue to position the wad inside his cheek. "I came to be with my friends."

"How do you think Douglas is holding up?"

"Well," Peck said, pausing to spit, "I think it is clear that ol' Meeker was threatening those boys pretty good. I heared they was scared they would be sent to Indian Territory. Meeker sayin' the soldiers would take them someplace else would cause them sizable concern."

"That would account for some of their anger," C.W. said, tapping the ashes from his pipe on a rock and putting it in his pocket.

The two of them stood and stretched. "Ready to go back in?" Collins asked.

Peck nodded and they walked together around the adobe building and quietly entered. They were surprised to find that the proceedings were ending for the day. The Utes were talking amongst themselves. Ouray remained at the table, resting his head in his hands. He appeared to be quite unwell. C.W. went over to him.

"May I get you some water?" he asked.

The chief looked up. "No, Mr. Collins, *gracias*."

"This seemed very brief."

"*Si*. But it is probably best."

"Is your wagon here?"

"Outside. Will you help me?"

Collins knew he must have felt very poorly to have made such a request. "Of course." He helped Ouray to his feet, noticing both ankles below his leggings were quite distended.

"My woman will come tomorrow. It will be a longer day with much testimony."

As C.W. walked with Ouray toward the door, Adams came over. "Mr. Collins. I am surprised to see you here."

"I am here as a friend to the Utes only, General."

"You are no longer a representative of Secretary Schurz?" the German asked.

"No."

Adams turned to Ouray. "Are you pleased so far with the proceedings?"

"They have only begun. We will see."

Ouray walked slowly through the door with Collins at his side. Collins bent and offered his clasped hands as a stirrup for the chief to climb onto the wagon seat. "I can tie my horse behind and drive, if you would like," he offered.

"Yes, that would be good."

C.W. fetched Ulysses from where he was tethered to a hitching rail by the post office. He secured him to the back of the buckboard and climbed onto the seat next to Ouray. He took up the lines and released the brake. The stout bay mare responded to a light slap of the lines and they pulled onto the road toward Ouray's farm.

"You must stay to eat," the chief said. Shortly after, he nodded off to sleep, his head rocking with the bouncing of the wagon.

57

The day dawned bright and clear. After spending time with his horse and mule, brushing them and giving them oats, he made his way to Ouray's house. Hannibal Peck was visiting and they drank coffee and reviewed the previous day's events. Peck and Collins then harnessed and hitched the mare to the wagon. Chipeta drove to the agency while they followed on horseback. Ouray was clearly suffering, wincing at every bump in the road.

On arrival, they saw at once that a number of white people had come from surrounding communities, hoping to spectate or interfere. Agent Stanley, Hatch, Adams and Valois were all in confrontation with them while Johnson, Sowowíc and the other Utes stood off to the side. Townsend and Sherman were conspicuously absent. Adams was in a standoff with a man who was threatening the Indians with a pistol. Several of the white men and women, and even children, were berating the Utes with vulgar epithets. Johnson and some of the others were braced for a fight.

General Hatch noticed Collins and motioned to him. He dismounted and walked over.

"I saw you yesterday," the officer said. "I knew you in the war."

He never expected General Hatch to recognize him. "Yes sir. I remember."

"Can you aid us in encouraging these people to depart?"

"I will try."

He walked over to the farmer menacing Adams and the Utes. Collins precipitously struck the man hard in the face, dropping him to the ground in a heap. C.W. reached down and picked up the revolver.

"*Mein Gott,*" Adams exclaimed. "Did you kill him?"

The crowd stood staring, dumbfounded into silence.

General Hatch took advantage of the moment. "All of you must depart immediately. If you do not, I will send for troops and have them use force in sending you away."

There was angry muttering all around, but the group began to break up. Children were called to wagons and men mounted their horses.

"Godless heathen!" one man bellowed as he rode away.

Lieutenant Valois, Agent Stanley, General Hatch and Adams were individually encouraging people to leave, while at the same time endeavoring to hold the Utes back.

A middle-aged woman came up to the man on the ground and helped him to his feet. She waved a finger at Collins. "Damn you for doing Henry like this."

"Get him the hell out of here," he told her.

Blood trickled from the man's nose and he was unsteady. "Come on, Fanny," he said. They made their way to a buckboard. Collins did not give him his gun and he did not ask for it.

General Hatch came up to him. "That was not what I had in mind," he said.

"Perhaps not, but it worked." He stuck the man's gun in his belt.

Hatch actually smiled at him and they stood together to watch the last of the unwanted visitors leave the vicinity. When they had gone, he adjusted his uniform and cleared his throat. "Well, enough of that. We need to begin the proceedings."

Collins walked to where Ouray and Chipeta waited in the wagon. Peck was by the adobe building conversing with some of the Utes. It looked to Collins as if he was attempting to calm them down. Chipeta and Collins assisted Ouray to his place at the table, then C.W. went back outside to unhitch the mare and secure Ulysses to the wagon. He slipped the purloined revolver into his saddle bags.

Peck joined him. "Goddamn that was a healthy poke. Pole-axed the fella."

"*Is minic a bhris béal duine a shorn.* Many a time a man's mouth broke his nose." Collins told him.

"True enough."

They went inside and found chairs next to Chipeta. Johnson was in the witness seat, being sworn in. Lieutenant Valois began the questioning, asking that Johnson recount in his own words the events leading up to and during the attack at the agency. Johnson told how Meeker wanted him to move to the new agency from the old White River location. He had already built a house and did not want to move. Then he saw how men were plowing the land all around. Johnson said he went to Meeker to tell him he had no right to plow up his land.

"I told the agent that it was not right that he should order the men to plow my land. The agent told me I was always a troublesome man, and that it was likely I might come to the calaboose. I told him that I did not know why I should go to prison. I told the agent that it would be better for another agent to come, who was a good man, and was not talking such things."

"Is this when Johnson hit Meeker?" Peck leaned in to ask quietly.

"He claims he never hit the man," Collins answered.

"Ol' Nick did like to tell tales."

Collins caught a glance from General Hatch and he felt momentarily as if he were in the presence of a disapproving schoolmaster. He nudged Peck.

The testimony continued with Adams, Hatch and Valois taking turns with the questioning. They especially sought to know who was involved in the attack on the agency, who fought the soldiers and whether there were Uncompahgre Utes at either location. Adams again became antagonistic, making accusations and demanding to know who took the women, who directed the fight at Milk Creek and what Johnson knew ahead of time. Johnson denied knowing anything or being involved in any of the violence. General Hatch then fired a series of questions at him.

> Hatch: Do you know the names of any of the Indians who were engaged in the fight at the agency?
>
> Johnson: No
>
> Hatch: Do you know the names of any of the Indians engaged in the fight with the soldiers?
>
> Johnson: No.
>
> Hatch: Do you know whether or not there was any fight with the soldiers?
>
> Johnson: No.
>
> Hatch: Do you know that the agency was burned up?
>
> Johnson: No.

After this last round of questioning, General Hatch adjourned the commission until two o'clock in the afternoon. Adams and Hatch appeared to be ill-humored and frustrated. Collins slipped out the door with Chipeta and Peck.

"You come to eat with us," she told them. They stepped off to the side and waited for Ouray, while the men of the commission filed out and headed for Agent Stanley's house. General Hatch paused a moment when he saw Collins.

"You are welcome to join us," he said.

"I appreciate it, sir. But I will join my friends here."

Hatch glanced at Chipeta and Peck and shrugged.

"Very well. I thank you again for your earlier assistance."

The officer moved off after the others. George Sherman came out of the door and recoiled when he saw C.W.

"Hello Sherman."

The man shot him a malicious look then headed for the agent's house.

"What was that about?" Peck asked.

"He viciously beat a team of mules on our way to Grand Mesa to rescue the women. I let him know what I would do if I caught him abusing animals ever again."

Ouray came out of the door. Chipeta took his arm and they went to the wagon. She spread a blanket on the ground and Collins and Peck lowered the chief to a seated position.

"Once I was a dangerous man," he told them. "Now I am a small child and will die soon."

"Aw come now, friend. It ain't so bad," Peck said.

"It is bad," Chipeta told him gravely.

She opened a basket and passed around cold mutton, tortillas, roasted green chilies and jars of cold coffee. They ate in silence, soaking in the sun of an unseasonably warm November day. Collins shared his tobacco pouch. Ouray smoked his pipe and Peck took a chew from his Navy plug. Yanco, Johnson and Sowowic came over. They spoke to Ouray in their own language.

"Sowowic is worried about the questioning," Ouray told Peck and Collins. "Johnson is telling him to just keep saying that he knows nothing."

"Good advice," Collins said. "But I think they are becoming angry."

"I know I made them angry," Johnson said. "But I am not going to give them bullets to shoot me with."

Collins walked the horses to the river to water them. When he returned, Ouray and Chipeta were napping. The others talked and smoked until they saw Adams and the others coming out of the agent's house. Collins patted

Sowowíc's back and nodded encouragement. They made their way as a group back to the building. Johnson and Yanco supported Ouray to his seat. Chipeta stayed with the wagon.

Sowowíc was sworn in and the questioning began. When asked about the trouble between Meeker and the Indians, he testified that Meeker had told him their land had been purchased with the shoes and blankets and clothing they received from the government. When the questions turned to the battle on Milk Creek and Thornburgh, he clearly avoided incriminating himself. Peck's name came up a few times in connection with providing information to the Utes. Collins glanced at him and he shrugged, grinning. After prolonged testimony similar to that of Johnson's, during which Sowowíc pleaded complete ignorance, General Adams accused him of being duplicitous. He was visibly irritated.

"I believe that he has not spoken the truth and does not want to speak the truth," the German said. "I believe also that none of them want to speak the truth, and it is, therefore, almost unnecessary to go any further."

"I cannot force them to say what they do not wish to," Ouray told him. "For that I brought them here. That they might speak for themselves."

Adams asked Ouray if either *Pi-ah* or Yanco could tell them anything about what happened at the agency or who was in the fight at Milk Creek. The chief answered in the negative.

Lieutenant Valois said, "No Indian would be safe from his own people, whether implicated or not, who testified against those who were guilty."

"Show me any act of law by which a man is compelled to criminate himself," Ouray said.

Adams took a deep breath. "Very well, I wish now to offer to the Commission the testimony which I took at Greeley, Colorado of the ladies who were captives."

The first statement to be read was that of Flora Ellen Price, the wife of the blacksmith at the White River Agency. Lieutenant Valois read the testimony aloud. Collins found it excruciatingly limited, plainly displaying the woman's low intelligence and unsophisticated character. She had apparently been led to making mendacious allegations by stronger personalities than her own. When the statement reached the place where she accused Johnson, whom he had found to be a dignified and honorable man, of committing outrage to her person, Collins got up and walked out.

Chipeta was sitting on the blanket by the wagon, beading a pair of moccasins. She looked up as he approached.

"How is my man doing?"

"He is suffering. But he is defending his people well," Collins told her. He leaned against the wagon.

"He can be very wise. Other times he has forgotten his traditional ways."

"It is a difficult time to be an Indian, I think," he said, taking out his pipe and filling it.

"It is an impossible time to be a Ute Indian."

YOU MUST ASSIMILATE

58

The next day, Ouray was too ill to leave his bed. Collins rode to the agency to inform General Hatch, president of the commission, that the chief would be unable to attend. The men of the commission met pursuant to adjournment. C.W. departed and found Peck down by the Indian camp on the Uncompahgre River, fishing.

"I believe I have heard enough," he said. "I am leaving."

Peck looked at him. "It will just be more of the bullshit we heared yesterday. How is Ouray?"

"Unable to leave his bed."

"I reckon he ain't long for this world."

"No, I guess not."

Peck reeled in a small trout. He took the fish off the hook and threw it back into the river. "Let him grow up and have babies," he said.

A small raft of ducks suddenly exploded off the river. C.W. noticed a bald eagle floating high above the trees. Peck baited his hook with another worm and cast his line into the water. The fragrance of moist earth rose from the riverbanks as the sun came out from behind some clouds. The serenity of the moment seemed sadly poignant.

"I believe this commission is meant to gather further evidence against the Utes...for use in expelling them from Colorado," C.W. told Peck.

"The Indians are sayin' these men plan to fault 'em with war dancing. With makin' plans for massacre ahead of time. They had a doings, you know a sort of church thing, a couple days afore the agency got burnt. It weren't no war dance. But that'll do 'em no good."

"I am surfeited with ignorance and prejudice," Collins said.

"Pardon?"

"Up to the gills with stupid."

"I hear ya pal."

Collins took his leave and rode back up to the agency. Adams and Hatch were walking together toward Agent Stanley's house. He rode over and dismounted.

"I came to bid you farewell," he said, shaking their hands.

"Is Ouray on the mend?" Adams asked.

"Seriously ailing, I fear. His constitution must also be weakened by apprehension."

"He is insisting that the Utes get a hearing in Washington," General Hatch told him. "Do you think he will last that long?"

"He is a determined man."

"*Ja* but I think he is played out," Adams said.

"So you are leaving us, Mr. Collins?" Hatch asked.

"I am. It is time to move on."

"It is a shame you and Gustavus could not have done more to fend off this calamity," Adams said.

Collins looked at him. "Remember when I was in your house at Mammoth Springs?"

Adams nodded.

"Well," C.W. said, swinging back into the saddle, "you never intended to come to the aid of these people, did you?"

"I did…I am," the big man protested.

"Farewell, General Hatch," Collins said, touching the brim of his Stetson in a partial salute. "Pay attention to what is transpiring here. I would not call it justice."

He rode away without waiting for a reply.

Ouray was sitting in a chair by the open door of his house, taking some fresh air. Collins rode over and swung down off Ulysses. He ground-tied his horse in a patch of dry grasses. Chipeta walked out of the house with Captain Jack.

"Hello Mr. Collins," Jack said.

"Hello."

They all brought out chairs and settled themselves comfortably near Ouray, enjoying the warmth of the noonday sun. Chipeta brought cups of coffee. C.W. offered his tobacco pouch to Jack and Ouray.

"*Gracias*," the chief said, taking out his extravagant meerschaum pipe, carved with galloping horses.

"Have you seen Peck?" C.W. asked Jack. "He is down in the Indian camp on the river."

"I will go there next. I wanted to talk to Ouray of my testimony."

"I am working to calm him down," the chief said. "Jack is too angry all the time."

"I am angry because these whites lie and cheat and steal. Meeker caused all the troubles. If he was not dead, I would cut out his tongue for all the lying and lying. The great trouble with Meeker was that he would tell one story one day and another the next, so that we did not know how to take him or when to believe him."

"I know he caused much difficulty," Collins said, "but there were others."

"Others?"

"I have good reason to believe that powerful men hired agents to commit crimes and leave evidence to implicate the Utes."

"Implicate?" Jack asked.

"It is to make us look guilty," Ouray told him.

"You know this to be true?"

"Yes. I even know that it was such a man who fired the first shot on Milk Creek."

Captain Jack was leaning far forward in his chair, intent on Collins' words. "So white men started the fight and we will pay."

C.W. finished his coffee and put the cup on the ground. He tamped his pipe with a thumb, taking out a match to relight it. "I believe this has been reported to Secretary Schurz, but I am not certain what he will do with the information."

Chipeta brought a plate of *biscochitos* and passed them around, after which she took a seat on a stump next to Ouray. Collins put his pipe away to eat cookies.

"I am curious. Did Meeker ever behave as if he cared about the Ute people at White River?" he asked Jack.

"Never. When he told me he had received information about Thompson's house being burned, I told him we should go together to see it was not burned. He answered me that it was none of his business to talk about these things and I asked him how that could be, as he, being Indian agent, was the man who should regulate such matters. He said the Utes were very bad men and that they should get out the best way they could; that he had no business to be worrying himself in talking for them."

It was his job to speak for you," Collins said.

"That is what I told him, but he told me that he was going to visit his home in that other town...Greeley. He had no time for me. Now Meeker is dead and his mouth is shut."

"*En este mundo ninguno escapa sin pagar lo que deben,*" Ouray said. "In this world, no one escapes without paying what they must."

"Some do not pay enough," Collins said.

"*La verdad.* But now that Meeker is dead, the whites will not believe he was at fault in any way. Nothing we say here in this place will matter," Ouray said. "We need to go to Washington. We are surrounded by enemies here. Even Adams is behaving as a puppet for big politicians."

"Are you leaving now, Mr. Collins?" Chipeta asked. "You will not stay to hear the rest of the testimony?"

"I have heard enough to know that Ouray is right.

Washington will be the only place where something might be done for the Ute people. There is nothing I can do here."

"We must see this commission through to the end," Ouray said. "But it is difficult to endure."

"When this is over I will go north," Captain Jack said.

"To hunt with Shavano?" Collins asked.

"No…to live with Sitting Bull in Canada."

"Did you not scout for Crook in Montana Territory? I am not sure you would be welcome."

"Then I will go to Wyoming. I have relatives at Fort Washakie."

Chipeta got to her feet and brushed off her skirt. "Will we see you in Washington?" she asked Collins.

"I will be there. I will want to talk to Schurz again and do what I can."

"We are grateful for your friendship," Ouray said.

"And I am most grateful for yours," Collins said, taking each of their hands lightly. Jack shook his hand in the white man fashion.

C.W. walked over to fetch Ulysses. He tightened the cinch and swung into the saddle. "Farewell, my friends," he said, lifting his hat. "*Ar scáth a chéile a mhaireann na daoine.* Under the shelter of each other, people survive." He spun the gelding and rode away.

WASHINGTON DC

59

Implacably grey monuments were overhung by an equally grim sky. The January afternoon was damp and chill. The surroundings and the weather did nothing to elevate his mood. Again negotiating the pretentious avenues of Washington D.C., a city he despised, Collins was reminded of previous visits and attendant despondency. This foray would be no different, steeped as it was in tribulation and uncertainty for the Ute people.

She had agreed to meet him in the lobby of the Tremont House, where the Ute delegation was housed. He found Josephine Meeker sitting primly on a settee by a window, attired in a rather odd costume reminiscent of the clothing worn at her release from captivity. He supposed she was quite enjoying her role as western heroine. Fictionalized accounts could be found in a multitude of newspapers, as well as in a book precipitously published at the end of November and penned by two *Denver Tribune* reporters. If anything, her outward smugness exacerbated the prudish attributes of her physiognomy.

Collins approached and sat in a chair across from her. Josephine perused him in amusement and he sensed she felt a sort of power over him. His ardent desire that she not author further mischief in regard to his Ute friends rendered this assumption predominantly accurate.

"Good day, Miss Meeker. Thank you for seeing me."

"You are welcome, Mr. Collins…Although seeing you again brings unbidden thoughts of my terrible ordeal."

"No doubt," he said noncommittally. He harbored far more sympathy for the Utes billeted under armed guard on a floor above them. He had, as yet, been unable to see Shavano, though he knew him to be present in Washington D.C.

"I will not disguise my purpose, Miss Meeker."

"Josie, please," she said waving a hand in a slight gesture that was affected to appear magnanimous.

"Yes, well, as I said…I will not equivocate. I need to ask you what your testimony will be in the forthcoming congressional hearings. Will you say you were raped?"

"Mr. Collins!" the girl said in mock chagrin. She went so far as to sit poised with her hand over her mouth for a prolonged instant. Observing that her dissembling produced no effect, she relinquished the pretense and gave him a calculating glance. "Why is this a matter of importance to you?"

"You know well that I maintain sympathy for the Utes, despite their recent offenses. Yours and your mother's statements in Greeley did terrible damage to the Ute cause. If you again repudiate your original statements to General Adams while in the Indian camp, in which you insisted no outrages took place, there will be enormous consequences for the Ute people. You have already, through your mythic fictions to newspapers and the Ute Commission, condemned the Ute people to calumny and persecution. Sentiment is roundly against them. Imagine if you pour fuel upon it in testimony to the United States Congress."

"I can imagine many possible eventualities," she said slyly. "I can well imagine a post as copyist here in Washington, as promised to me by Senator Henry Teller."

Collins examined her as if she were a specimen in a museum. "You would destroy an entire people for the sake of personal gain?"

Her smile bore no mirth. "And vengeance."

"What do you have to avenge?" C.W. asked disdainfully. "Your life is infinitely more fulfilled and interesting than before. Now, as you say, there is opportunity for you in Washington. You have fame, the sympathy of thousands, the attention of an entire nation. If your father had not met his fate, what would your lot have been? Frontier drudgery with some blemished youth of no ambition?"

Josephine Meeker contemplated him momentarily. "Perhaps we may strike a deal."

There was a crawling sensation at the nape of his neck. "A deal?"

She focused on him keenly. "You are a remarkably handsome man. I could never hope to light upon one such as you, despite all the public accolades in the world. Offer me matrimony and I will not heap further ignominy upon your savage compatriots."

"You jest," Collins said, truly discomfited by the creature before him.

"I do not," the girl said with complete aplomb. "That is the future I desire."

"I cannot credit your proposal, Miss Meeker."

"You are a hired agent, Mr. Collins," she said, coyly. "Did my proposal strike so far off the mark?"

Collins turned to gaze out the window at the relentlessly bleak buildings that encompassed the hotel. He realized she was again being counterfeit. "I will not be toyed with," he said, turning back to the woman. "I take it you will proceed with your specious testimony?"

"I will. My father was a sanctimonious fool, but he has at last, through his own folly and demise, given me my future. The more lurid the story, the greater the appetite. I will enjoy several years of public appearances while I take up a lucrative post here in the nation's capital. I have already received monetary remuneration of epic proportions."

" 'When they will not give a doit to relieve a lame beggar, they will lay out ten to see a dead Indian,' " he quoted.

"Precisely," she said, as if comprehending the literary

allusion.

Collins purposed upon one final attempt to dissuade the spiteful young woman from her aims. "Has it occurred to you that your tales of rapine may not earn you the matrimony you profess to desire? Men do so like their virgins," he said, embracing brutality over gentlemanliness.

She laughed coarsely, causing a nearby woman to glance in her direction. "How ungallant of you, Mr. Collins. I offered matrimony only to you." She lowered her voice. "In answer to your query, however, it is far too late in the game to think any man would want to marry a ruined woman, such as myself, no matter how much sympathy I engender. Even if it were true that the heathens did not outrage me, let us just say…" She raised an eyebrow pointedly and leaned closer. "That particular ship has sailed long ago and would not bear scrutiny in any event."

Collins stood. He no longer cared to bandy words with this Gorgon. He wordlessly contemplated her disagreeable visage a moment, as she sat gazing challengingly up at him, then turned on his heel and exited the hotel.

He met Gustavus Jocknick in a restaurant around the corner. They ordered two dozen oysters and a plate of shrimp. C.W. poked at an oyster absentmindedly, thinking about his interview with Miss Meeker.

Jocknick skillfully slid an oyster into his mouth without disturbing his decorous moustache. "You saw her?" he asked, pressing a linen napkin to his lips.

"I did. To no avail." C.W. ate a shrimp. It was excellent, but he found he had no appetite.

"She will continue to accuse the Utes of rape?"

"She will. And, I feel certain, to slander them in every other way possible."

Jocknick shook his head. "This is larger than the White River Commission. This will make potent propagandism. And she cares nothing for her own reputation?"

"None at all. She has received offers from Teller and, I

would hazard, others in similar positions. She also alluded to massive pecuniary rewards."

"How distasteful."

There was a lapse in conversation as they each entertained private musings. Jocknick busied himself with partaking of more oysters and sipping chilled white wine. Collins ordered coffee and abandoned all thoughts of food.

"What of your meeting with Commissioner Hayt?" he asked after a while.

Jocknick shook his head. "His clerk, Leeds, will be testifying to the fact that Hayt withheld monies and supplies and this led to the uprising. As you can imagine, when we met, he was neither sympathetic nor forthright."

"Why in hell can no one in the office of Commissioner of Indian Affairs ever execute their due diligence toward the Indians?" Collins asked in frustration.

"Too much money involved. Too many hands in the pot." Jocknick shrugged and took a sip of wine.

"And they do not have any vested interest in duty or integrity in their dealings with Indian tribes."

"Too true. Perhaps when you meet with Secretary Schurz, you may find some gratification. However, as I told you in Denver, he will bend with prevailing political winds if he seeks to remain in power."

"Even though he is also charged with the care of Indian peoples...Yes, this is all too reminiscent of past dealings with him."

"Come, come, you must certainly be aware of the intricacies of politics by now."

"I suppose so," C.W. conceded.

"Josephine Meeker's false testimony to Congress will be the finish of the Utes in Colorado."

"Will I not be allowed to meet with Shavano or Ouray?" Collins asked abruptly.

"It will be difficult to arrange. Ask Mr. Schurz. You are aware that Otto Mears is present as interpreter? He has them in his grip and will not relent."

"The man is implacable."

"And has much vested interest in the Utes' expulsion from Colorado, as we surmised."

Upon leaving the restaurant, the men walked along the streets with no particular aim. Eventually, they came in view of the capitol building.

"They will have their way now," Jocknick said ambiguously, twisting one end of his moustaches pensively.

"Yes."

"What are your plans?" he asked, turning to look at C.W.

"I will soon be withdrawing from this festered calamity. I can be of no further use." Collins laughed ironically. "Not that I was of any use to begin with. You set me on an abortive path, Mr. Jocknick."

"Not I, Mr. Collins," the man said, raising a forefinger in a disciplinary manner. "Not I."

"Yes of course," C.W. said, smiling with piqued amusement. "You are scrupulous in your accuracy. Secretary Schurz sent me on this futile commission."

"Was it not lucrative?"

Collins sighed. "Quite lucrative."

"Then not futile, Mr. Collins. Not futile."

He was forced to concede Jocknick his point, Collins thought. A man remunerated for this type of employment should not nurture too many misgivings. He came to a decision.

"I must go and see Schurz, at the very least to receive final compensation," he said. "I will take my leave."

Jocknick bade Collins farewell as he turned to walk away.

60

His meeting with Schurz was brief after a prolonged period of waiting. He received a letter of credit drawn upon the National Savings Bank from his secretary and was subsequently ushered into the large office, full of oak filing cabinets and leather covered chairs. Schurz sat behind his impressive mahogany desk, reviewing a document. He looked up when Collins was announced.

"Did you receive the amount owed?" Schurz asked.

"I did."

"Sit down. How are you, Mr. Collins? What may I do for you?"

C.W. removed his Stetson and took a chair beside the desk. "I wished to learn if you were fully informed of my discoveries whilst in the field."

Schurz raised his eyebrows. "Why, I believe so. What omission most concerns you?"

"That Mears, Pitkin, Vickers, Teller *et al* did, in fact, contrive to vitiate the Utes, as you suspected. But I believe the most significant and duplicitous player is Otto Mears."

"I know they have made unflattering statements in the newspapers. I assume they will do so again in their testimony to Congress."

Collins smoothed his moustache, pausing a moment to formulate his remarks carefully. "I have firsthand information that they hired representatives to create conflict between white settlers and the Indians. These agents have set fires and attacked ranches, making all to appear to be the work of the Utes."

"Oh come now," Schurz said, "I can hardly countenance such an idea." He removed his pince-nez, wiped them with a handkerchief and returned them to the bridge of his nose.

"I was severely beaten by an operative of Otto Mears in Cañon City. This same man fired the first shot that prompted the battle on Milk Creek."

C.W. now had Schurz' complete attention. "And you know this how?"

"I spoke with him. He told me."

"Where is this man?"

"Dead."

"That is a convenient end for such an improbable figure," Schurz said condescendingly. "You can hardly prove his existence if he is dead and cannot testify to anything."

"My word carries no weight?"

"I did not mean to intimate that, Mr. Collins. I simply cannot employ any intelligence that is not verifiable."

"I thought surely Mr. Jocknick informed you of these circumstances during your stay in Denver."

"Perhaps he did. I do not recall."

C.W. strongly suspected that the man was dissembling. "It was my impression that unearthing such a discovery was the import of my original mission."

Schurz stroked his beard. "With the ultimate goal of preventing tragedy."

"It was not possible," Collins said, disputatiously.

"So I have surmised. Be easy, Mr. Collins. I am convinced you did everything you could, under the circumstances."

Collins changed his tack. "The women are mendacious, Mr. Schurz. I was there when Adams first interviewed them in the Indian camp. The Ute men did not violate them. And they showed no outward signs of privations, other than the wound old Mrs. Meeker had received in her leg."

Schurz appeared discomfited. "I cannot outwardly challenge their statements in any manner," he said.

"Not even if their falsehoods spell catastrophe for the Ute people?"

"I am sorry…most sorry. There is nothing I can do about the women's testimony." Schurz leaned back in his chair and locked his hands behind his head. "Is there anything further I may do for you, Mr. Collins? I must attend a meeting with Mr. Hayt in a few minutes."

"Might I trouble you for a pass to visit my Ute friends at the Tremont?"

"Of course," he said and wrote on a sheet of paper. He blotted the note and placed it in an envelope.

Schurz got up and walked to Collins, who also stood. He handed the envelope to Collins and they shook hands. "Good luck to you. I am most grateful for your efforts." Schurz said. "Pray, do not take these events too much to heart. We do what we can. As you and I have witnessed before, white settlement has always been an inexorable tide. Unfortunate, but inevitable."

"Yes, I believe you counseled me in this regard after the devastation at Fort Robinson." Collins put the envelope in his jacket and placed his hat on his head. "What was it President Lincoln said? 'Those who deny freedom to others deserve it not for themselves.' Good-bye, Secretary Schurz."

"Farewell, Mr. Collins." Schurz assumed a dismissive manner. "Do not tie your fate too closely with the Utes. I advise you to use discretion."

C.W. left the offices and made his way toward the Tremont House. He passed through the lobby, where he had met Miss Meeker earlier that day, and climbed the stairs to the fourth floor. A discernably mature private stood in the hallway. He held an army-issue Springfield rifle.

"I would like to visit the Ute delegation," Collins told him.

"I am sorry, sir, but no visitors allowed. Members of the press have been pestering me all day."

"I have a pass from Secretary Schurz," he said, removing the envelope from his jacket pocket and handing it to the soldier. Collins wondered idly how this man remained at such a lowly rank at his advanced age.

"Which Indian did you want to see?" the private said, handing back the pass.

"Ouray."

"Third door down," he said. "Son-of-a-bitch has a suite."

"That son-of-a-bitch is a friend of mine."

Collins left the man muttering to himself and walked down the hallway to knock on the door. In a few moments, Chipeta opened the door and beckoned him into the rooms.

Ouray sat on an absurdly ornate divan. He appeared to be feeling better than he had in November. "Collins!" he exclaimed, standing to greet him. "I am so very happy to see you."

"And I you. Hello, Chipeta."

"Hello, Mr. Collins. Come and sit. There is tea. We like the English tea now."

C.W. placed his hat on a sideboard. They sat around a low table. Chipeta poured tea from a floral pot and handed them cups on saucers. There was an assortment of pastries on a cake stand. She left the room and returned with Shavano.

"Here you are again," he said to Collins.

"As you see."

He sat next to Collins and slapped him hard on the back. The woman poured Shavano some tea. He balanced the cup on his knee and helped himself to a large and sugary tart.

"I like these," the Indian said, when the entire pastry

had been consumed.

"I see that. How is Washington?"

"I dislike the noise, the stink and all the white people. They are all *KatÙsuYa.*"

"He came because I needed him," Ouray said. "He did not want to come here."

"Neither did I," C.W. said honestly.

"Did you speak to Mr. Schurz?" Chipeta asked. "He will not see us."

Collins took a sip of tea. "I did. I do not believe he plans to defend you very stringently. It seems he will acquiesce to the wishes of Colorado factions."

Shavano was eating another pastry. "Perhaps if he knew of the men hired by Mears and the others?"

"We discussed this. He told me we have no proof."

Ouray set his cup on the table noisily. "None of them intended to help. It is strange Schurz hired you."

"Perhaps he merely needed to assuage his conscience… to be able to tell himself that he had attempted to come to your aid. Perhaps he actually sought to ward off disaster."

"Will you be staying for the hearings?" Shavano asked.

Collins shook his head. "I have done all I can. Besides, Washington is an expensive city. I cannot afford to stay long."

"Do you have your medicine?"

"Always." He pulled the pouch from his shirt.

"Keep it close. It will protect you from those who would harm you."

Finishing his tea, Collins stood and retrieved his Stetson. "My friends, I will come to see you when this is resolved…however it is resolved."

Ouray stood to embrace him. Shavano followed suit, giving Collins such a bear hug as to squeeze the breath out of him. They grinned at each other. Chipeta held his hand a moment.

"We will look for you," she said. "Wherever we are, we

will look for you."

He smiled at her sweet face, feeling water rise in his eyes. He pulled his hat down low on his head. "Farewell," he said and swiftly exited the room.

Later, standing outside on the street in front of his hotel, with carpetbag in hand, night had fallen. He found a policeman.

"Can you please direct me to the train depot?"

"I can that," the officer said. "It is not far. Just turn left at the next street and follow New Jersey Avenue south." The constable looked Collins over. "To where are you bound at this late hour?" he asked conversationally.

"West."

"Good luck," the man called after him as Collins departed the glow of a street lamp. He was absorbed by the gloaming.

The End

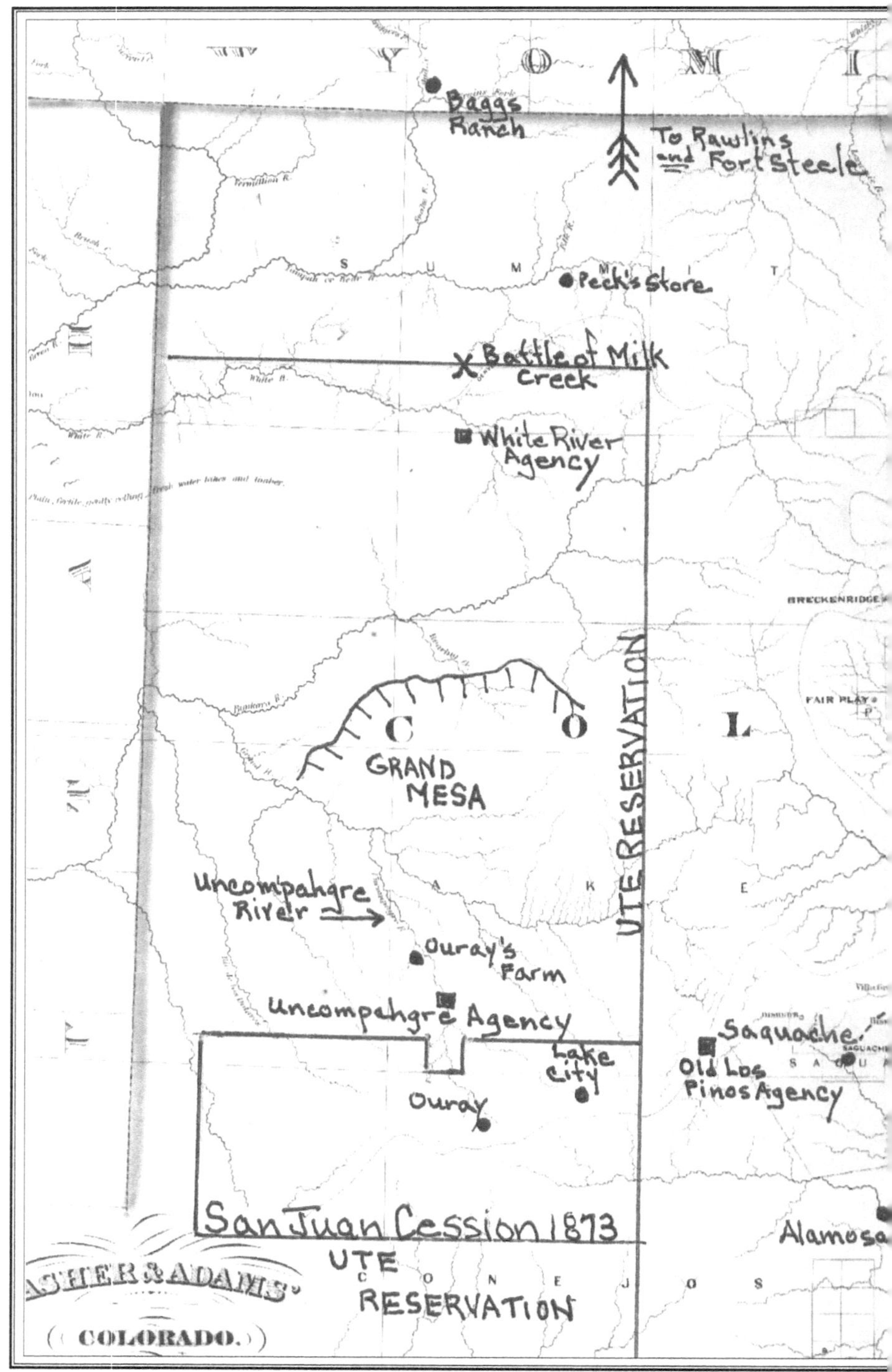

'Asher and Adams' Colorado, 1873, Courtesy of Denver Public Library,

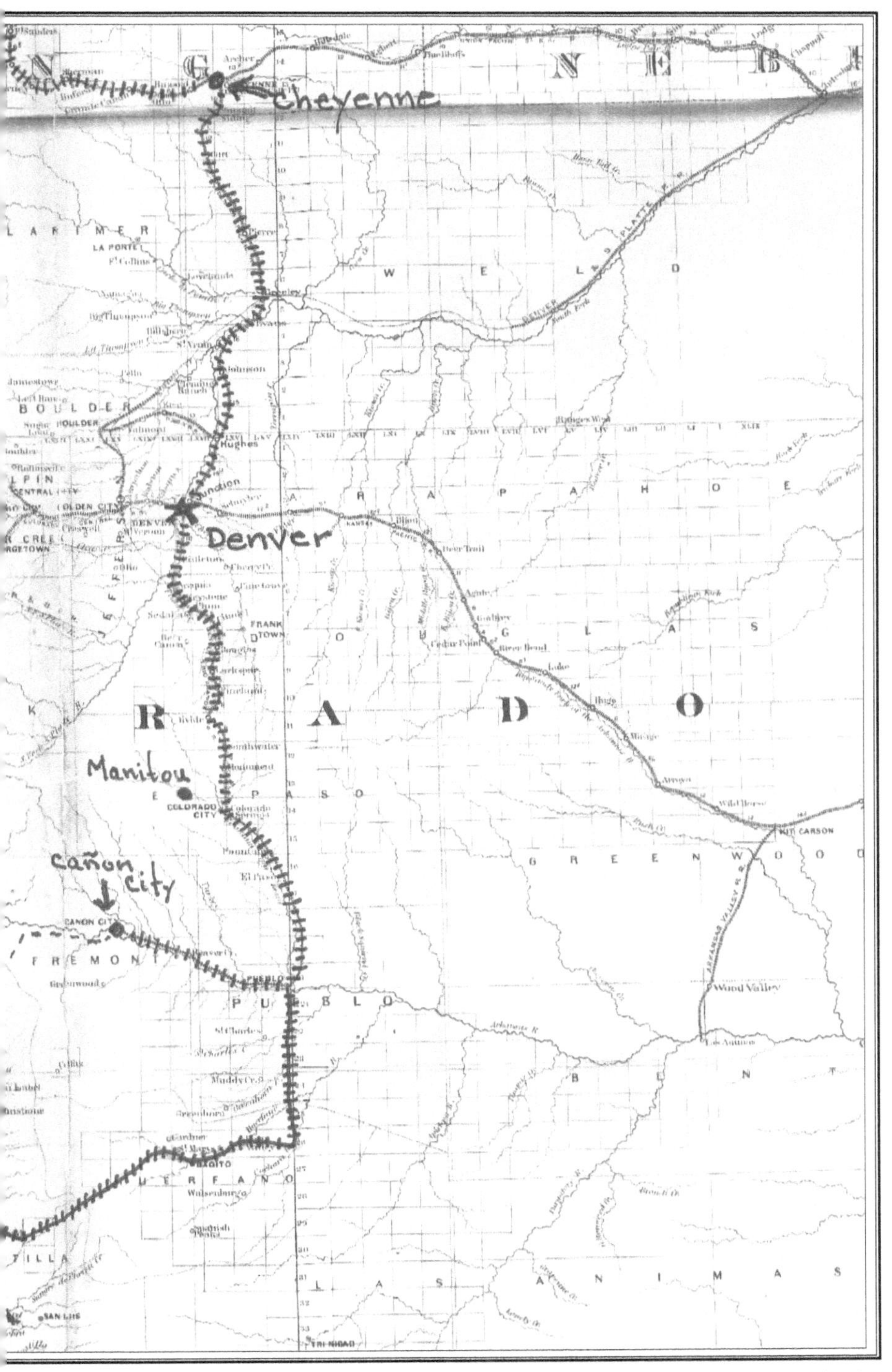

Western History Collection. Call # CG 4310 1873.A8 (Annotated by author)

Epilogue

During November and December of 1879, a series of hearings took place at Los Pinos Agency (on the Uncompahgre River) under the auspices of a Major General Edward Hatch. It was charged with apportioning blame for the military conflict on Milk Creek and the killings on the White River Agency. The commission came to the conclusion that the Utes could not be held accountable for the battle on Milk Creek. Twelve Ute men, however, were held culpable of the murder of agency civilians and abuse of Arvilla and Josephine Meeker and Flora Price, based solely upon the women's accounts of their experiences. Several of these men subsequently disappeared, unwilling to place their faith in the justice of the U.S. government. Ouray, Chipeta, Shavano, Sowowic, Ignacio, Captain Jack, Buckskin Charlie, Blanco and Severo agreed to travel to Washington D.C. to help resolve the situation. Meanwhile, vitriolic anti-Indian sentiment in Colorado was systematically encouraged by political statements made by Governor Pitkin, a multitude of local and state politicians and their instruments; the newspapers.

On December 30, 1879, a Pueblo newspaper, the Colorado Chieftain, published a letter from Arvilla Meeker stating she had endured the most "humiliating misfortune that can befall a woman."

From January through March, a series of hearings were held by the House Committee on Indian Affairs in Washington D.C. regarding the events of White River. Ultimately, little new information came to light.

In April of 1880, Senator Teller launched a vicious verbal campaign against Secretary Schurz before the U.S. Senate. He blamed Schurz for the capture and subsequent outrage of the Meeker women, Major Thornburgh's untimely demise and the murders at White River Agency, as well as a myriad of other crimes. Meanwhile, Secretary Schurz and a dying Ouray were attempting to author a viable agreement for the protection of the Colorado Utes. This agreement failed to protect anything but white interests, as it resulted in the surrender of all Ute lands within Colorado except a narrow strip of land in southwestern part of the state occupied by the Kapuuta, Moughwach and Weeminuche. Senate Bill 1509 required the signatures of three fourths of adult Ute males. In order to achieve this, it was rumored that Otto Mears used his own money to coerce many of the Ute signatures of ratification. Supposedly, only 110 signatures were procured, hardly three fourths of the total number of Ute men at the time. Bribery charges were eventually brought against Mears and he admitted to paying two dollars per signature, but justified the payment as necessary to ameliorate the incendiary situation in Colorado between the Utes and whites. He was exonerated by Secretary Schurz' successor, Samuel J. Kirkwood. For their journey out of Colorado, the Utes traveled upon one of Otto Mears' toll roads. It was estimated that the U.S. government paid him the sum of $100,000 for use of the road. Subsequent to the relocation of the Tabeguache and White River Ute people to Utah, Mears received the contract to build the new Indian agency there. He also accrued vast wealth through construction of railroads throughout Colorado and remained a powerful figure in Colorado politics into the next century. His image adorns the Senate Chambers of the state capitol building.

Secretary of the Interior Carl Schurz May 11, 1880 made this statement to the 46th Congress, House of Representatives a few months after the "Meeker Massacre" at White River Agency:

> It has seemed to me, and, I think, to a great many who have studied the Indian problem with care, that the system of large reservations, as has hitherto prevailed, is not only no longer desirable either in the interest of the Indians or of the whites, but will, in the course of time, become utterly untenable. As our white settlements in the West multiply, as the development of the country advances, available lands become more and more scarce and valuable, and so it is not unnatural that the withholding of large tracts from settlement and development so as to maintain a savage aristocracy in the enjoyment of their chivalrous pastimes, should be looked upon by many a system incompatible with the progress of civilization and injurious to the material interests of the country.

> As an inevitable consequence, we have witnessed many encroachments, lawless and wrongful in character: upon Indian lands and rights, and constant efforts to drive the

red men from the reservations belonging to them. This has kept the Indians in a state of uncertainty and restlessness, and led to many deplorable outrages and Indian wars. As a matter of course, this state of things has retarded the progress and impaired the well-being of the Indians themselves. However well disposed the government may be to maintain the title of the Indians to their reservations-and undoubtedly the government is and will remain so disposed-still it is evident that the government will not always be able in all things to control the action of our Western people, and as sensible men we must make up our mind to the fact that a long as the Indians hold very large tract of land, in great part useless to themselves and useless to other people, their tenure will, under existing circumstances, become practically more and more precarious. It is most desirable for the interest of the Indians themselves, therefore, that we should substitute for the system of large reservations another system that will protect the rights and interests of the Indians without standing in the way of the progress and development of the country.

On September 1, 1881, the final group of approximately 1,458 Ute people began their three-hundred-mile journey to their new reservation, situated on lands unwanted by Mormon settlers. The exodus was overseen by General Mackenzie and his cavalry, infantry and artillery. Thousands of whites were poised to take control of the relinquished Ute lands. General Mackenzie's troops were more necessary in keeping whites from swarming onto the White River reservation lands before the Utes had departed, than in keeping discipline among the Ute population as originally intended.

In 1881, John Coulter of Clear Creek County, Colorado introduced House Bill No. 178. Section 1 of the bill read as follows: "That any person who shall produce the scalp of any Indian or skunk found in this State, shall receive a reward or premium of twenty-five (25) dollars for each Indian or skunk scalp produced, to be paid out of the State treasury, as hereinafter provided."

Chief Ouray succumbed to Bright's disease on August 24, 1880 at approximately 11:00 am. He had made one final journey to the southern Ute people to visit Chief Ignacio and Buckskin Charlie, two other men of vision and integrity. His body was hidden in a secret location near present day Ignacio, Colorado. On May 24, 1925, what may have been his fragile remains were reinterred near the Ignacio agency, supervised by Buckskin Charlie. A Ute ceremony of four days celebrated the event, as well as a service encompassing both Protestant and Catholic components. Apparently, this took place due to arguments regarding his spiritual beliefs. In 1939, a monument was erected in Ignacio dedicated to Ouray, Buckskin Charlie, Ignacio and Severo.

After Ouray's death, Chipeta returned to traditional Ute customs and gave away all material vestiges of white ways, including a substantial amount of money. She spent time with Colorow's band, soaked her rheumatism in Glenwood Springs and visited her relations (and Ouray's grave site?) in Ignacio. Chipeta died on August 16, 1924 at a place called Bitter Creek, Utah, having survived Ouray by forty-four years. Her life ended in poverty and privation. She was buried on the Uintah Reservation in a shallow grave and soon after, citizens of Montrose, Colorado worked to bring her remains back to Ouray's and Chipeta's farm, south of the town. She was relocated on March 25, 1925. Chipeta's grave is now near the site of the Ute Indian Museum and adjacent park. Until 2022, the Montrose High School football team was called the "Indians."

On September 29, 1880, War Chief Shavano's son, Johnson Shavano, and a companion, rode into a whiskey trader's camp and asked for food. The trader, John Jackson, shot and killed Johnson and wounded Indian Henry, his friend. Witnesses later recounted that the white men had been drunk on their own goods. Chief Shavano asked the agent at Uncompahgre agency to arrange the arrest of Jackson for murder. William Berry, the agent at the time, went with several other men to arrest John Jackson. En route to Gunnison for trial, the party was ambushed by Ute warriors and Jackson was taken away and killed. War Chief Shavano was killed by a friend in 1886. Shavano, an accomplished healer, had supposedly advised the use of the wrong medicines for his friend's child, thereby causing the child's death.

Jane (Red Jacket Jane) moved to the Uintah Reservation and built up two successful farms. She remained steadfastly ill-disposed toward whites. Jane lived until 1908.

Nicaagat (Captain Jack), exonerated after the Milk Creek battle, refused to move into Utah. He was hired as a teamster on the Rawlins-Fort Washakie freighting road. In 1882, he was accused of horse theft and, refusing to surrender, fought a single-handed battle with troopers from Fort Washakie. After Jack killed a sergeant, the commanding officer ordered that a mountain howitzer be fired into the lodge where Nicaagat was sheltered among bales of robes and hides. He did not survive.

In the summer of 1882, Josephine Meeker was promoted from copyist to assistant private secretary for the new Secretary of Interior, Henry Teller. An extravagant salary of seventeen dollars a week was provided. At the same time, she was also receiving a five-hundred-dollar annuity from the Ute treaty that provided for the victims of the White River "massacre." Not surprisingly, although many of the provisions of the treaty were never honored, this stipulation was adhered to with regularity. Her value as news item and public speaker eventually diminished. By the winter of 1882, Josephine was unwell and spent Christmas in bed. She died of pneumonia on December 29, a mere three years after her captivity with the Utes.

Arvilla Meeker died of senility in 1905.

General Charles Adams was made United States Minister in Bolivia by President Hayes in gratitude for his courage in retrieving the captives. He returned after two years to become Post Office Inspector for Colorado. By 1885, he was a private businessman in Manitou Springs. He died the same year when a boiler exploded in a Denver hotel where he was staying. More than twenty people were killed in the accident. He was only fifty years old. His wife, Mrs. General, survived him by many years.

Gustavus Jocknick remained in the employ of the Office of Indian Affairs. He later moved to Ouray County, Colorado and tried his hand at farming. Sidney Jocknick wrote a book, published in 1913, entitled Early Days on the Western Slope of Colorado, dedicated to the honorable Otto Mears.

As for the unknown provocateur...

> "The soldiers also discovered in the fortifications of the Indians, the body of an unknown white man sitting in a squatting posture, with his gun in his hands as if ready to shoot."
>
> *- The Ute War, written and compiled*
> *by Thomas F. Dawson and F.J.V. Skiff*
> *of the Denver Tribune, 1879 -*

Epilogue

UTE WOLVES

Author's Note

Special thanks are given to Alden Naranjo, Cultural Director for the Southern Ute Tribe, in gratitude for his permission to use words and phrases of the Ute language and for the words themselves. He is gone now, but his generosity and wisdom will always be greatly appreciated. It is to him this book is dedicated.

Native American readers will hopefully understand that any denigrating or otherwise objectionable terminology in this text is used to illustrate prejudices and attitudes of the historical period within which this story occurs.

THE (**INDIANS**) INTERIOR **DEPARTMENT** COMING TO ITS SENSES.
SECRETARY SCHURZ. "Wilful waste makes woful want."

PROPAGANDA

Additional Reading

Early Days on the Western Slope of Colorado by Sidney Jocknick

Otto Mears and the San Juans by E.F. Tucker

History of the State of Colorado, Volume 2 by Frank Hall

Frontier Regulars, the United States Army and the Indian 1866-1891 by Robert M. Utley

Bury my Heart at Wounded Knee by Dee Brown

Massacre: The Tragedy at White River by Marshall Sprague

The Last War Trail, the Utes and the Settlement of Colorado by Robert Emmitt

The Ute War by Thomas Fulton

The Ute Massacre! Brave Miss Meeker's Captivity! Her Own Account of It by Miss Josephine Meeker

Being and Becoming Ute, The Story of an American Indian People by Sondra G Jones

...and various nineteenth century Colorado newspapers archived online at https://www.coloradohistoricnewspapers.org.

~ PLEASE NOTE ~

In considering the list of sources, be advised that none of them contains the complete or objective story of the events portrayed in *Small Light of Discretion*. Much of the additional reading reflects the dominant perspective of Colorado settler society, steeped in racism and bigotry. This particular episode remains a highly charged historical event in Colorado for Ute people and the white citizenry. I have done my utmost to filter the incident and attendant history through years of research involving similar historical events, as well as taking into account the vagaries of human nature. In perusing the materials listed above, the reader will easily surmise that each tends to be quite subjective.

For the Utes' own words, see the transcripts of the White River Ute Commission - understanding that translations may be suspect: https://digitalcommons.law.ou.edu/cgi/viewcontent.cgi?article=6987&context=indianserial-set

   Also visit the Ute peoples' own websites:
      https://www.utetribe.com/
      https://www.southernute-nsn.gov/
      https://www.utemountainutetribe.com/

GOING EAST

Juliana "Hoolihan" Clayton

About the Author

Juliana "Hoolihan" Clayton is an indigenous woman of Turtle Island (First Nations Plains Cree/Nehiyawak) who was adopted by a white family and raised on a cattle ranch in Wyoming. She has lived and worked with Native Americans and cowboys throughout the West during her years as a ranch hand and wildland firefighter. With a degree in history and education from the University of Montana, it has long been her goal to create a series of entertaining novels that are rife with impeccable research, unflinching veracity and forthright cultural perspectives on American history.

A member of Western Writers of America, J. Hoolihan has been published in western historical magazines, such as "True West" and "Wild West." During her extensive research, she continues to accumulate an abundance of topics for a succession of factual stories pertaining to the 19th century American West. *Commendable Discretion*, the first book of the Discretion Series, was published in January 2021. It was a finalist in the High Plains Book Awards. *With Great Discretion*, the second book, was published in February 2022. *Small Light of Discretion* is the third book of the series.

"Throwing the hoolihan" is a technique that old time cowboys used for roping horses. It has been Juliana's nickname for many years.

SAN JUAN MOUNTAINS

List of Illustrations

Illustrations from *Harpers Weekly* are used with explicit permission. Illustrations from *Frank Leslie's Illustrated Newspaper* are in public domain and were never copyrighted. All images are available through the Library of Congress Prints & Photographs Reading Room, Prints and Photographs Division, Prints & Photographs Online Catalogue.